DAMAGE IN AN
UNDEAD AGE

A.M. GEEVER

ZBZ-1 PRESS

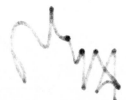

61C Days Turned to Nights lyrics courtesy of Justin Sane, Copyright © 2002

For Mom & Dad

And I'm not going to tell myself that I will ever find you glowing in those lights again, 'cause I don't know if I will ever have that chance.

JUSTIN SANE, 61C DAYS TURNED TO NIGHTS

1

"I'M LIVING PROOF YOU CAN DIE OF SEASICKNESS."

Miranda rested her sweaty forehead on the icy metal of the yacht railing. The raw wind lashed from the north, needles of cold sinking deeper into her chilled bones. She clenched her teeth to stop them chattering, wiped her mouth with red knuckles, then spat into the choppy waters of Puget Sound. The bitter taste of bile still filled her mouth. Three weeks of feeding the fish. One more and she would be dead for sure.

"Miranda, come see."

Mario's voice sounded a thousand miles away. She did not want to come see anything. She wanted to be left alone to die in peace.

Doug's voice this time. "Miri, you're going to want to see this."

She straightened up. Another wave of nausea hit her, but what she saw through the morning fog caused a dizzy head rush of relief. The white spire of Seattle's Space Needle raced up from the earth to pierce the sky, its flying saucer observation deck hovering just below the iron-gray clouds. In the fog, the Needle's graceful tripod legs seemed to melt in and out of focus, but the dark band of the observation deck's windows hovered in place.

The Space Needle.

If she had not been so exhausted, Miranda would have whooped for joy. Instead, she leaned against the rail and gave Mario a wan smile. They were almost to their destination. They could start looking for a marina and meet up with the Jesuits at Seattle University. They might even get word of what was happening at home. A shiver of apprehension raced up Miranda's spine. They did not know what had happened in San Jose after they had tried to smuggle out the zombie vaccine serum. Doug's contacts in Santa Cruz had not heard from anyone at Santa Clara University. She wanted to know if Father Walter was all right, hear his lilting Irish brogue. That something might have happened to him sent a shot of fear through her, so deep she almost could not breathe.

Get your shit together, Tucci.

She pushed the worry and speculation aside, shoved it down deep where it could not distract her. She would concentrate on what she could control, on what they were here to do. Since they had lost the zombie vaccine serum they had smuggled out of San Jose, Mario would need to develop another at Seattle University. The Jesuits had a lab ready to go. The madman Jeremiah, with his naturally immune blood, was imprisoned below. He would make a new vaccine possible.

She looked over to Mario and Doug, standing in the yacht's cockpit. Father Doug Michel's skinny six-foot-four frame stood ramrod straight, as if the wind, cold, and rain did not affect him. His blue eyes were vivid patches of color against his pale skin and the grayed-out horizon. He kept tossing his head to get his sandy-colored hair out of his eyes and looked as if his restless energy might make him burst. Miranda could tell he was excited to finally get here. Mario only reached Doug's ear but looked shorter with his shoulders hunched against the wind. His dark, wavy hair reminded Miranda of Medusa's writhing snakes with the wind whipping through it from every direction. He watched her expectantly, his dark eyes filled with excitement, and a very different kind of shiver flitted down Miranda's spine.

She limped over and took Mario's hand as she carefully stepped down into the cockpit, ignoring the lurch and swoop of her stomach. He gathered her in his arms and held her tight against him, pressing his cold cheek against her own. He was beyond stubble but not quite sporting a full-on beard. It had surprised her that it suited him. She looked over his shoulder at Doug, whose beaming smile would match the brilliance of the sun had it not been so cloudy. He reached over and rubbed her auburn peach-fuzzed head like he was shining a lucky penny.

"See, Coppertop? You did live long enough to get here," he said, his blue eyes twinkling.

Miranda grinned at him over Mario's shoulder. "Saying 'I told you so' is bad form."

"It probably is," Doug answered, "but so is making our boat smell like a vomitorium."

HALF AN HOUR later in their cabin, as she watched Mario getting ready to leave, Miranda thought, I just got you back. Mario stopped zipping his jacket and looked up, his brown eyes filled with concern.

"Did I say that out loud?"

"Yeah," he said, and smiled, just a little.

He sat next to her on the edge of their berth, his warm callused hand slipping comfortably around her cool red ones. She had grown tired of taking off her gloves every time she threw up over the rail but was paying the price. At his touch, she could feel her dread lighten by the tiniest fraction. He looked haunted for a moment, as if the years they had spent apart were waiting to pounce and snatch her away again.

"If your knee was okay, you would be going with Doug to make contact with the Jesuits, not me," he said. "I know you would rather do anything else than be the one who waits."

She sighed. "How's that for karmic payback?"

In the grand scheme of things, the guy who could make a new vaccine was far more valuable than she was. Mario would never be going with Doug to find their allies if she was not still recovering from her sprained knee and hairline-fractured shin bones. She had lost fifteen pounds if an ounce since they started their voyage. Being sick all the time left her weak, which made her feel useless and helpless. To add insult to injury, she had to mind whack-job Jeremiah. Life wasn't fair sometimes, but she already knew that.

"I promise, Miri. I'm coming back."

Miranda gave herself a mental shake.

"Of course you will," she said, but her forced cheerfulness sounded hollow.

She stood up as Mario shrugged into his backpack. He pulled her close, and when his lips brushed hers, the feeling that she would never see him again overwhelmed her. She wanted to hold him tight and never let go. She wanted to pull him to their bed and make love, knowing it would be the last time, so she could commit to memory every contour of his body, the firm and the soft, the rough and the smooth. She wanted to feel their bodies move together one last time, feel the gratitude that they had found one another again crackle and snap as it ricocheted between them until it could not be contained.

When the kiss ended, she took a step back and smiled at him. "You should go. Doug's waiting. Don't get dead."

WHEN SHE HEARD THE MOANS, Miranda knew they were in trouble.

She had known for hours that the day was not going to plan but had made herself ignore it. The sun would be setting in thirty minutes and the moans were the first sign of anything since Mario and Doug left that morning. No calls on the radio. No flares. Not even a fucking smoke signal.

She climbed to the highest point of the yacht's deck above the cockpit seats, keeping hold on the canopy rail, and raised the binoculars with her free hand. The moans were faint but growing louder. She could not tell how serious the trouble was from their slip at the end of Bell Harbor Marina's pier. Across the roadway, cookie-cutter low-rise condos blocked her view.

"We hear Our children!"

Jeremiah's voice, coming from the parlor below deck. He must have heard the zombies moaning.

"Your blasphemous treachery against Us will end, and God the All-Father will judge you as you deserve," he continued. "But first We will teach you submission and obedience! Perhaps We will keep you for Ourselves if you can learn. You will be an example of Our power and truth..."

Ignore him, she said to herself as he kept ranting. The moaning might not mean anything. The zombies could be chasing a shadow for all she knew. The growing noise did not mean squat. Not yet.

Sure it doesn't... Just keep on telling yourself that.

She strained to see beyond the condos, standing on tiptoe as if it would help her catch a glimpse of the streets between or see through the tall buildings that climbed the steep hills of Seattle. Improvised bridges—ladders, fire escapes, scraps of metal, rope, or combinations thereof—connected clusters of buildings. People had lived there at some point, but she had not seen any signs of life so far.

Farther up the hill, walls snaked out of sight. Most seemed intact, but one had a section that had collapsed a long time ago if the weeds and saplings growing among the jumble of fallen concrete blocks were any indication. Along the waterfront some buildings were intact while others, like the aquarium, had caught fire at some point. The aquarium wall facing Puget Sound had fallen in. The roof was gone. The steel beams that had supported its weight sagged despite being relieved of their burden. Seattle oozed emptiness and decay. Without people to maintain them, the artifacts of civilization that had seemed so permanent when humanity fell almost eleven years ago had begun to fall apart almost immediately. Miranda's knee twinged as she set her foot flat again. She looked up the mast. Another fifty feet of elevation might let her see enough to make the difference between—what? She had no idea. But she knew she had to hurry or she would lose the light.

She limped to the other side of the yacht and stepped into the mast-climber harness, securing it around her hips. She shoved her feet into the foot straps, then bent her knees and straightened them.

"Son of a bitch," she hissed, tears springing to her eyes at the sharp slice of pain that bisected her kneecap and shot down her shin. She winched her way up the static line attached to the mast, opening and closing the top line clutch, the pain worse every time she pushed against her body weight. It still beat how old-time sailors had done it: free-climbing hand over hand with their bare feet shimmying along the ropes.

Midway to the top of the mast the wind picked up, threading its way through the fibers of her clothes. She thought she saw movement beyond the harbor-front condos. The setting sun behind her cast long orange and pink shadows between the buildings. The wind gusted, and the harness twisted right, away from the city.

She fought the swiveling harness as she cursed everything: this boat, the unknown city, staying behind to watch Jeremiah, Mario and Doug being gone so long, and the fucking zombies that had made all of this happen. Finally, two more pushes up the static line and she was sure. A dark shadow of zombies, a tidal wave of putrefaction, staggered toward Puget Sound. They weaved and reeled, stumbled and shuffled, unsteady yet determined like a group of drunk revelers intent upon reaching the dilapidated Ferris wheel at the south end of Waterfront Park.

Then Doug and Mario burst into the open from the shadows below the elevated freeway, hauling ass, the dipping sun illuminating them with a translucent pink glow. Miranda nearly choked as they slowed when they saw what lay ahead. They glanced at one another before they turned northwest on Alaskan Way, toward the marina, and picked up the pace.

They had emerged on the roadway just a few seconds ahead of the great mass of zombies descending on the Ferris wheel at Waterfront Park. Retreat to the south was cut off. On the path to the marina, from every street that tumbled down the hillsides of Seattle, zombies spilled onto the road the two men sprinted along. When they disappeared from view behind the aquarium, Miranda released the top rope clutch and worked her way back down the static line. If she cast off and got the boat moving toward them, maybe she could get close enough to make a difference, to help them make it.

I should never have stayed behind!

She wriggled out of the mast-climber harness and released the docking rope, knowing the sentiment was ridiculous. She just hated how helpless watching them made her feel. Jeremiah's zombie repellant effect would have let them move safely through the infested city, but Doug had not been willing to risk Jeremiah's escape. Doug had made the right call. Besides, she would not be able to run for her life the way they were now.

She cast off the mooring ropes keeping the yacht at the dock and hurried back to the cockpit. She looked at the controls, her hands slick with sweat.

You can do this.

Since she always got seasick, Miranda avoided boats, which made her the least experienced piloting watercraft. She pumped the shift lever and made sure the boat was in neutral. She turned the key to the on position.

Nothing happened.

"What the fuck!"

She looked up at the shore. Zombies began to stumble up Piers 62 and 63, one pier down from the marina. With a city's worth of the undead coming from three sides, Piers 62 and 63 were the closest, most direct route for Mario and Doug to get to the water. She fought against panic as the moans grew louder and more excited.

If you panic, you cannot help them.

She checked again. The motor was in neutral; she had pumped the shift lever. She pumped it again and turned the key.

Nothing.

Then she remembered the kill switch.

She almost laughed out loud with relief when she saw it was in the off position. She turned it on. This time the motor began to power up. By rights she should wait half a minute to let the engine power up all the way. Instead, she applied a little choke, then some gas, and let out the throttle out in five seconds. The sputtering from the motor sounded awful because she had rushed it, but it did not stall. She depressed the button on the shift lever and pushed it forward. The motor's hum gained strength, and the yacht slid through the water.

When she looked up, she felt the blow to her stomach as if she had taken a punch. At least fifty zombies were on the pier, sniffing the air, trying to locate the men. She turned the wheel away from the dock as Mario and Doug came into view. At least as many zombies were on Alaskan Way, between the two men and the pier.

It was the most helpless moment of her life, being consigned to the role of spectator while Doug and Mario fought for their lives. With that many zombies, the fact that both of them were vaccinated against the ZBZ-1 virus did not matter. If they stopped for anything, if they even slowed down, they would be ripped limb from limb.

Blurs of motion.

Decomposed figures lurching and swaying.

Flashes of metal that glinted in the setting sun.

Doug and Mario were trying to push, duck, and deflect rather than stop and fight. A knot of zombies stopped, churning together like sharks in a feeding frenzy. Was one of them down? She gaped at the pier, struck dumb at the idea that one or both of them might be gone. Then a sudden burst of movement, black blood spurting in all directions, and both men surged into view. They hurtled down the long pier with the zombies swarming close behind.

They'll follow like lemmings, she thought, impotent anger rising at the relentlessness with which the zombies pursued them. They're both wearing chain mail, she remembered, her heart sinking even more. She did not think Doug would have a problem with the extra weight. Normally Mario would not either, but he was recovering from a gunshot wound to his arm, and his shoulder on that same side had almost dislocated. That had been almost two months ago, but he was still not back to normal.

She jammed the shift lever forward, and the yacht sped up, eating the distance to the pier. She eased off thirty seconds later, not wanting to get too close to the zombies that would soon be in the water.

Doug and Mario jumped. As they splashed into the water, the first zombie fell off the pier. A torrent of the undead followed, churning the water, but she still had not seen Mario or Doug surface.

"Where the fuck are you?"

Miranda kicked off her boots and grabbed a life ring. She hurled it over the side, climbed over the handrail, and dove into the dark, choppy water. Every muscle in her body contracted from the shock of cold, but by the time she surfaced, her limbs were cooperating with her brain. She stuck her arm through the life ring and looked toward the pier.

The water churned with the zombies' flailing limbs. They lacked the coordination to do anything besides splash, but they could still bite, or depending on how waterlogged, drag a person under. Lack of mobility never stopped them being dangerous.

Just as she was starting to panic because she still had not seen anyone break the surface, Doug's head bobbed into view. His dark clothes blended into the water, making him hard to see.

"Over here," she shouted, waving the life ring over her head. She swam toward him.

Doug shouted back. "Where's Mario?"

She was now close enough to shove the life ring at him. He latched on to it.

"I can't see him!"

"There," Doug said, pointing.

She saw Mario's head slip beneath the choppy water. She dove for him, unable to see in the dark water. Then a light flickered, descending beneath her.

His flashlight!

It was him, had to be. She swam after the light, lungs burning, kicking harder, and caught an arm. She held it tight and pumped her legs hard, but with his pack and the chain mail, it wasn't enough. She flipped back and caught him under both arms, then kicked her rigid legs to propel them up, toward the fading light above. The weight of Mario's body got heavier the higher they climbed. Her lungs pushed against the inside of her rib cage, the instinct to breathe impossible to resist. Her head broke the surface. Icy water rushed down her windpipe as she opened her mouth to suck in air. She gasped and coughed, struggling to keep her head above the surface, and pulled on Mario as hard as she could. He broke the surface beside her, his head lolling to the side.

Miranda's arms and legs were jelly, all strength depleted. She couldn't stop coughing as she flailed, and she felt Mario slip under the water again. She couldn't keep him up, didn't have the strength, and felt herself going down.

Doug shoved the life ring at her and pulled her arm through. She clutched it feebly, wrapping her other arm around the opposite direction, violent coughs still racking her body, throat and lungs raw. Through the dark water splashing in her face, she saw Doug pull Mario to him. Mario coughed, then retched up water as Doug slipped his arm through the life ring. Miranda clung to the life ring, unable to do anything but let Doug do the work for all of them.

Miranda's whole body shook by the time they reached the yacht, her body heat wicked away by the frigid water. Doug heaved himself over the edge of the swim platform, then reached back for her. She kicked her legs feebly, trying to help him get her out of the water, only now noticing how much her knee hurt.

"You're in my way," Doug said, pushing her aside when she tried to help him get Mario on board.

Delilah barked from the cabin below deck. Miranda's teeth chattered, in counterpoint to her shaking body, as Doug heaved Mario onto the swim platform. She could see he was shielding his shoulder, holding his arm tight to his body. They all lay gasping, muscles depleted from the cold and the sudden subsidence of adrenaline. Mario reached out and caught her hand.

"Th-thanks," he said.

"Y-you two o-okay?"

Doug pushed himself upright, squirmed out of his backpack, and pulled himself up the guardrail to his feet. "Never b-better."

Mario pushed himself up to sitting and started to speak to her, but Miranda cut him off.

"I already k-know, babe," she managed through her chattering teeth. "S-Seattle's gone."

2

As they dropped anchor near Bainbridge Island, Miranda looked back at Seattle's dark skyline one last time. She could just make out the shapes of the oversized letters attached to the skeletal frame over Pike's Place. The last time she had seen the giant PUBLIC MARKET sign, it had been illuminated in pink and red neon. Now it was dark and almost unrecognizable if you didn't already know what it was.

The warm water of the shower felt almost sweltering, like tropical rain. She thanked God again that they had this swanky yacht, not some basic sailboat. She stood underneath the light but steady stream, soaking in the heat. She heard Mario enter their cabin, then the suck and plop of removing his wet overclothes followed by the metallic slurp of wet chain mail hitting the floor. The shower curtain pulled away, and he stepped into the small shower stall with her. She shifted to make room as he wrapped his cold arms around her.

"That was close," she whispered.

Mario nodded, his cold lips pressed against her shoulder, and held her tighter.

AFTER THE SHOWER, Miranda inspected Mario for cuts and bites. She trailed her fingers over the welts on his arms and legs from zombie bites that the chain mail had fended off. A welt on his calf dribbled blood from a tiny cut, and there was a hole in Mario's chain mail in the same spot that needed to be repaired. There was no way to be certain if the cut was from a bite or from the chain mail. Mario was vaccinated—they all were—so if it was a bite, he would not become a zombie. He would need to take antibiotics, however, because zombie bites always went septic. They had a pretty decent store of antibiotics for now. Her hollow stomach twisted inside out at the thought of not having any, of watching him die of septic shock. She took a deep breath, shoving the morbid thought aside.

"You've got a cut on your right calf. More antibiotics and chain mail repair, but you'll live," she said, taking his hand.

He grinned at her, and she felt the familiar flutter in her chest. What would she do without him? He kissed her, then pulled away and shrugged into a robe.

"I need to look Doug over."

"Naked priests. They never let a girl have any fun." She pulled on a pair of sweats, then a t-shirt. "As his best friend, I'm deeply wounded."

She gave it five minutes before heading to the lounge area. Mario stood in the galley, sucking down a bottle of water while nimbly avoiding Delilah's uncanny ability to be underfoot when there was any possibility of food. She kissed the back of his neck as she squeezed by, trying to ignore the swooping sensation in her stomach when she leaned over to catch the dog's collar and pull her out of the way.

Doug huddled under a blanket on the long built-in couch. Miranda sat beside him, stealing some of the blanket and snuggling close. When he protested, she said, "Payback for choosing Mario to inspect your hot bod."

Mario joined them, sitting on the floor at Miranda's feet. He rubbed Delilah's batwing ears, and the dog's leg started jiggling like crazy. Even as discouraged as the slump of Mario's shoulders showed him to be, the way he looked at her warmed Miranda from her toes to her nose.

Carnal warmth notwithstanding, she was not able to tamp down the despair taking root behind her sternum, so powerful it ached. Mario and Doug were safe; that was what she had to focus on. She just could not fucking believe it. She could not believe that Seattle University, their safe harbor, was gone. She did not understand how she had the capacity to *be* surprised by this kind of setback anymore, but she was. This was supposed to be it. Their destination, their goal. The warm embrace of allies and the chance to let others mind the whack job for a little while. A chance to get off this nausea factory that masqueraded as transportation. Instead, their refuge was gone, and zombies roamed its grounds as freely as they did the rest of the city.

"You two were gone so long I was hoping it was because you were with people," Miranda said. She leaned her head back against the cushions and concentrated on her breathing so she wouldn't throw up.

"Just hard to move around, you know how it is. Clear one minute, a block party the next," Doug said. His lips were still tinged blue from Puget Sound's cold waters.

Mario tipped his head toward the fore cabin. "He give you any trouble?"

"Nah," she said. "The asshole behaved himself."

Delilah settled her head over Mario's thigh with a contented sigh. He scratched her head absently with one hand. With the other he found Miranda's foot under the blanket and wrapped his hand around the back of her heel, running his thumb back and forth over the top of her foot.

He said, "Of all the problems we might run into, I have to admit I did not see this one coming."

Miranda nodded her agreement. "Do we set up shop here anyway? If we took Jeremiah with us, it would be easier to move around. We could see if the lab is salvageable."

"You didn't see the campus, babe," Mario said. "Half the buildings were burned down."

"I don't want to take Jeremiah off this boat unless we have a destination in mind," Doug said. "He'll try to escape first chance he gets. I don't want to risk it if we don't have to."

A stronger wave of nausea rose in Miranda's throat.

*I will not puke, I will not puke, I will **not** puke.*

Mario stopped petting Delilah and rubbed his eyes. "We should try Portland."

Despite her joy at their miraculous deliverance, Miranda bristled. "You mean the place we passed six days ago? Six days that I could have been on dry land?"

Doug leaned forward and spoke to Mario across Miranda. "Where's the stuff we got for her?"

"Oh, right, I forgot."

Mario unglued Delilah from his leg and got up. He rifled through his oversized wet backpack, still in the corner where he had dropped it earlier. He pulled out bottle after bottle of pills, each ensconced in vacuum-sealed plastic bags.

"Oregon Health and Science University is in Portland," he said. "It was a teaching hospital, and there was a vaccine institute. We'll probably have an easier time finding the equipment we need there. I almost said something when we were approaching the Columbia River, but they were expecting us here with a lab that was ready to go. I don't know what we'll do for power, but, ah, here we go."

Mario held up a huge white pill bottle, and Miranda knew she was going to be sick.

"Oh shit," she moaned, bending double to put her head between her knees. A second later, a bucket was shoved under her face. She heaved into it, the meager contents of her stomach riding an acid-tinged wave the wrong way through her esophagus. Sweat chilled her skin as she spat into the bucket, waiting to see if any more was coming.

"Take this," Mario said, kneeling beside her. He handed her a pill and some water.

Miranda swallowed the bitter pill. She swished the water in her mouth before spitting it into the bucket.

"What is it?"

"Metoclopramide," Mario answered.

"Not helpful," she said more sharply than she meant to.

Doug patted her back. "It's prescription strength Dramamine." He grabbed the bucket as he stood up. "We got stuck in a CVS on the way back. You're welcome, Miri."

Miranda sighed. They had only just been delivered from death's door, and she was already snapping and crabby. "I'm sorry. Thank you, both of you."

Mario pulled her to her feet and turned her toward their cabin. "You should lie down till that kicks in. You look green. I'll be in as soon as I sort through all the meds we picked up."

She made it to the galley before he said, "Your limp is worse."

"I know," she said, but did not stop.

"What happened?"

Miranda turned back to face him. Between the fear, the icy water, and her stomach's latest act of rebellion, a deep exhaustion had settled over her, weighing her down like a heavy cloak. She wanted to lie, tell him she had tripped, but they had promised no secrets this time. It wouldn't be a big lie, but little lies made the big ones easier. If she wanted him to hold up his end of the bargain, then she had to hold up hers.

Besides, she had a work-around.

"I jumped into Puget Sound to save your ass, that's what."

Mario's eyes narrowed. "What else? Swimming would not screw it up that much."

Fuck, she thought. Resigned, she said, "The zombies started

moaning when you were coming back, and I couldn't see anything. I thought I might be able to see if I climbed the mast to—"

"You climbed the mast?" Mario said, interrupting her. "Are you *trying* to permanently screw up your knee?"

"Of course not," she said as Delilah began to whine. "Not any more than you're trying to screw up your shoulder."

Mario took a deep breath, his nostrils flaring. "A bum knee might kill you."

She could tell by his tone he was forcing himself to stay calm.

"So might a bum shoulder," she said, annoyed. She was not giving him a hard time about his injuries or how he might be making them worse. Why was he giving her one?

"Be reasonable, Miranda—"

"Be reasonable?"

If there was one thing that made Miranda see red, it was a man telling her to be reasonable because she did not agree with him. Mario was out of practice; that was for fucking sure.

"I was trying to see if I could help you."

"Watch Jeremiah and don't do anything stupid," Mario snapped, shouting at her. "Jesus Christ, Miranda! That's all you had to do!"

She took a step back, Delilah covering her retreat. The dog did not exactly growl at Mario, but the rumble in her throat was close.

Miranda looked at Mario, puzzled. She could count on one hand the times he had lost his temper like this and still have fingers free. Something else was going on; she just did not know what, but her temper was up, too. Trying to figure it out was not something she had the bandwidth for, tired and nauseous as she was. Mario and Doug had just given her the fright of a lifetime and he was giving her a hard time about saving him?

Her voice became a growl. "Don't take that tone with me."

"Or," Doug said, raising his voice, "you could just admit that maybe climbing the mast was not the brightest idea, Miri, and that you'll do a better job convalescing from now on. And you could try being less judgy, Mario, because you're deep in hypocrite territory."

Doug shook his head at them like they were unruly children.

"You two love each other, and unlike long-suffering Father Doug here, haven't taken a vow of celibacy. Why don't you do what normal people do when they've just cheated death and get a room?"

A pink flush of embarrassment crept up Mario's face, despite his narrowed his eyes and fierce glare. Served him right, Miranda thought. Doug smirked at her, his blue eyes brimming with good cheer.

"Oh fuck you both. I'm going to lie down."

3

Mario watched Miranda hobble off to their cabin, Delilah at her heels, not quite sure what had just happened. What the fuck had that been about? He should not be surprised that her own safety would be the first thing out the window if she thought he or Doug were in danger, but he had only just gotten her back. She had forgiven him, which he didn't deserve after what he had put her through, and he was fucking it up. Fear flooded his belly at the thought that he was driving her away. He followed as far as the galley, then stopped. If he tried to talk to her now, it would just prolong their argument.

Doug made an extravagant display of yawning and stretching.

"I'm going to let Jeremiah out,"

Doug went to the fore cabin. A minute later, Mario heard him say, "You wanna stay here and mope, fine by me, but you won't get your book."

Jeremiah muttered something Mario could not make out.

"Just put the damn things on," Doug said.

A smile quirked Mario's lips upward. After three weeks, even Doug's patience with their captive was wearing thin. Doug stepped backward into the lounge area far enough to clear a path from the fore cabin to the table across from the couch. Jeremiah shuffled through the door, the metal of the shackles that bound his hands and feet clinking.

Jeremiah looked smug when he said, "Your failure to impose discipline and obedience, to tolerate such willfulness, is why your woman behaves as she does. If you believed in Our judgment, in the truth of Us, God the Heavenly Father on Earth, it would be a simple thing to banish her defects of character."

Mario sighed. The guy was like a skipping record.

"I happen to like those defects of character. They keep things interesting."

Doug pointed to the built-in bench that curled around the table at a ninety-degree angle. A book sat on it.

"Sit. Read." Doug put his finger to his lips. "And for the love of God, shhhh."

Jeremiah shot Doug a venomous glare. "We shall mete Our judgment eventually, apostate. It will be swift and merciless."

But he did as he was told, eagerly scooping up the paperback. Jeremiah's man overboard escapade the third day out from Santa Cruz had almost derailed everything they had fought so hard for, that their friends had died for. They had clamped down hard. A few days later, they discovered they could extort him into middling-good behavior with books. It was a surprising discovery at first since there had been few books in New Jerusalem. But Jeremiah was crazy, not illiterate, even if reading popular fiction undermined his claim of rejecting everything to do with the 'fallen world' beyond his mountaintop cult. Luckily, the yacht's owner had been a voracious reader. Paperback novels were crammed everywhere, and letting him read made watching him less labor intensive. Jeremiah liked thrillers and mysteries, especially Jack Reacher.

Poor Jack, Mario thought, having read some Jack Reacher books himself. He was certain Jeremiah identified with the honorable hero of the series; he lacked the self-awareness to realize he was anything but. If Jack Reacher were here, he would kick Jeremiah's ass and not lose a wink of sleep over it.

Doug joined Mario in the galley. It was far enough away that they could keep a watchful eye on Jeremiah but still converse without being overheard.

"Way to go, slick. You better make up with her. The world is too small when you two are fighting."

Mario sighed. "I will."

A pause, then Doug said, "That was about the CVS."

"Fuck me," Mario said softly, because Doug was right. He hadn't realized it until Doug said it, but he had lost his temper because of what had happened earlier today.

"I really thought that was it."

"I've never seen you fight like that."

Mario could still hear the plate glass window of the CVS crack and shatter, the stress of the pressing horde finally too much. When he and Doug had broken the other window to escape, he had known they were already dead. But they could die inside like trapped animals, or die outside and go down fighting.

"Knowing I spent the last few hours of my life in a moldy drugstore instead of with Miranda made me angrier than I've ever been."

"Harness that, grasshopper. It saved us today."

Mario scrubbed the back of his neck with his hand.

"She makes me so fucking crazy. Climbing the mast when her knee is only just starting to heal? I know what she's like, I know, but... It's like she goes out of her way to make herself as vulnerable as possible."

"You know it's all about I-statements, right? No one *makes* you feel the way you do. It's more like *she* does shit that might get her killed down the line, and then *I* feel afraid, but it feels safer to get angry than admit it scares the bejesus out of me."

Mario looked at Doug for a moment, his brow wrinkled.

"What are you, my therapist?"

Doug laughed so loud it came out as a bark. He shushed himself almost immediately, mindful that Miranda might be asleep. "I think of it more along the lines of a couples counselor."

Mario smiled despite himself, but it faded almost as soon as it began.

"She has no idea how close she came to being on her own today. The pier was a breeze compared to getting out of that drugstore. She has no fucking idea."

"Then *tell* her."

Mario's eyes narrowed, and he pursed his lips, skeptical. "When's the last time you shared that close a shave with someone you care about?"

Doug opened his mouth to answer, then closed it.

"Ha! I knew it!" Jeremiah said softly.

They both looked up, giving Jeremiah their full attention. He was nodding his head as he read his book, oblivious that he had attracted their attention.

"Thank God for Jack Reacher," Doug said. "Otherwise, I'd have killed him by now."

"Jack does tamp down the crazy." Mario sighed. "Guess I'm sleeping out here tonight."

"You'll be fine. Tropical Storm Miranda never lasts long."

A soft smile curled the corners of Mario's mouth. Furious and intense but blowing over quickly—Tropical Storm Miranda indeed.

"I know," he said, sighing. "But I learned a long time ago that when a woman is angry with you, if you have to ask if it's okay to talk to her, it's too soon."

———

MARIO CROUCHED NEXT TO ANTHONY. The calico cat that Anthony had finally coaxed into the mudroom was nestled in the blankets that lined the birthing box. Six kittens suckled with small squeaks, continuously kneading their mama's stomach with their tiny paws.

"See, Daddy. There are three regular calicos, one tortie, and one black and one gray."

"I see them," Mario said. "They're so itty bitty."

"She had them while I was at school. They won't open their eyes for at least a week. See how their ears are flat? They're so cute."

Mario ruffled his son's dark hair. He never tired of getting the blow-by-blow of kitten development with the latest litter of Anthony's rescue kittens. Anthony was so serious about it. He had no idea how cute he was.

"They can't walk yet. Like, at all," his son continued. He turned to look at Mario. "I wanted you to see them but we can't be in here too much at first or the mama won't like it and she'll move them and how can I take care of them if that happens?"

Anthony took a deep breath, sucking in air after fitting so many words into one breath. Mario stifled a laugh.

"We don't want that," he said.

"No, we don't," Anthony said, agreeing with a seriousness beyond his years.

A high-pitched squeal came from the door to the kitchen.

"Daddy!"

Mario stood and took three steps, intercepting the streak of blond hair and pure energy that was Maureen, while Anthony cried, "Stop her!"

Mario lifted the three-year-old up in the air.

"How's my girl?"

Maureen wriggled in his grip, straining to see over his head.

"Wanna see kittens!"

"No!" Anthony said, sounding desperate.

"It's okay, Anthony," Mario said. He shifted Maureen to his hip and headed for the kitchen. "No can do, kiddo. They're too small. So are you."

"Wanna see kittens," Maureen shrieked.

Behind them, the door to the mudroom closed. Mario glanced back in time see Anthony's frowning face through the pane of glass before he disappeared.

"No kittens for you," Mario said.

Maureen's face had flushed dark pink on its way to deep red. Emily entered the kitchen, followed by nine-year old Michael, who had stuffed his fingers in his ears.

"What is going on?" Emily asked.

"She wants to see the kittens."

"Oh." Emily smiled. "Someone didn't get her nap today."

"Yeah, I can—"

MARIO JERKED AWAKE.

Disoriented by the dream, it took him a moment to figure out where he was. As soon as he remembered the yacht, he felt the crick in his neck and the cramped muscles in his back, hips, and legs. Sleeping on the lounge floor had not caused the stiffness—running for his life through Seattle had that honor—but it hadn't helped.

The dream had been so real. He could still feel the weight of Maureen in his arms, the softness of Anthony's hair, and the serious expression in his dark eyes. Michael had been wearing a t-shirt with the logo of his favorite band, Vegan Zombies.

How the hell do I dream t-shirts, he thought.

The yearning for his children reared its head, a physical ache that throbbed in his chest. He sat up, replaying the dream in his head because he didn't want to forget it. The slightly musky smell of the newborn kittens. The birdsong outside, the sunshine that had illuminated Maureen's blond hair so that it glowed. Even Emily's smile once she realized the crisis was only an overtired toddler.

Mario pushed the covers back and sat up. The chilly morning air sent prickles of gooseflesh racing over his bare chest and arms. He would never walk Maureen down the aisle at her wedding. Never know if Anthony became a vet, or what sort of man Michael would be. Better than his old man, Mario hoped. He had as good as orphaned them, leaving as he had. And while he knew he needed to go, for his safety and theirs, it didn't ease the guilt one iota. The only person who had not been in the dream had been Dominic, his brother.

Christ, he thought. If this is how the day is gonna go, I might as well kill myself and get it over with.

His brother's fate was the completely predictable consequence of the choices he had made, but Mario was the one who dropped him in it. Dominic was surely dead. Even though he hadn't been involved in the plot to steal the vaccine, the rest of City Council in San Jose would never believe him. He would be guilty by association, and someone would have to pay.

"Stop," Mario whispered to himself, taking his head in his hands. "Stop, stop, stop. Now."

He climbed to his feet, his eyes adjusting quickly to the gloomy predawn light. He stretched for a few minutes, mindful to not wake Doug who slept on the long built-in couch. Doug had offered it to him last night, but Mario refused. Doug wasn't the reason he was sleeping on the metaphorical couch after losing his cool with Miranda. He shouldn't be the one to suffer the consequence. Besides, he was already sleeping in the lounge instead of the fore cabin because they needed a secure place for Jeremiah.

Carefully, he walked to the galley and got a drink of water. After hitting the head and brushing his teeth, he decided now was as good a time as any to eat a little crow.

Gently, he opened the door to his and Miranda's cabin, easing it shut behind him. He could tell by the soft rise and fall of her breathing that she was still asleep. From the floor on Miranda's side of the bed, Delilah's wagging tail thumped softly against the floor, but she did not get up to greet him.

Mario stripped off his boxers and crawled into bed, curling his body against Miranda's bare skin like water sliding around a rock. The warmth of her body comforted him. He slipped his hand over her waist. She stirred, arching her back, which pressed her hips against him. His cock stiffened, and he was overcome by the sharp need to make love. He wanted to lose himself in her, be reassured that they were both alive and whole and together.

She rolled over to face him, blinking and scrunching her eyes as she woke. Even in the dim light he could see the pink flush of sleep on her face. And the downward pucker of her lips, which meant she wasn't mad anymore, but her feelings were hurt.

"I'm sorry," he said softly. "I was out of line."

She looked at him a moment, stifling a yawn, then said, "What happened out there?"

Every instinct shouted at him not to tell her. You didn't burden others with almost stories, unless they were fueled by bravado and alcohol, when you tried like hell to one-up the last guy. You didn't burden others, especially the people you loved. The rule was unspoken, but everyone knew it.

Mario choked over the words, forcing them out. "We almost didn't make it back."

Miranda sighed. "You think I don't know that? I saw the whole—"

He cut her off. Now that he had begun, the urgency to make her understand swept over him like a tsunami.

"No, Miri, you don't. The pier—*fuck*," he said, tears surprising him. "The pier was the easy part. The drugstore. There was no way we could make it. No way. I still don't know why we're not dead." His voice cracked, and his eyes welled up, but this time he didn't care about the tears. "I was never going to see you again. I was leaving you on your own. I wasn't afraid it might happen, Miri. I knew it already had."

"Oh, sweetheart."

Her comprehension of why he had acted like such an ass, the instant forgiveness that filled her eyes, bathed him in absolution. Her lips touched his, and he fell into her headlong—her caresses and soft whimpers, the silk of her skin, and the heady musk between her thighs. Her urgency matched his own, consoling him, reassuring him that she loved him no matter his flaws or mistakes, until the fiery conflagration of their desire and conciliation burned away to nothing.

Afterward, she nestled in the crook of his shoulder, the warm weight of her body half sprawled over his.

"You're not going anywhere without me," she murmured drowsily. "I promise."

Mario squeezed her shoulder, then resumed stroking her hair. It was unlike her to make such a promise, one she could not be sure to keep, but he appreciated the gesture. He drifted toward sleep, the solidity of Miranda's body tethering him to what was real, to what he could count on, but it could not quash the wisp of worry that would weave itself into his dreams.

What if they failed in Portland, too? What would happen then?

4

DOUG SCOWLED AT THE SKELETAL CRANES LOOMING OVER THE
Willamette River's east bank, relics from a time when cargo ships
were filled with goods or relieved of them. Even though iron-gray
clouds blanketed the sky, an attenuated glare suffused the gloomy
morning light enough that he squinted. The good weather of the past
week had ended, and it would be this way all day, he could tell
already. He wished again that he had his polarized sunglasses. He
was not sure where he had lost them. In New Jerusalem, most likely.
Another reason to hate that shithole and every fucked-up thing Jeremiah had done there. That the delusional leader of a post-apocalyptic
cult might be the missing ingredient for a cure to save humanity made
their mission feel like a bad movie.

You need an attitude adjustment, Doug told himself.

A growing sense of dread had taken root as soon as Doug
glimpsed the ruins of Portland this morning. Such moroseness was
unlike him, but zombies had taught him to pay attention to his
instincts and feelings rather than logic them away. He was not
exactly embracing the dread, but he wasn't pushing it away, either.

The decayed state of the buildings was evident even at this

distance. It looked more desolate than Seattle had. There were no signs of life, past or present. The makeshift bridges strung between buildings in downtown Seattle, even those that had fallen into disrepair, were evidence of life. Someone had held on, at least for a while, but here? Nothing. No thin wisps of smoke from campfires or stoves, no glimpses of motion behind windows so dirty they were almost opaque. So far, even zombies were absent instead of shuffling in the streets.

Portland felt dead in a way that Seattle had not.

But it was more than that. Seffie had come up last night while he and Mario talked, and Doug realized he hadn't thought of her once since they left Santa Cruz. Seffie had saved Connor's life, however briefly, and his, Mario's, and Miranda's as well. She'd been informing on them at first, but Doug had believed her when she said she stopped as soon as she knew the mission was about the vaccine. Seffie had more than redeemed herself but almost as soon as she was gone, she had become out of sight, out of mind.

When he first became a priest, Doug had cultivated the habit of reciting the names of the most recently departed when he said or went to Mass every day. There were so many who had died, too many to remember everyone, but Doug had felt that he could manage the recent ones at least once. For people like Seffie, who literally had no one, it had felt like a moral obligation to acknowledge that they existed at all. But Doug had not thought much about anyone who'd died to get them this far. Perhaps it was just a coping mechanism, but the realization bothered him. He could not even remember the last time he'd said Mass since they left Santa Clara, something all priests are obliged to do every day, even if just to themselves. The disconnection he felt from his vocation left him feeling like a ship without a rudder.

"I'm really starting to suck at priesting," he muttered.

He turned at the squeak of approaching footsteps. Miranda was cocooned inside a drab green jacket. The shadows under her eyes had receded, and the green tinge to her skin had been replaced by a rosy glow. And an air of contentment and obnoxious well-being. She had probably gotten lucky last night.

"You look a lot better," he said. "I think you've even gained a pound or two."

Miranda smiled. "I haven't needed a Dramamine in days. I love rivers as much as I hate open ocean."

"You were pretty pathetic."

They stood in silence as more of Portland's derelict buildings slipped by. The yacht rounded a gentle curve in the river, and a bridge came into view. The first of six, maybe eight, before they reached Ross Island? Doug couldn't remember.

He sighed, then said almost under his breath, "This fucking place."

Miranda looked up at him, eyebrows knitted together. "What do you mean by that?"

"I don't know," he said, shifting his weight from one foot to the other. "Two days ago I was so restless I couldn't wait to get off this boat, but now?" He shrugged. "You haven't been puking and the rivers are beautiful. Even Jeremiah's been less of an asshole."

"But?"

"I don't know," he said again. He knew that some of it was the feeling of disconnection from his vocation, but he wasn't going to get into that with Miranda. She'd just tell him that he shouldn't have become a priest in the first place. "It feels deader here. I know Seattle was the same but here it feels...more. It's like every place is deader and emptier than the last."

Miranda looked at him with appraising eyes. Her face became thoughtful as she looked back to the river.

"We thought people were waiting for us in Seattle. No one is waiting for us this time, either, but we know it. Last time we didn't."

Doug let her words settle for a moment, felt the truth of them slip into place like the last piece of a puzzle.

"I think you're right."

"You're agreeing with me just like that? No smart-ass anything?"

At his nod, she snorted in disgust. "I refuse to do all the heavy lifting. You better step up your game, buddy."

A tiny smile curled Doug's mouth and crinkled the corners of his eyes. A bridge was only three hundred yards ahead now, abandoned cars visible through crumbled sections of concrete parapet. Movement caught his eye, followed by a moan. Soon a small group of zombies gathered. First one, then another, walked off the crumbling edge and splashed into the river.

"And the welcome wagon arrives," Miranda said.

Doug gripped the pulpit rail tighter when the yacht tacked starboard to avoid the dropping zombies.

"Come under the canopy," Mario called from the cockpit.

Miranda headed to the cockpit to join Mario, but Doug watched the zombies a moment longer. The first few to fall from the bridge flailed in the water. More followed, pummeling into them like a slapstick routine. The voyage from Seattle had been pleasant, even restful, especially since Miranda had not been on death's door the entire time. Instead of puking, she had spent her time scribbling in a journal and grumbling about how hard it was to find a pencil that didn't smudge. When he thought no one was looking, Mario had spent an inordinate amount of time watching Miranda and looking content. Doug hadn't done much more than sleep, read, and tease Miranda.

They had needed the time to recoup and to plan, but most of all, to rest. Doug knew that he was always connected to God, because the door on God's side was always open. He would feel it again. He just needed to find the door on this side.

"I just needed downtime after what it took to get us here," he murmured to himself. "It'll come back. It always does."

Miranda's right, he decided. Knowing no one waited for them had made the lifeless city feel more desolate. Its loneliness had spooked him, and he had worried the feeling of disconnection like a dog worried a bone. He just needed to relax and recognize the disconnection and loneliness for what it was: a feeling that would pass.

Doug looked one last time at the hapless creatures falling off the bridge, at the decaying city that awaited them. A lightness began to fill his chest, chasing out the dread, and he grinned. There was nothing to be apprehensive about. It was just another dead city filled with zombies.

He could do that shit all day long.

THEY LANDED the yacht's dinghy almost directly across from the tip of Ross Island, a teardrop-shaped atoll in the Willamette River that proved an ideal hiding place to moor the yacht. Doug had studied maps of Seattle so much that he felt he could find his way most anywhere there. Portland, not so much. The only map of Portland they had was ripped in half, which might have felt indicative of how things were going if Doug believed in omens. Miranda had spent summers in Portland with her grandparents, and Oregon Health and Science University was on their half map. It was good enough for now.

Doug saw Mario check the five-foot-long length of nylon rope that attached Jeremiah to him for what seemed the zillionth time.

"Are you okay with that length, Mario? We can change it."

Mario shook his head. "It's fine," he said, the slightest trace of dissatisfaction in his voice.

Miranda rolled her eyes at Doug. Mario had wanted Jeremiah tied to Miranda 'because of her knee,' but Doug had overruled him. Mario had conceded with grace, which Doug could tell Miranda had appreciated. After the continual test of wills between she and Connor over her safety, Mario's faith in her ability to gauge risks, the mast-climbing incident notwithstanding, had to be a relief.

"Then let's go," Doug said.

Jeremiah shot Doug a venomous glare as Mario led the way. He was gagged, but it was self-inflicted. Jeremiah's predilection for shouting when the gag wasn't in place in order to attract zombies made it necessary. Otherwise, Doug might have felt bad about it.

Doug and Miranda brought up the rear, to both stay near Jeremiah and to prevent him from getting any bright ideas about using the rope to incapacitate Mario. Delilah trotted alongside Miranda but occasionally took off into the high grass to chase a rabbit.

"Welcome to Portland, kiddos," Doug said. "It's going to be great day. I can feel it."

5

MARIO BEGAN TO RELAX WHEN THEY REACHED THE ELEVATED pedestrian bridge where they could cross I-5 without incident.

"Miranda," Doug said, pointing straight ahead. "Is that it?"

They followed Doug's pointing finger. A graceful curve arced the bridge to the left, its end hidden by a riot of greenery. On a high bluff several miles beyond, a cluster of buildings poked over the tree line.

She nodded. "That's it. OHSU."

The buildings were miniaturized by distance but still tantalizingly close. If everything went right, they would be there in a couple hours. If they were lucky, they would find the right equipment so that Mario could begin his work to recreate the vaccine using Jeremiah's immune blood. If he could do that, they could make the San Jose vaccine and the corrupt political system it propped up irrelevant. And potentially save the human race from extinction.

That's a lot of ifs, he thought.

Miranda said, "The tram overhead went straight up there. I took that ride so many times as a kid."

Everyone, even Jeremiah, looked up. Sagging aerial tram lines that ran the length of the bridge and then ascended to the bluff in the distance were dotted with two suspended passenger cars.

"The damn thing could have at least fallen down by now instead of rubbing it in that we can't use it," Doug said.

Miranda unzipped her jacket and pulled out the map, then crouched down to spread it out.

"I want to make sure I have this route down. There are lots of twists and turns. We need to take at least one staircase that we can't afford to miss."

While Miranda studied the map, Mario took in the gridlocked I-5. Some cars were in their own lane, while others skewed across the dotted lines where they had smashed into other cars. Someone had probably tried to squeeze into another lane before someone else thwarted not only the offending driver, but everyone else. Or maybe the driver had turned into a zombie, and safe navigation of a vehicle no longer commanded its attention. Countless car doors were permanently rusted open with springs sticking through weather-beaten upholstery.

"So many still have zombies inside," Mario said.

The muffled thumps of desiccated faces and mummified limbs banging on dirty, rolled-up windows grew louder.

Doug nodded. "Stuck in traffic forever because their spouse who never listened just had to take the fucking freeway."

Mario snorted, even though the spectacle below them was depressing. So many people had died.

"They lived such small lives," he said softly.

"What do you mean?"

Mario shrugged. "Most people never changed the world in big ways. They just lived their lives. Went to work, paid their taxes, got married and had kids. Not many people founded the next Microsoft."

"Oh," Doug said, sounding amused. "Like you, you mean."

"That's not what I meant," Mario said, laughing.

"Sure you didn't," Doug said, giving him a mocking side-eye. "They did most of the living, though. And it's all gone."

Mario looked at the trapped zombies. They had been people once, and their regular, workaday lives had been everything to them. The good and bad, the ups and downs, the questions and confusion and messiness of life had been the same for every single one of them. What does this life mean? Am I loved, and do I have people to love? Did I leave this world a little better than I found it? When all those small lives with big questions were put together, they were as vast and significant as the universe. And almost all of them were gone, as if they had never existed in the first place.

The rustle of the map pulled Mario's attention from the poor souls trapped in the cars below. Miranda looked up at him, expectant, completely unaware that she was more than the woman he loved. She was his answer to the questions people still asked about their small lives.

Am I loved, and do I have someone to love?

Yes, I do.

Will I leave this world a little better than I found it?

If I'm lucky.

Miranda represented every undeserved blessing bestowed on him these past few months.

Love.

Forgiveness.

The hope of redemption.

She tucked the map inside her jacket as she stood. She took his hand, her smile driving away the last whispers of the dead, lost world.

"Come on," she said, grinning. "Let's go save the world."

NINETY MINUTES LATER, Mario was beginning to indulge in cautious optimism that they just might make it to OHSU without any mishaps. They had encountered zombies along the way, necessitating some backtracking, but so far, their journey had been almost uneventful. The bridge had deposited them in a residential neighborhood that looked so much like the Bay Area that he could have mistaken one for the other. Snug Craftsman bungalows, rambling Prairie style homes, and Victorian Painted Ladies lined the streets. Their bright colors had faded; shattered roof slates littered the sidewalks, and sagging porches and broken windows abounded, but once they had been beautiful.

They were looking for a park near a second set of stairs that would take them up to Terwilliger Boulevard. Portlanders had loved their pedestrian staircases. They were not going to bother with the stairs since they were sure to be overgrown. They would scramble up the adjacent hillside, but the stairs were the landmark that would tell them they were in the right place. From the top of the stairs, it was just half a mile farther.

She tried to hide it, but Miranda had developed a slight limp in the last ten minutes. They needed to get somewhere safe and rest, and not just because of Miranda. If he remained tethered to Jeremiah much longer, Mario was going to lose his mind. Five feet of rope had seemed long at first, but when they climbed over a wall or barricade made of cars, it required contortions that Jeremiah made harder than necessary. He was also unable to move out of earshot when they had to remove the gag to give him a drink of water.

This neighborhood had more zombies than the last. The undead staggered into the streets as they detected the live prey. Hopefully, there would be fewer zombies once they made it up the hillside. So far they had handled the numbers without needing to huddle around Jeremiah for protection, but that could change in a heartbeat. A heartbeat was how long it had taken him and Doug to get trapped in the CVS in Seattle.

Mario tipped the water bottle to take a sip. He heard a sudden patter of feet, then Jeremiah banged into him so hard he had to pinwheel his arms to stay upright. The water bottle landed on the asphalt with a dull clunk, followed by a wet *glug-glug-glug*. Mario whirled around as soon as his balance stabilized, expecting to see an influx of zombies behind them, but the street was clear.

He rounded on Jeremiah. "What the fuck?"

Jeremiah started mumbling unintelligibly through the gag and gesticulating at the ground with his bound hands.

"You want a drink of water?"

Jeremiah nodded. The muscles of Mario's chest and abdomen tightened, flooding his body with energy. A flush of heat swept from his chest to his hairline, and his hands balled into fists.

"Do not fucking do that again," he said, voice sharp and anger mushrooming. If they did not need Jeremiah so much, he would wrap the rope around his neck and strangle him, right here, right now. "You don't need to almost knock me over to ask."

"Everything okay back there?"

Mario looked ahead as he picked up the water bottle. Doug and Miranda had gotten ahead of them. Delilah pranced about, a stick in her mouth. She shook her head as if killing it, trying to entice someone to play with her.

"Everything's fine," he said to Doug.

He loosened the gag, and Jeremiah pulled it from his mouth. Mario shoved the water bottle into his hands and watched Jeremiah suck on it greedily, practically snorting like a piglet at its mother's teat.

Then he started talking.

"We have been meditating on the punishments We will mete out upon you when Our Justice is served."

"Omifuckinggod," Mario muttered, his desire to scream with frustration instantaneous.

He stuffed the gag back into Jeremiah's mouth and tightened it before he gave in to the impulse to beat their captive to a pulp. He grabbed Jeremiah by his upper arm and strong-armed him double-quick to the corner where Miranda and Doug waited. Mario realized his face must reflect his murderous anger when he saw how amused Miranda looked. Doug's grin meant that whatever was about to come out of Doug's mouth was just going to piss him off more.

"Don't say it, Doug," he said. "Just don't."

Doug schooled his features into innocence and flipped his palm upward in an airy 'Whatever can you mean?' gesture.

"This is it. Almost there," Miranda said. She gestured to the hillside in front of them. The overgrown trees, shrubs, briars, and grasses looked as impenetrable as the deep, dark forests of fairy tales.

"Awesome," Mario said through gritted teeth.

"Miranda and I will bushwhack," Doug said, pulling a machete from its sheath. "You probably shouldn't have a big blade when you're attached—"

"Agreed," Mario cut in, working to calm himself. Miranda looked at him through narrowed eyes, her brow wrinkled. "I'll be fine," he said. "I'm just— I'm fine."

She leaned in so close that Mario could see the gold flecks in her eyes. Nestled within the cornflower-blue iris, they looked like tiny dapples of sunshine.

"You *are* fine," she said, her eyes flicking down to the rope, then back up. She bit her lower lip, then smiled. "Maybe we play with that later, Doctor Santorello."

DOUG AND MIRANDA took turns so that they would not tire at the same time. They worked as quickly and efficiently as possible, but there was no way to make bushwhacking quiet. The hillside proved as impassible as Mario's first impression. The upside was there were no zombies wandering the hillside to worry about. The downside was a growing group of zombies milling around in the T-shaped intersection at the foot of the hill. Unable to follow because of the steep hillside, their moans, coupled with the noise of the machetes, attracted more zombies. But they were a secondary concern. It was what might be in the road above that concerned Mario.

Deal with it when we get there, he reminded himself.

You worked the problem in front of you before you worked the next one. His job right now was to bring up the rear of the line and mind Jeremiah. Future problems would be waiting for them like the nasty little bastards they were.

Doug turned back just as Delilah's tail disappeared into the scrub ahead. In a low voice he said, "We're almost there. I can just make out what's left of the road."

Miranda punched a fist into the air in silent celebration. Relief flooded Mario's nervous system, relaxing muscles that he had not realized were filled with tension.

Jeremiah turned back and looked at him. Something about the way he moved set off alarm bells. Something was very wrong. Mario didn't know what it was until Jeremiah leaped.

He had cut the tether.

His shoulder slammed into Mario's solar plexus, knocking him to the ground. Mario rolled down the path, ass over teakettle. The sharp, stumpy remains of shorn saplings stabbed at him. Remnants of brambles scratched his face. He threw his arms out, scrabbling against rocks and loamy soil. A blur of movement flashed by.

Mario scrambled to his feet. Jeremiah was almost at the foot of the hill. A flash of yellow nylon rope fluttered into view. The other end hung limp from where it was threaded through the belt loops of Mario's jeans.

Mario crashed down the hillside, Miranda and Doug shouting behind him. The moans of the zombies below grew louder with the noise of his and Jeremiah's reckless flight. The zombies in the intersection below rippled away as Jeremiah's feet hit the pavement.

"Come to Us, Our children," Jeremiah shouted, now free of the gag. "Come to Our defense! Be Our Judgment!"

Mario crashed into the street, barreling into the waiting zombies. He struck out blindly, pushing and shoving. A cold hand clamped over his wrist, twisting him around. He reached for the knife on his belt.

The sheath was empty.

He shoved his index and middle fingers into the zombie's eye socket. It had been a woman, slight of frame. He didn't know if his fingers were long enough to reach the brain. And if they did, were they deep enough to kill it? The eyeball parted under his fingers like jelly, his gloves sparing him the slimy mess but not the cold. He wriggled his fingers, still on the move so that other shambling zombies could not catch hold of him. The weight of the zombie sagged against his hand. The grip on his wrist relaxed. He pushed the limp form away and raced after Jeremiah.

Jeremiah reached the first intersection ahead. Mario shrugged out of his heavy pack, never slowing down. Without the pack he felt faster, lighter, arms and legs pumping to narrow Jeremiah's head start. He darted around zombies, ever intent on his target. At the dead end ahead, where they had scrambled up a small earthen embankment, Jeremiah hesitated. He looked right and left for a different escape route before scrambling over the embankment and dropping out of sight.

Mario gained ground, blood rushing in his ears. He vaulted over the embankment, crashing through the overgrowth. He tumbled to the wide road, the crumbled asphalt loose beneath his feet.

Jeremiah looked over his shoulder. Delilah flashed past Mario, a blur of tawny golden-brown. Mario dredged up a final, desperate burst of speed, forcing his body to bend to his will.

Ten feet behind.

Nine.

He could hear Jeremiah's labored breathing. Delilah was almost at Jeremiah's heels.

Seven feet.

He could see the runnels of sweat running down Jeremiah's neck.

Five feet.

Delilah leaped. Jeremiah cried out as the pit bull collided with the small of his back, causing him to stumble.

Mario slammed into the fleeing man, tackling him to the ground. Delilah yipped, caught between the two men whose combined momentum sent them tumbling. Mario held tight, arms yanked and twisted as they rolled over the pavement. Pain slashed through his injured shoulder, radiating down his arm and side and up into his neck. When they finally stopped rolling, he dragged himself over Jeremiah, too exhausted to do more than use his body weight to detain him.

They lay on the road, gasping for breath. Delilah sniffed his ear, panting against Mario's skin, then began to lick his face. A few moments later, Miranda and Doug's feet echoed on the crumbling asphalt. The sound of their footsteps drew near. They both dropped to their knees beside Mario and Jeremiah.

No one said anything at first. After a full minute Miranda said, "That was a...hell of...a steeplechase."

Mario tried to answer but was gripped by a hacking cough. A searing pain ripped through his side. He rolled off Jeremiah, onto his hands. Delilah nudged his side with her nose and whimpered.

"You're bleeding," Doug said.

A steady, heavy drip of blood hit the pavement under the right side of Mario's body where Delilah had nudged him. Gently, he moved the dog away and touched his side. His hand came away bloody.

I really need to get new chain mail, he thought.

Aloud he said, "I think I found the knife Jeremiah lifted from me."

6

Miranda sat beside Mario, inspecting the stitches Doug had sewn along his rib cage. The bleeding had been steady but never increased before Doug stitched him up. Mario was not experiencing any shortness of breath, so they were pretty sure that the knife had not nicked or collapsed his lung.

They had retreated to a two-story house a block away from where Mario had caught up with Jeremiah. Between the noise from cutting the trail and then chasing Jeremiah, along with Mario's bleeding wound, they had attracted so many zombies that it would have been dangerous to keep going. They needed to see how badly Mario had been cut, and the cortisol crash once they recaptured Jeremiah left everyone exhausted.

The patient lay on the canopy bed in a little girl's room filled with pink and fairies and unicorns and butterflies. And sparkles, lots and lots of sparkles.

Doug entered the bedroom, wiping dry his washed hands.

"Jeremiah's still locked in the closet?" he asked.

As if she knew what Doug had said, Delilah began to thump her tail against the floor. The caramel-colored pit bull had staked out a spot just outside the closet they had locked Jeremiah in without anyone telling her to.

"He hasn't gone anywhere while you were taking a leak," Miranda answered. "You always do such even stitches, Doug. How do you get them so neat?"

"Talent," Doug said. "At least you got stabbed on the side without the cracked ribs, Mario."

"They just stopped hurting, and now this," Mario said.

Doug stretched his arms high over his head, groaning a little.

"Let's see what's here that might be useful and get some rest. We can head out in the morning if it's clear out there. Maybe a good twelve hours tied up and gagged in a closet might do our problem child some good."

"That's not very Christian of you, Father," Miranda said, winking.

"I have zero fucks to give for Christian duty right now," Doug muttered.

"You know what you need, Doug?" Miranda asked. "A good chat with Sister John Ignatius."

Doug wrinkled his brow. "Is this one of your inspirational stories, Miranda? Because you suck at them."

Miranda ignored him. "Sister John was my sixth grade religion teacher, and believe it or not, I loved her. She managed to work forgiveness into every lesson and always said, 'I'm big on forgiveness because Jesus was, too.'"

Doug looked at Miranda, a mixture of confusion and astonishment on his face. Irritation filling his voice, he said, "If you're suggesting I forgive Jeremiah for leading us on that merry chase earlier, no way. Besides, you flunked that lesson."

Frowning, Doug stalked out of the room.

"He's pissed," Mario said.

"Oh, he's just tired."

Miranda stood but could not stifle a wince.

Mario said, "How's your knee?"

Miranda arched an eyebrow, a mischievous gleam in her eye. "I know the stab wound hurts, but how's your shoulder?"

"Touché," he said. "It hurts. Must have smacked against the ground ten times when I tackled him."

"My knee hurts, too," she said, glad that the guy she found it so easy to talk to had returned. Miranda squeezed his hand. "I'll come snuggle up when we're done and rest my knee."

"Okay. But no talking. All this breathing hurts."

AN HOUR LATER, they had pretty much finished scouring the house for supplies. Everything was in its place in this house. Miranda adjusted the clothes in the master bedroom closet so that they were straight and neat like she had found them. It seemed wrong to leave them bunched together when everything was so orderly. Apart from the obvious signs of abandonment—ten years of grime, water damage from a leak in the roof, the tree growing through the sagging front porch—it felt like the people who lived here might walk in at any moment.

Maybe they were on vacation, Miranda thought. There were no zombies, no bodies, no cars in the garage. A lot of canned and dried food filled the shelves in a pantry so full and organized it looked like something out of a magazine. It didn't look like supplies had been removed in haste. Nothing about the house was out of place. Not even a dish in the sink.

The lady of the house had liked to shop. Half the clothes in the closet still had tags attached. Miranda could picture the clothes on the willowy blonde in the pictures around the house. The little girl had her mother's smile but not her coloring, which favored the dark-haired man in a picture of the three of them. He had been on the homely side, but his face was friendly. All of the things that this family had valued just left to rot. Partly because there were not enough people left in the world to ever use up everything, and partly because strappy sandals and cute summer dresses were pretty much obsolete unless you had a death wish.

Or if you're like Karen, Miranda thought to herself. Her fashion-obsessed best girlfriend back in San Jose seemed intent on tempting fate with the high-heeled shoes she had started wearing again. Even inside a safe zone, they were a bad idea as far as Miranda was concerned.

Miranda pulled open the top drawer of the last dresser in the room and froze.

"Oh my God," she whispered.

The drawer could have been mistaken for the stockroom in a lingerie shop. Bras in every color nestled against one another. Smooth, sensible bras. Sheer, almost see-through bras. Silky satin and lace third-date bras. Push-up, demi-cup, balconette, strapless. She pulled one out and checked the size—34D.

"No way," she said, feeling light-headed. She checked another, and another, but the size stayed true. Half of them still had tags attached.

She yanked the next drawer open. A rainbow of matching panties filled it. Bikinis and cheeky shorts, thongs, G-strings. The kind with no crotch and several with elastic straps instead of a back panel of fabric that she could only surmise were meant to leave the back door open. The next drawer held bustiers, corsets, and garters, and unopened packages of thigh-high stockings, both those used with garters and the kind with elastic hidden behind the lace at the top that stayed up on their own. The last drawer held wispy negligees made of filmy fabrics that wouldn't reveal so much that it ruined the surprise of what lay beneath.

"Holy shit," Miranda muttered. "This woman has an entire dresser of lingerie in my size."

She felt like a dragon atop its hoard of gold. And then reality crashed the party, dousing her already-anticipating-getting-warmer tingly body with a vat of ice water. She was in the fucking wilderness. Her legs had not seen a razor in over a month. She had sweat like a pig while bushwhacking, which had also covered her in tiny flecks of wood and mud and leaves, never mind running after Jere-fucking-miah. The chance to get properly clean out here might not happen for a very long time. What was the point of all this if she smelled to high heaven? Or if she was somewhere so insecure that she would not feel safe wearing it?

"Nothing will take up much room," she said to herself, thinking of her pack that was strained at the seams. She held a pair of satin panties in her hand, the fabric silky soft between her fingers. I don't have room, she thought, slipping the panties into a pocket.

It was beyond unfair. Even Harold, her forced-intimacy, bound-ary-pushing lingerie connection in San Jose had never hooked her up like this. She pushed the drawers closed, bitterness filling her mouth, her throat, her *heart*. She had always loved lingerie. All these pretty, soft, beautiful things dangled in front of her like shiny new toys. She felt like a kid who had been naughty enough that ashes were all she could look forward to in her Christmas stocking.

She opened the bra drawer again and picked one up, a soft lilac satin with a cream lace overlay. It had literally been years since Mario had seen her in anything like this, since she had watched his reaction to seeing her wrapped up in a bow for him to untie. A flush of heat spread through her body as she imagined how his eyes would darken with desire. She could feel his hands settle on her waist. Hands that knew exactly what they were doing and where to do it. His breath hot against her skin and his mouth on her—

"Find anything?"

Miranda jumped at the sound of Doug's voice from the doorway. She shoved the bra inside her unzipped jacket and pushed the drawer shut so hard that the mirror on the dresser vibrated.

"No," she said, turning away from the dresser. "Nothing essential."

"Sorry, I didn't mean to scare you," he said. His eyes narrowed under scrunched eyebrows. "Are you feeling okay? You look...funny."

"You just startled me," she said. She looked down, trying to compose herself. The bra's strap poked out of her jacket. She walked to the door to join Doug, surreptitiously tucking it out of sight while she fiddled with her jacket zipper.

Fuck it, she thought. She could not take everything, but she would take as much as she could. This lingerie was also about survival—of her spirit. This world's ruthless practicality was going to have to shove over and make a little room.

7

"I don't need all that detail, Mario," Doug said. "What you're saying is we need to go to the other site."

Inwardly, Miranda groaned. After a week and a half at the main OHSU Campus, it looked like they would soon be leaving.

Mario nodded. "Yes. There's a West Campus with another Vaccine Institute site there. The equipment I need isn't here. I'm guessing it's there."

No one said anything as they digested this new information.

Doug said, "I'm not crazy about the water situation here, anyway. It looks like the other site has several creeks nearby. Where's that map you found, Miri?"

"Next door. I'll get it."

Miranda pushed back from the small table and left the office of Mallory Setajjei, Ph.D. She stuck her head into Alexander O'Donnell, Ph.D.'s office next door. The map Doug wanted was brightly colored, with ads for tourist attractions but not as much emphasis on anything besides major roads. After a week of rummaging through the effects of the people who had once worked here, Miranda felt like she knew them a little. O'Donnell had liked chewing gum, to judge from the wrappers in the wastepaper basket. Setajjei had been a WASP-y blonde woman married to a man whose skin was so dark it had an almost purple hue. The background of the picture of them on her desk was filled by the snow-capped peak of Mount Kilimanjaro. And one of the other professors down the hall had kept an emergency bottle of gin, still half-filled, in his desk.

Miranda grabbed the map. The guys had cleared off the small table so she could spread it out.

"About thirteen miles to Beaverton, we think," Doug said, almost to himself. "D'you think your knee is up to it, Miri?"

"Should be," she said. She had been doing the exercises assigned to her a few years ago when she broke her leg. "It feels a lot better. Stronger, too."

Doug said, "That's great. How's your shoulder, Mario? Feel any better since you've had a break from carrying your pack?"

"It does. A lot. She's got me stretching and doing strengthening, too." He grinned at Miranda. "We're becoming less decrepit by the hour."

Doug nodded. "Good. We can add more to mine and Jeremiah's packs if need be and leave tomorrow."

"More trekking," Miranda said, grinning. Even after resting up, she felt tired just thinking about it. "What expeditions are made of."

MIRANDA COCKED her head to the side. "What is that noise?"

The screeches of animals got louder with every step. According to the atlas they had found at the library, they were almost at the Vaccine Institute.

"Some kind of animal," Doug said.

"I know that," Miranda said. "What kind?"

"I can see an open space through the trees ahead," Mario, once again tethered to Jeremiah, said.

Mario gave Jeremiah a nudge to keep moving. Then Delilah

streaked away, breaking through the tree line ahead. The screeching detonated like a bomb. A minute later, they stepped into a parking lot. It was the usual kind, with weeds growing in the cracks and small copses of trees where the asphalt had disintegrated entirely.

And monkeys.

Delilah zigged and zagged across the parking lot and through patches of tall grass, chasing brown monkeys.

"What the..." Doug said, his voice trailing.

Miranda looked across the parking lot, jaw slack. Delilah was chasing *monkeys*.

"Delilah!" she shouted, shaking off her surprise. "Come!"

It took another thirty seconds of shouting to get Delilah to return so that Miranda could put her on a leash. Monkeys that had scampered up trees and into hiding places were beginning to return. The largest were maybe two and a half feet tall, but only when standing on their hind legs. Most had brownish fur, though some were lighter, and they all had close-set eyes that regarded their human cousins with wary curiosity. Some had fur all over their faces, while others had pink skin covering the *T* of their faces from eyes to upper lip.

They were everywhere: the parking lot, the large brown brick building opposite them, the overgrown grounds, and the roofs of low-slung buildings that stretched into the distance on the parking lot's west side. The loud screeches had mostly died down, but they still chattered, seemingly from every direction.

"Monkeys," Doug said slowly. "Huh. I did not see this one coming."

"There must be thousands of them," Mario said, sounding thunderstruck. "They're everywhere."

Miranda looked over to Jeremiah, who was still tethered to Mario. He too looked shocked and confused.

"Do you think they'll attack us?" Miranda said.

Mario shrugged.

"Only one way to find out," Doug said, and began to walk forward.

THE NEW DIGS WERE NICE, if chilly. After ten days of trekking to get here, Miranda would have set up in a ditch if it was safe. Beaverton was even more bucolic compared to the campus they had left in Portland. Overgrown Bucolic, she thought. It sounded like a school of art, like Impressionist or Cubist.

This Vaccine Institute building on the OHSU West Campus was newer, with better light and windows that didn't open, which was a plus these days. The lack of zombies wandering inside made Miranda think that whoever had been here when zombies first appeared bugged out fast. So much for diligent scientists working feverishly to save humanity.

They had set up their common area in the atrium, against a wall underneath the wide, curved staircase to the second floor. A section of the atrium roof was glass which meant the light was good. With glass doors at the front and back of the atrium, it wasn't an ideal setup, but the lab that Mario needed was on the first floor. The lab was off one of the hallways, which had doors at either end, so they had done as good a temporary reinforcement job as possible for now on the main doors. They would sleep upstairs, Doug in the lab adjacent to where they had locked Jeremiah away. Miranda and Mario had set up in a nearby office.

The second floor was open to the atrium, with a balcony that functioned as the main hallway. The building was big, but not too big. Like the porridge from *The Three Bears*, it was just right.

Miranda sat at the table they had dragged from an office while Doug prepared a cold dinner. She pulled the blanket she had found around herself even tighter. Her hat was pulled down almost to her eyebrows. They had found so much water in the many hot water heaters in the cluster of buildings that they'd decided to bathe. Miranda had scrubbed and primped everything she could—she had even shaved—even though the water was freezing and the air in the building was worse. Now she couldn't get warm, but for the first time in weeks, she was clean.

She tapped the brochures in front of her. "According to these brochures from the other building, this campus included the Oregon National Primate Research Center. That's why we have monkeys. Macaques, from India and Japan."

Doug's nose wrinkled. "Animal testing...yick."

Miranda shrugged. "Their keepers set the monkeys free, so they must have cared about them. You saw those enclosures and cages. They didn't get out on their own."

"If you say so," Doug said, sounding unconvinced.

"Did you know the ones from Japan were those snow monkeys that bathed in hot springs in the winter? That would be so cool to see."

"*Hot springs* would be cool," Doug said. "This food is as good as it's gonna get until we have something to cook on. Why don't you go get—"

The door across the atrium clunked open.

"Mario," Doug finished.

Mario crossed over to them, grinning like a kid at Christmas. He dropped into the seat beside Miranda.

"I still can't believe there's a BSL-3 lab here," he said.

Miranda smiled. It was only the millionth time he had said so since they arrived. It was nice to see him so excited.

Doug set bowls of food in front of them, then picked up a fourth. "I'll run this up to Jeremiah. Be right back."

"Do you still think the lab is salvageable?" Miranda asked.

"Oh yeah," Mario said around a mouthful of food. "There are things that need to be fixed, but I've already pulled some equipment from other labs. We need power of course. By rights I need a Biosafety Level Four lab, but my expectations of what we'd find were pretty low. A BSL-3 is way better than I expected."

Miranda took a bite of the mushy whatever it was. Doug had

added dehydrated apricots. It wasn't horrible, but it was close. The apricots on their own would have been better.

"We're going to look for solar components tomorrow," Miranda said, poking at her food. "We should be able to rig up something."

"Find some heaters," Mario said, pulling up the zipper on his jacket. "And something to cook with. This mush is dreadful."

A FEW HOURS later while she was killing time before Mario came to bed, Miranda wrote in her journal. She had not kept one since her angst-filled teen years. What she wouldn't give now for those problems. If their mission was successful, a firsthand account of their journey might be of interest to people. Miranda did not kid herself that this was on par with the journals of Lewis and Clark, but it didn't hurt to keep a record.

She realized she was dragging her hand and smudging the graphite. Goddammit, she thought, checking the pencil point. It was no longer sharp. She needed a good pencil sharpener. Pencil tips blunted too quickly but carrying ink for a fountain pen was impractical. The ink in ballpoint pens had dried up years ago, and the fine point uni-ball pens she had loved were a distant memory. Pencils were the best option for traveling, but the smudging drove her crazy.

Just as she was finishing her entry, the door to the office they had set themselves up in opened. She set the journal aside, next to the small camping lantern. Its soft light was just enough to read and write by, and it was perfect for what she had in mind.

"I thought you'd be asleep by now," he said.

"And miss a chance to smell clean you? No way."

His smile was everything she had hoped for. She got up from their bedrolls and met him halfway.

"I was thinking along the same lines," he murmured.

Miranda arched an eyebrow, a seductive smirk raising the corner of her mouth. "Took you long enough to get here."

She leaned in, desire crackling between them as their lips met. The anticipation that had been building inside her ricocheted through her body. Mario pulled her close, his lips on her neck, scorching it with caresses and nips. She unbuckled his belt and worked on the button and fly. He made quick work of unbuttoning her shirt. She gasped when his lips moved to the swell of her breast. Then he pulled away abruptly and raised his eyes to hers.

He pushed her shirt off her shoulders and slid his hands down her arms. They settled on her waist while he held her at arm's length. He traced a finger along the edge of the black lace bra. Slowly, down one breast to the dip in the center, then up along the other.

"Where did you get this?"

She felt aflame as his fingers traced her skin along the edges of the lacy confection of satin and lace. His touch, and the way he looked at her, filled her with heat. She wanted him to keep kissing her, keep touching her everywhere, but his reaction was worth the interruption.

"There was an entire dresser of lingerie at that house."

Mario's expression changed from wonder to expectation.

"You mean there's more?"

She nodded, a crafty smile on her kiss-swollen lips.

He ripped his shirt over his head and pulled her to him. She thrilled at his shudder when her hands slid over the sculpted muscles of his chest and stomach. He gasped as she slid them inside the waistband of his loosened pants. His heat ensconced her hand as she wrapped it around his stiff cock. He groaned into her mouth as he claimed it again, his tongue seeking and lips urgent. Miranda almost cried out when his mouth latched on to a nipple, a lightning bolt of electric pleasure racing from his nipping teeth directly to her tingling sex. Her head fell back, breath hoarse in her throat.

He released one nipple to push her bra aside and suckle the other, sending more heat rushing through her body. She worked her hand along the shaft of his cock, the smooth elastic surface sliding over the hardness within. He groaned when her other hand slipped down and cupped his tight balls. When she stroked her fingers along their underside, a violent shudder ran through his body. He released her nipple and gasped.

"Miri, stop or I'll come."

She stopped. After a moment she withdrew the hand that cradled his balls but left her other hand in place around him, not moving but not letting go. They looked at one another, breathless and flushed, the lust on his face stoking the fire inside her even higher.

Miranda enjoyed holding him in her hand, knowing that she could listen to him and drag it out. Or not.

"Hmmm... What's a girl to do?" She moved her hand an inch up his hard cock. He groaned, and she smiled. God, she could do this all day long. "Worked up a little, baby?"

She let go of him and stepped back. After a few moments he took a step toward her, but she touched a finger on his chest and pushed back.

"Stay there."

A slow smile crinkled the corners of his eyes.

"Yes, ma'am."

She took several steps back and undid her pants. Slowly, she slid them over her hips, revealing the microscopic lace G-string. She would pay for it later, but when he saw her smooth skin around and beneath the G-string's lace, she knew she would shave it again in a heartbeat.

"Holy shit," he said. When the lacy band of the thigh-high stockings appeared, he laughed. "My God, woman. You. Are. Gorgeous."

Miranda licked her lower lip, his reaction so much better than she had imagined. She wanted to jump him right now, shove him down on the floor, feel his hardness inside her, but this was a moment to savor. She reached behind her back with both hands and unhooked the bra, letting it fall to the floor. His face looked like a kid's at Christmas, a kid who had just unwrapped the best present ever. She stepped out of her pants and kicked them away.

"Pants," she said. "Off."

He complied immediately, removing his socks and boots, too. She closed the distance between them, never taking her eyes from his, and dropped to her knees in front of him.

Mario's breath hissed in when she ran her tongue along the underside of his cock. She laughed softly when she reached the extra sensitive bunching of skin just below the tip, and his cock sprang up of its own volition. Then, slowly, she took his hard length in her mouth, sliding her wetted lips forward millimeter by millimeter.

He started to shake. He lasted about two more seconds before grabbing the back of her head and setting a more robust pace. She matched it, slicking his cock as she sucked forward and back. When his breath started to rasp unevenly, she took a deep breath through her nose, relaxed, and swallowed him so deep that her lips touched his body. His cock filled her throat. When she swallowed again, her throat's deep embrace encircling him, his half-strangled cry was accompanied by his pulsing release. He stood shuddering, holding her head in his hands as his hips flexed forward.

Then he let go and staggered back. Miranda stood up, thoroughly pleased with herself. Mario looked at her, eyes glazed.

"You're going to be the death of me."

"But such a nice way to go," she purred.

Mario took her hand and pulled her over to their bedrolls. "Let me see what I can do with you."

Miranda lay on her back. Mario began at her toes, trailing his hands up her silky stockinged legs. When he reached the lace bands halfway up her thighs, he pushed her legs apart. The feather-light kisses on the inside of her thighs made her breath catch in her throat. He kissed higher and higher and then completely skipped where a natural progression should have taken him.

Trailing kisses and swirls of his tongue started again on the tiny swell below her belly button. He moved up her writhing body at a snail's pace. She tangled her fingers in his hair, both wanting him to hurry and take his time. A soft cry escaped her when he took a pebble-hard nipple in his mouth. He licked and nipped, going back and forth from one breast to the other, teasing with his tongue and teeth.

The rushes of pleasure electrified her clit, like there was a high-voltage wire connecting them. He climbed up her body to kiss her, his hunger palpable. She wrapped her legs around him, his cock trapped between them. He nibbled the edges of her earlobe and nuzzled her neck just below her ear. By the time he stopped, she lay gasping, her body humming from tip to toe.

He raised himself up from her enough to slip a hand into her panties. His fingertips stroked the smooth skin beneath, skating back and forth over the curve of her bald pubis, velvety soft under his fingertips, before continuing on to the creamy wetness between her thighs. She moaned as he slipped his fingers inside her, teasing her clit with soft flicks of his callused thumb. He worked his way back down her body, kissing and nipping. When his mouth reached the band of her panties, he pulled down on the lacy straps. Miranda lifted her hips. The panties disappeared. As she lowered her hips, Mario pushed on them, rolling her onto her side.

"Goddammit, Miranda," he said, cupping the cheeks of her ass in his hands. "We have to come back to this later."

Her throaty laugh was infused with desire. She rolled onto her back. Mario continued where he had left off, nuzzling his way over the smooth rise of flesh.

"I can't believe you did this," he murmured.

His tongue slid into the soft cleft of her naked pubis. Miranda groaned as his tongue circled her clit, then whimpered as it flicked back and forth. Then he moved away to kiss and nuzzle the bare skin that nature had meant to stay covered.

Back and forth he went, driving her wild, his ministrations lifting her higher and higher, only to stop when he lazily licked away to nuzzle and kiss the soft flesh just adjacent, or to stroke his fingers over her soft, bare skin. Ragged gasps of air barely escaped her throat. Her heart thrashed against her sternum. He teased her to the precipice, the pleasure and pressure and heat unbearable.

His tongue slipped away.

"Don't *do* that," she gasped.

He returned to where she bid. Her heart hammered, the eruption building, she could feel herself tipping...

He moved away again.

"You...fucker."

Miranda felt his deep laugh against her as he once more slid his tongue right where she wanted it. Her engorged clit throbbed, the thumping pulsations of blood distending the tiny organ, making it quiver in time with her pounding pulse. She craved the mercy of release, straining toward his tongue and lips, his hot breath on her skin. She climbed higher, faster, blood rushing in her ears, heart about to burst, tipping, tipping, half expecting to have it snatched away as she hovered at the edge.

She exploded into Mario's mouth, bucking wildly, her orgasm engulfing her. She could not tamp down her cries as she was sent falling and flying, shockwaves of pleasure detonating through her. Mario's lips and tongue surfed along with her body, never losing contact as she came, one orgasm tumbling into the next. When finally spent, she twisted away from him, now almost too sensitive to bear the lightest touch.

Mario lifted himself over her. She opened her legs to meet him. He pushed into her constricted slickness, its warm embrace tight from her orgasms. A trill of triumph fizzed through her when he moaned as he entered her. Her hips rocked to meet his; his harsh sighs grew more urgent. She knew he loved to be inside her after she came as much as she wanted him there, when her eager body gripped him even tighter. She kissed him as they moved together, tasting herself on his lips. Their passion burned hotter, each pulse of pleasure building on the last until she spasmed around him with a final cry, her orgasm triggering his.

Mario collapsed on the bedroll beside her, sweat mixed with the sharp musk of sex heavy in the air. Miranda wheezed as if she had just run a marathon. Mario rolled on his side and pulled her to him.

"Yell much?" he asked, his lips tickling the back of her neck.

"You got me so worked up I *couldn't* be quiet. I can't believe Doug hasn't knocked the door down thinking we're being eaten alive."

"No danger of that," Mario said, already sounding sleepy. "I told him I planned to jump you."

Miranda flipped over to face him, mortified. It was ridiculous to feel this way, but a part of her did.

"You told him?"

"Honey, it's okay," he said, laughing softly, but not in a way that made her feel like the laughter was at her expense. "Doug knows we're sleeping together."

Her burst of laughter filled the room. She knew that she should not care if she was unable to stay quiet sometimes in close quarters, even if she felt awkward afterward. She had never begrudged anyone she had heard over the years. The pleasures of their world were so often fleeting—you had to make hay while the sun shined. The sun shone? She could never keep those stupid things straight. She had trouble keeping most things straight after a fuck like that. Doug would razz her without mercy tomorrow, but even that could not penetrate her drowsy contentment.

"We need to get some clothes on," she said, a deep wave of sleepiness threatening to pull her under. "Because zombies."

"I know," Mario murmured. He did not move, except to pull her closer to him. His dark eyes seemed to peer straight into her heart. "I love you so much."

Miranda's heart felt overfull, happiness splashing over its edges. She wanted to fall into the depths of his brown eyes, into the love and tenderness she saw there, and stay forever. Instead, she dragged herself to sitting through sheer force of will. She smoothed Mario's half-damp hair from his face. He was so relaxed that the crow's feet at the corners of eyes almost disappeared. He looked like a twenty-year-old, hardly more than a boy she had snatched from a cradle.

"I love you, too," she said. "Now move your sorry ass and get your clothes back on."

Mario looked at her through squinted eyes, his enthusiasm to comply markedly absent.

"You're way less bossy when we're fucking."

Miranda smiled. "So are you."

8

THE NEXT DAY, MIRANDA STAMPED HER FEET, TRYING TO WARM them up. They were out of the wind on this side of one of the solar power manufacturing facilities that she and Doug had found on a map, but it was still cold enough to turn her breath into a white mist.

"Thank God we're on the West Coast," Doug said. He crouched on his knees as he tried to pick a lock to a building big enough to be an air hangar. "At least solar was commonplace out here before the Green New Deal so we don't have to go twenty miles to find this stuff."

"Even with bikes, that would be a drag," Miranda agreed. She felt a little surge of joy over the mountain bikes they had found halfway here. "I didn't expect to find a factory so near." She sighed. "I am not looking forward to figuring out how to install this stuff."

"I expected you to be more of a know-it-all, Miri, what with the solar at the Farm."

"Converted residential is my specialty, not these commercial systems. And I haven't done much with it the last couple years."

"Well, let's get inside first and see if there's anything worth using."

They fell silent again. Miranda swept her gaze back and forth over the usual landscape of broken parking lot asphalt with copses of trees and abandoned cars and trucks rusting into immoveable hunks of steel. They'd been lucky so far today—no zombies.

She glanced at Doug, then surreptitiously adjusted the crotch of her jeans. She had known it would be uncomfortable for a few days when she shaved her lady parts, and the other night had been more than worth it, but she hadn't expected that it would be this miserable this quickly.

"What is going on with you and your jeans?" Doug said, never taking his attention away from the lock he was picking.

"What?"

"Your jeans. You keep pulling at them like a little kid who doesn't know better than to scratch their crotch in public."

Miranda felt her face get hot and tried to sound as dismissive as possible. "Nothing's wrong."

Doug stopped moving his pick tools and looked at her. "Then what gives?" He squinted his eyes. "Are you blushing?"

She glared at him. "There's nothing wrong." The speculative look on Doug's face meant that he thought there might be something to harass her about, so she lied. "I got my period this morning. Happy?"

"Oh."

"So unless you know where to find some tampons, put a sock in it."

"Okay, sorry," he said, looking contrite.

Several minutes passed before she heard a click and Doug's triumphant, 'Hah!' Doug packed his pick kit, then pulled his machete from its sheath while she screwed the suppressor into the barrel of her gun. When zombies popped out from behind closed doors, she preferred the speed of using firearms. She also preferred to not lose her hearing.

"I'm ready," she said.

"Here goes nothing."

SEVERAL HOURS LATER, Miranda felt moderately hopeful that they could make the equipment they had found work, assuming they could figure out a way to transport it. She was also so cold that the roots of her teeth ached. Outside was chilly enough. The refrigerator effect of this closed, unheated building dropped the temperature another ten degrees. She blew into her hands, trying to warm them, and kept working her way through the boxes of installation instructions.

"Ready to pack it in?" Doug said from across the darkening room. "We can pull some of the sheet metal into that break room and make a temporary firepit. If we vent it through the high windows, we can burn the wood pallets we saw on the way in here. I don't know about you, but I'm freezing my ass off."

"Sounds amazing," Miranda said. She straightened up and arched her low back, sighing at the welcome release of tension. The concrete floor beneath the industrial carpet had done her hips, legs, knees, and every joint in her feet no favors. "I want to eat something and crawl into my sleeping bag. No heat sucks."

"Being outside with no heat sucks more," Doug said. "We should check out their delivery trucks in the morning, see if any are in good enough shape to repair. Maybe we'll get lucky, and one of them will be solar-powered."

"Dude, you're smoking crack," she said. "Let's go use beautiful, combustible fuel to warm up."

"It'll be like a camping trip. We can braid each other's hair." He winked, then his face became serious. "Besides, I need to talk to you."

"About what?"

"About what Mario does in the sack that makes you scream like that."

"Oh, go fuck yourself," she snapped, Doug's peals of laughter filling her ears. "You're a real asshole sometimes. You know that?"

"I know," he snorted, and laughed harder.

"DOUG, WAKE UP."

Miranda's voice through a fog of sleep.

Something was wrong.

Doug reached for his Glock as he bolted upright. It was not where he had left it, just outside his half-zipped sleeping bag. He whipped his machete from its sheath. He kept that on his hip no matter how uncomfortable it made sleeping. After all these years, it wasn't much.

A woman and three men stood fifteen feet away from him and Miranda. Their firearms, the heavy-duty kind, were pointed at the floor. He saw his Glock and Miri's handgun and rifle on the table the woman sat on.

"Hello, sunshine," she said. "We've been waiting over an hour for you two to wake up. Why didn't you keep a watch?"

She was pretty, willowy and tall. And strong. He could see that just by looking at her even though she was bundled up against the cold. Silvery-gold blond hair peeked out from under a black knitted hat.

He glanced over at Miranda, who sat on an overturned filing cabinet a few feet away. She gave him a thumbs-up. They had not harmed her, nor confiscated her machete. But they put her just far enough away that she could not do anything useful, like toss him a hidden weapon. They had waited for them to wake up, presumably so they would not be injured if he or Miranda had weapons that they couldn't see. Or maybe they were just considerate. Stranger things had happened.

All speculation aside, they were definitely not amateurs.

"Usually we do, but it's pretty deserted out here. It was sloppy of us," Doug conceded casually, as if he knew her well.

Doug lowered and resheathed his machete, which was either a fantastic goodwill gesture or a huge-ass mistake. He gestured at the woman and her companions. "Case in point."

When she laughed, Doug realized that he knew who she was.

"Holy shit," he said. "You're Skye Swanson."

The woman blinked in surprise.

"And that means what?" Miranda asked.

Doug looked over to Miranda. "This woman holding us at gunpoint is one of the best women rock climbers in the world."

"Guilty as charged," the woman said. "But I'd like to point out that our guns are not pointed *at* you."

"Don't tell him who you are," one of the men beside her snapped.

"He already knows who I am, Rocco," she said, then returned her attention to Doug. "It's been a long time since someone recognized me. And you are?"

"Father Doug Michel. My friend is Miranda Tucci."

"A priest? What are you doing here?" Rocco demanded, his eyes flickering to Miranda. Almost imperceptibly, his posture softened.

Rocco stood as tall as Skye but was heavy set—linebacker heavy set. His dark eyes were still narrowed in a suspicious squint, but his frown had receded when Doug said he was a priest. He had looked at Miranda when Doug said her last name. So...Catholic, probably Italian-American. His name and dark olive skin looked the part.

"What we're doing is none of your fucking business," Miranda said.

"Listen up, sweetheart," Rocco began.

Miranda cut him off. "I am not your sweetheart."

Skye put her hands up and talked over both of them.

"Enough! Let's dial back the pissing match a little," she said, shooting Rocco an annoyed stare. "You don't want to say, and I don't blame you." She shrugged. "But you're on our patch."

"Are any of you in charge?" Doug asked.

"I am," Skye said.

Doug shook his head. "I mean *In Charge* in charge. You're well fed, you're clean. You're living somewhere nearby, and not rough."

Skye's mouth twisted to the side, then she shook her head and grinned. "Not just a celebrity watcher, huh?" She turned to her companions. "Let's take them home, guys. They can talk to the commander."

Rocco still looked suspicious. The other two stayed silent.

Doug saw Miranda bristle from the corner of his eye, but she did not say anything. There was nothing *to* say. They were outnumbered, outgunned, and had been caught with their pants down.

Doug sighed. "Can you at least reassure me you're not a bunch of crazy people? I've had enough of that to last a lifetime."

"Do we look like crazy people to you?" Skye asked. Then she winked at him. "Trust me."

9

A TWINGE OF QUEASINESS BURBLED IN DOUG'S STOMACH JUST after they crossed some railroad tracks. He, Miranda, Skye, Rocco, and the two silent types were on their way to where these people lived. Doug and Miranda were in the back of a pickup truck with Rocco and Mister Silence One. Skye drove, joined in the cab by Mister Silence Two.

He and Miranda had been relieved of their weapons, which Doug had expected. And if they were a bunch of crazies, they were at least nice enough to bring along the bicycles that he and Miranda had found.

"We're almost there," Rocco said.

"Good," Doug said, shivering. It had not been a long drive, perhaps twenty minutes, but in the low forties, it did not take long to get chilled to the bone. "I'm getting queasy with this hood over my head."

"Me, too," Miranda added.

"You know how it is," Rocco said, sounding unsympathetic but less hostile.

Doug did know how it was. If their captors turned out to not be

New Jerusalem-level crazy, he was fully prepared to be understanding. They turned...right. He had to think about it since he was facing the truck's tailgate, his back tucked against the cab.

Rocco said, "Just hang on. The hoods do not come off early if you puke."

Less hostile is a relative measure, Doug thought.

The truck slowed, the brakes squeaking softly, then stopped. Voices shouted a greeting, which were returned by their captors. Then came a sound he could not identify. Creaking, but not the usual creak of a gate. Nor did it have the rolling sound of a garage-style door. What it did have was a faint mechanical whine that Doug couldn't place. After a minute, there was a loud thud, like a huge door being slammed shut, but hard enough that he could feel it. Then the truck started moving again. The sound of the tires became hollow with the repetitive clunking sound that tires used to make when they rolled over adjacent sections of concrete on an interstate highway. But this rate of repetition was quick, more like a road made of stone Belgian Block, but not that bumpy. What the fuck was it?

He felt Miranda lean against his shoulder.

"Drawbridge?"

"Could be," he said. It made sense. The creaky, metallic whine might have been winches, and the thud had been made by something big.

The truck resumed its route but at a much slower rate of speed. Gravel crunched under the tires. There were less bumps and jolts, so a well-maintained road compared to those outside their compound. Casual greetings rang out, louder than those at the entrance. The voices faded as the truck passed. Maybe because people had seen the captives? That could go either way. People were not accustomed to seeing people in hoods, or they knew what horrible fate lay in store. Doug had followed Skye Swanson's meteoric rise in the professional rock-climbing world. She had always seemed down-to-earth and nice, not creepy, and had been friendly enough while taking them captive. He decided to trust his gut and go with not creepy.

The brakes squealed again as the truck stopped. The cab doors opened and closed.

"You can take off the hoods," Skye said, her voice on the far side of the vehicle.

Doug pulled the black hood off, squinting for a second. Beside him, Miranda did likewise. Skye stood near Miranda.

"Hop out, stretch your legs," she said. "I'll be right back."

They hopped over the side of the truck bed under Rocco's watchful eye. Miranda whistled.

"Nice setup," she said before blowing on her hands.

Doug did a three-sixty, taking in their surroundings. The pointed green metal roof of a building peeked over the top of overgrown shrubbery and younger trees straight ahead of them. Maybe on purpose, maybe not. A line of huge hardwood trees ringed the parking lot as far as Doug could see, with no discernible fence or barrier beyond.

On this side of the overgrown landscaping were display boards sheltered with the same green metal roofing, with benches below and several light poles. A flagpole sans flag sat at the end of a concrete walk in good repair. A green-and-white sign warning that dogs were not allowed was next to a full bike rack. Miranda pointed out two weathered six-by-six stubs sticking an inch out of the ground at the corner of the sidewalk. They had cut down whatever sign had been there, presumably to make the location harder to identify.

They were in an old park, a big one.

People walked by—young and old, men and women, a group of children minded by two teenage boys. All were openly curious, but no one engaged beyond a returned smile or nod. Within minutes, foot traffic picked up. Word had spread. Their method of arrival or that they were outsiders, or both, appeared to make them news. Rocco chatted with a woman just a few feet from Doug, relaxed but watchful. Mr. Silent One and Two leaned against the truck bed behind them.

Miranda leaned in close. "No one seems scared. I'm not picking up creepy undercurrents."

"Me neither," Doug answered. "It helps that we're not coming off an adrenaline rush like when Finn and Dalton got us through those zombies."

"Makes me trust my first impressions more," Miranda agreed, picking up on his line of thinking.

Doug sighed. "Either way, we're at their mercy."

Skye came into view farther down the walkway.

"Rocco," she called. "The commander's coming. Wants us to wait in her office."

Miranda and Doug glanced at one another. A female commander. Not unheard of, and usually a good sign.

"You heard the lady," Rocco said, gesturing to where Skye waited for them.

———

TEN MINUTES LATER, the chill had started to loosen its grip on Doug's bones. They sat in the commander's office, the smallest of such rooms in the hallway of offices at the park's Visitor & Nature Center. The room felt cramped despite the high ceilings and skylights because of everything packed into it. It looked like maps were affixed all over one wall, but Doug could not be certain since they were covered. Bookcases lined the wall behind them where Rocco had parked himself. Skye stood in the doorway, making small talk with passersby while acting as a surreptitious gatekeeper. Doug got the impression there was more foot traffic than usual.

He and Miranda sat facing the small desk, their backs to the bookshelves, but Doug had taken a moment to check out the books and binders before taking his seat. Entire shelves were devoted to organic farming methods, irrigation systems, solar energy systems design and installation, and a few volumes of the City of Beaverton building code. Books on law, political theory, governance, consensus

building, and communication styles were also represented. Stacks of
paper, pencils, and bound journals littered the commander's desk,
along with a picture of a black mixed-breed dog, its wagging tail a
blur as it looked up into the camera.

"Hi, Anna," Skye said.

Doug perked up and looked to where Skye stood in the doorway.
She pushed herself off the jamb to stand straight. Perhaps this was
the commander, since Skye was not hurrying her along.

"I hear you brought home some strays," a voice said.

A short, slight woman followed Skye into the room and shut the
door. Doug got to his feet; Miranda followed his lead. The woman
pushed her short brown hair streaked with gray out of her hazel eyes
and looked up at Doug.

"No one told me you were so tall," she said, extending her hand.
"I'm Anna Smith, pleased to meet you. I help run this place."

Mid-fifties, Doug guessed. Anna's hand was small in Doug's, but
her grip was firm. Direct eye contact with an air of easy authority.
Sure she 'helped' run the place.

"I'm Doug Michel," Doug said. "And this is Miranda Tucci."

After introductions were completed, Anna Smith sat behind her
desk. She shifted a stack of papers to see better, triggering an
avalanche.

"That's what I get for trying to organize things," she muttered.
When Skye crouched to pick them up, she waved her off. "Leave it,
Skye. I'll get them when we're done here." She looked Doug and
Miranda over. "I hear you're a priest."

"I am," Doug said. He grinned. "Catholic. Or as I like to say, The
One True Church."

Smith smiled.

"And what are you?" she asked, shifting her attention to Miranda.

"I'm a farmer," said Miranda.

Anna Smith nodded. "You look like a shit kicker to me, but the
two aren't mutually exclusive. So. What are you two doing in our

neck of the woods? They tell me you were looking for solar components. Where are you hoping to set up shop?"

She doesn't fuck around, Doug thought. She did not seem crazy, and her bookshelf indicated someone with a genuine interest in governance, not power. He decided to play it as straight as he could.

"We're over at the vaccine institute. We're planning to stay, but only short term. A few months, hopefully."

"You're a scientist?" Smith asked.

"Yes," Doug said. He was, after all. Just not the kind that worked on vaccines.

"And you're doing medical research?"

"The kind that needs a lab, and that's all I'm going to say. No offense, but I don't know you people."

Smith nodded, then leaned back in her chair. "I appreciate your position, but that's not an answer I can live with. What kind of research? A vaccine, maybe?"

Doug shrugged.

"For the zombie virus?" she prompted. "Maybe the flu?"

Doug stayed silent.

"Is anyone else with you?"

Doug shook his head. "No. Just the two of us."

"This is your lucky day, Father Doug Michel," Smith said. "I'm a biologist. I'm gonna go out on a limb here, but I can probably be of some assistance with whatever vaccine you're working on. You are at a vaccine institute, after all."

Fuck.

Aloud Doug said, "That's a generous offer."

"But you're going to have to tell me what you're working on."

Silence filled the room. Doug glanced at Miranda, who had become very interested in her fingernails. After a minute or two, Smith sighed. She leaned forward, putting her elbows on her desk. The look in her eye reminded Doug of his most unfavorite high school teacher, Brother Anthony. Brother Anthony had been an excellent math teacher but had no use for class clowns like Doug Michel.

"Okay, Doug. Let's cut the bullshit. I did not become a full bird colonel in the United States Air Force without picking a few things up. We've had eyes on you for days now. There are three of you, at least. And if your pal's deep interest in the floor the whole time we've been talking is any indication, she has no poker face, and you are no scientist."

The woman did not miss much; he had to give her that.

"I am a scientist," he said, relenting. "An astrophysicist."

"Ah," Smith said, sounding pleased. "A rocket scientist. Now we're getting somewhere. So the other guy is working on your vaccine."

"He's doing the research."

"For?"

"No offense, Commander, but I am not giving it up on the first date. I appreciate your position, I do, but that's as much as I am willing to say."

Smith stared at him, hard. "Are you at liberty to share his name?"

This question, more than all the others, was a problem. If Doug was sure of anything, he was sure that a community as well organized as this one seemed to be had at least a passing knowledge of what had happened in San Jose with the vaccine. People he had come across in remote parts of the wilderness had often heard about it. Smith would know Mario's name and what everyone thought he had done. It would undermine any credibility they had built with her so far.

"James Gideon," Miranda said.

"Or Jimmy, if you want to annoy him," Doug added, sounding far calmer than he felt.

A tidal wave of relief crashed through Doug's body. She had no poker face, but if the stakes were high enough, Miranda could lie with the best of them.

Smith leaned back in her chair. "I'm happy we can have a productive conversation, even if it took a while."

He knew it was coming as soon as Smith relaxed back into her chair.

Smith continued. "We have to verify all of this, of course. I'm sure you understand."

Doug nodded. "I do."

If Doug were in Smith's shoes, he would be verifying their story, too. The problem was they had to keep Jeremiah's existence a secret. Maybe his initial assessment of Smith and this community was correct. Maybe they were what they appeared to be—decent people just trying to survive. But Jeremiah repelled zombies. He was the only person who did, in Doug's experience with the undead. It was harrowing to use him to walk through a horde, but it beat the alternative. Even decent people did bad things to survive, and in a world as hostile as theirs had become, Jeremiah offered a unique survival advantage.

Anyone could want such a thing for their own. Doug understood, he really did, but they needed Jeremiah. At least until the vaccine was finished. Now they had an even higher tightrope to walk. One with a frayed net.

"Skye," Smith said. "Are you willing to take Father Doug here over to the Institute and check it out?"

"Please," Doug said. "Call me Doug."

Skye said, "Sure thing, Anna."

Smith nodded. "Okay. Doug it is. You'll be staying here, Ms. Tucci, until—"

"No," Miranda said at the exact time Doug said, "That's not happening."

Smith gave it a few seconds, then said, "Ms. Tucci will stay, just to keep things honest. She will not be harmed. She won't even be confined. She'll have minders but will be our guest."

"You mean your hostage," Miranda countered.

"In the technical sense, yes," Smith said. "But my read on you two is that while you aren't entirely forthcoming, your motive is an abundance of caution. I understand that. Mine is the same."

Doug did not like it, not one bit. But he did not see that they had a choice.

"Or you can stay here, Doug, and she can go," Smith offered. "No offense meant to Ms. Tucci, but you seem to be in charge. I thought you would prefer to do the introductions."

Miranda sighed. Her disgusted I-give-up sigh. "Fine. I'll stay."

"Are you sure?" Doug asked.

"Yes." She looked at Smith. "But please quit calling me Ms. Tucci."

Smith nodded. "Done."

"Don't fuck us over," Doug said, his manner still friendly, but the threat lurking below the surface clear as crystal.

"I have commanded airmen and women in three different theaters of conflict, Doug," Smith said. Her affect was also friendly, but a flinty resolve came through. "I have never ordered anyone under my command to violate the Geneva Convention, nor did I tolerate it. I'm not going to start now. Ms. Tucci be fine. You have my word."

He believed her. Maybe it was Smith's directness and no-nonsense manner. Even so, he didn't like leaving Miranda behind.

Skye said, "I'll round up a few people to take Doug back."

"Make sure you all get some lunch," Smith added. She stood, then stooped to pick up the papers that had fallen on the floor. "I'll see about getting Miranda situated."

Smith gestured at the books and papers that filled the room with a handful of papers.

"You know the kicker of all this? I retired a year before. My husband and I had just moved to the prettiest little house on the Lost Coast. I was *so done* with command." She laughed and shook her head, bemused. "I guess command wasn't done with me."

10

MARIO COCKED HIS HEAD, HIS HAND STILL HOLDING THE DOOR of the outdoor latrine. He heard the rumble of a vehicle engine, faint, but getting louder. Delilah cocked her head, also listening, and the macaques began to shriek.

He jogged toward the building, his hand resting lightly on his holstered Sig P226. In every direction, macaques streaked to the safety of hiding places. Once he and Delilah were inside, Mario snatched up the nearby chain and strung it tight through the door-width push bars and snapped the padlock shut. He knew the doors on the opposite side of the lobby were already padlocked but checked anyway. He took the stairs two at a time to the second floor. The main parking lot sat at the rear of the building. Whoever was driving the vehicles would end up there, assuming they did not go off-road.

Would the chains and padlocks keep someone out? No. A person only had to break the glass. But it would slow down anyone who did not want the integrity of the building compromised. Even transparent glass doors could keep zombies at bay unless they pressed against them enough to break the glass.

Could Miranda and Doug have found a vehicle in working order?

Highly unlikely. Mario settled in next to the window facing the parking lot. A few minutes later, an old pickup truck and a late model Honda Pilot came into view. He could not see through the Pilot's tinted windows, but two people were in the truck.

The truck and the Pilot drove behind a dense copse of trees that had grown through the center of the parking lot's broken concrete. The vehicles did not re-emerge on the other side. Several minutes later, Doug appeared, followed by a woman and a man, both heavily armed. Doug did not appear to have his Glock or rifle, but he did have his machete. He was also wearing a drab-green knitted hat and gloves that he had not left with yesterday. His body language was relaxed. Another woman emerged from behind the trees, but it wasn't Miranda.

Mario's pulse skyrocketed.

Doug led the group up the sidewalk to the rear lobby doors. Mario left the window to meet them. When he emerged from the stairwell, Doug and the others waited outside the door. Delilah pranced in place, warbling, tail wagging at the sight of Doug. Doug was listening to whatever a tall, slender woman was saying to him. The other woman, shorter, with a pointy chin and nose and a pinched look to match, shifted her weight from one foot to the other. Behind them stood a man built like a brick shithouse, dark eyebrows pulled down over even darker eyes, his mouth twisted in a suspicious scowl. They were all dressed for the weather and looked well fed.

"Open the door," Doug said, his breath frosting the glass.

Doug scratched his chest in a circular movement, which signaled that the strangers were okay so far. Scratching your nose meant danger, but had that been the case, Doug would have started scratching his nose as soon as he had come into view of the building. So, Doug was reasonably sure these people were okay, but the lack of Miranda and Doug's semi-weaponless state meant the strangers were holding the cards.

"Where's Miranda?"

"She's fine," Doug said.

"That's great," Mario said. "But where is she?"

"James, it's freezing out here. Open the door, and I will tell you all about it."

James was Mario's middle name. Miranda was not here. So far, Doug was not inspiring confidence.

"I'll lock Delilah up if it's going to be a problem. I don't want her getting shot."

"I love dogs," the tall woman said, looking shocked. "We aren't going to shoot her! She's wagging her tail."

Mario shrugged, noncommittal. He unlocked the padlock and pulled the chain loose. He gripped Delilah's collar and pushed on the bar.

He didn't unholster his handgun. He was clearly outgunned, but he wasn't going to hand it over until he had to. And he didn't want there to be any misunderstandings about his intent if he reached for it. Doug and the strangers entered in a gust of cold air.

"Are you sure she's all right?" Mario persisted.

Doug reached to pet Delilah.

"James, she's fine. She stayed behind with Commander Smith. We didn't have a lot of choice about that, but we had the same take, that they're good people. They offered to send Miranda back instead of me, but she insisted. Our new friends want to make sure we're doing what I've told them we're doing."

Mario bit back an unhelpful retort, annoyed at Doug's lack of alarm that Miranda wasn't here. He didn't know what Doug had told these people—he was better off keeping his mouth shut and listening.

"I'd feel better if she was here," Mario said truthfully.

"Then let's get this over with," Doug said. He let go of Delilah, who immediately began making the rounds. "Skye, Rocco, Tessa, this is James Gideon. Tessa's their solar expert. Skye and Rocco were part of the group we ran into."

"We caught you guys sleeping," Skye said.

"Well, yeah," Doug conceded. He looked down, his cheeks turning light pink.

Great, fucking great, Mario thought. These people had gotten the drop on Doug and Miranda. Either Doug and Miranda had been very sloppy, or these people were very good. Doug was introducing Mario by his middle and his mother's maiden name, which made Mario one hundred percent sure that Doug had not told them about Jeremiah.

"Enough with the small talk," the man named Rocco said brusquely. He ignored Delilah, who rubbed against his leg. He pulled off his knit cap and stuffed it in a pocket. "You two," he said, pointing a football-sized hand at Doug and Mario. "Sit. Now. James, give me your gun."

Mario handed over his Sig and sat on the floor next to Doug as instructed.

"Liley, come," Mario said. Two repetitions later, the excited Delilah complied. Mario put the pit bull on a down stay beside him and held her collar again.

"Any surprises you want to tell us about before we find them?" Skye asked, looking at Doug.

"Not a thing," Doug said.

She looked at Mario, head cocked quizzically to the side.

"No," Mario answered, trepidation building with every second that passed.

The room where they had stashed Jeremiah off the second floor's main lab was easy to miss, small, relatively soundproof, and locked. They might find the room, but Mario doubted they could get inside.

"Tessa will keep an eye on you while Rocco and I look around. Ready, Rocco?"

Rocco grunted.

"He gets nicer, I promise," Skye said.

FORTY MINUTES LATER, everyone but Delilah was in the second floor main lab that Mario wanted to use for non-biohazardous work when they got things up and running. Mario studiously avoided looking in the direction of the door to Jeremiah's cell. Rocco and Skye had not missed it, had asked about it, and tried to pick the lock to the outer door. They'd been unsuccessful, thank God. Both he and Doug had pleaded ignorance, saying they had not been able to get into the room, either.

Tessa stood on a ladder they had scrounged from the basement, the top half of her body hidden by the drop ceiling. Light from her headlamp flashed down through the removed sections punctuated by pings, bangs, curses, and requests for a different type of pliers, diagonals, or screwdriver. Doug held the ladder like a regular Boy Scout.

Rocco's interest in the room where Jeremiah was hidden was plain. His suspicious glances were followed by thoughtful scowls, restless shifts of his body weight from one foot to the other, and deep rumbles of dissatisfaction in his chest. The only saving grace was that there were two doors. The first here in the lab, which had a window, opened to a short passageway before the second door, to the room where Jeremiah was. Luckily, the second door didn't have a window. Mario didn't understand the original function for the double doors, but they were the only reason their situation was not more precarious.

Tessa's descent of the ladder pulled Mario's attention back to the here and now. She flicked the headlamp off, then pulled it and her cap off her head when she reached the floor.

"Good and bad news, I'm afraid," she said, untangling her hat from the headlamp. She pulled the hat back on, covering her mussed jaw-length brown hair. "We can set this lab up to run on solar no problem, but I'm not qualified to deal with the electrical on a building like this. We need to get Erik—"

Rocco groaned. "Shoot me now."

"Oh, please," Skye said to him, rolling her eyes. "They're just people, Rocco. You act like you're allergic to them."

"I *am* allergic to them," he said.

Tessa continued as if she had not been interrupted. "We obviously don't want to burn this place down because rats have been chewing on cables. Erik will be able to direct repairs and come up with the right modifications for amps and current and whatever else."

"Who's Erik?" Mario asked.

"And why is Rocco allergic?" Doug added.

"Erik's the electrician at P-Land," Skye said, ignoring Rocco's even louder groans of distress.

"And P-Land is?" Doug asked.

Rocco sighed. Loudly.

"It's the other settlement in the area," Tessa said. "*Portlandia*. P-Land for short."

"I used to live there. It's fine," Skye added.

Rocco snorted. "I don't see you making plans to go back."

Skye shook her head. "They just do things more collaboratively there."

Mario glanced at Doug. From the look on his face, he appeared just as mystified.

"So do they call themselves P-Land," Mario asked, intrigued. "Or is that a—"

"They talk everything to death," Rocco said, interrupting Mario. "Let's see how many ways we can consider keeping chickens before we take seventeen votes on it, because the vegans don't think it's ethical to keep chickens in the first place. The vegetarians don't think they should be slaughtered after they quit laying, but buried. But not in the garden, where they might do some good. That just doesn't seem right after all those chickens have done for us."

Tessa began to laugh. Skye looked on the verge of joining her.

"And the bees. Don't get me started," Rocco continued, his previously stormy countenance a mixture of annoyance and amusement. "Some of the beekeepers there are into vegan beekeeping, which is a thing, apparently. They don't harvest the honey, and were a little too sanctimonious, even for P-Land."

Mario was not sure if Rocco was pulling his leg, but Rocco did not strike him as the kind of guy who pulled your leg unless he was ripping it from your body.

"Are you serious?" Doug asked, looking like he wanted to join in the laughter but not quite sure if this was for real.

"Oh my God," Rocco said, shaking his head as he warmed to the subject. "The bees were a pitched battle. The sourcing people backed the vegans. The humane meat eaters backed the other beekeepers but were ridiculed by the vegetarians for being hypocrites. The gardening crew just wanted the bees and didn't give a shit. Their Council took it to a vote how many times, Skye? Six, seven? You were still living there then."

Skye's face was flushed pink from suppressed laughter. She lost her battle with it when she squeaked, "Nine."

Beside Skye, Tessa's giggling was interspersed with hiccups. Mario felt a smile forming, despite his anxiety at the intrusion of these strangers, and Miranda's absence, and the need to keep Jeremiah a secret.

"Nine votes," Rocco chortled. "For bees!"

When the laughing had ratcheted down to snickers and giggles, Doug said, "P-Land is your nickname for them, isn't it? It's not what they call themselves. What do they call you?"

Rocco grinned. Skye's giggles ramped back up until she laughed so hard she needed to wipe tears from her eyes. It took Tessa three tries before she managed to say, "LO. It's short for *Law & Order*."

This time, Mario laughed with them.

———————

AN HOUR LATER, they were almost ready to depart for P-Land.

"It'll take an hour to get there, three days to get the deal settled, and an hour to get back," Rocco said.

Mario looked at Rocco, alarmed.

Skye said, "He's joking."

Rocco socked Mario on the shoulder. "So serious, this one."

Mario suppressed a wince. Rocco's playful punches smarted, but the ice had been broken. With no evidence of treachery, even Rocco seemed to have decided that he and Doug were good guys. Good guys Rocco and Skye never let out of their sight or left alone with one another, and whose guns were not returned to them.

Affably watchful Rocco was preferable to suspiciously scowling Rocco, but Mario would feel a whole lot better about their impending departure if he or Doug could check in on Jeremiah before they left. He definitely had enough water for a few days, but not food. Doug had tried twice without success to shake Skye. He had not tried again as it might make her suspicious.

It was up to Mario.

"Let's hit the road, then," Skye said.

Mario visibly hesitated as Rocco walked ahead of them, then said, "I know this sounds stupid, but I'd feel better padlocking the main door. I know we can't do much about the other after we go. I'd just hate to lose anything, being here on our own."

He watched Skye take a quick look at their belongings. They didn't have much, which meant they couldn't afford to lose anything. Rocco had already walked ahead, out the rear doors, which left Skye to watch Doug, and Tessa to watch Mario.

"Tessa," Skye said. "Want to help Mario?"

Tessa nodded. "Sure."

"Doug," Mario said. "Do you mind taking Delilah while I get this?"

"No problem, James," Doug said.

Delilah darted out the door ahead of Doug and Skye. Delilah had taken a shine to Skye and looped back to prance around her. Mario turned toward the front doors on the other side of the large central lobby, not hurrying nor dawdling. He stooped to pick up the chain, checking to see that Doug and Skye were well on their way to the parking lot. He started to attach the chain, then looked at Tessa.

"If it really takes an hour to get there, then I better hit the latrine before we go."

"Okay," Tessa said.

Mario knew that Tessa had used the latrine before, so she knew it was a thousand feet from the front doors, off to the side of the building. He handed her the chain and padlock.

"We both know you're not here to help with the door, but I can handle the latrine on my own," he said.

He ducked out the door and strode toward the latrine before she could respond. He glanced back. Tessa hesitated, then decide to wait for him. As soon as he was out of her sight line, he ran to the building's side entrance. They had unlocked the door after clearing the building in case they needed a quick escape route. It was insecure as far as people went but even unlocked, zombies could not open a heavy metal door that swung out. Mario ducked inside the building and took the stairwell to the second floor two steps at a time.

He hurried to the lab, grabbed the key to Jeremiah's cell from a cabinet along with a few Meals Ready to Eat, and opened the door. He hated opening the second door on his own without a weapon in his hand, but he did not have time, and he didn't want Jeremiah getting a weapon. He unlocked the door and pushed it open. Jeremiah looked up from where he lay on the cot by the far wall, under the small window. The composting toilet near the inoperable sink smelled okay. Paperbacks littered the floor around Jeremiah. He stuck his finger in the book he was reading as he sat up.

"What do you—"

Mario tossed the MREs in Jeremiah's direction.

"Might be a few days, don't fret."

He pulled the door shut, locked it, repeated with the next. Last stop was to reach below a table top by the sink and feel for the grip of his back up handgun—another Sig P226. The tape pulled away clean. He tucked the gun into his waistband at the small of his back, out of sight under his outer layers.

He was sweating by the time he exited the building. His detour had taken him two minutes, maybe, but it felt like ten. If Tessa had become suspicious or investigated, the situation was about to get sticky.

When he rounded the corner of the building, he saw Tessa

standing just outside the main doors. Mario saw her shoulders relax when she saw him.

"Thought I fell in, huh?" he said when he got closer.

She snorted. "Not quite, but let's get a move on."

THE DECELERATION of the SUV woke Mario up.

Shit, he thought. He had not meant to fall asleep. He had meant to stay vigilant until he had a better read on these strangers. He straightened up and looked around. Skye's attention was on the road as she guided the SUV through a hairpin turn. Rocco sat in the front passenger seat opposite her, head against the window, snoring softly. Tessa and Doug sat in the middle row of seats. Delilah had managed to wedge herself between the driver and passenger seats and snuggled up to Skye, her head on Skye's lap. As the road straightened ahead of them, Mario could see a gate in the distance that straddled the road.

"Rocco, wake up," Skye said.

Rocco sat up and stretched his arms, wiggling his fingers in Skye's face. She swatted his hand away.

As they pulled up to the gate, Mario could see that it stuck out from the exterior wall—a double entry like San Jose. Skye waved out the window, shouting a hello to people in the tower, but the other side of the conversation was unintelligible.

"There's a truck in the screening gate area. They're opening up the people door for us," Skye said.

Mario called Delilah to him as they exited the SUV and put her on a leash. They headed for a door in the timber gate, where they were met by a red-haired woman who stepped through.

"Hey, Skye, Rocco. Tessa, good to see you! Who's this lovely girl?" she said, putting her hand down for Delilah to sniff.

Delilah's tail wagged so furiously it smacked on Mario's leg like a wire whip. The woman smiled pleasantly at Doug and Mario, looking curious, but didn't ask who they were.

After giving the dog a few pets, the woman said, "Come on through."

Once they got through the gate door, the scene inside was chaotic. A box truck with supplies was parked, cab doors open wide. At least fifty people were crowded around a tall man with blond hair. He looked to Mario like a corn-fed midwestern farm boy who had been through the wringer. His clothes were filthy, his color sallow, and his brown eyes held such haggard rage that Mario took an involuntary step back. It looked like he was almost arguing with another man in front of the large group of people.

"Shit," Skye said.

"Come on, Skye. Put on your big girl panties," Tessa said, grabbing Skye's hand and pulling her along. "He won't see you, anyway, with that many people."

"Any idea what that's about?" Mario murmured to Doug, tipping his head at Skye.

Doug shook his head. They joined the others at the edge of the crowd.

"...tole some of their vaccine serum a couple weeks before we arrived. I barely managed to bribe our way into the city. They weren't going to part with anything. They had been fighting with another group set up at a college, but that had died down. The prick I talked to said, 'even if recent events were different, we don't sell vaccine to outsiders.' What does it matter where we're from?"

Murmurs whooshed through the crowd. Mario and Doug looked at one another. He was talking about San Jose.

The tall, older man he was conversing with shook his head in disbelief. The wire-rimmed glasses perched on his hooked nose wobbled. He put a hand up to steady them.

"It's hard to believe," he said. Hastily, he added, "Of course I believe you, Brock. You hear the stories of what it's like there, but it's hard to believe we have nothing of value to them."

"They don't give a shit about anyone."

There were more murmurs from the assembly. When it became apparent he had no more to tell, people drifted away in twos and threes.

"Come on, let's go," Skye said. "I don't want to—"

"Skye!"

The man named Brock was working his way through the thinning crowd toward them. Skye's posture stiffened, and her shoulders hunched as if she was steeling herself. For a moment Mario thought she was going to ignore the guy and keep walking, but she stopped.

When he reached them, Brock said, "Skye...it's so good to see you."

He wrapped his arms around her. Skye returned the hug, barely. She began to wriggle out of his embrace almost immediately, but he did not let go right away. When she did manage to extricate herself, he kept hold of her hand.

Delilah began to strain at her lead, her attention focused on Brock. Mario heard a low rumble in the pit bull's throat.

"Brock," Skye said, taking a step away from him. "I didn't know you were back."

Brock's bloodshot brown eyes were interested only in Skye. He looked at her like she was an oasis in the desert. He had not bothered to acknowledge the rest of them.

He said, "We just got back. It was a disaster."

"I caught the end of your story."

"That's a tough break, man," Rocco said.

Brock finally tore his gaze from Skye. "Hey, Rocco, Tessa." His eyes skittered over Mario and Doug, then went back to Skye.

Skye pulled her hand away, her unease so evident that Mario found it hard to believe the guy did not notice.

"We've got business, Brock. I've got to go," Skye said.

"Jennie's dead."

All three of the LOers gasped. Skye's eyes widened.

"What?" she said.

"Jennie's dead," Brock repeated. Tears began to leak from his eyes. "On the way back, we got caught by a horde, and she...she..."

He broke down completely, unable to go on.

Mario saw that Skye also had tears in her eyes.

"Oh my God. Brock," she said. "I'm so sorry."

She stepped toward him and put her hand on his shoulder. Everything about the way she moved and interacted with him had softened. When he put his arms around her again, she held him. He wept on her shoulder like a bereft child.

Doug asked Rocco, "Who's Jennie?"

"His sister," Rocco said, still looking shocked at the news. "She was Skye's friend. I can't believe it."

The rumble in Delilah's throat was just below a full-on growl. Mario tipped his head toward the side of the enclosure between the gates to P-Land. He wanted to get Delilah away from the others to get a little breathing room. She didn't seem to like Brock, and she really didn't like him holding Skye close.

"We need to see what we can find out about home," Mario said softly. He leaned against a section of exterior wall a few feet from the door they had entered by.

Doug nodded. Skye still held Brock. Even though she was about five foot ten, the man crying in her arms dwarfed her.

"At least we know they're not fighting anymore," Doug said. He looked at Skye and Brock. "I wonder what the story is with those two. She wanted no part of him until he told her about his sister."

"Delilah sure doesn't like him."

They lapsed into silence. A minute later, Tessa and Rocco joined them.

"We're going to take you to see the Council," Rocco said. "Skye's going to stay with Brock for a while."

"Did they go to San Jose hoping to bring back some of their vaccine?" Doug asked.

Tessa nodded. "Yeah, but it sounds like it didn't go so well. I met some people from San Jose a couple years back. It sounded pretty fucked up considering they have the only cure."

"You would think they'd want to share it," Doug said.

They were all silent for a moment. Mario was grateful that Doug had not told anyone that they were from San Jose. Things could have gotten a little awkward. Brock had looked murderous while telling his story. The last thing they needed was the guy deciding they were a good punching bag to vent his frustration on.

"Do you mind me asking what the story is?" Mario asked. "Skye did not look happy to see him at first."

Rocco shook his head. "Brock is Skye's ex. It was a nasty breakup. But she was really tight with Jennie."

WHEN HE SAW Miranda as they arrived at the Institute the following morning, relief would have bowled Mario over if he had not been sitting. Delilah bolted from the SUV ahead of him. Miranda stooped to greet the enthusiastic dog, petting her while trying, without much success, to avoid getting a full-on lick on the lips.

"Hey, beautiful," Mario said when he reached her.

Miranda wrapped her arms around him. It had only been two days since she had stayed behind at Commander Smith's invitation that could not be refused, but it felt like years.

She kissed him, and the spark of heat behind it took him by surprise. She must have been worried about him, too. Delilah tried to wriggle between them.

"Okay, you two, break it up," Doug said. "How ya doing, Coppertop?"

Miranda hugged Doug, then jabbed him in the ribs. "I was a little worried when they said you had to stay at P-Land overnight. They took very good care of me, but even New Jerusalem didn't seem too bad at first."

"You got an extra day with three squares and a cot and hot water, and still you were suspicious," Rocco said as he and Skye joined them, but his tone was joking.

Miranda shrugged. "You can never be too careful."

"It was just late by the time we finished up there," Mario said. "Smarter to spend the night."

"We got an electrician and a crew lined up," Skye said. "So I guess it's official that we're neighbors."

Mario nodded, excited at the prospect of soon getting to work, and also at the idea of spending some time alone with Miranda. Their kiss had made him hungry for more. But allies were important, and even after the end of the civilization as they had once known it, manners were too.

He nodded and said to Skye, "Nice to meet you, neighbor."

11

To hear Miranda tell it, LO sounded like a theme park. Doug laughed to himself at the face she would make at this characterization. He had to remember it for later.

For a smaller outpost, LO had a lot of things going for it. They had a doctor, a nurse practitioner, and a dentist: the trifecta of post-apocalyptic healthcare. They had a two-layer palisade that was twenty-five-feet high. Its poles were whole trees nestled beside one another, with the second layer behind the seams where every tree on the outer layer met. Miranda had come away with a very positive impression of Commander Smith. Smith ran a tight ship but worked hard to get buy-in from the residents. The people Miranda had met seemed happy to be there.

They were not just in Tualatin Hills Park. Miranda seemed to have passed whatever Smith's character tests were, too. When Smith had learned that he and the others were going to be delayed overnight in P-Land, she had pulled out the maps and showed Miranda where they were as a show of good faith. Along the park's southern border was a small housing development, a residential Catholic Boys' Home, and an apartment development. LO had expanded into all three.

Two creeks ran through the former park, so they did not lack for water. They had even set up some windmills, but Doug wasn't sure where. Along with solar, they provided electricity for stoves in the housing plans and the kitchens at the Boys' Home.

The windmills also helped power LO's defense system. A week later, Miranda could not shut up about it. Doug was itching to learn more. Since one of the things that attracted zombies was sound, LO had figured out a way to use it against them. They'd set a perimeter that encircled their settlement about two miles out in all directions. Along the perimeter were Station Houses that broadcast white noise. The levels weren't high, just enough to attract zombies within approximately a quarter mile. The system was designed to funnel zombies from the north and west and most importantly from the east —where Portland was located—southwest of LO to a kill zone. Amplification was normally set at the same level throughout the system, but when they wanted to funnel zombies to the kill zone, the volume became progressively louder from station to station, luring the zombies where LO wanted them. They killed zombies at every Station House, of course, but the bulk were redirected to the kill zone on a regular schedule. If the density of zombies was getting too high in the kill zone, they could amp the sound up elsewhere to redistribute them.

It explained the overall lack of zombies in the area that they had noticed once they got inside the ring of Station Houses. They just hadn't known that the Station Houses were there. The Station Houses were no more than one mile apart, which was the major weakness of the system. If a Station House went off-line, zombies got through the gap, and when there were enough zombies heading one direction, it caught the interest of others. So it was not a question of if they would end up going through the gap, but how quickly that happened and how many.

There had only been two system-wide failures in the five years the sound defenses had been operational. LO was still here, and they still used the sound defense system, so clearly, they had been able to bounce back and refine. The good old-fashioned trench and chain-link fence, and the tall log palisade, were the low-tech backup.

Doug checked his compass again. He only had about half a mile left, assuming he was going in the right direction. He was. Now that he knew where LO was, he had decided to try the route that he had mapped out from the Institute. Their location at the Institute was northwest of LO and a little over an hour's journey on foot. He had needed to adjust course a few times but only needed to kill four zombies.

Smith had promised to get them a working vehicle, but he wanted to know how to get to LO on foot, just in case. He also wanted to thank Smith for their assistance brokering the deal with P-Land. As of yesterday, after five days of almost nonstop work, the Institute had power. Mario had spent the last day giggling like a kid in a candy store despite the still-long list of repairs.

Five minutes later, he had reached the correct spot on the map. Doug looked around at the trees, shrubs, briars, and grasses gone wild for ten years.

"Where the hell is it?" he said softly.

After ten minutes of searching, he noticed a fallen tree. He could tell that the tree had snapped and fallen some time ago, its fat trunk still attached to the stump by jagged, broken edges that had been sharp but were now worn and crumbling. About a third of the way up from the trunk the bark had worn off. The oval of wood underneath was smooth, as if it had been rubbed for years by the legs of people climbing over.

"Bingo."

Doug scrambled over the tree and saw another worn spot on the next tree in front of him. Alongside the second tree a worn depression meandered through the deep, overgrown thicket. He would have mistaken it for a game trail if he had not known there were people living nearby.

Several twists and turns later, he emerged on a one-lane gravel road. To the left the road ran out of sight back toward the road he had just been on. He headed the other direction, and a few minutes later, he saw the drawbridge gate.

The first obstacle was the trench that encircled the settlement. He had been driven over it the other day—once with a hood and once without. Beyond the trench was the chain-link fence, then the palisade. There were three guard booths along the catwalk over the drawbridge, at its center and in the simple towers the drawbridge was nestled between. Doug had not been up there, but the winches for the drawbridge were in the towers on either end. The whole set up was impressive.

That must have taken forever to build, Doug thought, taking in the palisade again.

Five of the six people in the guard tower trained rifles on him. The other spoke into a radio.

"Hello," Doug called from the far side of the trench, hands held open in front of him. "I'm Doug Michel. I was here the other day with Skye, Rocco, and Tessa. I'm hoping to see Commander Smith."

"Wait right there," a silver-haired woman with a rifle said.

Doug stopped. The person on the walkie-talkie was looking at him and speaking into it. A few minutes later, Skye appeared in the guard booth. Doug saw her nodding to the others, and the drawbridge began to lower.

Once inside, Skye introduced him to the guards before they set off for Smith's office.

Skye asked, "You came on foot? Alone?"

"I haven't sprouted wings."

"Well, just so you know, that is against protocol. She's gonna read you the riot act."

"Oh," Doug said. "You have a protocol for traveling on foot?"

"We have a protocol for everything."

The gravel road opened up to the wide gravel-covered parking lot. A tiny corner of the asymmetrically slanted roof of the former park's Nature Center peeked up past the trees in front of the building.

"Wow," Doug said as the doors to the Nature Center closed behind him. "This is a beautiful building."

The roof slanted up from behind him to a height of two stories. Windows nestled under the high eave in the far wall that plunged straight down from the roof. The ceiling was timbered in honey-colored pine, knots casting a speckling of freckles. Unlike the other day, the sun shone brightly, flooding the lobby with light. He was also not being held captive, which made it possible to appreciate the architecture. On the far side of the lobby to Doug's right, floor-to-ceiling windows displayed a patio nestled in the ninety-degree corner of the building's two wings.

"It is pretty," Skye said. "It's a bitch to heat with all the windows, though."

He followed Skye around the reception desk to the offices. He could see Smith sitting at her desk, reading the papers in front of her. She looked up as they approached the door.

"Look what the cat dragged in," Smith said, smiling. "What can I do for you, Father?"

"Please, call me Doug," Doug said as he stood in the doorway. "I just wanted to thank you in person for getting P-Land to help get the power on."

"Not a problem, happy to do it," Smith said, dismissing his thank you with a wave of her hand. Her eyebrows scrunched together. "How did you get here? Did you walk?"

"He did," Skye said, nudging his ribs with her elbow. "Alone."

"Thanks for the backup," Doug said, glancing sidelong at Skye.

The barest of smiles quirked the corners of Skye's mouth as Smith began to speak.

"Walking alone is dangerous, Doug. That's not how we do things around here. The protocol here is..."

———

WHEN DOUG EMERGED from Smith's office half an hour later,

he saw Skye lounging sideways across a love seat in the lobby, her long legs bent at the knee over its arm. When she saw him, she propped herself up on her elbows.

"How was your chat with the commander?"

"You are pure evil," he answered. "I'm never coming here on my own again just so I can avoid that lecture."

Skye's head fell back as her peal of laughter filled the lobby. She swung her legs off the couch and swiveled up to standing in a movement so smooth Doug realized he was gawking. He had never seen anyone move with such an easy, fluid grace.

"What?" she said, looking at him. "Do I have something in my teeth?"

"Do you, what? No," he said. "Nothing in your teeth. I've just— never mind."

She's one of the best rock climbers in the world; of course she's coordinated... You need to quit talking, or you're going to make a fool of yourself, he thought.

Skye regarded him with a mixture of confusion and amusement. "Well, okay. Let me make it up to you. I'll give you a tour since you didn't see anything last time."

"You mean when I was your prisoner?" he said. "I think a tour is the least you can do."

They exited the building. Once out from under the covered walkway with its concrete sidewalk, the path became earthen, covered with trampled down layers of leaves and pine needles. They entered the woods. A soft hush seemed to fill the space around them. The pines were straight and easily a hundred feet tall, like spears planted in the earth that wanted to fly into the sky. Oaks with branches gnarled and twisting were covered in moss and lichens. The plants on the densely tangled forest floor were low to the ground, in more lush shades of green than Doug ever knew existed. Sunlight filtered through the canopy, dappling the path Skye had chosen with golden pools of sunlight. Doug took it all in, feeling the glow of the colors and sounds and smells surrounding him.

He said softly, "This is beautiful."

"Isn't it?" Skye agreed. "We call it The Big Woods."

"Is it old growth?"

"I doubt it, but it feels like it could be, you know?"

Doug nodded in agreement. "Miranda told me about the woods, but she didn't mention how dense they are. I had this idea that you had lots of little cabins among them, but that wouldn't work at all."

Skye nodded. "A common misconception, so you're totally average, Father."

He opened his mouth to tell her that his friends called him Doug, but she winked at him. Then he took a mental pause. This was maybe the second time he had ever seen Skye, let alone spent time with her. Was he already thinking of her as a friend?

After a few minutes of walking, he said, "Where are we going?"

"My favorite place in The Big Woods," Skye said. "I like to show it to new people. I'll show you the boring stuff after."

They passed a sign on the right that pointed out Tadpole Pond, but from the path it was impossible to investigate, and Skye did not stop. The terrain dipped low and grew marshy, but the built-up path was higher and stayed dry. Velvety brown cattails studded the wetted ground, standing proud on thin stalks adorned with tall, pointy green leaves. Soon the cattails grew so thick it was impossible to see through them. They rounded another curve in the path where the marsh edged into a pond.

"This is it," Skye said. She crouched down and motioned for Doug to do the same. "We might not see them. It's the wrong time of day."

"Might not see what?" Doug asked. If he knew what he was looking for, it might increase the likelihood he would spot it.

She shushed him. A few minutes later, she leaned in and whispered, "There, on the far side."

Doug looked to where she pointed. A long, dark critter, sleek and glistening, sliced through the water against the creek's gentle current. Its dark-brown fur looked almost black, and its eyes seemed full of good-natured mischief. It dove before the cattails along the creek obstructed Doug's view. A few moments later, several more swam after it, chirping to one another. On the far side of the cattails the group emerged, whiskers twitching, the smaller ones splashing noisily in a flurry of squeaks. They dove below the water's surface, flashing the pointy tips of their long tails, before their dark heads popped up again.

"River otters," Doug said softly.

Skye nodded, grinning, as two of the smaller otters began to wrestle, dunking one another in a quick succession of flips. A third little otter joined the dunkfest so that they resembled a splashing, tumbling ball of glistening fur. Then the first otter squeaked. The tumbling dunkers quit playing, heads turned attentively in the first otter's direction. With another splash of their slender tails, every otter ducked beneath the surface, trailing bubbles as they raced away.

"That was so cool," Doug said as they stood up. "I've seen otters before but never this close. A group is called a raft, right? Since they hold paws when they're sleeping?"

"I'm not sure that river otters do that as much as sea otters. You can also call them a romp. I love how playful they are, so that's what I call them."

"A romp of river otters," Doug echoed, beginning to chuckle. "That's perfect."

Skye said, "If I could choose an animal to be, I'd be an otter."

"I can see it," Doug said. "A squeaky blond otter. I'd be a shark."

"Really?" She sounded dubious. "I don't see you as a shark."

"Then what do you see me as?" he asked. "I'll run it by Miranda and see if she agrees."

Skye stopped and looked him over from head to toe.

"You're tall and skinny, but you're strong." She narrowed her eyes while she thought, then said, "A praying mantis."

"A bug?" Doug said. "You think I'd be a bug?"

"It's a bad-ass bug."

"That the female eats after mating!"

"I don't think you're gonna have that particular problem."

"Oh my God," he groaned, his head falling back. "On second thought, I won't run it by Miranda. And you're not allowed to be friends with her. I don't think I can take it."

AN HOUR LATER, Skye had shown him all of LO. The Big Woods' south side adjoined three housing developments—an apartment complex, a residential boys' home, and a single-family homes and townhouses development. Once the park buildings had been secured, the small community kept expanding until it had all three housing complexes behind the main palisade. Now they were close to seven hundred people. He and Skye rounded the last corner of the single-family home/townhouse plan, which was pretty in a faux Craftsman, cookie-cutter sort of way.

"That last house on the corner, by where the original entrance to the plan was, is the medical clinic," Skye said. "We'll stop in, and I'll introduce you to Doctor... Fuck."

"Doctor Fuck?" Doug said. He had to turn around because Skye had stopped and was now behind him.

She grimaced. "My ex is over there. He's seen me."

The guy from the gate at P-Land, Brock, walked toward them. The ginormous farm boy looked better than last time, clean and lacking the fury he had emanated as he told the tale of his disastrous trip to San Jose, but still haggard. Like he had not slept well. A pang of sympathy welled up in Doug's chest.

He lost his sister. Of course he's not sleeping well.

"Hey, Skye," Brock said, then pulled her in for a hug.

Skye said hello with markedly less enthusiasm.

"It's good to see you," Brock continued, breaking the embrace. "I haven't been sleeping well since I got back. I can't stop thinking about Jennie."

"Have you been to see the doctor?" Skye asked. The concern in her voice sounded genuine.

"That P-Land quack?" he said, sounding annoyed. "I came here to see Doctor River. She gave me this tea to help me sleep. Wouldn't give me any real drugs since she said insomnia is a normal reaction to grief." He held up a small paper bag, rolling his eyes.

"What kind of tea?" Doug asked.

Brock looked over at Doug like he had only just noticed him. "Valerian Root."

"That's actually a good sleep aid," Doug said.

Brock said to Skye. "Are you free? It helps being around people who love—loved Jennie—as much as I did."

"I can't," Skye said gently. "I'm in the middle of showing Doug around."

Brock glanced at Doug, a flash of hostility flitting over his face.

"Oh," he said, his voice chilly. "I didn't realize you were showing *Doug* around."

"Doug's a priest, Brock," Skye said.

"I don't think some company is too much to ask, especially now," Brock said sharply, his voice rising.

"I'm busy, Brock," Skye said, beginning to sound angry, too. "I can't right now."

Doug watched the escalating exchange, not liking what he saw. Brock was clearly jealous, of him of all people, but Doug didn't know either of them well enough to say anything without, he suspected, making it worse.

"I just miss her," Brock said angrily. "I guess you don't."

"You know that's not true," Skye said, then softened her voice. "I'm just busy right now."

He's using his dead sister to manipulate her, Doug realized, his opinion of Brock getting lower by the second.

"Whatever," Brock said dismissively. He directed another dirty look Doug's way as he turned on his heel and stalked away.

"Brock," Skye called after him, placating. "Don't be like that. I'll come see you later."

Brock kept walking. Skye sighed, looking troubled.

"He's so unreasonable," she muttered.

"I know his sister just died, but he seems like a dick," Doug said.

Skye almost smiled but looked troubled. "Now I have to go see him, or he'll make things difficult. Small communities, you know how it is."

Doug did know 'how it is' in small communities, but he did not like the way Brock had tried to intimidate with anger and when that did not work, use his grief to manipulate.

"It's none of my business," he said slowly, which caused Skye to quit watching Brock's retreating figure and look at him. "But is he why you moved to LO?"

"You're right," she said evenly. "It's none of your business."

He *is* the reason she moved, Doug thought. Skye started walking again. In two quick strides of his long legs, Doug caught up.

"I'm sorry. I shouldn't have pried."

He didn't want to just say he was sorry, though. He wanted to make sure she had some way to deal with her creep of an ex. After what he had just seen, Doug thought she might need it. He reached out for Skye's wrist and pulled her toward him. She turned, looking both startled and angry, and tried to pull away.

"That's your first mistake," Doug said, still holding on to her wrist. "You should step into me. Someone pulling on you won't expect that, and then you can use your momentum to knock them off balance."

The annoyance leached from Skye's blue eyes. He had her attention, so he continued with his unorthodox olive branch.

"Like this," he said. "Grab my wrist and pull."

She did as he instructed, her grip even stronger than he had expected. He turned into her, wrapping her arm around him as if they were dancing. When his shoulder reached her chest, he leaned in.

"Hit their chest with your shoulder, but as hard as you can. And if you want to be really slick—"

He nudged against her sternum just enough to almost unsteady her balance, then turned in a little more so that he almost faced her. His outside foot swung behind hers. He planted it solidly on the ground, then he pushed on her exposed left shoulder with his free hand. Not as hard as if he were really trying to fend someone off but enough to trip her. When she realized she was falling backward, Skye released his other wrist. He darted low, sliding his right arm around her to catch her waist like a dancer dipping his partner.

"Don't worry," he said, grinning, his face inches from hers. "I've got you."

Her eyes had gone wide with shock. She narrowed them and smacked his shoulder.

"You jerk!"

He could feel her ribs shake against his arm as she laughed. Her breath tickled his ear. She smelled like mown grass and honey, and her eyes were so blue that the sky above them looked drab. A flush of heat raced through Doug's body as he pulled her up to standing. As her smile faded, he realized her lips were the velvety pink of rosebuds.

My God, she's beautiful.

He held her a moment too long, his heart pounding, then let go as if she were a hot coal.

"Your...uh... You let go. Of me—my hand. I mean, my wrist," he said, stumbling over the words as he tried to regain his equilibrium. "To break your fall."

She nodded, her mouth forming a tiny 'O.'

"Yeah," she said, sounding breathless.

"When you thought you were falling, you let go. To break your fall."

"Right." She nodded. "You already said that."

Oh my God, shut your mouth, he thought.

"Right," he answered, his mouth-words not getting the memo

from his mind-brain. He could feel a hot blush creeping over his face. "Right, of course, you— I did."

Doug looked away. The rush of attraction was as surprising as it was unexpected. He could not remember feeling this nonplussed —ever.

"Doug," Skye said.

He looked up, not wanting to make things any weirder by not looking at her when she spoke to him.

"That was nice of you. And useful. But if you grab me again, I will knock you on your ass."

"Fair enough," he said softly.

He tried but could not tear his eyes away from her. Something— surprise, maybe?—flashed in hers.

"Let's go see River. She's the doctor here."

She turned without waiting for his reply. A few seconds later, Doug followed.

12

Mario looked up from his notes. Outside, the macaques' screeching indicated something out of the ordinary. They were better than any alarm system humans had ever devised.

Mario pushed the notes aside and walked to the rear entrance that faced the old parking lot. A Jeep, the old kind like you saw in World War II movies, tooled into view. Doug, Skye, and two people Mario didn't know were inside. Mario pulled on his jacket and walked out to meet them.

The watery winter sunshine did not do much to counter the cold and damp, but the weather was milder than the day before. Still, it had to have been a chilly ride. The Jeep squeaked to a halt, Skye behind the wheel, Doug in the passenger seat with cheeks rosy from the cold.

"Hi, Skye," Mario said, approaching the Jeep.

"Hey, James," she answered. "How's it going?"

"It's going," he answered, almost turning around to see who Skye was talking to. He was still not used to the people here calling him James. "On the right side of the grass, so it's a good day." He looked over at Doug as he hopped out of the Jeep. "See you got a ride."

"Smith read me the riot act for walking over there by myself, so I said yes to a lift."

"James, let me introduce you," Skye said to Mario as she stepped out of the Jeep. "Phineas, this is James."

Phineas, a fresh-faced kid in his early twenties with kinky, close-cropped hair, stood up and reached over the roll bar to shake Mario's hand. Freckles spattered the bridge of his nose, darker speckles against his dark skin. He was one of the first African Americans Mario had seen since they arrived in the Northwest, which some-times felt like the Great Northern Whitewash. Phineas was medium height with broad shoulders but a wiry build.

"Hey, man," he said, his quick smile flashing white, even teeth.

"Mathilde," the woman sitting next to Phineas said as she extended her hand. The slight purr of what most people might think was a French accent softened the consonants of her speech, but Mario didn't think she was French. She looked about thirty, with dark hair and eyes. "Very pleased to make your acquaintance, James."

"Enchanté," Mario said, deciding to take his best guess. "Swiss?"

Mathilde smiled. "Très bien! Most people cannot tell the differ-ence and assume I am from France."

"Coup de chance," Mario said. At Phineas' raised eyebrows, he added, "Lucky guess."

Mathilde shook her head. "La fausse modestie ne vous convient pas, James."

Mario laughed. "Je ne contredis jamais une femme charmante."

"We better hit it," Skye said, climbing back into the driver's seat. Phineas swung under the roll bar to take the passenger seat.

"What's the rush?" Doug said. "At least let us give you some tea or something. I'm freezing after riding in a Jeep *in January*, even if it is wimpy West Coast January. You must be, too." His voice became sing-songy as he said, "We have power now, so it's mosty-toasty."

After a moment's conferral, the trio agreed.

"Besides," Phineas said, "I gotta take a dump."

"Phineas!" Mathilde scolded.

"Overshare much?" Skye said.

"Sorry," the young man said, but he did not look it.

Mario pointed him in the direction of the latrine, then followed everyone else inside.

"We're set up near the reception desk," Doug said, leading the way.

Mario filled and flicked the switch on the electric kettle while the others claimed seats. "Using appliances never gets old," he said. "Electricity is the best."

"What's this?" Miranda called down from the mezzanine balcony across from reception.

"Come join the party," Mario said to her, noticing she looked less pale than earlier. "You feeling better?"

Delilah scurried down the stairs, nails clicking on the terrazzo floor, and made a beeline for Skye.

Miranda joined them, and Mathilde was introduced.

"Not sick, I hope," Skye said to Miranda.

Miranda shook her head as she settled in next to Mario. "Nah, just wiped out so I took a nap. I'm glad you stopped to visit. I get tired of these two."

"Absence makes the heart grow fonder, but familiarity breeds contempt, or so they say," Mathilde said.

Miranda leaned against Mario, the weight of her body against his better than a warm blanket.

"You sure you're not coming down with something?" he asked, sidebar from the group conversation. He put the back of his hand against her cheek, but she didn't feel feverish.

"I'm fine," she assured him, resting her head on his shoulder. "Just needed some rest. I wrote in my journal, too."

While Skye was telling them about the otters she and Doug had seen, Mario realized Phineas had not returned from the latrine yet. He checked his watch. It had been almost twenty minutes, and it wasn't like they had magazines there. He pulled his hand out of Miranda's and stood up.

"I'm going to go check on Phineas. It's been a while," he said.

Miranda straightened up. "I checked the perimeter earlier. It was okay."

"I'm sure it's nothing," Mario said, not wanting to alarm anyone. "Probably got waylaid by macaques."

"I don't think that's it," Skye said slowly.

Phineas' voice floated down from the mezzanine. "Rocco was right, Skye."

Mario's head snapped up. Phineas stood at the mezzanine rail, looking down at them. Jeremiah stood beside him.

"Our deliverance is at hand."

JEREMIAH'S DELIVERANCE proved short-lived after Mario, Miranda, and Doug's vociferous protests were followed with calmer, if circumspect, explanations. He was once again safely locked up at the Institute.

Miranda stayed behind with Phineas and Mathilde, while Mario and Doug went to LO. Mario looked around the lobby of the Nature Center. It really was as beautiful as Doug had said. He just wished his first visit, not to mention his first introduction to LO's commander, was for any reason other than the secret of Jeremiah being exposed.

Doug sat on the chair next to him, mostly scowling at Skye in a very un-Doug-like display of pique. Skye leaned against the reception desk, her face mostly impassive but also, Mario thought, a bit amused by Doug's demeanor.

"I still can't believe you distracted us so he could sneak around and spy on us," Doug said. "Even pretending like you weren't going to stay."

Skye shrugged. "You'd have done the same in our shoes."

"That's beside the point..." Doug muttered, then lapsed into silence.

A few minutes later, a short, trim woman, brown hair shot through with gray and authority radiating from her like the sun, walked through the entrance.

"So," Anna Smith said a few minutes later. She sat on the corner of the desk in her office, having shoved a stack of papers out of her way first. Mario wondered if she had opted for sitting on rather than behind her desk to make their conversation less confrontational. "It seems we have a little bit of a situation here."

"It's none of your business," Doug said.

Smith shot an exasperated look at Skye, who stood just inside the closed door. Skye shook her head as if to say, I can't help you this time.

"Holding someone prisoner against their will on my patch without a damn good reason is definitely my business," Smith said. "Get your side of the story in before I get his."

"He's crazy," Mario said. "Delusional."

"Unless he's dangerous, that's not a reason to hold him prisoner," Smith countered.

Doug's bark of laughter was loud enough that Mario jumped in his seat.

"He's completely dangerous," Doug said. "He's the most dangerous whack job I've ever met, and I've met some doozies."

"So?" Smith said.

"He's a rapist and a murderer, for starters," Doug said, ticking off Jeremiah's crimes on his fingers. "He thinks he's God's messenger, has some *very* fucked-up theology, and refers to himself in the third person. That alone is enough to lock anyone up."

Smith looked at Doug evenly. "Then maybe we should just shoot him and be done with it."

"No," Mario said quickly. He had not meant to let her see the panic that her suggestion sent through him, but he failed spectacularly. "I need him for my research."

"Ah...he's immune to the zombie virus," Smith said, somewhere between a question and a statement. "I can't think of another reason for you to go tromping to the ends of the Earth with him in tow to find research facilities with a BSL-3 lab."

Doug threw his hands up in the air.

"Yes," he said irritably. "He's immune. And he doesn't see any reason to get rid of zombies because his little cult where he terrorized the people *he* held hostage suited him just fine. That's why he's a prisoner. Good enough for you?"

"Almost," Smith said. "But it doesn't explain why you're working with Mario Santorello."

The sensation of the floor falling out from under him was so strong that Mario did not understand why he was still sitting upright in his chair. From Doug's stunned expression, he had not seen this one coming either, but the set of his jaw quickly became defiant.

Mario realized he better speak before Doug's uncharacteristic belligerence made things worse. He took a deep breath.

"How long have you known?"

"Rocco recognized you."

Mario nodded. "As long as we're fessing up, he also repels zombies, which we've never seen before."

"Oh, *come on*," Doug said. "You're killing me here! Why don't you tell them all our secrets?"

"Better now than later," Mario said to him. He looked back to Smith. "The truth about me is a little more complicated than everyone has been led to believe."

An hour and two rounds of bourbon later, which was exceedingly generous of Smith, Mario thought, the LO commander looked at him and Doug thoughtfully.

"That's quite a story," she finally said. "I understand why you're cranky, Doug, but I have to admit, I am not sure what to make of you, Mario." She looked over at Skye. "What do think? Does it play?"

Skye swished the last of the bourbon in her glass before polishing it off. She set her glass down.

"It plays," she said. "Maybe 'James' here," she said, "isn't as altruistic as he's making himself out to be, but it makes more sense than a vaccine developer throwing in with the bad guys. People who make vaccines want to protect people from disease. It's usually not about the money."

"I think you've got a pretty good sense of Miranda by now. She would not be with a creep," Doug said. "What Mario did wasn't easy. He's *more* altruistic than he's letting on."

Smith said, "Or he's at least trying to make amends."

She's got that right, Mario thought. He had been a victim of circumstance as much as anyone else, but he still felt like he had to make amends for what he had done to Miranda, his wife and kids, and all the innocent people caught up in the power struggle between the Council's greed and the Jesuits' ministry. People whose names he would never know.

"Okay," Smith said. "Here's what we're going to do. You're going to keep doing your work, but we need to beef up security over there."

"How about setting up a mini-sound defense perimeter around the Institute?" Skye said to Smith. "I know Station Ten and Eleven aren't far north of it, and Nine is southwest, but Larry has the equipment."

"It's overkill," Smith said, a faraway gaze in her eyes as she considered the suggestion. "But it's a vaccine to protect against the zombie virus, so better safe than sorry. Good idea, Skye."

Smith continued. "We need a more humane lockup for the prisoner. I hear it's basically a closet."

Doug shrugged, looking discomfited. "It was just the three of us, and he's really devious."

Smith waved his protest away. "I'm not criticizing. Skye will pull together a detail, and they'll be at the Institute tomorrow. It's too late to send them over now," she said, glancing out the window at the rapidly fading light. "You'll have to stay the night, too. Don't worry," she added when Mario started to object. "We'll get in touch with Miranda. Phineas has a radio."

"Let's hold up a minute," Mario said.

The conversation was going well, perhaps too well. If there was any possibility that things might go pear-shaped, he would prefer to know now, or at least get a read on Smith's reaction.

"The whole point of what we did was to change how things went in San Jose. To break the monopoly. The vaccine must be free to everyone, no matter what. That is non-negotiable. If you don't agree, then this conversation is over. Lock me up if you want, but I will not do any more work unless I'm convinced you understand that."

Smith's look of surprise was all the assurance that Mario needed.

"I thought that was what we were talking about," she said. "But you're right. It never hurts to be clear. The vaccine is free, and everyone gets it, no exceptions."

Mario's body relaxed. This entire episode was nerve-racking, but he had not realized just how much until now.

"I don't want nonessential personnel at the Institute," Smith continued. "It's probably overcautious, but there will be more back and forth between here and there now. Might as well keep as low a profile as possible, given those parameters. Anyone nonessential to the research or security should come stay here."

"Miranda's not gonna like that," Doug said. "She'll want to be on the security detail."

"*I* don't like it," Mario protested.

Smith was silent for a moment, then said, "Well, I'll talk to her. We should keep calling you James Gideon," she said to Mario, then said to Skye, "We need to flash his picture around to see who might recognize him. Maybe we'll luck out there."

"I could use a research partner," Mario said. "Or an assistant, if there's anyone here who knows what they're doing. Experience with primate research would be a plus."

"What's that girl's name, Skye?" Smith asked. "You know, with the long hair and the brutal laugh? Isn't she a biochemist or a virologist?"

"Alicia?" Skye said. "I think she's one of the two, but I'm not sure. She was all but dissertation on her Ph.D."

"That would be perfect," Mario said, a thrill of excitement

making his brain buzz. A good lab partner would make all the difference. "If she's either of those things, she probably knows who I am."

"All the more reason to pull her in," said Doug.

They sat quietly for a moment, then Smith said to Mario, "How good are your chances of doing it again?"

Mario shrugged. "I should be able to with enough time. The biggest difficulty I see is his repellant ability. The person we developed the first vaccine from couldn't do that. It might be a different strain or just a mutation of the same strain. Until I've done more work, I just won't know."

Smith picked up the bourbon and splashed some more into everyone's glasses. She raised hers up. "To the successful repetition of reproducible results. That's what good science is, after all."

They clinked their glasses, grinning at one another, and a lightness filled Mario's chest. Even though they had failed to keep their mission secret, Mario felt more encouraged than he had in a long time. Skye had believed them, believed *him*. Smith knew who he was and was still willing to help, even if she had a healthy dose of skepticism about some of the details. His infamy stemming from the official story was so firmly entrenched that Mario had never expected that anyone would ever give him the benefit of the doubt.

He sipped his bourbon, its smooth but fiery bite flooding his mouth.

It felt good to have allies again.

13

MIRANDA FELT MARIO'S HEAD FALL ONTO THE PILLOW BY HERS as he lay beside her. She felt breathless, her body tingling and heart still hammering. She opened her eyes and turned to look at him. His dark features were flushed, a satiated haze she was well acquainted with enveloping him.

"How did you get so good at this?" she said.

He pulled her to him, skin warm against hers as he kissed her forehead, and said, "Practice. And natural talent." She nudged him with her elbow when he boasted. "I'm going to miss you."

"LO isn't far."

"I'll still miss you."

Miranda smiled. "I'll miss you, too, but admit it. You're looking forward to having me out of your hair so you can concentrate on your work."

He ran his fingers along her body until his hand rested on her hip. "I wouldn't go that far. It *will* be easier to concentrate without the distractions you create."

"You love when I distract you," she said, grinning, then sat up.

She stretched her arms over her head and ran her fingers through her short hair.

"I *am* looking forward to doing something useful," she said. "Refusing to go there when Smith first suggested it was dumb."

Mario laughed, the corners of his eyes crinkling. "I can't believe you lasted a week."

"Yeah, well, the last three days were not wanting to admit I made a mistake."

"Oh, believe me, I know."

Miranda stood and threw Mario's pants at him, scoring a direct hit to his face. "Brat."

He tugged the pants away. "Do you promise to get more rest? You've been dragging since we got here."

Miranda pulled on her shirt. "Less rest, not more, and exercise is what I need. All I've been doing here is loafing and napping. It's indecent. I usually never nap."

She tucked in her shirt and started searching for her boots. After so much time apart, she hated not being together even if she was putting a good face on it.

"Get this vaccine done quick, okay?" she said.

Mario smiled at her. "I'll work as fast as I can."

AN HOUR LATER, Miranda checked on Jeremiah one last time before departing. She was not entirely comfortable with the new brig arrangements even though she had to admit they were secure. More people from LO onsite to assist allowed for more fail-safes and consistency. Given what they were trying to achieve, they needed every advantage they could get.

They had a welder at LO, so Commander Smith had ordered improvements using retro-fitted iron bars from some of the abandoned primate enclosures. The new brig was in the old animal hospital on the grounds nearest to the main Institute building. There was no reason for Jeremiah to be in the main building now. As Smith had pointed out, if Jeremiah was kept there and escaped, he might set fire to the building or sabotage equipment. Losing the BSL-3 was an outcome they could ill afford, especially considering that it had taken so much work to get it operational.

Macaque monkeys squawked and chittered at Miranda as she walked the path, her shoulders hunched against the damp, chilled air. You're adaptable little buggers, she thought as they scurried about. How the desirability of roosts was determined was beyond her, but as she became familiar with the monkeys, she had started to figure out which were higher status and which were lower. The lower-status monkeys rarely enjoyed the prime locations for long before they were bullied out of the way by more dominant members of the troop.

She smiled a greeting to Axel, the taciturn guard at the main door, as she entered the building. He looked about nineteen even though she knew he wasn't. Inside the Brig Lab, as it had come to be called, sat a metal cage similar to the kind used in zoos before natural habitats became popular. It had been constructed along the far wall of the low-slung, one-story building. The twelve-foot-square cage was close enough to the windows to allow for natural light, but not so close that Jeremiah could reach them, even if he had something in his hand. All of the furnishings were constructed of iron and welded to the frame: the tabletop and bench chair, the slab for the mattress, even the improvised sink and composting toilet. Nothing could be taken apart to be used as a tool or weapon. The only things he had access to were paperback books and the clothes on his back, not even shoes. If he somehow managed it, they were not going to make escape any easier. The dishes for his meals were used under direct supervision and immediately collected by the guards, who were there twenty-four hours a day.

Miranda heard voices as she entered the brig.

"So you had a village in the trees," a female voice said skeptically. "And how did you manage that?"

At the far end of the room, this shift's guard, a twenty-something woman named Courtney, sat in a chair several feet from Jeremiah's cell. Miranda could see her in profile as she leaned forward, elbows on her knees. Jeremiah sat on the floor inside his cell.

"Hard work," Jeremiah said in an uncharacteristic display of humility instead of his usual delusional narcissism. "Everyone worked together."

"Hi, Courtney," Miranda said.

Courtney looked away from Jeremiah's cage. Her delicate features—dark-brown eyes, olive skin, impossibly high cheekbones and bow lips—did not quite match her sturdy frame. But still, she had an unusual beauty and an almost palpable intelligence. Over the past few weeks, Miranda had seen several of the male LO guards go out of their way to speak to or assist Courtney, but she did not seem to favor any one of them in particular.

"Hi, Miranda," Courtney said. She stood up and walked over, pushing her curly chin-length bob behind her ears. "What can I do for you?"

"Nothing really," Miranda said, looking past the young woman for a moment at Jeremiah. "Just heading out for your neck of the woods soon. Thought I'd stop by the zoo to see the animals before I go."

"He's still here."

Miranda sighed. "Jeremiah in a cell never gets old."

Courtney's perfectly plucked eyebrows drew together as she frowned. "We don't imprison anyone lightly around here."

Confused by Courtney's reaction, Miranda said, "I never said you did. I'm just glad he's locked up."

"Oh," Courtney said. "We weren't told much about why he's in the brig apart from a history of being violent toward others."

"I can vouch for that," Miranda said.

She understood why Smith had to keep some details of Jeremiah's past secret, but some of his crimes could be revealed without giving anything away. Then again, Smith knew her people. She must have her reasons for proceeding as she had, but Miranda figured she could give some general information without treading on the commander's toes.

"I don't want to speak out of turn and get on Smith's bad side," Miranda said. When Courtney leaned forward, Miranda continued. "He's clocked me a few good ones, actually. I know I can be a pain in the ass, but still. He's also a rapist."

Courtney looked at Jeremiah askance. "I'll keep that in mind."

In for a penny, in for a pound, Miranda thought, then added, "He can be very charming when he wants to be. Never forget that he's dangerous."

Courtney nodded as she seemed to reassess Jeremiah in light of this new information. Miranda left her and walked closer to Jeremiah's cell.

"What's this?" she said when she was several feet away. "Cat got your tongue? I'm going to start thinking you don't like me anymore."

Jeremiah opened a paperback he had picked up while she and Courtney talked.

"Not one word of welcome? You must be trying to make a good impression on the people who don't know you."

Jeremiah glanced at Miranda, seeming as if she was not worth the effort of responding to, but he couldn't hide the anger percolating underneath his calm facade.

"That's what I thought," she said. "You try that on for size, but I guarantee you, no one here is buying."

She turned on her heel, said goodbye to Courtney, and left.

Jeremiah in a cell would never get old.

14

THE LIGHT SEEPING THROUGH THE BEDROOM BLINDS LOOKED A
lot brighter than it should. Miranda forced her slitted eyes fully open.
Beside her, Delilah yawned and stretched. Miranda sat up. After
looking for her watch on the bedside table, she realized it was still on
her wrist.

"Oh no," she groaned, pushing the blankets aside. "Why didn't
you wake me up, Liley? We slept all morning!"

Miranda dragged herself out of the warm bed, feeling the prickle
of gooseflesh travel over her skin in the chilly air of the townhouse,
and picked up her jeans off the floor. She padded to the dresser,
pulled out a long-sleeved shirt and a sweatshirt, and pulled them on
as she walked to the kitchen. After three weeks at LO, she was beginning to get into a routine. First—and no matter how early she had
gone to bed the night before—she overslept about half the time, but
usually not like this.

Mornings were spent helping Rocco with the winter vegetable
crops. She liked the loudmouth farmer. He reminded her of another
loudmouth farmer except that Rocco was more tactful than she had

ever been. He had the Italian-American well-meaning but patriarchal male chauvinism thing down pat. She had dealt with that growing up, so it didn't faze her. She had also noticed that he laid it on thicker around people who would bite at the morsel dangling in front of them that let him yank their chain.

After lunch, which she wolfed down like a starving person since she had arrived at LO, she often hung out with Skye. Skye had managed to get a climbing wall built in what they called the Community Room at the Nature Center. In addition to learning how to climb herself, she was helping Skye during her lessons for the kids. Different grades came on different days. Miranda liked the second graders best. They were too little to know they should be afraid to scamper fifteen feet up a wall and possibly fall into the cushy, thick mats when they climbed free hand.

Afternoons that she didn't help Skye were her own, and she kept them free. Then she could do whatever happened to be going on that day or help in the gardens again. Or nap, which was something she never used to do, but did now on a pretty regular basis.

She padded downstairs and opened the townhouse blinds facing the street. January was not the brightest month in Portland, but it was better than inside with no lights on. Outside, people were busy going about their day, walking by in twos and threes.

River stood on the porch of the house where her office was located, kitty-corner to Miranda. She often wore her long black hair in two braids that hung over the front of her shoulders. Miranda had almost made a wisecrack about how she must have had hippie wannabe parents when River said she was three-quarters Northern Paiute Native American. Miranda had reexamined River's high cheekbones, dark eyes, straight ebony hair, and tawny skin, and wondered how the hell she had missed it. The braids still seemed like overkill, but the white Italian girl knew when to keep her mouth shut. The neighbor from the other side of the townhouse, whose name Miranda could never remember, pushed her daughter's stroller in front of her as they left the townhouse. Miranda waved at the toddler, who waved back.

Miranda thought of this place as 'the townhouse.' It wasn't home, or even her place. It was temporary. When Mario finished recreating the vaccine, they would need to distribute it and kill a shit-ton of zombies. After that, who knew?

She would love to go home. She wanted to see Father Walter and Karen, even Harold, if only so she could kill him for selling them out to the City Council. She wanted to be there when the assholes on the Council realized their days of holding the people of Silicon Valley hostage were over. The idea of watching the light drain from their eyes as it had from every doser she had ever met, to see the moment they realized they had no power to insulate themselves from the wrath of those they had oppressed... Good God! Finding out that Santa Claus was, in fact, real would not come close.

For Mario, it was more complicated. He wanted to be with his children, but it would probably never be safe for him there. His years of being a double agent had entrenched him as a bad guy in the minds of the populace. The demands of keeping his cover intact meant that a lot of people had turned into zombies while the Jesuits' long con against the Council played out. To their loved ones it would not matter if Mario helped get the vaccine back and made freely available to everyone. Miranda understood why Mario would be a bad guy forever to those people. For him, going home just wasn't smart.

Going home would also mean dealing with Emily, which was complicated for both of them. One of the last things her friend, Mario's wife, had said to her before they left San Jose was that she should forgive herself. Self-forgiveness was not something Miranda was good at. She wasn't sure if she ever would be. That early Catholic conditioning of right and wrong ran so deep, even if it did not necessarily apply in the same way to her lived experience in this world as it would have in the one before. She and Mario were finally together again. Miranda would never give up this precious second chance. There would not be a third, of that she was certain.

She shook herself. There was no point in thinking about any of this now. She was planning the future she wanted, with Mario. There was no guarantee it would be the future she would get, but that was what you did—delude yourself, then adjust.

She fed Delilah, brushed her teeth, grabbed an apple that tasted sour on account of her commitment to good dental hygiene, and headed to the Nature Center.

THE NOISE as she entered the rock-climbing room was tremendous. Nahesi Andrews, a scrawny eight-year-old girl with kinky hair and freckles, was the highest up the wall. Skye belayed her from below, calling out to the girl with suggestions.

"A little more to the left, Nahesi," Skye said as Miranda stepped in beside her. Skye gave Miranda a sidelong stink eye. "That's it! Good job! You want a fist lock now."

A high-pitched squeal preceded Nahesi falling off the wall. Skye hit the belay brake.

"Nice of you to join us, *Coppertop*. You're only an hour late," Skye said to Miranda. To the young climber she called, "I'm letting you down, Nahesi!"

The child bounced her feet off the wall as she descended, then unclipped her harness.

"Fifteen-minute break," Skye announced.

Like cockroaches when a light is switched on, the children who were not climbing scattered. Those on the wall ignored the summons, unwilling to let their turns be cut short, so Skye and Miranda stayed nearby.

"I overslept," Miranda said, while Skye extricated herself from the belay gear. "And quit calling me Coppertop. It's bad enough when Doug does it."

She looked around to see what had become of Delilah. Through the door to the lobby, she caught a flash of brown rounding the reception desk, which meant Delilah was off to hit up Commander Smith for treats.

"I can tell you just got up by the bedhead," Skye said irritably. "You obviously did not look in the mirror."

Miranda liked Skye, even though she had found her a little stand-offish at first. Helping Skye with classes had helped with that. She had never seen Skye so cranky.

"Is something wrong besides me being late?" she asked.

Skye sighed. "I've got cramps, and they're *killing* me. Not liking Coppertop and oversleeping *through lunch* don't compare to dealing with these little monsters on my own."

Skye arched her back as she continued, groaning. "And Rocco gave me an earful at lunch about you not being there to help him with the onions and garlic shoots."

"Oh God, I'm so sorry," Miranda said. As if on cue, her stomach growled to remind her she had only eaten an apple. She was, as Father Walter would say, perished with the hunger.

Skye had to be feeling pretty bad because she never called the kids monsters. She didn't call them angels, either, but people who dislike children generally do not volunteer to teach them.

Skye grimaced as she straightened up. "I got you a box of Mitsubishi pencils; they're in my bag. They stay sharp, and they don't smudge."

"Oh," Miranda said. She didn't even remember saying anything to Skye about the pencil she was using for her journal, though it really did suck. "That's really nice of you, Skye."

"I would kill for some ibuprofen. I tried to get some from River, but we're out right now."

"We probably have some at the Institute. We picked up a lot of meds in Seattle."

"Are you serious? Does it still work?" Skye sighed. "Apart from zombies and sexual predators and no plumbing and no restaurants and terrible heating in winter, dealing with my period is the worst part of all this."

Miranda barely smothered a laugh at the list of complaints. Not that she didn't agree with Skye, but restaurants had never been on Miranda's list, and heating was not as much of a concern in the Bay Area as it was here. Skye looked so miserable that Miranda could swear her own back was beginning to have sympathy pains.

"I'll radio and tell the guys to bring ibuprofen the next time one of them—"

"Hey! Coppertop!"

Miranda turned around. Doug stood in the doorway of the community room, his skinny frame not beginning to fill the door at all.

"Hey you," she cried. She met Doug halfway, and he swooped her up in a hug. She had not seen Doug or Mario since moving to LO three weeks ago. Seeing Doug made her realize just how much she missed both of them.

When he set her down, she asked, "Did Mario come with you?"

"Nice to see you, too."

Miranda snorted. "You know what I mean."

"No, just me. He's in that lab almost twenty-four seven."

"I guess I'll manage with just you somehow," she teased.

"Hi, Doug," Skye said, joining them.

"Hi, Skye," he said.

Doug and Skye looked at one another.

"So," Miranda said, because both of them seemed to have been struck dumb. "How long are you here?"

After a three-second delay, Doug looked at Miranda like he had forgotten she was there.

"Uh, just overnight. Needed a change of scenery." He looked back to Skye. "How much longer till this class is over? I found some beer. Home-brew, so I don't know if it's any good—"

Skye turned back to the room before Doug finished his sentence.

"Hey, kids," she shouted. "Class is over!"

Some of the children looked delighted, some not, but they streamed out of the community room as raucously as a herd of rhinos. A tiny dark-haired girl shot Skye a dirty look as she passed. Miranda recognized Bebe, who at seven was small for her age.

"Hey, Bebe," Skye called after her. The girl turned around, glowering. "I promised you another turn, didn't I?"

No answer from Bebe, whose lower lip jutted out.

"How about tomorrow morning, after breakfast," Skye said. "Just you and me."

Bebe's face lit up for a moment before she remembered she was angry. The glower returned. Skye crouched down. She extended her hand, making an O with her thumb and all but her pinky finger, which stuck out.

"Pinky swear. But you have to turn that frown upside down."

Bebe's face split into a grin. She wrapped her pinky around Skye's. "Pinky swear," she said, then threw her arms around Skye's neck.

Skye smiled as she stood up. "That kid."

Miranda said to Doug, "Bebe's the teacher's pet."

"You didn't have to end class early," Doug said, trying not to sound pleased and failing. Miserably.

"My assistant is unreliable, and my back is killing me," Skye said. "You had me at beer."

Doug hooked his thumb like a hitchhiker to point over his shoulder. "I have ibuprofen in my pack. It's old, but it still works."

Miranda laughed at Skye's dumbfounded expression. "There's a reason he's my best friend," she said to Skye. "Even if he does call me Coppertop."

A FEW HOURS LATER, the party at Skye's was in full swing. Word of five cases of beer got out after they stopped to tell Rocco Blabbermouth Giorgini. About ten people invited themselves in addition to those Skye invited, but as she had said, the more the merrier.

"All I'm saying is that if you say you're gonna be somewhere, you gotta *be* there."

Miranda finished her swig of beer and set the bottle on the table with a bang.

"Rocco, *I overslept.*"

"For five hours?" His dark eyes were sincere...tipsy sincere.

Miranda shrugged. "Maybe you should get me an alarm clock instead of lecturing me."

Rocco slung his arm around Miranda's shoulders in a gesture so expansive it nearly knocked her off the sofa. "That's what I like about you, Miranda. You're always thinking outside the box."

"Outside the— *what* are you talking about?"

Miranda didn't know how many beers she had drunk, but it wasn't so many that she had forgotten what outside the box meant.

Rocco shrugged. "I was harassing you; you pushed it back on me... It's outside the box."

Miranda laughed at him. "You're drunk."

"And what if I am?" he said, rising from his seat. He walked away on unsteady legs. A minute later, he came back with four more beers and handed two to Miranda.

"These are my last two," she said.

"You said that three beers ago."

"But this time I mean it."

Rocco landed on the couch with a bone-rattling thump. After a loud slurp of his beer he leaned in and whispered, "What's the deal with Doug and Skye?"

"They're friends?"

Rocco's mouth scrunched to one side, and he looked at Miranda sidelong, incredulity in his dark eyes.

"They aren't friends?" Miranda whispered. "What hap— but he invited her for beer."

"I'm not the only one who's drunk," Rocco muttered. "They're over there, in the kitchen."

Miranda looked across Skye's apartment. The living room and kitchen were separated by a bi-level countertop island with barstools along the living room side. Candles were spread across the counter, their flickering light making the people gathered around them look cozy. Skye sat on one of the stools, an elbow on the counter, smiling at whatever story Doug was telling, as were River and another man Miranda didn't know. Doug began waving his arms over his head.

"What are you talking about, Rocco? He's telling—"

Then she noticed how Doug's eyes flickered to Skye more than the others. Skye leaned in the barest fraction. She didn't even know she was doing it. It was suddenly apparent to Miranda that Doug was not telling the story to River or the guy. He was telling it to Skye. The others just happened to be there. Then Doug hit the punchline because all of them erupted into howls of laughter. Skye's head fell back, her long silvery-blond hair falling down her back, and a charmed curiosity flitted across Doug's face.

"Oh," Miranda said.

"Yeah. Oh," Rocco said. He took another swig of his beer. So did Miranda. "Is he a priest for real?"

"Yes. Of course he is."

Shit, she thought a moment later. She turned to Rocco and whispered, "You don't like Skye, do you? Like, more than a friend?"

Rocco's belly laugh erupted with a frothy spray of beer. From around the room, heads turned.

"Jesus, Rocco," Miranda said, wiping beer from her face, but starting to giggle. Rather drunkenly, she noticed. "What's so funny?"

"I play for the other team, Tucci."

"You play for—oh. *Oh*," Miranda said. "You're gay?"

Rocco nodded, still laughing.

Miranda shrugged. "It's not like it was tattooed on your forehead. According to," she stopped just as she was about to refer to Mario as Mario. "According to James, I regularly miss things that are obvious to everyone else. 'You're so smart, Miranda. How did you miss that?' He recognizes that I'm smart, so I'll probably keep him."

Rocco squeezed Miranda's shoulder, smiling broadly. "You kill me, Tucci. You really do." Then his voice dropped low, and he leaned closer. "But Doug, being a priest? He doesn't look too serious about it."

Miranda looked at Doug and Skye again, feeling kind of stunned in the way one does when their alcohol-infused brain is slow to process information.

"Lots of people here care about Skye," Rocco continued. "Are protective after what Brock put her through. Doug better watch his step."

In the flickering candlelight, Miranda could almost see an embryonic *something* flutter between them. She had known Doug before he became a priest, even liked one of his girlfriends enough to consider her a friend. Before a zombie bit her... *That* had sucked. The girlfriend after had disliked Miranda, but Miranda had not liked her, either.

"It's a crush." She paused. "If it's anything."

She could not remember Doug ever having a crush this obvious, though. He was a priest, but he was still a man and not blind. And Skye really was stunning.

It had to be a crush. But she'd never seen him so...what the hell was it? She peered at him intently. He must have felt it because he looked her way.

"Having fun, Miri?" Doug said, raising his voice.

"Yep," she said.

"Good."

He winked at her, then looked back at Skye. The corners of his mouth quirked up to form the tiniest Mona Lisa smile, but the way it lit up his face...

Enchanted.

That was what it was. She had never seen Doug so enchanted by anyone.

Miranda leaned back against the cushions and took a deep swig of beer. Rocco's head had fallen back, and his breath sighed in and out just shy of a snore.

Rocco was right. Doug would be wise to watch his step, but she was afraid it might be too late for that.

15

MARIO LOOKED AT THE STREET SIGN AND SIGHED.

"I'm going in circles."

The problem with places like this cookie-cutter pre-apocalyptic housing plan that LO had annexed was that everything looked alike. The houses and townhouses were all painted the same colors and similar to one another. Worse yet, the names were variations of the same thing: Audubon Street, Audubon Way, Starling Place, Sparrow Whatever. It was not as bad as Atlanta had been, where everything was a variation of peach tree, but couldn't they have come up with names that were more distinct from one another?

"The urban planner who approved these street names was probably a day away from going postal," Mario muttered.

"Are you lost?"

Mario looked up from the slip of paper at the question. A raven-haired woman with dark eyes, bronze skin, and broad, high cheekbones had walked up behind him.

"Yeah. I am," Mario confessed. He held out his hand. "I'm James, James Gideon."

"River Swifthawk," she said, shaking his hand. "I'm the doctor around here. And you're new."

"Kind of... I'm trying to find where Miranda Tucci is staying."

River's eyes lit up. She looked at him with renewed interest.

"Oh. You're *that* James. You're at the Institute with Doug Michel. I've heard about you."

"All bad, I take it?"

River laughed. "Nah, she's crazy about you. I met Doug when he was here a few weeks back. That guy can spin a yarn. I haven't laughed that much in ages."

"Doug's stories are always hilarious," Mario said.

"I'm on my way to my house. It's just down the street from Miranda. I'll walk you that far and point you in the right direction."

Mario fell in beside River, matching her brisk pace. "Do you mind me asking what your ethnicity is? With your last name, I'm assuming Native American?"

River smiled. "I'm three-quarters Northern Paiute. The rest is European mutt."

"That's the southeast part of the state?"

"Very good," River said, looking impressed.

"I did two years as a JV after graduating college. One was at a residential middle and high school on the Pyramid Lake Reservation."

"Pyramid Lake? That's the middle of nowhere. What's a JV?"

"Jesuit volunteer. That's what they called people who served in the Jesuit Volunteer Corp. It was sort of like the Peace Corp but Catholic, and here in the States."

"What did you do?"

"Helped the teachers in the classrooms and the kids with their homework and college applications. Made sure they went to bed on time and brushed their teeth, ate their breakfast, spoiled the homesick kids a little. Broke up a few fistfights. That sort of thing."

"A do-gooder from a young age," she said. "Hush-hush research is right up your alley, then."

Mario looked at her sharply. His work was not supposed to be common knowledge.

"Don't worry," she assured him. "Anna, the commander, filled me in. Broad strokes only, in case my services are needed."

"I have no comment."

"Anna will like that, James, even though you only confirmed it." She pointed ahead. "You're taking a right at the corner."

Ahead, Mario could see what had originally been the plan's main entrance, now blocked by the palisade. When they reached the corner, River stopped and pointed at the house across the street.

"My office is in that house. I live there, too, in case you need the services of an endocrinologist turned general practitioner. Front door is always open, and my office is the first room on the left." She turned right and pointed up the street. "Miranda's in the third building up on this side, the left side townhouse. Nice to meet you, James."

"Nice to meet you as well," Mario said, shaking her hand again. He gestured around them, "And thanks for rescuing me. It all looks the same."

"I know," River said. "We really need to fix that."

———

THERE WAS no answer to his knock, so he tried the door. Unlocked. He stepped across the threshold, the doorknob still grasped in his hand.

"Miri?" he called out.

He pulled the door behind him, then heard a bark and a descending thumping on stairs. A moment later, Delilah appeared at the far end of the hallway. She barked again, tail wagging like crazy, and headed for him like a high-speed train. Ran into him like one, too.

"Oh, man, Liley," he said. "Maybe I should bring you back with me. You'd barrel right through that roadblock I can't seem to get past."

After sufficient jumping, zoomie circles, warbles, pets, licks, and belly rubs had been completed, Mario kicked off his boots. He dropped his pack and jacket, leaving everything in the entryway. He followed Delilah down the hallway. Miranda did not seem to be home, because Delilah had definitely made enough noise to alert her. Strange that she would leave the dog behind, though.

Delilah waited for him at the bottom of the stairs, then raced up them. When he did not follow quickly enough, she darted back down, barked at him again, and cocked her head as if to ask, are you coming or not?

"Okay, I'm coming."

He followed the dog up the stairs, across the landing, and poked his head into the room directly opposite the stairs that Delilah had disappeared into. Miranda lay on a chaise lounge near a window, dead to the world. A lined notebook and a maroon pencil were on the floor below her arm that dangled over the chaise lounge's side. He recognized Miranda's tight, neat handwriting on the pages.

How did she sleep through that racket? Mario wondered.

Delilah nudged and licked Miranda's hand.

"Liley, no," Mario whispered.

He hurried over to Delilah, quietly shushing the excited pit bull so that she would not wake Miranda. If Miranda was sleeping, then she must be tired. Barring illness, she had never been much of a napper.

Except since we arrived in Portland, he thought.

He had attributed it to being so seasick on the journey here and needing time to rebound, but worry began to niggle at him. What if she was sick? Like something really wrong with her sick? He planned to be here a few days, so he would pay attention and see for himself, he decided. He had already met the doctor. Perhaps he could enlist her aid if necessary. Miranda was terrible about admitting she was ill. She seemed to regard illness as a moral failing. Or maybe it was just that it made her feel more vulnerable.

Just as he caught Delilah's collar and gently closed his hand around the dog's snout, Miranda stirred and opened her eyes. When she saw him, her eyes opened fully, and a smile spread across her face.

"When did you get here?" she asked, her voice heavy with sleep.

He did not answer right away. He was too busy noticing that the cornflower blue of her eyes was so much brighter than the usual shades of blue. The way her freckles spattered across her nose was more charming for his having missed them, and her lips positively cried out to be kissed.

He dropped to his knees beside her. "Just now."

"ROCK CLIMBING, HUH?" he said. "Not sure I'd be any good at it."

Mario pulled Miranda's hand into his pocket as they walked, shoulders hunched against the damp Northwest winter breeze. Her hand felt like a block of ice inside his, even through his gloves. Miranda had elevated losing non-leather gloves to an art form, and he had never been able to figure out how she did it, nor how to help her hold on to them. In Northern California it had not mattered so much, but the winters were a lot colder here.

"Like Mathilde said, false modesty does not suit you, James," she said, nudging him with her elbow.

"You're learning from the best, according to Doug."

Miranda nodded. "What has he said about her?"

"Not much," Mario answered, trying to remember anything that Doug had said that stood out. "He thinks she's cool, though. He didn't say so, but I can tell. Why?"

"No reason," Miranda said. "He's just kinda fanboy about the famous rock climber."

They emerged from the narrow band of trees that separated the housing plan from the campus of the former St. Mary's Home for Boys. Wider, more manicured lawns and vegetable gardens surrounded buildings arranged in a semi-circle. Institutional buildings, but nice. Soft light from lanterns studded the building windows, but one had a lot more along the ground floor.

"That's where we're going," Miranda said, pointing to the well-lit building.

As they got closer, Mario could see people in twos and threes entering the building. They stepped onto the path, which crunched beneath Mario's feet, and joined the procession.

When he pulled the door open, the smell of garlic, tomatoes, and thyme almost knocked Mario over. A loud gurgle emanated from Miranda's stomach.

"Was that you or me?" she asked.

"You," he answered. "How could you not tell?"

She didn't answer, just smiled, as they walked into a large dining hall with long, crowded tables.

"You're in for a treat," Miranda said, sounding excited as they got in line to get their food. "That's Rocco's sauce. It's amazing."

As they exited the line and began to look for somewhere to sit, Mario recognized Rocco, who had accompanied him and Doug to P-Land. Rocco stood by a table on the far side of the dining hall.

"Tucci," Rocco called, waving his hand. "Saved a seat for you."

"Hey, James!"

Mario turned around. Alicia, his research partner, waved. A man joined her, and she smiled at Mario.

"Enjoy the pasta," she said, laughing.

Mario tried not to outwardly cringe at the horrible screech of Alicia's cackling laughter. The only downside to working with her was her laugh, which always grated against his aural senses like baby bunnies being tortured. Judging from the flinches, squints, raised shoulders, and swiveling heads around him, he was not the only one. Alicia was either oblivious to the effect her laugh had on everyone around her, or lacking the ability to do anything about it, just didn't care. Mario was pretty sure it was the former, not that latter. Alicia was too sweet to not care, especially if she was doing something that made others uncomfortable.

Mario followed Miranda to their seats. They set their carb-overloaded plates of spaghetti and crusty white bread at the places Rocco had saved for them.

"Heard you had a visitor," Rocco said to Miranda. "How you keeping these days, James?"

"You guys are worse gossips than at home," Miranda said, but her smile belied her protest. She looked at River as she sat beside her, then to Mario. "Have you met River yet?"

Mario nodded. "We've met. I'd still be looking for your place if she hadn't saved me."

"He was close, but he was clueless," River said.

Mario twirled the spaghetti onto his fork and took a bite. An explosion of savory flavor filled his mouth. Miranda had not been exaggerating. Rocco's sauce was amazing. When he had finished the bite, Mario looked across the table to Rocco.

"This is better than my nana's sauce."

"Bite your tongue!" Rocco said, looking scandalized. "You never say that about your nana's sauce, even if it's true!"

"I'm the oldest grandson," Mario replied.

Understanding dawned in Rocco's dark eyes.

"Oh. Well, you're forgiven anything then, since you could do no wrong as far she was concerned. And you have better manners than your girlfriend. You savor the fruits of my culinary skill." He pointed his fork across the table at Miranda. "She eats like she's never seen food."

It was true. Mario had taken five bites in the time it took Miranda to almost clear her plate.

"Don't food shame me," Miranda said around a mouthful of spaghetti.

Skye plopped into the seat beside Rocco. "Who's shaming who?" she asked cheerfully.

"Rocco says I eat too much," Miranda said without missing a beat.

"Miranda, you eat more than anyone I've ever seen," Skye said.

"More than me when I was competing. And you wolf it down like you're starving."

Laughter drowned out Miranda's protests before she left to get seconds. Rocco heckled her retreating form until she flipped him off.

Mario shook his head. "She's got a good appetite, but until just now, I've never seen Miranda eat anything that fast."

"I don't believe you," River said. "The woman can eat."

"And sleep!" Rocco said. "How can anyone take so many naps?"

"She's napping?" Mario said. "Like regularly?"

"Don't go covering for her," Skye said. "Because this one," she elbowed Rocco, "gave me an earful when she slept through helping him with the garden a few weeks back. Like it was my fault or something."

"I had five hundred onion and garlic starts. I needed the help! And I knew you'd see her later and deliver the message, especially since you were Miss Crabby Pants," Rocco said. He looked at Mario and said, sotto voce, "Skye was cranky that day...that time of the month, if you know what I mean."

Skye rolled her eyes. "What are you, fourteen?"

"But she got real cheerful when Father Doug showed up," Rocco added.

Skye choked on her drink. Between coughs, she said, "So were you when he invited us all to drink beer."

"She's got you there, Rocco," River said.

Mario noticed a pink blush working its way up Skye's face since Rocco's comment about Doug.

"I'm getting some water," Skye said, hastily leaving the table.

Huh, Mario thought, remembering how Miranda had asked him what Doug had said about Skye.

This place is like an old CW show. They're all attractive, even, but the conversation is too intelligent.

He looked across the dining hall at Miranda as she refilled her plate. She looked tired. Not sick but worn out. Maybe a vitamin deficiency? Mono? He didn't know what to make of the appetite change because hunger did not suggest illness. He leaned over Miranda's empty spot between him and River.

"Can I talk to you later?" he asked, his voice low. "I think I'm going to need your help."

River raised an eyebrow. "With?"

"Not sure," he said. "But Miranda's been dragging since we got to Portland, and she never naps. She also hates to admit when she's sick."

"You've just described the predominant type of person to survive the end of the world," River said. "Let's talk later. I'll get her sorted."

ON THE WAY back from dinner, they lay in the field just before the woods to look at the stars.

"There's Orion's Belt," Miranda said. "See the three really bright ones in a row?"

Mario nodded, then realized she couldn't see the gesture. "Yeah, I do. What's the story of Orion?"

"No idea," Miranda said. "There are more stars to that one, but the belt is all I can ever find. Mythology is one of those things I always meant to get around to reading."

"No time like the present. D'you know any more?"

Miranda yawned. "There's Canis Major."

Mario followed the line of her pointing arm. All he saw were stars.

"What's it supposed to be?" he asked. If he knew what he was looking for, he might have a better chance of seeing it.

"No idea," Miranda replied. "My dad knew them all, but I don't remember the stories. I never paid attention."

"That's a golden childhood memory."

Miranda snorted. "He used to drag us out with that stupid telescope for hours, like it made up for him being gone most of the time. I'm surprised I remember any of them since I hated it so much." She paused, then sighed. "Wouldn't mind stargazing with him now."

Mario squeezed her hand in his. Like most people, they rarely spoke about the people they had lost. Which was ironic, since it was one of the first things they had connected over.

"What's going on?" Miranda said. "You seemed a little distracted before dinner."

"That was your fault."

She elbowed his ribs lightly. "After that. You were laser-focused then."

"We've hit a roadblock," he said, his amusement at her teasing at odds with how frustrated thinking about the delay usually made him feel. "I'm not sure what the problem is yet."

Miranda sat up. "I'm cold. Let's go." As they scrambled to their feet, she said, "It's not a different strain of virus, is it? Not that I know if that makes a difference."

"Maybe, but there's something weird going on. Which makes sense because Jeremiah repels zombies. Alicia leans toward a different strain and a mutation, so that's probably what it is."

"Deferring to Alicia's assessment? That's high praise, coming from you," Miranda said.

They entered the thin strip of woods, Miranda leading the way along a path she was obviously familiar with. Mario could see one or two lights from the housing plan through the trees.

"Alicia is a talented virologist. She made the shift from epidemiology to vaccine development without missing a beat. She'll probably figure out what this hitch is before I do."

He could see better as they neared the tree line and the little housing plan. Miranda turned to stand in front of him, her face in shadow.

"So you're here to clear your head for a few days and go back to it fresh."

She reached for his hands. Hers were like ice again.

"And to see you."

He couldn't see her smile but could hear it in her voice when she said, "So I'm a distraction."

"My one and only."

She laughed, then leaned close. Her lips were cool, but her kiss crackled with heat. He tugged her to him, the fullness of her breasts pressing against him through her jacket. Her icy hands found their way inside his unbuttoned coat. She slipped them down and inside the back of his jeans, her thumbs anchoring over the waistband.

When their lips parted, she said, "Your one and only, huh?"

Mario said, "You know you are."

16

MIRANDA STARED AT RIVER, DUMBFOUNDED.

"That's impossible," she said.

"The rabbit died, Miranda, metaphorically speaking. You are definitely pregnant, about eleven or twelve weeks."

"But my tubes are tied!" she protested. "I can't *get* pregnant!"

River's mouth twisted in a frown. She pushed a lock of glossy black hair behind her ear.

"Yeah, you told me. A tubal ligation makes it highly *unlikely* that you'll get pregnant, but not impossible. When did you have it done?"

River's face was a study in professional sympathy. It made Miranda want to punch LO's doctor in her face.

"What difference does that make?" she snapped, her temper flaring. "The whole point of permanent contraception is that it's permanent!"

"Okay," River said, beginning to look determined to get the information she sought. "I'm assuming you had this done after zombies, so within the last ten years."

Miranda tried to think, but her mind was whirring like one of those cheap metallic pinwheels little kids play with.

Pinwheels.

Little kids.

"Michael's birthday," she said. "I did it right after my godson's third birthday, so seven years."

"Okay," River said, nodding. "That makes sense. The failure rate for tubal ligations is two percent in the first ten years."

"But two percent, that's practically zero. It's supposed to be permanent," she insisted.

River sighed. "Unfortunately, you are not the first person I have had this conversation with. I'm assuming someone qualified did the procedure?"

Miranda nodded.

"You would have been better off with an IUD. You have to replace them periodically, but they're more effective. Someone who can do a tubal ligation should have been able to do an IUD insertion. I'm surprised you weren't steered in that direction."

"But it's supposed to be permanent," Miranda repeated, her voice softer than before.

"Have your breasts been sore lately?"

Miranda thought for a moment. "Yeah, but my bras have been tight... Oh my God."

"Your womb is already expanding, Miranda, and your cervix has softened. You're tired all the time, which is common during the first trimester. So are appetite changes. And you missed your last period."

Like an automaton, Miranda nodded. She never gave the missed period a second thought because her tubes were tied. And with having been seasick and losing so much weight on the journey here, and the stress of being out in the wilderness...

"Even if there was no test to confirm it, I would feel confident in this diagnosis," River added.

"Wait a minute," Miranda said. "You aren't a gynecologist. You could be wrong."

River sat down on the other end of the exam table.

"I'm a medical doctor, Miranda," she said gently. "Every M.D.

gets the same foundation, the same education and training. Or we used to. I've had to do everything the last ten years, including obstetrics. I am one hundred percent sure that you are pregnant. I was sure during the exam, but just on the off chance, I wanted to do a test."

"What if the test is wrong? It must be expired by now."

But she was tired all the time, and irritable. Well, more than usual. Her appetite had changed. Some foods tasted funny now. She knew that she was grasping at straws, but she couldn't help it. This could not be true.

"I did a blood test, Miranda. And I'm an endocrinologist. Testing for elevated human growth hormone is not difficult."

"Fuck," Miranda said softly. "Fuck, fuck, fuck, fuck, *fucking* Mario."

River half-smiled and shrugged. "It's not entirely his fault."

"Not that," she said. "Going behind my back and tricking me into seeing you. He comes to visit, and then a week later I'm pregnant?"

"That's not the right math, Miranda. He was worried about you. He thought you had mono."

"Mono," Miranda muttered. "I fucking wish. You can do an abortion, right?"

River nodded. "Sure."

"And then I can get an IUD."

"Yeah, that's not a problem." She paused. "Don't you want to talk to Mario first?"

"Talking to Mario is not going to change anything. I am not bringing a kid into *this*," she said, gesturing out the window to the world at large—zombies, disease, assholes run rampant. "That's why I got my tubes tied in the first place."

River nodded. "Look, it's not my job to tell you what to do, but for what it's worth, I think you should talk to him."

Miranda wanted to scream. At River, at Mario, at everything.

"I don't need his permission, and you should mind your own fucking business."

"Okay," River said, nodding. She slipped off the exam table.

Silence filled the room, disturbed only by a riffling of papers as River stuffed her notes into a file.

"I'm sorry," Miranda said. "I didn't mean that. It's just—"

Just what, she thought. Unexpected? Unwelcome? Completely fucked?

River set the file folder down.

"No offense taken. This is obviously the last thing you expected me to tell you today. I think you should talk to Mario because then he can be there for you. I know he's gone back to the Institute, but he can come here and at least be with you for the procedure. I don't know him well, but he doesn't strike me as the kind of guy who's going to be an asshole."

Miranda's mouth pursed into a scowl. River was right, of course. Mario wouldn't be an asshole. He'd be great.

And he missed his kids, felt guilty about leaving them. If she told him she was getting an abortion, and she was, he would never say he wanted her to do otherwise, but she would know some part of him would want it. He'd never want her to do anything other than what she had already decided. He was too practical to entertain impossible scenarios, and a baby was as impossible a scenario as it got. Even if she wanted to, they were unsettled and far from home and their mission was not over. If they did something that used to be normal, like have a kid, they were stuck here for at least a few years and—

She gave herself a mental shake. What anyone may or may not want was beside the point. What you wanted and what you got were very different things. She had learned that a long time ago. And there was no way she was bringing a kid into this. No fucking way. She had never understood why people felt the need to bring totally helpless, vulnerable children into the clusterfuck the world had become. She had sworn to herself that she would never be so selfish and irresponsible.

River said, "What are you plans right now? I cleared my schedule in case you wanted some company."

Miranda gave the doctor a weak smile. "That was really thoughtful of you, but I think I'd rather just hang out with Delilah."

"Okay. But if you change your mind, I'll be here."

Miranda nodded to River and got down from the exam table. She felt like she was floating above her body as it walked out of River's office, crossed the street, and entered her townhouse. Delilah thumped down the stairs, all tail wags and wiggles, and Miranda felt herself being sucked back into her body. Into boobs that felt one thousand percent more sore than they had before her appointment. Into a waist that felt thicker and jeans that were snugger, even though she had not noticed before. Into a body that felt exhausted and ravenous and hijacked.

She stepped outside with Delilah so that the dog could take a pee. Miranda realized that she had been peeing more, now that she thought about it. That was probably a pregnancy symptom, too.

"Motherfucker."

She bit her lip while she did the math. She must have conceived right around the time they got to Seattle, or not long after. After a five-year separation, she and Mario had a lot of sex while they were on the yacht—a lot of unprotected sex. While they were having sex was pretty much the only time she hadn't felt ill. Neither one of them thought about birth control because she'd had her fucking tubes tied.

She did the math again. It had definitely been seasickness during the journey, and after Seattle she had the prescription Dramamine. If she'd also had morning sickness, she wouldn't have noticed it.

Christ, she thought. What a clusterfuck.

"Coppertop!"

Miranda looked down the street. Doug strode toward her, his never needing to think about getting pregnant male insouciance surrounding him like a cloud. The nickname, which she secretly liked, set her nerves on edge today. She did not want to deal with anyone just now, even her best friend in the world.

"What are you doing here?" she asked when he reached the walk in front of the townhouse.

"Again with the warm welcome. I'm beginning to feel unwanted," Doug said, but he grinned. "But since you asked, I haven't seen you in three weeks and I am bored out of my skull at the Institute. Apart from monkey watching, they're pretty entertaining. But when I started giving them names, I realized I needed a change of scenery. You were right to come here. There's a lot more going on."

"Yeah, I'm sure there is," Miranda said, thinking of Skye. She leaned into the escape from her own problems that Doug's presence gave her. Hard. "Any reason you didn't come sooner? Anyone you've been avoiding?"

Guilt flashed across Doug's face for a split second, like a kid with his hand caught in the cookie jar.

"What are you talking about?"

"Oh, you know exactly what I'm talking about. Absence makes the heart grow fonder, though. I don't think you need to worry about a less-than-warm welcome."

Doug began to blush rather spectacularly, which was not his usual modus operandi. She opened her mouth to really lay it on thick, then stopped. She cocked her head, suddenly aware of a buzz of background noise.

"What is that?" Doug said, turning around to look in the direction the buzz seemed to be coming from.

"Zombie moans," Miranda said, already walking past Doug and into the street.

A siren blasted. Once it faded, Miranda took a moment to orient herself to the noise. It was louder to the east. She took off for that side of the housing plan, Doug on one side, Delilah on the other. Small observation platforms were built into the palisade at regular intervals, which was where Miranda was headed. In the two minutes it took them to reach the closest one on the southern palisade, someone had already climbed up. Miranda started up the ladder.

"How many?" she asked as she neared the top of the ladder.

The woman already on the platform turned toward her. It was

her next-door neighbor, whose name Miranda could never remember. She looked pale and scared.

"A lot," she said.

Miranda stepped onto the platform, now able to see over the top of the palisade. "Whoa," she said.

The scent of decay wafted over them. Perhaps a quarter of a mile away she could see zombies. Tens, maybe hundreds, of them tripped through the overgrown trees and disintegrating parking lots and roads. Accurate numbers were impossible to estimate in the overgrown greenery of the Northwest, but even so, Miranda could see that it was a lot more zombies than usually wandered outside of LO's immediate defenses.

She looked down at the trench on the other side of the palisade. How deep had Smith said it was? Ten feet? Fifteen? She couldn't remember. An emerald ribbon of grassy earth made a twenty-foot buffer between the palisade and the chain-link fence. The trench was on the outer side of the fence, lined by another strip of ground between the fence and trench. Both sides of the fence were kept clear of brush and trees, but the far side of the trench was as overgrown as everything else. That was one thing they had going for and against them. Unlike the first few years after zombies appeared, the overgrowth of trees and scrub was a natural impediment for zombies. Much more so here than at home on account of the wetter climate. But it was impossible to tell exactly how many zombies there were based on sight. Sound was often a more reliable indicator.

"Damn," Doug said, stepping next to Miranda. "Good thing I was traveling here from the north."

Her neighbor said, "The sound defenses must be malfunctioning."

No shit, Miranda thought, looking at the woman askance.

The siren wailed again. Miranda's neighbor whimpered, her hand leaping to her mouth. "I can't believe this. I've got to get back to Gemma."

So that was the kid's name, Miranda thought, a little confused by the woman's reaction. Being unable to grasp that she herself was pregnant after taking steps to ensure it would never happen? Sure. Being unable to believe zombies might get close to your fortified community after the undead had roamed the planet for ten years? That she did not understand. The unbelievable part was that it did not happen more often.

Miranda turned to Doug to suggest that they get back to the ground and find out how they could pitch in, but he had already stepped onto the ladder.

"I'm going to head up to the Nature Center to see what's going on," he said.

Miranda waited for him to start down, then stepped on the ladder to follow.

The jog through the Big Woods was creepy as fuck when you could hear zombie moans. Miranda began to revise her reaction to her neighbor's disbelief after realizing she had gotten used to these woods being quiet and safe. She and Doug, with Delilah following, emerged into a crowd of people milling outside the Nature Center under the awnings of the covered sidewalk. They threaded their way through them to the main doors just as Skye emerged.

"What the hell are you all doing here?" Skye demanded. "Get to your posts!"

Immediately, a babble of protests and questions—was this a drill, what had happened to their defenses—erupted. Skye used her thumb and middle finger at the corners of her mouth to produce a piercing whistle.

"It's real, and you are endangering all of us by not being at your posts! Get going right now, or I will make sure you're all thrown in the brig when this is over."

Eyes widened, and a ripple of fearful electricity zipped through the small crowd. They quickly dispersed, and Skye turned back to Miranda and Doug.

"I didn't know you pulled that much weight," Miranda said, impressed at how quickly Skye had whipped everyone in line.

"I don't." Skye looked to Doug. "When did you get here?"

"About ten minutes ago," he said.

This time, Skye's smile was shy as she glanced down at her feet and then back up at him. She looked relieved that Doug was here. Doug looked like he wanted to say something but couldn't get it together enough to formulate a sentence.

Oh, for Pete's sake, these two are in *trou*-ble, Miranda thought.

"How can we help?" Miranda said.

Skye took a step back. "Uh, well, the commander asked me to go to the control shack and find out what's going on. Why don't you come with me?"

Ten minutes later, they were inside a small outbuilding that maybe once had been a storage shed. All except Delilah, whom Miranda had ordered outside because she got underfoot. The shack might still pass for a storage shed if not for the high pole behind it with a crazy number of cables that ran from the shed to the pole. The pole also had small boxes with blinking lights and something that looked like a speaker near the top. Skye and a red-faced, middle-aged man named Larry were hunched over a control panel console that looked as state-of-the-art as the shed did not. Larry kept stabbing at two readouts on a map, one to the south, the other to the west.

"I don't know, Skye." He shook his head, beads of sweat glistening on his bare pate. "It's showing an intermittent disruption at Station Eight, which must have caused a cascade through at least part of the system. It's still showing Station Six is online, but that's the direction the zombies are coming from, so it's got to be off-line. Everything was okay when we went to Eight this morning," he said, looking to Skye for confirmation.

Skye nodded. "You're the expert, but yeah, as far as I could see."

"Why were you there this morning?" Miranda asked.

"A regular inspection. Skye always gives me a lift," Larry said. He then said to Skye, "Were things okay when you went back?"

Skye nodded. "Yeah. Everything was normal. They offered me breakfast, but I had things to do here." At Doug and Miranda's quizzical looks, she added, "We were back here when I realized I forgot my sunglasses. I went to get them on my own. Don't rat me out to Anna."

Larry frowned. "I'm worried another station besides Eight and Six is off-line, and we just don't know it. For there to be this many zombies here at LO...that would take eight, maybe ten hours. Six never radioed that there was a problem, but something is going on in their direction."

"That doesn't sound good," Doug muttered.

Larry nodded, his face anxious as he continued to explain. "Every station has a noise diffuser. End result is basically a big speaker playing white noise. It's loud enough to keep a zombie's attention but not so loud that it brings all of Portland and the surrounding area down on us. Most funnel south to the kill zone, and the ones that fall into the trenches around the stations are dealt with in place. That keeps the two-mile radius around us in place. That's really important on the Portland side especially. We get the highest number of zombies from that direction."

"So the systems in all the stations are hooked up to one another?" Miranda asked. "Wouldn't it be better to have them operate independently to avoid this?"

Larry shook his head. "We networked it a few years ago to get the amplification consistent at all the stations. We're using different equipment across them, depending on what we could find at the time and who we had to work it. If the amplification is off, you get some stations louder than others."

"And they get too many zombies, which messes up the funnel to the kill zone?" Doug said, looking to Larry for confirmation.

Larry nodded. "Yeah, that's right. We have to figure out what's going on at Six and what's causing that failure at Eight, or this will keep happening. Even if Six is off-line like I think, we've had problems at Station Eight before. I'm sure it's the root of the problem. We're still waiting for all the other stations, including Eight, to radio in."

What Larry had just explained sounded like an accident waiting to happen to Miranda. "Why haven't you gone out to get the right equipment so that it's standard across the stations?"

"It's on the list," he said, then sucked his gaunt cheeks between his teeth. "You know how it is. There are always more immediate problems. And it's been working like it should until now."

"Okay," Skye said. "I'll update the commander and check back in with you. Let us know at the Nature Center as soon as Eight and the rest radio in, okay?"

"Of course, Skye," Larry said. He dug in his pocket and produced a threadbare handkerchief, which he pressed against his face. "We've been so lucky here. Feels like it's running out."

"It's not luck," Skye said to him. "A lot of work has gone into all this, and neither Six nor Eight are on the Portland side. We'll get it figured out."

She patted Larry on the shoulder, then motioned to the door. Once they were outside, Doug said, "You're going to need to send someone out to check at least those two stations."

Skye nodded, and they started down the path to the Nature Center.

"How long before the zombies surround us?" Miranda asked.

"Hard to say for sure," Skye said. "Depends on how many stations go out. They're all about a mile from one another, so it won't take too long for them to start getting through any gaps. Twenty-four hours, tops. That's what makes a possible failure at Station Six so troubling. If it has been overrun, it happened so quickly that they couldn't radio in."

Miranda could see the buzz of anticipation in Doug's eyes. He wanted to get out there and see it himself, to run into the danger. There was definitely something wrong with people like him.

"You in?" he asked her.

Miranda nodded. She wanted to see it, to run into the danger, too, if it meant she might be able to make a difference. She had known for a long time that there was something wrong with her.

17

A CRACKLE OF STATIC ON THE HEADSET, THEN PHINEAS' VOICE said, "It's just ahead."

Now we see, Miranda thought. Her pulse sped up a little, enough to beat back the chill from the heavy, damp air. She tried not to think about the zombies and how the noise of the motorcycles had attracted them along the way. They had been the right choice for transportation, since more than once their maneuverability had outweighed how loud they were. Right now, they did not have time for delays.

Miranda saw the sign for a Quality Inn as they approached from the north on Southwest 189th Avenue, Doug and Skye following behind them.

Doug's voice came through the headset just as Miranda saw it. "Whoa."

The motorcycle slowed, then stopped as they pulled abreast of Doug and Skye.

The intersection of 189th and Alexander Streets at the Quality Inn, about half a mile down the road, was completely jammed with zombies. Zombies spilled up the road from Highway 8 ahead of them. It looked like they were also coming along Alexander Street from the west. Station 8 was two-thirds of the way down Alexander Street from that intersection.

Skye flipped the visor of her helmet up.

"Let's take Johnson, see if we can get in from the back," she said, her breath frosting out from her helmet like cold dragonfire.

The next ten minutes were so full of backtracking that Miranda felt completely turned around by the time they left the motorcycles to continue on foot. The last street sign she had seen, peeking out from overgrown shrubberies and trees with stamped metal letters so faded she could barely read them, had said Almond Street.

Miranda was still blown away by how overgrown the terrain in the Northwest had become. While visiting her grandparents, she had taken many trips on the aerial tram in Portland that traveled up to the OHSU campus to take in the incredible view of the city. The only part she had disliked was when the degree of the tram cables had changed, making the car rock back and forth. Her stomach had always swooped, no matter how many times she made the trip. What had struck Miranda every time was how green Portland was. She knew that below the swaths of trees were houses and neighborhoods, but even then it had seemed wild and untamed compared to what she was used to in San Francisco.

San Jose had become overgrown despite the more arid climate, but Portland's rate of overgrowth, with its wetter, more temperate climate, was to the tenth power. Even so, Skye and Phineas moved with quiet assurance.

The moans of the horde to the south started out as a buzz, but were soon so loud Miranda wondered if a nearby zombie would even be capable of hearing them. A shiver burrowed into the base of her skull. Some things were so unnatural that you never got used to them.

Skye crept behind a row of tall, shaggy cypress trees that blocked the road.

"The station is in the house behind this one. There are two fences around the property with a trench between them, similar to LO but not as big. There's a shallow tunnel, a wiggle space really, under both fences. That's how we'll get under the fences without making too much noise." She looked from Miranda to Doug. "How turned around are you?"

Doug snorted softly when Miranda said, "Very."

Skye nodded. "It's a rabbit warren back here. It might not have looked like it, but we left the bikes at a rendezvous point with three different ways to get out from there that are usually pretty clear. If we need to fall back, stay with me or Phineas. If we're separated, we might not find you before we need to fall back. I don't want to go back without you." She glanced at Doug, her expression pained. "But we will, if we have to."

Doug grinned at her. "Don't worry, Skye. Miri and I are like a cheap suit. We'll be all over you."

"Oh my God," Miranda said with an exaggerated eye roll. "Don't include me in that."

But Doug's teasing words, she noticed, had chased the pained look from Skye's face.

They followed a trail through the tall weeds and grasses. As they reached the back of the yard, Miranda could see a chain-link fence. On the other side of the fence was a narrow strip of land, then a braced and reinforced trench about eight feet deep and four feet wide, with a mirroring strip of land and fence beyond it. On both strips of land inside of the fences, aluminum ladders lay on the ground alongside the chain-link mesh.

The area surrounded by the inner fence on the far side of the trench, where Miranda saw a garage, a house, and a patio, looked clear. The defense system's speakers, along with other smaller components, were bolted to the roof. The equipment on the roof was bigger and more complicated than Miranda had envisioned. Cables connected to the components were fastened down with clamps that disappeared through the roof.

It was well fortified, but something about the place felt off. Miranda couldn't account for the feeling since she had never been here before, but she also couldn't shake it

Phineas dropped to his knees beside a gray, pebbled, two-by-three-foot paving stone that lay longwise on the ground abutting the fence. Beside it were two cinder blocks. Skye picked one up and set it on the other. Phineas flipped the paving stone up and leaned it against the cinder blocks.

A metal-framed piece of chain-link stuck up from the ground, blocking the smoothed-out hole lined with bricks under the fence. Upon a closer look, Miranda could see it was fitted into a frame buried in the ground. The frame had fine mesh screen on both sides, presumably to keep the worst of the mud out when the weather was wet. Phineas tugged the piece out, clearing the way for them to wiggle through the opening underneath the fence.

"That's ingenious," Doug muttered.

Skye stuffed her machete and small pack through the opening. Then she lay on her back, head to the fence, and wriggled underneath.

They followed, Phineas bringing up the rear. He reached his fingertips through the chain-link and pushed the paving stone. It landed across the hole with a squishy thud. By the time he had replaced the screen, Skye had the ladder across the trench. It just fit, ends perpendicular against both fences. Miranda looked to the next fence. The paving stone, metal-framed square of mesh, and cinder blocks weren't in place. She pointed it out to the others.

"Where are the dogs?" Phineas asked.

"That's what I was thinking," Skye murmured.

That's what's been bothering me, thought Miranda.

"How many dogs are usually here?" Doug asked.

Skye shrugged. "Two or three. Let's go."

Miranda saw a flash of movement from the corner of her eye. As she turned to look, a zombie staggered into view in the trench below. It began to moan as soon as it saw them, slipping in the mud as it rounded the corner of the trench. The moans of the horde of zombies on Alexander Street beyond them provided cover, robbing this zombie of its chance to raise the alarm and blow their position.

But it also meant that zombies had gotten through the first fence.

Skye swore softly, then said, "Phineas, stay here in case we need to get out fast. Kill anything in the trench that comes close, and be—"

"I know, Skye," he said, sounding a little insulted. "I'll be careful."

Miranda grinned as Skye crawled across the ladder. She guessed Phineas was about twenty, which was just about the age she had been when she began to think she knew everything there was to know about killing zombies and going on missions. She appreciated that Skye's instructions were so explicit, especially with a young man. Sometimes their testosterone got the better of them and they did stupid shit like letting zombies stack up and then timing how quickly they could kill them all.

As she started across the ladder, Miranda heard Doug say, "Don't be insulted. Miri let them stack up once when she was your age and..."

"ITS THROAT IS SLIT, just like the other," Doug said, looking up from the German shepherd he knelt beside. "What kind of asshole does this to a dog?"

Skye's frown deepened as she left the shabby garage behind the one-story ranch. Doug wiped his gloved hands on his pants as he stood, then reclaimed his machete from Miranda.

"Something fucked up happened here," he said.

As they approached the house, Skye stopped, motioning for them to do the same. She pointed to the roof.

"Those cords there, on the left side of the largest component on the roof. Have they been cut?"

Miranda squinted. The shingles were black, as were the cords, and she was not familiar with the equipment. She reached for the small binoculars she kept on her belt. It took a few seconds to find the cords. Two of them were sliced clean through.

"They've been cut," she said, a chill running down her spine.

She handed the binoculars to Skye. Skye looked for a moment, then wrinkled her brow as she passed the binoculars to Doug.

"Jesus," Skye said. "Everything was fine this morning."

By the time Doug gave the binoculars back to Miranda ten seconds later, Skye's mouth had settled in a hard line.

"We're entering into the kitchen," Skye said, gesturing to her left with her machete. "There's a dining room to its left. It's open to the main living room, like a big L-shape. The main room is the L's long end and wraps back around the kitchen along the front of the house. A hallway that runs to the opposite end of the house opens off that main room to the bedrooms and bathroom. There's a reinforced entry at the front door. I'll go straight through the kitchen after we clear it and check the entry. You two go through the dining area. We'll meet in the main room, then check the rest together. Ready?"

At their nods, she banged on the door, waited, then eased it open. How anything inside would hear over the racket of the zombies at the front of the house Miranda didn't know, but she was reassured to see Skye playing it safe. When no zombies appeared, they crept inside.

The tiny kitchen was clear. Miranda turned left and paused in the open doorway to the dining room. The spartanly furnished room had a crammed bookshelf on the opposite wall, its contents overflowing on the floor. A small table with two mismatched chairs was between Miranda and the bookshelf. The bowls on the table still had spoons jammed into the food.

"Whatever happened surprised them," Miranda murmured.

They turned toward the main room. A beat-up table—heavy and old-fashioned—with a piece of electronic equipment that looked like a sound board, was flipped over onto the worn and blood-stained carpeting. The sound board stuck out from under the table, next to an old Mac laptop with a screen that had snapped off. The table had smashed the sound board beneath it. On the floor next to it lay a man's body. From ten feet away, Miranda could tell he was dead.

Skye emerged from the reinforced entry room at the other end of the long living room. She glanced at the body, pain flashing across her face, and jerked her head toward the hallway. Miranda and Doug joined her.

"I could see the fence through the front door window," she said. "One section is damaged. Not that many are through yet, but it'll fall eventually." She indicated down the hallway. "Bath and one bedroom on the right, two bedrooms on the left."

They nodded, then followed her into the dark hallway. The doors to the rooms were closed. Skye gripped the doorknob of the bathroom door, then looked at Doug. He nodded, hefting his machete in his hand. She twisted the knob. Doug kicked the door open. Nothing visible. He stepped in quickly and checked the tub and the partition for the toilet. He shook his head as he turned around.

Miranda heard a moan. She turned around, trying to locate it. The first door on the other side of the hall? She stepped closer and leaned her ear to the door.

"Goddammit," she whispered.

She turned back to Skye and Doug. Just as she pointed at the door, something banged against it so hard that she jumped. Then scratching, more banging, and moans.

Somehow, a zombie had gotten in, even though every window in the house that Miranda had seen was bricked in. Doug joined Miranda at the door.

Skye touched Doug's shoulder. "If it was Crystal, she was chubby. Not enough to turn fast, I think, but maybe."

Doug crinkled his brow at Skye. "You sent a chubby person out here?"

She raised her hands in front of her, palms up. "I'm not in charge of staffing the stations."

"Okay," Doug muttered, looking unimpressed with Skye's explanation. "Want me to go first?" he asked Miranda.

Miranda shook her head. "As long as I know it's coming, I've got it."

The zombie scuffled against the other side of the door. Doug put his shoulder against it, twisted the knob, and shoved. Not enough to open the door, but enough to get the zombie off of it. A loud growl, followed by another hard thump.

This time, Doug shoved for all he was worth.

The smell hit Miranda as she darted past him into the room. The damn thing had not lost its footing, which was the point of using the door against it, and it was a lot more than chubby. The room was smaller than she and Doug had realized. Not more than ten feet and long and narrow, like a shoebox. Miranda had just enough time to get her arm up. She heard the clatter of her machete hitting the Pergo floor as the dasher chomped on her upraised forearm. It shook her like a cat with a rat.

Pain radiated from Miranda's arm as the zombie tossed her like a chew toy.

"Kill it!"

"I'm trying," Doug said, but it kept shaking her, its head bobbing back and forth.

"Goddammit, Doug," Miranda shouted. She hammered on the zombie's face, trying to gouge an eye. "Chop its fucking head off!"

"Get your hand clear!"

Miranda whipped her free arm away. She saw a blur of silver, short and controlled. The head seemed to wobble, then fell away from the zombie's body. She ripped her arm out of the now slack maw so hard that she smacked herself square on the nose with the back of her fist. Black blood spattered the walls and ceiling and most of Miranda from the shoulders up.

"Fucking hell," Miranda said, shaking out her arm and wiping her face.

Doug walked over and shoved his machete through the zombie's eye. On the floor under the bricked-in window, Miranda saw a pistol. She stooped to retrieve it and sniffed, careful to keep the barrel pointed at the floor.

"Unfired," she said, looking at Doug.

She set the pistol down so she could check her arm. The zombie's teeth had left deep indentations on her leather jacket's sleeve. She peeled her glove back enough to free the jacket tucked into it, undid the zipper that ran from wrist to elbow, and pushed it up. She twisted her arm, checking her chain mail and the long-sleeved thermal shirt underneath it. No blood on the cloth, and the chain mail was intact.

"Looks okay," she said. "I'll have River check me out when we get back."

River.

Holy shit, I'm pregnant! River's going to read me the riot act.

Not that it mattered in the long run, and doctors always seemed to be yelling at her for something she did that was hazardous to her health. But how had she forgotten the development in her personal life that had floored her just hours earlier?

"You okay?" Skye asked.

Miranda rounded on her, suddenly furious.

"What the fuck, Skye?" she demanded, pointing at the headless zombie on the floor. "She was at least thirty pounds overweight! That's more than enough to turn as a dasher. And you didn't think to tell us the room is a fucking shoebox? We would never have entered that way if we had known!"

"Last time I saw Crystal she wasn't, I didn't— I'm sorry," Skye stammered, unprepared for Miranda's anger. "I forgot how small—"

"You for— Are you a fucking amateur? What if I hadn't been wearing chain mail and leather? Maybe you should put layout diagrams on the doors as reminders!"

"C'mon, Miri," Doug said, his voice placating. "Honest mistake. And we're fine." He jerked his head at the door. "Let's clear the other rooms, Skye."

Miranda's mouth hung open as she watched Doug's retreating form. Honest mistake?

"Who the hell does he think he's kidding," she said under her breath, wiping zombie muck from her cheek. "Honest crush on the pretty girl is more like it."

By the time she joined them in the hallway, they had cleared the other two bedrooms without incident. Miranda turned on her heel and stalked to the main room. They had not stopped before to see how the man in there died. Miranda had a sneaking suspicion it was not because he had become a zombie.

Miranda crouched next to the body of the man by the overturned table. The blood was dried and brown.

"He's been shot," Miranda said.

Doug crouched next to Miranda and helped her check the rest of the body. He grunted with effort as he turned the man over. "I don't see a bite mark anywhere on him."

"And where is Derek," Skye said softly. "He was the third person here. He might be able to tell us what happened, but he must have taken off."

Still annoyed, Miranda stood up.

"It's obvious what happened here. She got bit and hid it from the others, and she killed the dogs so they wouldn't give her away because she was that kind of asshole."

She pointed at the dead man. "I'm guessing he found out, they fought, and she shot him." Miranda paused. "But her gun wasn't fired, so your other guy, Derek, must have shot him to protect her, or she used a different gun, and then Derek took off before she turned. And then she shut herself in there and wimped out."

Skye shook her head. "I can't believe Crystal did this. I don't disagree," she added hastily at Miranda's frown. "But she knew better."

"What people know and what they do are two different things," Doug said. "That door wasn't locked. If I knew someone was going to turn and was idiot enough to not put them out of their misery, I would at least put a warning on the door."

Skye's breath whistled through her teeth. "We need to get to the bottom of what happened here, especially those cut cords, but right now, we need to report the situation to Anna," she said. She pulled the broken laptop out from under the sound board and stuffed it in her pack. "Maybe they can get something off the drive. Let's go."

Skye headed for the door. Miranda grabbed Doug's arm and pulled him back when he followed.

"You're making excuses for her fuckup?"

Miranda searched Doug's face. She wanted to just be angry, but what she felt was betrayed. Doug always had her back, including when he told her that she had made a mistake. He had backed her up physically this time, but not in the way that really counted.

"I didn't think assigning blame would help, Miri. She knows she screwed up. We all do at some point."

"If it was anyone else, you would never let this slide. You'd say *something*."

Doug's voice was defensive. "If it was anyone else? What the hell does that mean?"

"It means if she was anyone other than your *girlfriend*," Miranda snapped.

Surprise filled Doug's face, but a pink flush crept up his face. "I don't know what—"

"Anyone can see you're infatuated with her! And I could give a shit. Fuck like bunnies for all I care. Just don't let it affect your judgment."

"Look," he began.

"Quit talking," she said through gritted teeth, brushing past him. "You'll only dig a deeper hole."

18

PHINEAS' HUNCHED FORM SCUTTLED ACROSS THE ALUMINUM
ladder over the trench when Miranda and Doug exited the house.

"That's not a good sign," Doug said.

Miranda stepped up the pace to a jog. When she first saw
Phineas, she had thought for a moment that he was a zombie, one of
the rare ones able to climb. Thank God they did not have that to deal
with, but something was up. He would not be abandoning his lookout
and coming to them otherwise.

They caught up to Skye at the fence.

"They just radioed, Skye," Phineas said. "The failure spread. All
of the stations are down. We have to get back now while we still can.
In a few hours, LO will be surrounded."

"This day just gets better and better," Skye said.

"Should we go to the Institute instead?" Miranda asked.

Both Skye and Phineas shook their heads.

"It's farther away," Skye said. "We'll head back to LO."

Miranda looked in the trench while Phineas wriggled under the
fence. He had killed ten zombies while they were gone. More were
turning the corner on her left, their grasping hands upraised and

mouths open. To the right another stumbled into view. Miranda turned to take her turn under the fence, then looked at the zombie again.

"Its hair is clean."

The zombie's dark, curly hair was shiny and hardly mussed. The blood from a gash on its forehead was still red. It raised its eyes to hers.

"Help."

"Someone's in the trench," Miranda said, hurrying over and dropping to her knees.

Doug paused beside Miranda long enough to assess the situation, then jumped into the trench. In two steps he reached the short figure, a woman, and boosted her up to the edge of the trench. Miranda and Skye reached into the trench, each catching the groggy, mumbling woman under the arms, and hoisted her up. Miranda reached back to help Doug while Skye dragged the woman out of the way.

Skye knelt beside her, pushing her hair aside. "It's Courtney," she said.

Miranda's brow crinkled. "Courtney? Wasn't she on guard at the Institute?"

"I haven't seen her in a while, so maybe," Skye said. She had already begun to check the young woman for bites. "I don't see any bites."

Phineas looked from the other side of the fence. "That's a hell of a whack on her forehead."

Skye dragged Courtney, who mumbled unintelligibly, to the opening. "Let's get her under the fence and back to LO. Maybe she can tell us what happened here."

As Phineas finished pulling the young woman to his side of the fence and Miranda began to wriggle through, he said, "What if she's bitten, and we just can't see it?"

"Our motorcycle is more powerful than yours. She can ride between us with one of our helmets. The helmet will protect us."

"Good idea," Doug said, fitting the screen into place and flipping the paving stone back over the crawl space. "She doesn't look sick though. I want to know how she ended up in that trench."

MIRANDA AND PHINEAS were on their motorcycle again, the landscape rushing by. Doug and Skye, with the now unconscious Courtney, drove ahead of them. They took a different route back than the one they had taken to the station. Already, there were more zombies. Without the noise of the Stations to stop and distract them, they just kept going. It was not that they were trying to get to LO in particular... Zombies simply wandered until there was a reason to stop or change course. Even with how wildly overgrown everything in the Northwest seemed to be, if it was happening this fast on all sides of the settlement, then LO would be surrounded within a day, tops.

Miranda's forearm that the dasher had chomped and then used to rattle her around like a chew toy throbbed. It was going to be a hell of a welt, she could tell already.

Doug, Skye, and Courtney turned out of sight a hundred yards ahead of them.

"Almost home," Phineas yelled.

Miranda's body swayed with the slight lean of the bike as it entered the turn in the road. Then it slid out from under her.

The ground rushed up. Every part of her body—arms and elbows, knees and hips, shoulders and back—were beaten without mercy as she rolled over the hard-packed earth, rocks, and fallen branches. Despite the muffling effect of her helmet, crashing proved incredibly loud. Finally she stopped, facedown. Her right arm was tucked close to her side, the other flung above her head. She had no idea where her legs were.

For a moment she lay there, catching her breath, tremors roiling her body. Then a twig snapped, followed by a shallow grunt.

Get. Up.

Miranda pushed her hands against the ground, levering up onto her knees. Her arms wobbled like jelly. Every movement, especially breathing, hurt. She looked up, her head throbbing, to see zombies staggering closer. They tripped and fell, lurched and swayed. They weebled and fucking wobbled but did not stay down.

She dragged herself to her feet, wincing at a dull throb across her hip, and felt for her handgun. Gone. Of course. But her machete was still secure in its sheath. She scanned the crash site for Phineas. He lay on the ground on his back a hundred feet away. The motorcycle was fifty feet beyond him where it had knocked down what remained of a side yard fence. The front wheel still spun like *The Little Engine That Could.*

Miranda grimaced at the protests from every inch of her body. She ignored the pain, stumbling to Phineas. The sharp bite of gasoline filled her nostrils. She looked at the motorcycle more closely and realized the gas tank was punctured and leaking. Shaky fingers took three tries to undo the snap on her helmet. It hit the ground with a dull crack of ceramic. The cold, damp breeze riffled her sweat-soaked scalp, chilling her shaking body. She listened for the sound of an approaching engine but did not hear one. Doug and Skye either did not realize they were no longer following them or could not afford to double back. Either way, it amounted to the same thing. And they didn't have extra room on their bike with Courtney on it already.

We are so screwed.

Phineas stirred as she approached.

"You gotta get up, kid," she said, dropping to her knees beside him.

Phineas looked at her, his eyes unfocused. He mumbled, but all she caught was, "We crashed."

The moans grew louder. Zombies were coming from all sides, the nearest just fifteen feet away. Phineas fumbled with the snap on his helmet, and Miranda pulled it off.

"Can you stand?" she asked. "We gotta move, and I lost my gun."

"Still have mine," Phineas said, reaching to touch his leg. His moans of pain as he rolled onto his hands and knees mingled with the encroaching zombies before he retched and threw up. It was only when she leaned to help him to his feet that she noticed the blood-stain on his lower leg. He was wearing a waxed jacket with matching pants. If the blood was coming through, he was bleeding badly.

The closest zombies were on Phineas' side, just ten feet now. Miranda pulled his arm over her shoulder and dragged him up. Phineas unholstered his handgun with his free hand, lifted it, and fired at the three zombies in their path. He got two, which was pretty impressive, considering.

"There's a...two-story safe house," he said, grimacing. "Around the corner."

Miranda picked up the pace, which admittedly was not saying much. Phineas did his best to keep up, but mostly Miranda dragged him. He kept taking out the zombies in their way, his aim remarkably accurate considering the pain he must be in. If he could keep that up, they just might make it. They turned the corner. The only two-story house was three doors down.

"Thank God," Miranda gasped.

The scuffle and scrape of dragging feet behind them sounded closer, the moans and grunts louder and growing more feverish. No zombies blocked their path to the third house, but they were stumbling to the road from the overgrown yards.

She dragged Phineas across the driveway of the third house. Almost at the front door, a shadow flickered in the corner of her eye. Before she could turn her head, Phineas lurched into her. The gun boomed in her ear, setting it ringing and stuffing it with cotton at the same time.

"Key's under the mat," he gasped.

A bark of laughter came from Miranda. "Of course it is."

Zombies stumbled over the lawn of the next house, just feet away. Phineas leaned against the door. Miranda flipped the mat up and snatched the key with trembling fingers. It slid into place, the action of the lock flawless. She pushed the door open, sending Phineas sprawling into the foyer. He pulled himself over the threshold by hands and elbows.

A zombie stumbled onto the porch, already stooping for Phineas, desiccated hands reaching, deathly maw stretched wide. Miranda shoved it back. Pain flared, sharp inside her elbow, as something popped. She stumbled through the door, slammed it shut, the snick of the deadbolt the denouement of their flight. She got Phineas up the stairs. He kept passing out and coming to. She didn't even try to get him on the bed. She knelt next to him, feeling along his shin. Definitely broken—badly.

"We are so screwed," he panted.

Miranda flinched, not having realized he was conscious.

"I think you have a compound fracture," Miranda said to him. "I need to cut your pants to see how bad it's bleeding."

Phineas nodded.

She opened the window blinds to beat back the gloom. As she knelt beside Phineas, Miranda drew the hunting knife she kept on her belt. She eased the blade into the seam of his waxed pants and cut along it. Phineas started to laugh but stopped with a wince.

"What?" she asked, her brow furrowing in puzzlement.

"I've finally got a beautiful woman tearing my clothes off."

"Don't get cocky, kid," Miranda said, but she couldn't suppress a smile. Cheeky little fucker, she thought. She cut his jeans underneath his outer layers of clothing to the knee to reveal the blood-soaked thermal underwear beneath them.

"Do you have chain mail on?"

Phineas shook his head. "Not with these pants. They're..."

Miranda saw his eyelids flutter.

"Phineas! Stay with me, okay?"

Head resting on the floor now, he nodded.

She was about to cut the thermal underwear, then hesitated. He was bleeding—she could tell just by looking—but not as badly as she had feared. As soon as she cut his thermals, she exposed him to even more germs. Gingerly, she felt along his shin. She heard his sharp

inhale, then a long exhale. When she reached the break, barely skim-
ming the ripped skin and muscle and bone that had definitely pushed
through them, he pounded the carpeted floor with his fist, whimpering, but did not cry out.

Tough little fucker, too.

"It's definitely a compound fracture," she said.

She unzipped her jacket, then pulled off her lightweight wool
sweater and the long-sleeved turtleneck underneath it. Her exposed
chain mail tunic clicked over the undershirt beneath it as she made a
few quick cuts to reduce the turtleneck to long strips. She wrapped
them as tightly around the break as she could without disturbing it
even more. By the time she was done, Phineas writhed in place, his
dark skin dusted with gray and his short-cropped hair sweat soaked.

"What are we going to do?" he gasped.

"We're gonna elevate your leg."

She pulled on her sweater and climbed to her feet. Even with the
layer of clothing below the chain mail, she could feel the difference
without the turtleneck. She limped to the window that faced the
street, her hip throbbing. If she didn't keep moving, it would stiffen
up and fuck her.

Zombies were congregating in the street in addition to the ones
that banged against the front of the house. More were coming, from
every direction that she could see, but there was still wiggle room.
Maybe. If she could slip out the back, swing wide and then backtrack.
If she left now, she *might* make it. She might not, either, but fifty-fifty
were not the worst odds she had ever faced.

"And then I'm going for help."

"There are too many," Phineas said, too weak to make his protest
sound like a protest. "You'll never make it."

Miranda left the window and pulled a nightstand over to where
Phineas lay, then pushed it on its side.

"We have no supplies, and you're going into shock. And it's fifty
degrees in here, maybe. This is gonna hurt."

He was three shades grayer and clammy to the touch by the time she had his leg elevated over the nightstand with a pillow beneath it. She pulled all the blankets off the bed and wrapped them around him, tucking them under as far as he could tolerate her jostling him. Then she went to the other bedrooms and grabbed those blankets, too. She stuck a pillow under his head and another blanket around it. He looked about twelve, so bundled up in blankets. She picked up her leather jacket and shrugged back into it, then pulled on her gloves.

"Take my gun," Phineas said. "I think I dropped it in the hall."

Miranda tapped her holster, where his gun already resided.

He smiled weakly. "That's how it's gonna be?"

"Half a mile, you said?"

"I didn't, but yeah."

"Sit tight. I'll be back with help as soon as I can."

Phineas looked scared and confused but was trying so hard not to show it. She remembered being his age. Wanting to prove herself, pretending she wasn't afraid in situations where fear was the only sensible emotion. He had so much life ahead of him if he was lucky. And if she was.

"You don't have to do this for me."

Miranda shook her head. Why were young men so *dumb*?

"That is one of the stupidest things I've ever heard," she said. "Try not to do anything stupid, like move. Or go outside. I'll be back."

"Don't die trying, Miranda."

For a second she thought he was teasing, but he looked too serious.

"Okay," she said. "No dying."

Phineas grinned faintly. "So it's a date?"

Miranda laughed despite herself. "Not in your lifetime, kid."

19

MIRANDA DUCKED AS LOW AS SHE COULD IN THE OVERGROWTH and still move at a trot, grimacing with every step. She cut through the yards of the next four houses before doubling back to the road. Moans came from every direction. She knelt between a rusting truck and minivan, both permanently parked in a driveway, and peeked around the truck's tailgate.

A steady stream of zombies shuffled toward the house where she had left Phineas, but just as many were wandering in every other direction, including near her. She could not stay here long.

Okay, think, she said to herself. If I'm looking north, then LO is east of here.

In just the past minute, she had counted over forty zombies coming from the east. As she had already suspected, going east immediately was a nonstarter. There were more zombie snacks east of here at LO, but she and Phineas had attracted a lot of attention locally. Zombies didn't make decisions about where they might get the most to eat because they didn't make decisions at all. They just responded to the stimulus at hand.

She could fall back again, but Phineas needed medical attention now. There was a small woods behind the houses on the other side of the street that would offer better cover. Woods were usually good at slowing down if not stopping most zombies if they were thick enough.

A loud moan ahead. At the end of the driveway, a zombie with no legs that dragged itself along the road had noticed her. It was so weathered and worn that she could not tell if it had been a man or a woman. Long, stringy hair dragged on the ground, and its clothes were so threadbare that it was impossible to tell what color they had once been. Its fingernails were long gone, the ragged stubs of its fingertips embedded with dirt and grit around nubs of bone.

Miranda tensed, her muscles coiled with energy. She unsheathed her machete and stood up straighter, taking in the street at a glance. There were a lot more zombies than she had realized. This little road had a lot of trees growing through the decaying asphalt that she could use as cover.

She jumped over the dragging zombie. The moans started immediately, loud and mournfully agitated. She zigzagged around a zombie that had turned around, alerted by her footsteps, then ducked behind a slender tree. She left the shelter of the tree, and the ground rushed up at her. Her foot had caught on a root. She landed on her side, barely getting her arm up in time to shield her head as she hit the ground. The impact sent shockwaves of pain through her bruised frame.

Before she could scramble up, a zombie grabbed her foot. Rolling onto her back, she kicked at it. It latched on to her boot, holding her foot in the air while it tried to bite through the sturdy leather. Miranda thrashed her leg, trying to shake it off, but with her foot in the air, she couldn't get any leverage.

More zombies closed in. Miranda wriggled toward the zombie that had her. She whipped her machete behind its ankles, the flat of the blade against them. She caught the other end of the machete in her hand and pulled. The zombie lost its footing and fell, pulling her along with it. Miranda whipped up to sitting, tugging the machete out from underneath the tangle of hers and the zombie's legs. She stabbed at its eye, finally hitting the mark on the third try.

Stumbling to her feet, she ran, hacking blindly. A cold chill of fear shot through her when she realized she was almost completely surrounded. Zombies closed in, hissing, arms outstretched. She ducked low and tackled a small zombie, perhaps a child once, with her shoulder. It toppled over, knocking into the zombie behind it.

She sprinted through the gap, crashing through the scrub of an overgrown lawn. Ahead, she saw a low chain-link fence. Not much, but something. She could hear the zombies pursuing her, their moans deafening. She quit hacking at branches. Zombies didn't care if branches slapped their faces and ripped at their clothes. Neither could she.

What felt like a freight train crashed into her from the left. She fell to the ground, a massive zombie next to her. She rolled away, but a hand closed over her shoulder. Miranda looked for her machete, but it must have been jarred from her hand.

The zombie dragged her backward. Zombies don't breathe, but it seemed she could feel its rank breath against her neck. Unable to get away, she rolled into it, catching the elbow of her captured shoulder behind the zombie's arm. She pushed, using her elbow and hand as a lever to roll over it.

The zombie's grip never loosened. It hissed, almost sounding angry at such unruly prey. Her other arm now free, she shoved her fingers into the zombie's eye. Her fingers slid through, the chill of the mushy, dead flesh penetrating her gloves. Her fingers were jammed up to the palm before the zombie let go of her shoulder.

Miranda leaped to her feet and crashed through the scrub. There *was* a chain-link fence, and woods just beyond it! She jumped the fence at a flat-out run.

She fell into a decaying cement staircase and tumbled down, smacking every part of her body that might have come through the motorcycle crash without injury. She hit the bottom face-first, tasting blood in her mouth when her teeth cut into her lower lip. She rolled over and looked up the staircase. Zombies were stacked against the fence above, unable to figure out how to get over it. She reckoned the fence was four feet high. Eventually the pressure from the zombies at the back might knock it down, but right now, it was enough of an obstacle to offer a reprieve.

She pushed herself to her hands and knees. The cement might be cracked and falling apart, but what was intact was still hard as hell. Drops of blood dripped from her nose. She wiped it with the back of her hand. Only drops, not the geyser that meant her nose was broken. She pushed up to standing and stumbled into the woods.

This must have been a park—no need for steps otherwise. She set off, following the faint remnants of a path as the gully descended. The temperature dropped a few degrees, enough that her breath began to mist. Her sweaty clothes stuck to her skin, chilled and clammy as the air grew heavier with suspended moisture. She stopped, cocking her head to listen. There was noise ahead...a low, slow gurgle that was almost musical.

Water.

She picked her way carefully through trees and overgrown ferns, her muscles beginning to stiffen. The loamy soil felt springy under her feet, decades of accumulated pine needles and leaves the first soft surface to cushion her body in what seemed hours. Ten minutes later, she stood on a bank above a stream.

"This has got to be the stream that flows through LO," she said aloud. "I just have to follow it upstream."

She couldn't be too far now. The ride to Station Eight had taken perhaps twenty minutes. They had been on the motorcycle almost that long when they crashed. She didn't know how the route there compared with the one back, but Phineas had said they were almost there.

Her body sagged with weariness. The idea of deliverance banished the last vestiges of adrenaline, amplifying every bump, cut, scratch, bruise, and wrenched joint.

I just need to get back, she told herself again and again. *I'm close. I just need to get back.*

She was so focused on keeping herself moving that it took her a few minutes to realize that the canopy of the trees—most of them deciduous—had climbed higher. These trees were older and blocked most of the sky. The undergrowth had thinned. She stopped, then turned around.

"Oh shit."

She took in the wide, open spaces between the trees. Even the pines and redwoods grew more sparsely here. There were logs and rocks, but zombies could move here with relative ease. She tried to jog, even walk faster, but everything was seizing up. It was easier to count what didn't hurt, which was exactly nothing.

She smelled them first. A moment later, she heard the moans. Above on her right, and on the far side of the stream, too. She peered through the trees, the light filtering through the tree canopy from the overcast sky more like twilight than midday. How did they get so close, she wondered, realizing that the zombies coming down the hill above her were only a hundred feet away. The soil, she realized. The soft loamy soil that felt like a caress had masked the sound of the zombies' approach. Now they were almost on top of her.

She had just passed a section of high creek bank. She turned around and forced herself almost to a trot, gritting her teeth against the pain. When she reached the stretch of creek, she inspected the bank. Three feet high, with a boulder jutting out over the water, creating a foot of overhang.

The water pooled below the overhang. She looked at the trees again, but the lowest branches were twenty feet from the ground, and she could not outrun them.

"If they walk into the creek... Fuck it."

She faced the bank as she slid her legs over the edge and into the water. Like a snake, cold water slithered between the tongue and lacings of her boots. The shock of the stream's icy temperature sucked her breath from her lungs as she sank into the water. She felt along the bank below the surface until she found a tree root she could hang on to in order to keep herself in place, then lowered all but her head into the water. Already, she shivered. When she could almost see the faces of the zombies approaching the far bank clearly, she slid all the way under, keeping only her nose and mouth above the water's surface.

She didn't know the temperature of the water apart from fucking freezing. The first minutes were excruciating as her body heat was whisked away by the current. She tasted blood again as she bit her lip to keep from huffing her breath out or chattering her teeth. Then, slowly, it got better. The aches and pains subsided, soothed by the water's chill. A full body ice bath, sans ice. The water between her torso and the leather jacket felt not warm, but not as cold, the jacket acting almost like a wet suit.

On the far bank, the zombies shuffled and groaned. Seventy-five, maybe more, it was hard to tell. The contours of the far creek bank worked in her favor. Instead of walking into the creek, its rise fed the zombies west, paralleling the creek.

Above her, what was left of a gnawed face swayed into view—the first zombie on this side of the creek. It inched toward the edge of the creek bank.

It's going to fall in.

Despair welled up in Miranda's chest. After all she had endured, all she had lost and been lucky enough to find again, they were going to fall in. When she was too cold and stiff and tired to run. The struggle to survive, do the right thing, not hurt others when she couldn't help hurting herself, would end right here.

Miranda waited for the zombie to take the final step. But it didn't. The zombie swayed in place, moving neither forward nor back. She gripped the root holding her in place tighter. The first zombie was joined by another, then another. She couldn't hear them, but their mouths opened and closed. They shuffled in place, those that wandered off replaced by others, or maybe the same ones circling back.

They know I'm here, she thought, panicked. For a split second she almost burst out of the water to make a doomed break for it.

Calm down, calm down, calm down.

The hammering of her heart didn't seem to lessen, but she managed to stay put. The zombies above shuffled almost at the edge of the creek bank. They could tell something was here, but being almost completely submerged in the creek was confusing them.

Shivers racked her from head to toe now. She felt her feet rise and tightened her abdomen, fighting to keep them in place. If her boots splashed out of the water, it was over. She knew she had gripped a tree root to stay in place but couldn't feel her fingers anymore. She wanted to turn her head to look, to make sure she really was holding on. Her toes had gone numb, too. She sucked on her lower lip to keep it between her chattering teeth. It ached faintly... Had she bitten it? She was too cold to tell.

Miranda opened her eyes. Had she drifted off? Who were those figures above her? She squinted through the two inches of water sliding past her eyes. Were they people? Had someone come looking for her? One of the figures lurched into another, and they both stumbled out of sight. They're zombies, she thought, her brain struggling to fit the pieces together. A person would never bang into another like that. She didn't think so, anyway. She couldn't remember how long she had been in the water, just that she couldn't stop shaking. She was so, so tired. If she could just go to sleep—

I'm hypothermic.

The thought swelled inside her muddled brain like the reverberation of a bell. If she fell asleep, it wouldn't matter if there were zombies nearby.

She had to get out of the creek.

She waited for what seemed like forever, but no more zombies came into view. It took every ounce of strength she had to lift her head out of the water. She heard a clacking sound she could not identify. She let go of the branch she thought she still held and struggled to her feet. The water splashed. It was so *loud*. She looked up the bank. One look at how high it was and she wanted to slip into the water again.

Wade down the creek.

She lumbered forward, splashing back into the water when her foot did not follow. She tugged it free of whatever it had stuck on and let the water's buoyancy push her up. She splashed through the water, stumbling and falling, the faint moans of zombies behind her. After forever, she saw the bank turn into a gentle rise. She was supposed to do something, she thought. What the hell was it?

"Get out," she muttered through her numb lips and aching teeth. "Supposed to get out."

She flailed out of the water and fell, gasping on the bank. She could see the far bank. There were no zombies on it anymore. She realized she had not even thought to check before now.

She crawled to a nearby log, water running out of her jacket, her sleeves, her pants. Freezing, wet clothes clung to her skin. The chain mail, cement heavy, pulled her down. The loamy soil felt soft against her hands and knees, its pungent scent of decaying pine needles, leaves, and earth filling her nostrils. She could see the dirt and pine needles clinging to shaking fingers, but she couldn't feel them. All she wanted to do was lie down, hug her limbs to her body, and sleep.

She was supposed to do something, she just couldn't remember what. She couldn't think with her teeth making so much noise. She couldn't keep going, she couldn't—

A thought bubbled to the surface.

Get. Up. Get up or you're dead.

She climbed the log, then pulled herself up the tree beside it. She leaned against the tree, spent and trembling.

Just try for a minute. A minute, and then you can rest.

She stumbled and tripped and staggered. She had never been so cold, so tired. She had never wanted to give up as badly as she wanted to give up right now. There weren't any zombies, but if they showed up, it would almost be a relief. The shivering, the ice in her veins, the titanic effort it took to put one numb foot in front of the other, would stop. She could lie down and sleep until they gobbled her up. She was so tired and numb she didn't think zombies devouring her flesh would even register.

From somewhere, she dredged up a chuckle. "T-that's s-s-so f-fucking m-m-m-morbid."

Her feet squished wetly inside her icy boots. She could hear zombies moaning but could not tell how close they were. She would never outrun zombies if they were nearby. Since she couldn't do anything about it, she ignored them.

I should count, she thought. It might keep her awake, even if she couldn't remember why that was important.

One, two, three, five, eight? No...one, two, five, four...

The sob welled up, rushed past her lips. Cold tears slid down her cheeks.

The creek veered to the left, but there was something straight ahead. She squinted, trying to see what it was. It was almost like a void, an absence, rather than a presence, except for the glow along the top. She kept following the creek. She had to keep moving, follow the creek, get to LO.

Miranda jerked to a halt.

"It's the p-p-palisade."

She turned back, trying to hurry but failing. She stumbled blindly toward LO's wall.

I have to tell them about Phineas.

The groans of zombies seemed louder. She tumbled through the tree line, then reared back, arms pinwheeling, and fell on her ass. A foot past her toes was a trench that she had almost stumbled into. Zombies writhed in it, snarling and snapping at the sight of her. Across the trench was a strip of land and a chain-link fence. And beyond that, the log palisade that bordered LO.

The zombies were louder on her right. She looked to see. A mob of zombies, hundreds perhaps, were coming toward her. Some fell into the trench, but those that didn't had seen her.

"M-m-m-m-motherf-fucker."

She forced herself to stand and walked on unsteady feet. The cold was knit into her bones so deep she would never get warm again. Could she walk as fast as a zombie? There were lights farther down the palisade. People would be at the lights. Maybe. Maybe everyone at LO was already dead. Maybe it was full of zombies. Maybe she should quit trying.

Light flared in her face. She couldn't raise her arm to shield her eyes. She squinted into the light, but it was too bright to see.

"Help me."

It came out a whisper, not the shout she had intended. The light moved away, then back. She tried to lift her arm, but its weight was too heavy to bear. She looked back to the zombies pursuing her. They were gaining ground.

The ground felt hard beneath her ass. She didn't remember sitting. Her jaw ached from the constant chattering of her teeth. Pain throbbed through her shivering body. The zombies were only minutes away, and she was tired, so tired. Too tired. She curled into herself, knees tucked, arms wrapped around them. Like a baby, she thought drowsily, which made her think of Mario. It took what felt like forever to figure out why.

A baby... That's right. I won't have to tell him.

She heard a distant crack, then another. And another after that, but they did not concern her. Approaching zombies were the last thing Miranda saw before her eyes slammed shut.

20

"I AM OPEN TO SUGGESTIONS," ROCCO SAID. "BECAUSE AS FAR AS I can see, we're fucked."

Doug turned three hundred sixty degrees on the cab roof of the truck they perched on. Apart from the south, the direction they had come from, everywhere around them was quickly becoming wall-to-wall zombies. South was going to look the same in a matter of minutes. Doug could *see* the palisade through the early morning mist that the sun was slowly burning off. LO was half a mile dead ahead, at most, but the zombies swarming ahead of them looked too thick to drive through, forget about reaching the main gate. They had to get the equipment in the truck back to LO, or the sound defenses might never be fixed. And if they weren't, the chances that LO would eventually be overrun went up—a lot.

They had to get back.

Skye stood next to him, shaking her head, as flummoxed as Rocco.

"We've got a two-ton Peterbilt dump truck," Doug said. "Radio them now. Tell them we're driving straight down, what is this, 160th? We are crashing into the trench, and there better be people to help get this shit unloaded."

Skye looked at him like he had lost his mind. "The zombies will use the truck as a bridge. With this many, they'll rip down the chain-link fence, and then they're at the palisade."

"How about we work the problem in front of us?" Doug snapped.

Skye flinched. There were already zombies approaching the truck. They had to move—now.

"Let's do it," Rocco said.

Ten seconds later, Doug dropped through the truck cab's open passenger window. He finished buckling up as Rocco hung up the radio.

"Your window open, Doug?" Rocco asked. "We might not have both sides to count on when we get there."

Doug nodded. "Yeah. It's down."

Skye sat between him and Rocco, grim determination wrinkling her brow and tightening her jaw. The engine revved, then the truck jerked, thumping over the curb—or maybe the first zombie.

First zombie, it turned out, because the thud was followed by another, and then another, and then more at once than Doug wanted to think about. They picked up speed. Every thud was a zombie that might get tangled up in an axle or damage the hydraulics that lifted the truck's bed.

The gravel track road ahead of them looked like a crowded dance floor. Doug laughed, despite the sweat-drenched terror that gripped his gut and made his breath feel tight.

Skye said, "What's fun—"

A loud bang made Doug jump. The upper half of a zombie flew up onto the hood of the truck. It smacked into the windshield with a loud crack.

"Fucking hell," Rocco cried.

The truck picked up more speed. The zombie against the wind-shield writhed, its rotting face smearing the glass. Its brown-gray skin was covered with cuts and bites, and its broken teeth scraped against the cracked windshield.

Skye cried out, "The glass is cracked! Watch—"

She just had time to get her hands up before the broken windshield collapsed into her lap. She pushed against the top of the windshield frame and six inches of jagged glass still attached to it, trying to keep the zombie from falling completely on her. The driver's side had pulled free of the frame, shattered glass studding Rocco's raised arm. The windshield in front of Doug had not broken free, but glass spiderwebbed inside the bending frame.

He broke out the cracked glass that was blocking him from helping Skye. Rank air gusted into his face. Rocco had, if anything, sped up. The constant thump-thump-thump of zombies being crushed under the truck's huge tires jostled them violently. The zombie writhing on the remnants of the windshield squirmed and tried to twist closer to Skye. She pushed herself back against the seat, leaning into Rocco. Doug could hear the crisp snap of the zombie's teeth.

He reached for the zombie to pull it free of Skye and shove it out, over the side of the truck's hood. The engine revved deep, black smoke from the forward exhaust stack blowing through the cab.

The truck jerked sharply, then tipped forward, and what felt like a two-by-four hit Doug's body from right shoulder to left hip, and from left hip to right, all at once. He gasped for air, suddenly suspended from his seatbelt, looking straight down at dark earth. The zombie that had crashed through the windshield had been thrown back through it. It squirmed on the ground at the end of the truck's hood, disoriented by its new location. Or maybe just hungry. It was a zombie. Anthropomorphizing was never a good idea.

"You guys okay?" Rocco asked, sounding stunned.

The truck stood on its front grille and bumper, held upright by the trench walls. Skye pushed back from the dashboard. Blood ran down her nose from a cut on her forehead. The truck had lurched into the trench so violently that Doug had no idea how she was still conscious after hitting her head on the dash.

"I'm okay," Skye said. "Let's get out of here."

Doug held on to the outside of the truck door, positioning his feet on the dash. Here goes nothing, he thought, pressing the button to release his seatbelt. If his footing wasn't good enough, he would fall through the missing windshield onto the zombie below.

He didn't fall, so he instead climbed out until he stood outside the cab, his feet on the door in the open window. The truck shifted and creaked, like distant thunder, and Doug froze. Then he scrambled over the hot exhaust stack as quick as he could, arms shaky from adrenaline, to get behind the relative safety of the truck bed's high sides. He hunkered down immediately behind the cab, the part of the bed that would tip up and back to dump a load if the truck was upright. Some of the equipment they had gotten from the audio supply warehouse was still in the truck bed.

Doug dropped to his knees to reach a hand down to Skye. From farther down the trench came a moan. A zombie, twenty feet away, staggered toward them. More followed.

Skye looked up to Doug, hand outstretched. The cut on her forehead had almost quit bleeding, so the cut itself wasn't serious. Pieces of glass stuck in her silvery-blond hair, and blood that had run from the cut across her forehead crusted along her hairline. Soot from the truck's exhaust that had blown through the cab smudged her cheek and chin. In the early morning sunlight just beginning to work its way over the lip of the trench, it was easy to believe that her light-blue eyes were the only points of color in a washed out, gray-and-brown landscape.

She raised her eyebrows at him. "There are zombies down here! Help or get out of my way."

Doug grasped her hand. She scrambled up past him, and he helped Rocco climb up as well. By the time he straightened up, Skye had climbed the high sides of the bed that now pointed skyward and hopped off to solid ground.

"A lot of the equipment is up here. It was thrown clear when we crashed," Skye said, looking toward the palisade. She turned back to the truck. "Pass it up—"

Her eyes widened, as big as dinner plates.

"Get up here now! They're coming!"

Then Doug heard the growing rumble. He hadn't noticed it before with all the noise of the crash and the creaking of the truck. He looked at Rocco, then they started to climb. It wasn't hard, with the square indentations of the high sides of the truck bed. Skye was already running over to the chain-link fence when he pulled himself out of the trench, carrying boxes of audio equipment under each arm.

"Holy shit," Rocco said.

Thousands of zombies were closing in. They would fill in the trench and reach the chain-link in minutes.

"Get the equipment," Skye shouted. "They're coming down to help."

Doug picked up the two closest boxes of equipment and ran for the chain-link fence. A rope ladder hung over the jagged top of the palisade, people already climbing down. A stretcher, the kind that had been used by helicopters to pluck shipwrecked survivors out of the sea, was being lowered from a winch.

Doug picked up more equipment and kept on doing it. By his third dash to gather up the components that had been strewn across the area between the trench and the fence, the leading edge of zombies were steps away from tripping into the trench. A woman cut the last link for a hole in the chain-link fence as he approached. Equipment components were thrust through, then carried and dragged and loaded onto the stretcher by the people who had climbed down to help.

A blur caught the corner of Doug's eye. Zombies were already inside the fence, moving toward them from the north. They had breached the fence somewhere else. Soon, the buffer between the fence and the palisade would be a churning horde of the undead.

They had to leave. Now.

"Did you see the master equalizer?" Skye asked, her eyes filled with desperation.

"I don't know," Doug said. "This has to do. We need to go."

She shook her head and dashed for the truck.

"Skye," Rocco shouted.

Doug sprinted after Skye. Zombies poured into the trench, a putrid, reeking flow of moaning death. When he reached the truck, he saw that the zombies falling into the trench were stacked almost to where the back of the cab met the truck's bed. One's head was split cleanly in two by what had to have been Skye's machete. A smear of black blood started just beside where Skye rooted through boxes and ended where she had pushed the zombie into the trench.

"Skye," Doug shouted. "We have to go!"

She ignored him.

"Goddammit," Doug swore, jumping down into the truck. "What are we looking for?"

"Look for equalizer on the box."

Doug shoved boxes and small crates aside as the banging on the sides of the truck bed got louder. Beyond Skye, on the other side of the truck, a zombie tumbled into the trench. But instead of disappearing from sight, it landed level with the back of the cab. Nothing blocked it from crawling onto the high back of the truck bed that curled over the top of the cab. The zombie lifted its head, cloudy eyes looking straight into Doug's. Its mouth opened, moans lost in the din of all the others, and started to wriggle and squirm their way.

"Got it," Skye shouted.

Doug's heart sank. The box was five feet long, about three feet wide, and two feet high. Not cardboard, but a wooden box—a shipping crate. And heavy as hell. He remembered moving it before.

"We can't—"

"Just push it up to me," Skye said, levering the crate up on its short end to lean against one of the reinforcing beams that lined the trench. She looked over to him, her eyes blazing. "You can do this."

She'd had the truck bed to use as a fulcrum to lever the crate, which made its weight easier move. Doug wouldn't. He was just about to tell her that when she scampered up the side of the truck and out of the trench like she climbed things every day—because she did.

"Fuck," Doug almost shouted.

He squatted low, getting both hands under the box, and pulled, screaming with the effort. The box moved an inch, then another. When it was high enough, he dropped to his knees to rest the end of the crate against his chest. Then he twisted and shoved his shoulder underneath it.

The cloudy-eyed zombie reached for his foot.

Thighs burning—from running and climbing and squatting—Doug pushed his trembling legs straight.

The zombie's hand wrapped around his ankle.

The box weighed two hundred pounds if an ounce. It stuck eighteen inches above the lip of the trench. Not enough to pivot it up. Skye leaned on it anyway.

The zombie was on its knees, one hand around Doug's calf. Another zombie slithered in behind the first. And another banged into the truck bed on the other side, behind him. Doug got his hands under the crate and pushed up, the most important press up of his maybe soon-to-be-over life.

Doug felt the zombie's teeth close on his pant leg as the crate lifted from his hands. He turned, slamming his fist into the side of the zombie's head, hard enough to shove its head sideways and kick his leg free. In two steps, he was hoisting himself up the side of the truck bed. Rocco's meaty hand gripped his and pulled. Doug crested the lip of the trench onto solid earth. Skye and three others were already on the far side of the chain-link fence, almost trotting despite the weight of the crate they carried between them like pallbearers.

The horde of zombies along the palisade were just fifty feet from the stretcher.

From Skye.

Doug sprinted, his long legs carrying him past Rocco, through the hole cut in the fence. He reached Skye and the others, slipping his hands under the crate to help carry it.

The zombies were forty feet away when they reached the stretcher.

"On three," Skye said.

Doug wanted to say that three was too long a count, but it would only slow them down.

"One, two, three."

They all heaved, the zombies ever closer. The crate thumped onto boxes already on the stretcher. Doug thought he heard the metal cable attached to the stretcher creak. Rocco reached them, grabbing some straps to help them tie everything down.

"Get out of here," Rocco shouted to the others.

Fifteen feet, the depth of the trench. The leading edge of the horde was only fifteen feet away. The rope ladder was another ten feet beyond the stretcher.

Then Rocco's arm lifted above his head, his upstretched hand whirling in a circle from his elbow. The stretcher lifted, smooth and steady.

"Let's go," he said, pivoting to the ladder.

Doug glanced at the horde, so close now that he could see the clouded gray eyes and flaky sores, hear the teeth snapping along with the moans. Skye pulled him along.

Everything about her was in crystalline focus. Her lips were so pink, her face flushed and filthy, smeared with soot and dirt and blood. Her eyes were the same shade as the lightest blue sapphires. Even now, she was beautiful.

The scream of twisting metal cut through the noise of the horde like a knife. The chain-link fence was down, and zombies stumbled over it.

Rocco was almost halfway to the top of the palisade when they reached the ladder. The rails were rope, but the rungs were wood, which would make it easier to climb. It twitched from the motion of those climbing ahead of them.

"Go," Skye said.

Doug shook his head. "You first."

But she didn't move. She stared at him, then glanced at the horde less than twenty feet away. She pointed to her leg. Her leather pants were torn. Doug could see the fabric of the layers beneath it, pulled out through the tear.

"I've been bitten, Doug. Go."

Doug couldn't breathe, couldn't move, couldn't think. The zombie he had seen when he followed Skye back to the truck. She had killed it, but it had killed her, too. She hadn't said a word, hadn't paused in her frantic effort to save LO and the people she loved.

Doug stared at her ripped pant leg, denying the proof of his eyes.

It couldn't be true.

He wouldn't *let it* be true.

"I don't see any blood," he protested.

"I can feel it running down my leg," she said, her voice trembling. "Go. *Please.*"

The horde tripping over the downed chain-link fence to their east was almost as close as the one behind them. Doug looked into Skye's blue eyes. She began to shimmer through the tears filling his own.

He held his hand out to her and said, his voice cracking, "Come die with the people who love you."

"There isn't time for us both to get up the ladder! You have to go!"

Resolve flooded Doug's body like a jolt of electricity.

"I'm not going without you. You climbed El Capitan. Climb the fucking palisade."

Skye's incandescent fury almost blinded him. She opened her mouth, then her fighting stance melted away.

"You're impossible!" she snapped at him.

She turned away, tugged off her boots, and wriggled her sock-clad toes into an almost non-existent space between two of the vertical tree trunk logs of the palisade.

Doug grasped the ladder. Skye's fingers gripped the rough bark of the logs. Her muscles flexed, her brow furrowed and her lips pursed as she looked for the next handhold.

Doug climbed the first two rungs of the ladder. Impotent rage at these mindless monsters who had stolen the fearless woman climbing the palisade just feet away from him detonated in Doug's chest. He wanted to jump off the ladder and kill as many as he could, pointless as it would be.

Instead, he climbed.

Skye was eight feet off the ground when the first zombie hit the palisade below her. She wriggled her toes and hands into the tiniest crevices of the vertical palisade logs. She reached and pulled with her arm, climbing another foot. She felt for a toehold so small Doug couldn't see it and pushed herself up another two feet. She moved with a fluid grace, unhurried and deliberate, as if there was nothing below her but grass and earth.

By feel, Doug kept climbing, his eyes riveted on Skye. When she reached the midway point up the palisade, she began to work her way over to the ladder.

"Get out of my way," she said, grinning.

Doug felt his heart rip and bleed as he watched Skye in her element one last time. She was only doing this because he had weaponized her affection for him. And he was rewarded by the sight of her moving with confidence and grace and joy, even now, on what she knew was her very last climb.

Doug tore his eyes from her and climbed. The ladder tightened with the weight of Skye working the rungs below him. It surprised him how heavy she felt below him but the gratitude that filled his breaking heart was impossible to deny.

A blur of faces and hands reached for him at the top of the palisade. He fell over the edge onto the large watch platform. Rocco helped him to his feet.

Doug pivoted back to the ladder. Skye's head crested the palisade. Doug clasped her hand in his.

"I've got you," he said.

Skye smiled wearily at him. And then she jerked down, her hand ripped from his, and disappeared.

Doug lunged over the palisade's edge, caught at the waist on the thick tree trunk poles. Skye clung to the ladder three rungs below, screaming and kicking at the zombie clinging to her feet. It had dragged her feet off the ladder and hung from her legs.

Doug had seen five zombies that were coordinated enough to climb, including this one. He hoisted himself farther over the palisade and grabbed Skye's wrist.

Behind him was an eruption of noise, jostling, the thud of running feet, and a shout of, "Someone shoot that fucking thing!"

Hands clamped around Doug's legs. Skye kicked one foot free of the zombie's clutching grip and got it on a rung. Her face contorted with effort, her eyes screwed shut, as she pushed and Doug pulled. Doug's fingertips brushed her other arm, pinching the barest sliver of her jacket between his middle and ring finger. He bunched the fabric until he could wrap his hand around her other arm above her elbow.

A rifle cracked, and Skye launched up at him. His grip on her wrist and arm never loosened as they tumbled back onto the platform.

Doug gasped, his chest heaving, covered in sweat and shaking. His heart pounded against his sternum, blood thundering in his ears. Skye looked over at him, the fear and panic in her eyes receding. Doug scrambled to Skye's feet, ripping the shredded leather of her pant leg as if it were cotton candy.

The mirror crescents of the zombie's teeth, so distinct he could see them individually, were red and angry against Skye's sweat-soaked skin. But her skin was smooth and unbroken.

Doug almost collapsed with relief. He felt the sob rush from his mouth. He looked up at Skye.

"You're okay. It was sweat you felt."

Her hand flew to her mouth. Doug could barely breathe. He moved to embrace her, but Rocco knelt beside her and wrapped Skye in his arms. Doug wanted to push him aside, but Rocco didn't let go, so he got to his feet, swaying on rubbery legs.

Skye broke hers and Rocco's embrace. Rocco almost got out of her way when he turned to look up at Doug. Almost, but not quite. He kept hold of Skye, his arm around her shoulders. Skye smiled at

Doug, relief and gratitude and something more, lighting up her face more than the morning sun climbing into the sky above them. She had pulled her leg close to her body and rubbed her hand over the unbroken skin that she had been sure was her death sentence.

Rocco said, his voice hoarse, "Nice save, Father. That direct line to God got us a miracle."

Doug squinted at Rocco. No one here called him Father. A vertical, anxious-looking line creased the space between Skye's eyebrows. Rocco's happiness over their safe deliverance was genuine, but a hardness lurked beneath his smile. His flashing eyes bore into Doug's, brimming with warning.

Doug got the message loud and clear. He was a priest, with nothing to offer Skye except friendship. And he needed to back the fuck off before Rocco decided to remind him again.

21

Miranda's eyes cracked open. The feeble gray light from the sliver between the curtains detonated an explosion of pain behind her eyes. She screwed them shut again.

Everything hurt. Her muscles ached, so tight that she had to strain to move. And when she did, she realized it was a bad idea. Her head throbbed, wrapped in bands of steel that radiated from her sternum and traveled up over her jaw and cheeks. Another band of steel-tight muscles began at the base of her skull, meeting the other at the top of her head before sliding down to bore through her temples. Her back felt no better, her hip and right elbow worse. Her toes, even the soles of her feet, pulsated with pain that matched the beating of her heart.

A wet snout nudged her. Delilah snuggled closer.

"Liley," she said, relaxing, even as the steel bands crushed her skull. If Delilah was here, then she was at LO. She snaked a stiff, sore arm out from under the blanket to scratch the top of the pit bull's head.

A door creaked open, then a figure approached.

"You're safe, Miranda. You're at LO."

"River?" she asked.

"Yep," River said, walking to Miranda's bed.

Phineas, Miranda remembered. Dread filled her chest. Had she even told them?

"Phineas. Did I tell—"

"Phineas is fine, he's here," River said quickly. "He's got a nasty fracture, but he's young and strong. He should be okay. Look straight ahead, keep your eyes open."

A bright light flashed into Miranda's eye. Pain stabbed her brain, then the light flicked away. Then the other eye—bright light, stab, relief.

"That looks good," River said. She pulled off the covers and skimmed the taut muscles of Miranda's body, ignoring Miranda's whimpers and gasps. "I'm going to give you another painkiller and see what I can dig up for a muscle relaxer. We'll try a hot bath and massage later today. You were hypothermic. That's why your muscles are so tight and sore, from your body shivering to stay warm."

"What about the... Am I still pregnant?"

"Yep," River answered. "Contrary to every soap opera you ever watched, the female body can take a pretty good wallop and not miscarry. Especially if there's not a direct blow to your abdomen."

A flash of relief made her body feel light for a second but was immediately displaced by crushing weariness. She still had to deal with getting rid of it. You would think the apocalypse would help me out, just this once, she thought. An overwhelming need to talk to Mario ambushed her so suddenly she wanted to cry.

She tilted her head from side to side, focusing on the misery of her painful muscles. Physical discomfort helped push the feelings aside so that the tears did not break through.

"How long have I been back?"

River pursed her lips, her eyes flicking down as she thought. "About eight, nine hours."

River turned at a soft knock on the door.

Doug's voice said, "River?"

Relief filled River's voice. "You're back. Is everyone okay?"

"Yeah," Doug said, stepping into the doorway.

The smell of rotten zombies, shit, mud, and blood poured from Doug's filthy clothes. Dark smudges circled his eyes. A clean strip of pale forehead came into view as he pulled off a bandana tied over his head.

"Someone's downstairs with your assistant," Doug continued.

"Thanks for letting me know. Five minutes, then let Miranda rest." River wrinkled her nose. "And go get a shower."

Doug approached the bed. "You look like shit, Miri."

"You *smell* like shit," Miranda said, wrinkling her nose. "What have you been doing?"

Doug petted Delilah as he looked around the room, then pulled a chair to the bed and sat down. River pulled the door shut behind her.

"I've been doing my part to save everyone instead of going swimming like some people," he said, but she could hear a grin in his voice. "We got the comm equipment to fix the sound defenses, but it was a near thing getting back."

For the first time, Miranda noticed a background hum. Despite the grin, she realized Doug looked careworn and exhausted.

"Are we completely surrounded?"

Doug nodded. "As far as the eye can see."

Tears filled Miranda's eyes. She sat up without thinking, gasping at the pain in her muscles. "What about the Institute?"

"They're fine. They've got their own mini-sound defense perimeter, remember? It's working. The zombies are a lot closer than they're used to them being, but they're safe. Besides, the monkeys screech like banshees when the wind blows. If they can't get to the damn roof in time with all the squawking, I'm not sure they're worth saving." Doug paused, his brow furrowed. "Are you crying?"

Miranda shook her head despite the tears that spilled down her cheeks.

"Everyone over there is okay, Miri," he said, no trace of teasing in his voice.

Miranda let the tears that would not fucking stop roll down her face. It hurt too much to move her arm to wipe them away.

"I'm fine," she sniffled, feeling like an idiot. "I don't know why I'm crying. I just need to talk to Mario."

"You can get him on the radio," Doug said, his tone encouraging.

Miranda bit the inside of her cheek to keep fresh tears at bay. "I need to talk to him in person."

"That's gonna take a while," Doug said. He got up, bandana in hand, then seemed to think better of it. He pulled at the bedsheet and used it to blot the tears on her face. "We can't get out to fix the sound defenses. There are too many of them. Smith is having everyone but the perimeter guards shelter-in-place starting at noon. They did it once before when a horde surrounded LO, early on. It took two weeks, but eventually the zombies moved off."

"Two weeks!" Miranda gasped, panicked. "But in two weeks I'll be... I can't wait that long!"

What had River said? Eleven weeks? Twelve? Two more weeks was cutting it close for a simple vacuum abortion. She didn't have to wait to get the abortion. It wasn't necessary to talk to him. Doug was right; she could use the radio. But not talking to Mario in person felt wrong. And she wanted his support, his in-person support, like River had suggested. Less than two days ago she hadn't seen the point in talking to Mario, but now she didn't want to deal with it alone.

"Miri, what's wrong?"

"I— fuck," she said. She opened her mouth, shut it. Opened and shut it again. Even though she knew it was true, she couldn't believe it.

"I'm pregnant."

Doug stared at her blankly. "But...I thought you got your tubes tied?"

Miranda laughed bitterly. "Yeah. I did."

"Holy shit."

"Tell me about it."

They were both silent for a few moments, then Doug asked, "What are you going to do?"

Miranda lay back, grimacing at the shriek of pain from her abs and back. It felt like she had done a thousand crunches.

"Have an abortion."

Even to herself she sounded weary, like this was the last thing on earth that she wanted to deal with. Which was true. But it was more than just ordinary weariness. She was exhausted by this world. She was tired of zombies and everything they represented—death and pain, mindless hunger and miserable choices. Of how relentlessly it ground everyone down, denying them the things that were normal—that were human—to want.

"How far along are you?"

Miranda sighed. "Eleven or twelve weeks. I was so shocked I don't remember half of what River said. I only found out the other day, when you got here."

"Oh." Doug's face became thoughtful. "It would have been nice to know I had a hormonal mess on my hands."

Her laugh came out as a half-strangled snort. Delilah whimpered and nudged Miranda's hand again.

"It's okay, Liley," she said, rubbing between the pit bull's eyes until Delilah closed them, warbling with happiness.

Doug said, "Makes sense that you want to talk to Mario in person." When she didn't say anything, he said, "Is there anything I can do?"

"Short of preaching a homily so bad that the stupid zombies run away?"

Doug smiled, then sobered, a flash of sadness in his eyes.

"Have you thought about keeping it?"

"No," she said, then paused. "A little. Mostly about what it would be like to be able to do something human and not have it come back and kill you. But just a little. Like a tiny speck of dust little." She paused, then said, "What if Mario wants it?"

"Do you really think he will?"

She threw her hands up, exasperated, and immediately regretted moving her arms. "I don't know. I don't even know why I'm worrying about it. Everything about this makes me want to find a razor."

Shit, she thought, watching Doug's eyes widen. She hadn't meant to say that. She didn't even mean it. Even though she knew that Doug knew, she had barely acknowledged to him that she used to cut herself.

"You're worrying me, Miri," Doug said.

She sighed heavily. "I'm not going to. You don't need to worry. I just... I just don't want to have to deal with this."

"You can always lean on me."

Doug looked so young, and as ready and willing to help her as a Boy Scout. Sometimes she forgot how earnest Doug could be when he wasn't being a smart-ass.

"I know that, Doug. I *am*. My mental health is already improving."

"Hot mess is what usually comes to mind," he said. "But, yeah. Maybe it is."

"Thank you for not going all forced pregnancy on me."

Doug snorted. "For crying out loud, Miri. I can barely figure out my own life. I don't need to control someone else's."

Miranda laughed, which made her stomach muscles hurt. "You're a terrible priest that way. Quit making me laugh; it hurts!"

Doug didn't laugh like he usually did when she teased him about not towing the patriarchal, priestly party line. Instead, he scowled down at the floor.

"I'm gonna go," he said, stretching as he stood. "I came straight here after we talked to Smith. I need a shower and something to eat. If I get a move on, I can catch Skye—the others—at the dining hall."

He looked sick at the mention of Skye, which was not the reaction Miranda was accustomed to seeing where Skye was concerned.

"Is Skye okay?" she asked.

"Yeah, of course," he said, a grin quickly put in place. "Just the usual close shaves all around."

His deflection rang as hollow as an echo bouncing off the sides of a well. Whatever had happened to Skye had scared him.

He cocked his head to the side. "I guess we'll hang out at your place for the duration?"

"I guess. Talk to River, see what she says. Maybe we can stay with her, so we don't drive each other crazy."

Doug shook his head, looking amused once more. "It's too late for that, Coppertop. No more refreshing dips in alpine streams."

"Alpine streams, my ass."

She watched as he moved the chair back to where it had been before he arrived. Everything about his manner, his body language, was off since Skye came up. Whatever was going on with them—or maybe just with him—had changed.

When Doug reached the door, she said, "I'm sorry for giving you shit about Skye when we were at Station Eight. That was the hormonal mess talking."

Doug turned back, the discomfort on his face plain. "You were right. I need to get my head on straight."

He looked as excited about getting his head on straight as she felt about being pregnant.

"It won't be the end of the world, you know. If you want something different for your life."

He stared at her, frozen in place, like an animal caught in a trap. When she saw the conflict and guilt that flashed across his face, her eyes filled with tears again.

Doug sighed. "You should keep that in mind, too, Miri. The waterworks are back on."

Miranda wiped at her face. Delilah wriggled closer, licking them away. Gently, Miranda fended the too helpful pit bull off. Delilah settled beside Miranda with a contented sigh.

Despite her worry for her best friend in the world, Miranda closed her eyes and slept.

22

DOUG FELT ONE THOUSAND PERCENT MORE HUMAN AFTER A shower. Exhausted and wrung out, but human. He checked his watch as he emerged from the wooded path next to the cluster of Boys' Home buildings near the dining hall. Seven thirty, the time they had agreed on. Skye would be there on the dot.

Five hours until shelter-in-place started.

When they reached LO not even two hours ago, Doug had known he was going nowhere for a while. But his relief at having responsibility for that decision taken out of his hands was matched only by his anticipation of spending time with Skye.

And his guilt.

A fingernails-scratching-on-a-chalkboard shiver slithered from the base of his skull along the length of his spine. The grasping hands and biting teeth. The flash of terrified panic in Skye's blue eyes when the zombie yanked her off the palisade, when they were literally home free. Or almost, since Skye had believed she was dead no matter what. The sheer scale of the smell and sound of the horde below them had felt almost as overwhelming as his panic. But he would have dived off the palisade into the horde after her, if that was what it took.

This kind of thing usually rolled right off his back, but not this time. Not with Skye. He had wanted to hold her close so badly, make sure she was really here, when he realized she had not been bitten. But Rocco got between them, literally and figuratively, with a back-the-fuck-off glare that was genuinely frightening.

Rocco was only trying to be a good friend.

And he was right.

Doug knew he had to get his head straight. He *had* to. Especially after seeing the look on Skye's face earlier, the little anxious line that had appeared between her eyebrows, and the tightness at the corners of her mouth. The way he was feeling, the way he was acting—seeking her out like a goddamned puppy, conversations that only deepened their connection—was not good for him and was definitely not fair to Skye.

Trying to pray for clarity was a joke that he had abandoned weeks ago. He inevitably wound up daydreaming about her, daydreams that were not PG-13. This infatuation...he had not had a crush like this in years. In ever. He told himself every day that was what it was: a hard-ass crush. Sooner or later it would wane if he could just back off enough to let it run its course. But the knowledge that it *would* wane was so depressing that he never did.

The way she moved had gotten under his skin. Whether she was teaching the kids how to climb or stacking dishes in the dining hall kitchen or, like today, climbing the palisade to escape a horde, she inevitably did something—a flick of the wrist while pushing her hair out of her eyes, the twist of her waist when she reached up to help a kid with a handhold—that literally took his breath away.

It won't be the end of the world, you know. If you want something different for your life.

Miranda's words had echoed in his head almost nonstop. And Miranda was pregnant. Holy ever-loving shit.

Doug had only known Miranda since the ZA. She had always

been one hundred percent adamant that she was never having kids. She was never bringing a kid into all this. She had even gotten her tubes tied to make sure it never happened.

"So much for permanent birth control," he muttered.

It didn't surprise him that she planned to get an abortion. What had surprised him was how ambivalent she sounded about it. Maybe that was just because she hadn't talked to Mario yet, hadn't gotten confirmation that he agreed. Doug had no doubt that Mario would be on board with whatever she wanted to do. But maybe it was one thing to not want to bring kids into this admittedly terrible world, but something else altogether to find out you actually were pregnant. By the man who was the love of your life, no less. Who you never thought you would get a second chance with.

I'm glad I'm not in their shoes, he thought, and not for the first time. That they were right for each other was obvious, but it had never been easy for Miranda and Mario. It had to be cool, though, to see how your DNA combined with someone else's. It was the natural world, natural selection, which was all part of God's design, at work.

I wonder what mine and Skye's kids would look like.

Doug froze in his tracks. The world around him seemed to spin.

"You can't think things like that," he hissed aloud.

It won't be the end of the world, you know. If you want something different for your life.

So many people depended on him back home. He was going home, back to reality, eventually. Ever since they left Santa Cruz, something had felt off. One day he was using his service to God to endanger the success of the mission to save the town, and then, within weeks, he felt disconnected from that same God in a way he never had before. And he hadn't been able to get it back.

Just now, thinking about a child he would never have with Skye, was the first time in months that he'd thought in terms of God's design, writ large or only his small slice of it. He hadn't felt that connection, had not been able to feel it, since Santa Cruz. That was the weirdest part of all. Downtime, which was what the voyage to

Seattle had been, had always been when Doug could relax into God's embrace. When he could feel God's purpose for him, and his calling to his vocation. But not this time, for months now. He hadn't been able to get the door on his side open.

Every time he thought of leaving Walter to handle everything on his own—safeguarding the settlement, keeping the City Council at bay—the weight that settled on his body felt physical. Felt like it would crush him. The only time it didn't feel that way was when he was with Skye.

"This ends today," he said.

He had indulged this crush long enough. Too long. He had to get his head together, and he had to do it now.

He pushed the dining hall door open. A day's worth of cooking and baking had not yet warmed the building. He picked up a tray, filled it with food, then looked around. Maybe five other people were in the dining hall besides Skye. She sat at a table in the far corner. Seeing her there, looking exhausted but alive and whole, sent a rush of dizzy relief through his brain. How was he supposed to get his head on straight when he wanted to shout from the rooftops because she was all right? He was just about to spin on his heel and take the food to Miranda's when Skye looked up and caught his eye. He couldn't duck out now, not without making things weird, so he walked over and sat down across from her.

"How're you feeling?" she asked. "How's Miranda?"

"I'm beat. Miranda looks terrible, but she'll be okay. It'll take more than hypothermia to kill her."

Skye smiled. "You'll be hanging around for a bit."

"Looks like."

"It'll be nice." When it was clear he wasn't going to respond, she said, "You'll be staying at Miranda's while you're here."

"Yeah," he said. "Well, I don't know if River wants to keep an eye on her, so maybe not."

As soon as the words were out of his mouth, he wanted to snatch them back. He had not meant it to sound like he might be looking for a place to stay. He was afraid to speak again in case he said something stupid or dangerous like 'Come stay with us.'

He had to shut this down. Ideally in a way that he and Skye might still be friends.

Skye reached over and touched his hand. "Thanks, for before. For insisting I not give up."

Her hand barely touched his, but the heat that radiated from it felt like lava flowing into his veins. She had come so close to not being here, sitting across from him, looking at him with those eyes that were so goddamned blue. Thinking about how differently this day could have gone made the room around him spin. An overpowering urge to reach over the table and pull her to him, to kiss her, caught Doug in its undertow. He wanted to feel Skye's lips on his, taste her, touch her, more than he had ever wanted anything.

"I was afraid—" he said, then stopped. He snatched his hand away. "It's what we do. No big deal."

Skye almost recoiled. "It was a big deal to me."

"You know what I mean," he said, brushing it off.

Hurt flashed in her eyes. He was being a dick, which was not how he meant to be. He shouldn't need to be a dick to disengage, but it was so much harder than he had realized.

What he needed was to leave. To get the fuck away from her.

"I'm gonna split," he said, standing, his tray of uneaten food still on the table. "I need to figure out where Miri and I are staying and get food and whatnot. I'm sure you do, too."

Doug walked away as fast as he could without running. He heard the scrape of Skye's chair being pushed back but didn't stop. He stepped into the cold, damp air outside. The sun had been crowded out by heavy clouds. A gun-metal gray mist hugged the ground.

"Doug! Wait!"

He kept walking, but Skye's footsteps grew closer until she caught his arm. He stopped but didn't turn around, so she yanked on his arm until he did.

"What is up with you?"

Her eyebrows were drawn together, the anxious, vertical line between them. Her pink lips puckered in a frown.

He feigned a nonchalance he did not feel. "Nothing."

"Then why are you acting like this?"

"Like what?"

"Like you didn't just save my life an hour ago. Like we don't even know each other. Like we aren't friends."

Doug took a deep breath. "Of course we're friends."

Skye's eyes filled with tears. Clearly, it was the wrong thing to say. Or maybe it was the way he had said it. Dismissively, like it wasn't worth mentioning.

This wasn't how he had meant this to go, and he wasn't sure how he had let it happen. But he had to fix this, and he had to do it now. If he didn't, he was afraid he'd chicken out.

"I just don't want you to get the wrong idea."

"What?"

"I get the feeling you might—"

He stopped.

Her eyes narrowed, any trace of tears replaced by wariness.

"You get the feeling I might what?" she said, her voice flat.

"It's just that I'm a priest, you know? And I get the feeling that you—"

Silence stretched between them.

After what seemed an eternity, she said, "Oh. Oh, I see. You get the feeling that I have this one-sided thing for you?"

Doug shifted his weight from one foot to the other. He held his hands up, helpless. "I— I think you might think something's going to happen here. Something that...can't."

Relief flooded Doug's body when Skye started to laugh. It was going to be okay.

"You *asshole*. How dare you try to dump this all on me." She waved her hand back and forth between them. "Whatever *this* is, it's not just me. *You're* the one always seeking *me* out. You'd do jumping jacks if you thought it would get my attention, and now you want to pretend it's me getting the wrong idea? If I have the wrong idea, Doug, it's not because I imagined it."

Doug took a step back, retreating from her anger.

"Look, Skye," he said, whiplashed from his delusional relief back into a conversation that had careened off the rails. "It's not like we can't be friends."

"Really?" she said, incredulous.

"But that's all we can be."

She stared at him, her eyes flashing. They were still so goddamned blue, but burned with the intensity of Mount Saint Helens' infamous eruption.

"You want to be a priest?" she spat. "Fine. Be a priest. But you have a lot of balls standing in front of me, hiding behind that Roman collar I never see you wearing and trying to shove whatever it is you feel for me into my lap, pretending it's not yours. I can own my part. I care about you." Her voice grew tight. "A lot. And I thought... Goddammit." She shook her head and sighed. "I thought maybe this could be more."

Doug's heart twisted at the pain in Skye's voice. She glanced away, blinking hard. A single tear escaped and rolled down her cheek. But when she looked back, her eyes burned with reproof.

"I can own that I want to be more than your friend, Doug," she said softly. "And that I'm a fool because of it. For thinking you wanted that, too."

"You're not a fool, Skye," Doug protested, desperate to backtrack. "I've never thought—"

"I don't care what you think! I know what I saw when you pulled me over that palisade, and it wasn't that I had gotten the wrong idea. And now you've got the balls to stand here and—no. No." She laughed, the sound like acid sizzling on metal. "You don't. You don't have the balls at all. Your God has them."

She turned on her heel, fury radiating from her like ripples of heat distortion shimmering up from desert hardpan. Doug could only watch, the air sucked from his lungs, every molecule of his body aching for her, shouting at him to follow and make things right between them.

He took a step, then another, before he stopped. The weight of his denial crashed down. His chest felt scraped out, and his empty stomach roiled. Loss snaked through his body like a contagion.

This was always how it was going to end. Thinking otherwise had been a fantasy.

Selfish.

Sin.

Painlessly undoing the wrong he had done Skye was impossible, just like the heartache he felt watching her walk away.

23

JUST ANOTHER MINUTE. YOU CAN DO ANOTHER MINUTE WITHOUT screaming.

Doug's jaw ached. For the first five minutes of the trip, he kept reminding himself to relax it, but he clenched it again so quickly he gave up. Skye sat in the front passenger seat of the SUV, her eyes straight ahead or looking to her right, where she would not accidentally catch sight of him. Her posture was so stiff she looked like she would break if jostled. She answered Rocco, who was driving, in one-word sentences. Normally the two talked up a storm. Doug had no idea why she had decided to accompany them to the Institute, but if her intent was to torture him, she was succeeding.

Next to him in the back seat, Miranda twitched and fidgeted like an unmedicated kid with ADHD hopped up on sugar and caffeine. Her anxiety was palpable, even with Delilah next to her. The pit bull had picked up on Miranda's anxiety and lay beside her mistress, her head resting on Miranda's knee instead of hanging out the window. The dog's presence usually relaxed Miranda, but several times already, Doug had asked her to loosen the death grip on his hand.

When the SUV finally came to a halt in the front of the parking lot at the Institute, Doug sagged with relief. Skye and Miranda were out of the vehicle so fast it might as well have been on fire, and Delilah was already on hind legs, peering up a tree at an angry macaque. Doug watched them go, feeling more demoralized than he could recall. His hand that Miranda had held was still blotchy red and white. She had left fingernail marks on his palm.

Miranda needed to talk to Mario. Her growing anxiety during the ten-day-long shelter-in-place at LO had been tough to watch, mostly because there was nothing he could do to alleviate it. Things had started off well enough as she brave-faced her way through the first two days. They had stayed with River, who busted out her emergency Blu-Ray player. She had everything from *The Godfather* to *John Wick*, which was impressive since Blu-Rays were obsolete tech before the ZA started. It had been an almost successful way for Doug to not think about Skye until River selected *Notorious* with Ingrid Bergman and Cary Grant. The combination of a secret, tortured love affair and Nazis had done him in. The movies lost their special treat charm. By day three, Miranda spent her time brooding or scribbling furiously in her journal and cursing when she needed to sharpen the pencil with a ferocity that was impressive even for her. There was, apparently, a better kind of pencil but it was at her place. Doug wallowed in self-recrimination and self-pity about how spectacularly he had fucked up with Skye. He had done the right thing the wrong way. He told himself he should feel relieved, but he was dying inside.

Doug got out of the SUV and shut the door. The monkeys were screeching as they scooted on the ground or leaped from tree to tree. Doug caught sight of Goldie, the large, blond, perpetually frowning male macaque on the roof of the one-story building directly opposite the main Institute building. Goldie seemed to find people lacking. Doug felt that he had validated Goldie's low expectations.

"She's pissed now, but you did the right thing."

So lost in thought of his inadequacies as a human being—never mind as a priest—Doug had not noticed Rocco lingering nearby. He didn't want to think about any of it, much less get compliments he did not deserve.

"I didn't mean to," he started. "I never— Christ, I fucked up."

Rocco shrugged. "She's a great person and a beautiful woman. It's been known to mess with many a man's head. Many a woman's, too."

"I've never felt so disconnected from it before. Being a priest, I mean. I got confused...and then I was selfish."

"You're human, and you fucked up," Rocco said. "Welcome to the club. What matters is you did the right thing, even if you were a little slow doing it."

Doug felt minutely less wretched knowing that Rocco did not hate him. Rocco had sent some distinctly unfriendly vibes Doug's way over the past weeks. Doug had known it was because Rocco was worried about Skye getting hurt, which made him like Rocco even more.

"Heading back right away?" Doug asked, looking at the brewing thunderheads to the south. "There's weather heading this way."

"As soon as Skye's done with the blood sample."

Doug's anxiety spiked. "They need a blood sample from Skye? Is she sick?"

"No, no," Rocco said, his tone reassuring. "She's got AB negative blood. They wanted some, don't ask me why. It's the rarest one, she said."

Doug nodded, but he didn't see why River couldn't have drawn Skye's blood and sent it over. He headed up the path, then realized Rocco hadn't joined him.

"Are you coming inside?"

"You didn't hear me tell Skye I'd wait for her here?" He continued at Doug's head shake, a knowing grin on his face. "Guess you were a little distracted on the ride here."

Doug turned back up the path. He should check in on Jeremiah later, make sure the whack job wasn't doing something he shouldn't.

Or maybe he just wanted someone he could take his shitty mood out on. Ixnay that welfare check for now, he decided. The person he needed to check on was Miranda, once she and Mario finished talking. Mario, too. He'd be as blindsided as Miranda had been.

Doug nodded to Rich, who stood just outside the main doors.

"How's it going, Rich?"

Smith had sent Rich over as one of the Watch Commanders when she beefed up security after learning what Mario was really working on. He exuded a quiet competence that usually relaxed Doug, but not today.

"I'm well, thank you," he said, his Southern drawl blurring the edges between thank and you. "Is Miranda okay? She looked a little out of sorts."

Doug said, "That seems to apply to a lot of people these days, but Miri'll be fine. She always is."

In the atrium where they had set up their common area, Miranda sat at a table. Her head was in her hands, and it looked like she was crying. Delilah hovered next to her, looking distressed.

Oh shit, Doug thought. He would never have pegged Miranda as a hormonal pregnancy crier, which showed how much he knew about women. There were people in the lobby she didn't know well, and she was still crying. This was not good.

"Miri, what happened?" he asked as he reached the table.

Miranda looked up, embarrassment filling her face. She wiped her eyes on her sleeve.

"I hate this crying shit," she said, her eyes welling up again. "He's in the BSL-3 running an experiment for the next twenty-four hours. Alicia's there, too."

"And you don't want an audience."

Miranda nodded. Absently, she reached down to pet Delilah's head. Doug sat in the empty chair opposite her.

"That's got to be an anticlimax."

Miranda's bark of laughter was so sudden it startled him.

"You got that right," she said, half crying, half laughing. "I got so amped up to finally talk to him, and now it's going to be another day. We said hi on the phones through the glass, like in prison."

She sighed, rolling her eyes. Her hand rested on her belly, which she had done a lot while they sheltered-in-place at LO. Doug knew she had no idea she was doing it, and he didn't think it was the kind of unconscious gesture that women planning on getting abortions made. It suggested protectiveness, not get the fuck out of my body, but he wasn't touching that with a ten-foot pole.

What I know about women got me where I am with Skye, he thought. What did he think he knew about being pregnant?

"Alicia came out to draw some blood for Skye, but one of them had to stay with the experiment. But she was going right back in; they both need to do things for the experiment. Ma—" Miranda caught herself, then continued. "*James* started talking, and I could tell he was just about to go on a tear about protein folds or whatever the fuck it was, and you know how he is when he gets like that. He is not in the space I need him to be. I held it together till I got out here. Now I'm crying—again."

"I'm sorry, Miri. You can always watch the monkeys. There's an orange-y one I'm thinking of calling Little Coppertop."

Miranda rolled her eyes. "I'm dragging my sorry ass upstairs," she said. "If I'm not crying, I'm falling on my face. Or stuffing my face. Going to annoy Jeremiah doesn't even appeal to me right now. I don't know why anyone would do this to themselves on purpose." She got up, then squeezed his shoulder. "Thank you for checking on me."

Doug smiled up at her, his heart not in it. "Any time."

Opposite them, the door to the hallway where the BSL-3 lab was located opened with a clunk. Miranda looked up.

"Hey, Skye. Hanging out a bit or taking off?"

Don't turn around, don't turn around, do *not* turn around, Doug said to himself.

He turned around.

The door sighed shut behind Skye. Her hair was pulled back in a severely tight bun. Dark circles smudged her eyes. She had pulled long hours getting the sound defenses back up, but Doug wondered how much of the pinched expression was because of him.

Skye glanced up through the atrium's glass roof, then back to Miranda. Outside, the macaques began to shriek.

"Heading out. The storms can get bad this time of year, but we should beat it home. I don't want to get stuck here for the night."

"I don't imagine you do," Miranda said, glancing sidelong at Doug. "Safe travels."

"Take care, Miranda. See you when I see you."

She turned and headed for the door.

"Be careful," Doug added softly.

Skye paused for a millisecond. Her body stiffened even more, but she left his remark unacknowledged.

Anxious dread pulsed through Doug's veins. He wanted to run after her, try to make things right, even though he knew it was impossible.

Miranda had not moved from where she stood by her chair. Outside, a sudden clap of thunder rattled the building.

"Are you ready to talk about—"

"No."

She gave him a have-it-your-way shrug. "Whe—" she yawned. "When you are ready to tell me how you screwed the pooch so bad..."

"Yeah, no," Doug said. He had no intention of talking to her about it. Ever.

"If he gets out of the lab early—"

"M—James is not going to need any help with wanting to see you, Miranda, but I'll send him your way if he doesn't find you first."

Miranda's and Delilah's footsteps receded up the main staircase. Squawks from the monkeys signaled Skye and Rocco were driving away.

How pathetic would it be if he went to the door to watch them leave? Exceptionally pathetic, he decided, rising to his feet anyway.

When he got to the main doors, the SUV was still there. Another vehicle, a truck that had not been there earlier, was parked on the closer side of the building, just around the curve of the O-shaped line of parking spaces in the center of the lot. Doug could see Rocco in the SUV, but he did not see Skye anywhere. The dark bank of thunderclouds was much closer. Rich had moved inside to get out of the weather.

"Who's that?" he asked Rich, indicating the truck with a jut of his chin. "Why haven't they come in?"

"It's Brock. From P-Land." Rich's soft southern drawl made him sound rueful. "He was on his way in, but he and Skye met on the walk and headed toward the pond. She didn't look happy to see him."

"And you didn't go out there?"

"You obviously don't know Skye very well. She would not have liked me sticking my nose in."

And Rocco is just waiting for her in the SUV, Doug thought, surprised. That did not seem right. Rocco nursed a deep dislike of Skye's ex, though he wasn't outwardly antagonistic. But the curve of the O that the parking spaces were arranged around, combined with the solid ingrowth of now mature trees at its center, meant that Rocco probably had not been able to see who had been driving the truck from where he was parked.

"Tell Rocco that Brock's here and to come to the pond," Doug said.

He pushed through the door. The wind had picked up, the air colder than before. He veered left off the path toward the pond. As he got closer, he heard voices over the wind and creaking trees.

"...can't believe you're being so selfish," Brock's voice said.

"I'm done with this conversation, Brock. I'm done with *you*."

"I'm not," Brock said angrily. "You owe me an explanation."

Doug did not care for Brock's tone one bit. He picked up the pace, crossing into view just in time to see Brock grab Skye's arm.

"Skye," he shouted.

A flicker of relief flashed across her face, quickly replaced with an annoyed this-is-all-I-need expression.

"Rocco's waiting for you," Doug said. "Brock. Didn't know you were here."

"I'm talking to Skye," he said, still holding on to her arm.

Skye shook him off. Above, thunder rumbled across the darkening sky.

"It's over, Brock," she said. "Leave me alone."

"I just wanted to see if you're okay. They said you were here when I radioed so I came. It's a long drive," he added, his tone implying Skye owed him for it.

A flash of lightning lit up the sky. Whatever had been holding Skye's temper in check snapped.

"Stalking me is what you're doing! I broke up with you, Brock, months ago. We're finished."

Brock's eyes narrowed. He stepped closer, using his size to intimidate. "What makes you think you get to decide that?"

Doug went from wary to enraged in a heartbeat. "Back the fuck off," he said, putting himself between them.

The heavens opened. A torrent of water fell from the sky, soaking Doug almost immediately.

"Oh yeah?" Brock said.

"Give me an excuse, man."

Guys like Brock relied on brute strength and always underestimated anyone who didn't. Doug knew he could toss him with a karate hold, find a pressure point, and immobilize Brock while he writhed in pain in under five seconds. He had done it more times than he could count.

"Goddammit, Doug, I don't need your help!" Skye said. She pushed him out of the way and rounded on Brock. "Smith offered to ban you from LO. Did you know that?"

Even through the rain, Doug saw Brock blanch.

"I told her not to, but I've changed my mind. I don't know what I ever saw in you, but you'll never set foot inside LO again."

A figure approached from the path. Rocco—finally.

Brock narrowed his eyes and looked from Skye to Doug. "You're fucking this asshole now, is that it? You cheating bitch."

Lightning flared bright, followed by a rip of thunder over their heads. Doug's hands balled into fists.

"You okay, Skye?" Rocco asked, trotting into place beside her. He wrapped his hand around Doug's wrist, above Doug's fisted hand. "What are you doing here, Brock?"

Over the hammering rain, Skye said, "He's leaving."

Brock glared at Skye, the fury in his eyes like nothing Doug had ever seen, even in Jeremiah. If he and Rocco weren't here, Doug knew that Brock would hit her.

"It's bad weather to travel, especially alone," Rocco said.

Skye fixed an angry stare on Rocco. "Either he's leaving, or I am."

"Okay," Rocco said, turning to Brock. "Come on, Brock. You're leaving."

"You'll get yours, you fucking cunt," Brock snarled. "Just wait."

He spun on his heel and stormed away. Rocco shot Doug a what-the-fuck look before following Brock. The two men were lost in the sheeting rain in seconds.

The storm howled around them. Another crack of thunder broke, so close that Doug flinched.

He raised his voice to be heard over the rain and wind. "Come back inside, Skye. It's not safe to travel in this."

She frowned at him, her fury on full display. Doug didn't think she could look more angry if *he* had been arguing with her instead of Brock.

"You don't get to fight my battles, Doug. I'm not anything to you."

She headed for the building without a backward glance. Doug followed, floored by what he had just witnessed and seething with the pent-up energy of not beating Brock within an inch of his life. He had disliked Brock before, but now he fucking hated the guy.

All things being equal, he would never let anyone leave in weather like this. It was already storm-dark, would be true dark in under an hour. In weather like this, you could drive into a group of zombies before you realized they were there.

But all things were not equal. Brock had threatened Skye. If she had not insisted that Brock leave, Doug would have. The creep would get what he would get.

Doug wanted it to be bad.

24

He wasn't worried. It was just...odd.

It's nothing, Doug told himself as he turned into the last corridor on the first floor, at the far side of the building.

But it was unlike Skye to not be somewhere when she said she would be. She was the most punctual person Doug had ever met. She had paced the lobby all morning and through lunch, only stopping when it was clear the storm was not going to pass until at least late afternoon. It finally started to clear up just past four o'clock. It beggared belief that she would do anything to keep them at the Institute for a millisecond longer than necessary after almost twenty-four hours of not wanting to be here. If she had not had that run-in with Brock yesterday, Doug might have the same attitude as the others, but the two things in combination did not feel right.

Doug had known that Brock was a creep the first time he met him. Even so, the depth of his venom when Skye had told him to get lost and leave her alone—again—and that she would take Smith up on her offer to ban him from LO, surprised even him. Smith was not the kind of leader to offer something like that lightly. Before last night, Doug had thought Brock was merely a manipulative asshole. Now, he was certain Brock was abusive. When he thought of Brock hitting Skye—whether last night if he had not been there or in the past—rage mushroomed through him so fast he thought his body would explode into a million pieces. Doug had joined Rocco in escorting Brock off the Institute grounds. Rocco had not been happy about sending anyone, even Brock, out in such dangerous conditions until Doug filled him in on what he had missed. Rocco's concern for Brock's welfare had evaporated instantaneously.

Doug knew the others were right; ten minutes was no big deal. Miranda was twenty minutes late for everything. But it niggled at him. There was no harm in looking around. When the few things he had the illusion of control over were out of kilter, it made Doug antsy. When it involved Skye, even more so.

He really didn't want to think about that right now.

Instead, I'm taking this pointless walk around the building because she's a few minutes late, but I'm not going to look at why that is, because if I don't, it's not real, he thought bitterly.

He was probably the last person on Earth she wanted to see. Who was he kidding? He was *definitely* the last person she wanted to see, except maybe for Brock. Being lumped in with that piece of shit was a low Doug could do without.

He cringed for at least the millionth time as he thought about the argument he'd had with Skye. Could he have fucked it up more or been a bigger asshole? He didn't see how that was possible. When she almost died, he got scared, and then tried to make his fuckup her responsibility. Tried to make it about her getting the wrong idea and she had called him on it. She had refused to take responsibility for his bullshit and insisted that he own it. And then she told him where he could shove it.

He loved that about her.

It had made sheltering-in-place at LO dreadful. The horde had already taken responsibility for being stuck in the same place as Skye off his shoulders and gobbled it up for its own. It wasn't his fault. He had not chosen it. Might as well enjoy the company. Except the only time he had spent with her was while he was being an asshole. Over a week knowing exactly where she was, and that she never wanted to see him again.

I could sell myself a bridge and fuck it up.

A sound ahead pulled him from his brooding. He heard it again, a soft thud. Even if it was not Skye making the noise, something was. He had to check it out. He padded down the hallway, his pulse thrumming in his temples a little faster. He stopped. Listened. A thud, followed by a grunt, from the last room along the long hallway.

"Fuck me," he said, pulse skyrocketing.

He grasped the smooth leather hilt of the stubby nightstick on his belt, pulling it loose. This will be really useful against a zombie, he thought, cursing himself for leaving his Glock behind with Rocco. He had mentioned the weird recoil that had developed over the last few days, and Rocco had insisted on taking a look while they waited. It was sloppy, the kind that got you killed, but he had handed the gun off without a second thought because he was distracted about Skye. Doug closed in on the heavy metal door and peeked through the diamonds of thin wire that reinforced the glass of the narrow inset window.

His blood ran cold.

Brock had Skye pressed back over a table. Her jacket was on the floor, the layers of her upper clothing gone. Smudges of finger marks were forming on her ribs and splotched her breasts. One of her shoes was missing, and her long, silvery-blond hair tangled around her head like a cumulus cloud. She was bleeding from a cut along her jaw. Brock's hand covered her mouth, the flesh whitening where it pressed against her face.

She struggled, trying to fend off his other hand that worked to unfasten her pants, but feebly, like she was really out of it. The puffy red marks on her temple and face registered, and Doug realized that Brock must have punched her. More brown smudges of developing bruises wreathed Skye's slender neck. If he had punched her and then choked her into unconsciousness, she might just be coming to now. There were scratches on Brock's face, but he outweighed Skye by at least a hundred pounds. If he had gotten the drop on her, she never stood a chance.

It took Doug half a second to process the scene in front of him, the other half to shove on the door.

It stuck.

His mind raced as he banged on the door. He looked down through the glass. A chair had been tipped back against it and jammed under the doorknob. Brock looked up. If he was surprised to see Doug, he did not show it. He released Skye's mouth, grabbed two handfuls of her hair, and banged her head off the table. Then he started working on her pants with both hands.

Skye's head lolled to the side.

Her eyes locked with Doug's.

She started screaming.

Doug did not remember breaking the glass. He shoved his hand against the top of the chair, felt it give way, and turned the lock on the knob. He pulled his arm back through the mangled diamonds of wire and glass and pushed the door aside.

In the time it had taken him to get through the door, Brock had pushed Skye's pants and underwear down around her boots and pulled her to him, her knees spread around his hips. He would have looked comical with his ass hanging out and erection bobbing in front of him if his intent was not so foul.

Doug plowed into him. Until that moment he had known Brock was imposing, but he had not realized just how solid the guy was.

But he had momentum on his side.

And rage.

They hit the floor hard, rolling over one another. The sharp edge of a table leg hit Doug's back across his kidneys. A blast of pain and light exploded around Doug's eye from Brock's fist. Another powerful punch connected with his cheek, bending him back over the table leg. If he did not unpin himself, Brock would beat him to a pulp.

He got his hands behind Brock's head and smacked their fore-heads together. He felt almost stunned, surprised by the stars in front of his eyes. Head-butts never seemed to affect other people like this, but at least he caught Brock off guard. Doug's fist connected with the bottom of Brock's chin. He heard Brock's teeth click when his jaw snapped shut. Doug kneed Brock in the groin, heard his groan of pain. He wriggled out from between Brock and table, blood pound-ing, adrenaline rushing through his veins as he stumbled to his feet.

A hand clamped around his ankle, and his feet shot out from under him. His elbows broke his fall, sending lightning bolts shooting through his fingertips. Doug rolled onto his back. He kicked at Brock's face with his other foot. His boot did not connect very hard, but Brock let go of his ankle.

They both scrabbled to their feet. Absurdly, Doug noticed that Brock had managed to pull up his pants before he charged. His arms wrapped around Doug's midriff. With a spine-rattling impact they rammed into the wall. Doug wrapped his foot behind Brock's foot, just like he had demonstrated for Skye, and lurched forward. They fell to the floor again with a crash.

Brock's elbow connected with Doug's jaw, the force snapping his head back. He brought his own elbow down on the top of Brock's head and rolled away, stumbling to his feet. His fingers closed around the first thing his hand came into contact with—a metal stool. Brock was halfway to standing when Doug slammed it into his face.

A hollow crunch that sounded like a gunshot penetrated the roar of blood in Doug's ears. Blood gushed down Brock's beefy face. Doug slammed the stool into Brock's face again, and again, until Brock fell to his knees. Doug swung the stool in a low arc into the side of Brock's head, and he toppled like a tree. Doug dropped down, strad-dling Brock's chest, and clamped his hands around Brock's corn-fed neck.

All of Doug's rage rushed into his hands. He leaned into them, tightening his grip on Brock's throat, heedless of the blood dripping over them from Brock's broken nose. Brock's face began to redden.

His hands pulled on Doug's wrists like Skye's must have done to his own before. Doug squeezed harder, savage joy rushing through him when he saw fear creep into Brock's eyes.

"Doug, stop! Stop!"

The voice sounded far off but broke through the haze of murderous fury. He looked up into Skye's face.

"Doug, stop! Please! Stop!"

He looked down at Brock, at his hands around his neck. It was almost as if he did not know how they had gotten there, except that he did. He didn't want to let go. He wanted to kill Brock. The asshole deserved it.

But Skye was kneeling beside him crying. Hysterical. Pulling on his arm and begging him to stop.

Skye.

He released Brock's neck. The downed man's chest still rose and fell. Skye knelt nearby, quivering like the papery rustle of a birch tree in the wind. Her terrified eyes hit Doug like a sledge-hammer. He pushed away from Brock and wrapped his arms around her. She pressed her face into his chest, tremors racking her body.

"You're all right, you're safe," he said, holding her tight, rocking her back and forth.

His right arm felt sticky against her back. His brow furrowed when he saw that it was covered in cuts and scratches he did not remember getting. He buried his face in her hair, so silvery-blond that it looked like the silver bark of birch trees, and his rage morphed. Like a chunk of carbon becoming a diamond, it transformed into something that could never be undone, unforgivingly hard but clear and true. It flooded him with a hunger to protect her, never leave her, so deep it would never be sated.

He would do anything for Skye. He knew that now.

When Brock stirred behind them, Doug realized that the battered man had been gasping and hacking for air, had been trying to sit up for some time, but his brain had not registered it as important. He looked over his shoulder. The son of a bitch was in no shape to do much of anything.

Voices and the echo of pounding boots in the hallway. Mario, then Rocco, skidded to a halt in the doorway.

"Holy shit," Mario said, at the same time Rocco said, "Jesus."

Doug took in their alarmed faces. "Get this piece of shit out of here, Mario. Before I change my mind and kill him."

More voices from the hallway, more people in the room. Hushed murmurs and whispers, a coat draped over Skye's shoulders. Someone helped Brock up, righted the stool, brushed the broken glass aside. All Doug cared about was in his arms. The rest was background noise.

His lips brushed Skye's ear when he whispered, "It's all right, you're safe. I've got you."

NINETY MINUTES LATER, Doug walked down the darkened corridor to the room where Skye was spending the night, making as much noise as possible with the least amount of movement. Which was fucking hard when almost every part of your body hurt, but he did not want to startle or surprise her. As bad days went, this one was right up there, but his portion of it was nothing compared to what Skye had been through.

Dim light spilled into the hallway from her open door. At least he would not wake her. Unless she had already fallen asleep and left the light on and he *had* just woken her up, which made him feel like a thoughtless ass. But if she was awake, she might want the company. Or maybe she wanted to be—

Stop it, he said to himself.

His only regret about almost killing Brock was the almost part. Doug could still feel Brock's fleshy neck in his hands, his windpipe under his thumbs. See the fear that had started to creep into Brock's eyes. Feel the blind rage that had blocked out everything but his desire to kill that motherfucker.

He should have finished it.

Doug gave himself a mental shake, banishing the thoughts from his brain. The last thing this mess of a world needed was a homicidal priest. If he even was—

Stop it.

"Skye," he said, pitching his voice so it carried. "You still up?"

"Yeah," she said, sounding breathless.

As Doug neared, he heard short, regulated exhalations. He reached the open door and saw why. She was doing push-ups next to the cot. He resisted the urge to tell her to rest, even though he wanted to.

Push-ups made sense, since it was Skye. She would feel in control, the focus and intensity, even the pain from her injuries, clearing her mind. He leaned against the doorjamb and waited. She did fifty more by his count before rocking back onto her heels in a crouch. Her tank top clung to her body, glued in place by a fine sheen of sweat. Reflected in the lantern's low light, her pale skin looked luminous.

"How many?"

"Two hundred," she said, her voice raspy from being choked.

"Just warming up."

Her wet hair was tied back in a loose bun at the nape of her neck. Her shiner was worse than his. That fucker had stepped into the punch, gotten his weight behind it, unlike the one Doug had taken. The fury percolating just below the veneer of Doug's calm sought a fissure to travel, to push against, so that it could erupt. His hands prickled, needing something to smash. He would murder that—

Stop it.

Skye picked up the worn towel on the cot as she got to her feet, blotting the sweat from her face and neck, wincing when she touched tender spots and the cut on her jaw that had needed stitches. Silence filled the space between them for so long that Doug began to feel uncomfortable.

"How are you feeling?"

She shrugged, wincing when she tried to smile. "I tried stepping in when he grabbed me but..."

It took Doug's brain a moment to catch up and process her words. "Jesus, Skye," he said, dismayed. How could she joke about this?

She sank to the cot, her movements stilted. Absent was the supple grace that always made his breath catch in his throat. She seemed to have folded in on herself, as if to present as small a target as possible.

"Thanks. For before."

Doug gaped at her. "Skye," he finally said. "You don't... I...*anyone* here would have helped you. I...I'm just—"

She looked up at him. Her furrowed brow made her aspect seem almost wistful, except for the anxious, vertical line between her eyebrows. Doug's stomach did a backflip.

"Not anyone would have killed him. And you would have if I hadn't stopped you." She coughed, then cleared her throat, a grimace of pain flitting across her face. "That's how it seemed, anyway."

Doug realized he was shaking. Not from anger, but fear. Fury, rage, the need for vengeance, he craved them like a junkie craves smack because they pushed away the fear. They subsumed it below their imperative to act, and giving in to that impulse would save him from feeling the bone-deep terror of what had happened, had almost happened. And how he had not been there to protect her.

Doug had never felt a helplessness this profound. She was not okay; anyone could see that. He wanted to take her in his arms, rock her back and forth, tell her that she was safe, that it would be all right, for as long as it took her to believe him. But now was not like before, when you did that kind of thing without thinking, on instinct. When no one noticed or cared that you were a priest holding a beautiful woman in your arms or suspected that you never wanted to let her go.

She swallowed hard, holding back tears, the deepening purple-black bruises engulfing her eye and skirting her temple, accentuating just how fragile she was. That angered him, too. Brock had robbed Skye of her confidence, of the strength that Doug knew she still possessed, but she didn't believe it anymore. It was written all over her.

He almost asked her to tell him what she needed, but how would she know? Why should *she* have to tell *him*? He should be able to figure it out, but the wretchedness he floundered in made it impossible.

Or I'm just a fucking coward.

Skye had been as vulnerable as a person can be. Completely at the mercy of Brock's pathetic, violent need to control her, as if she were a thing and not a person. When Doug had held her in his arms, she clung to him as if her life had depended on it. Maybe it had. In that maelstrom of emotion, he knew that he would do anything for her. He had also had time to think about what that meant.

It scared him shitless.

He was afraid of how easy it would be, because Miranda was right. It wasn't the end of the world if he wanted something different for his life. If zombies had not been the end of everything, then the future of Father Doug Michel sure as shit wouldn't be. He was afraid he was failing the people at home who counted on him, but what about Skye? She had captivated his imagination almost from the moment they met. Watching her struggle to keep herself together felt like someone had sawed his sternum in two and was cranking on a rib spreader without bothering to put him under.

She looked up at him as her face crumpled, the shimmer of tears finally overspilling.

"Do something, or leave me alone," she whispered. "Don't just stand there."

Her words challenged him to make up his mind. Of course she did. She didn't have time for bullshit.

"Neither do I," Doug whispered, and the fierce love that had twined around his heart swallowed him whole. The fear and uncertainty that had felt paralyzing just moments ago, irrelevant. If this was out of bounds, pushing him closer to something he was not supposed to want, he was powerless to stop it...and he didn't want to.

Doug went to her, the rightness of his decision growing stronger with every step. Skye curled into him, finally surrendering to the need to get it out. Sobs racked her slender frame. The viselike grip that terror and worry had clamped around Doug's gut began to ease as he folded her into his arms. Tension drained from tendons and ligaments connecting his muscles and bones. He needed the reassurance of her body against his, soft and warm and strong, at least as much as she needed his.

He could not—he *would* not—explain it away anymore. This thing between them, his feelings for her, were real.

He stroked her wet hair, his shirt growing damp where her head rested on his shoulder. The antiseptic scent of the lye soap that she had tried to wash this violation away with still lingered on her skin.

"I'm here, Skye," he whispered. "I'm not going anywhere. I promise."

25

COMMANDER SMITH'S SHOCKED VOICE CRACKLED OVER THE radio. "Is Skye okay?"

Next to Miranda, Mario snorted derisively and muttered under his breath. Rocco scowled, his eyebrows drawing together as he answered.

"He beat the shit out of her, Anna! She's got a concussion for sure, and I wouldn't be surprised if she's got fractured ribs. I'll feel better once River checks her out. If Doug had been a minute later, he would have raped her, so no. She is *not* okay. Her breathing seems normal. I don't think she's got a collapsed lung. She isn't showing signs of internal bleeding, thank God."

Smith didn't respond right away, but voices could be heard murmuring in the background. "Do you know how he got inside?"

Rocco said, "We found an open door on the west side of building. No one is fessing up to leaving it unlocked, but someone did. If I find out who..."

"Where is Brock now?" Smith asked.

"Under lock and key," Rocco said. "But I want to bring him back right away. I'm afraid Doug might—"

Rocco stopped, shooting a quizzical glance at Miranda, a question in his eyes. She nodded yes.

"We need to get him out of here unless we're okay with not guaranteeing his safety," Rocco said.

"Okay, here's the game plan. You're going to take Brock to P-Land."

"No!" Miranda, Mario, and Rocco said at the same time. Rocco looked over to them, as if he appreciated the backup.

"Hear me out," Smith said. "My next radio call will be to P-Land. They will be in the loop by the time you get there. Brock did this on neutral ground. Jurisdiction isn't clear cut."

Miranda grabbed the handset from Rocco. "He beat her up, tried to rape her, and might have killed her. We ought to be taking him out back and putting a bullet in his brain, not worrying about jurisdiction!"

"I understand your frustration, Miranda, but there's a reason there's never been a serious conflict between LO and P-Land. We've always worked together, unlike a lot of places. I am not going to jeopardize that now, no matter how terrible the crime."

Smith's response was calm. Reasonable. And it pissed Miranda off. She felt hot all of a sudden, as if her blood had begun to boil. It must have showed because she felt Mario's hand on her shoulder.

"This is not our first violent crime," Smith's voice continued. "Brock will be punished. Of that I can absolutely assure you."

Rocco held his hand out for the handset. Miranda gave it to him. She turned back to Mario, whose offered hand felt comforting as it closed around hers.

"Are you sure about this, Commander?" Rocco asked.

"It's not just the politics. The sound defenses are working, thank God, but problems equalizing the levels have cropped up in the last few hours. We were just about to radio you to stay put when you called us."

"How long to fix it?" Rocco asked.

"Not sure," Smith answered. "It's not staying in the same place, so we don't know which Station will be affected, or for how long. We still have a baseline, but the fluctuations are making presence over here hard to predict. Density is still higher than we're used to dealing with because of that horde. P-Land is not having these kinds of problems. It's the safer place to take him right now—for all of *you*. If Brock was killed, I wouldn't give a shit. And that is *not* a nudge and a wink, just so we're clear."

Rocco sighed even as he nodded his head. "Okay, Commander. I'm going to wait for confirmation that you've contacted P-Land before setting out."

"Give me thirty minutes," Smith said. "Over and out."

Rocco put the handset in its cradle.

"This is bullshit," Miranda said, wiping tears from her eyes. Anger ricocheted inside her, gaining momentum, made worse by the fact that she could not stop crying. Every time she thought she had it under control, her tear ducts made it abundantly clear that she did not.

"I don't like it either," Rocco said. "But she's right. That piece of shit is not worth a shooting war with P-Land. As much as I like to make fun of them, when they need to bust out the big guns, they do."

"Do you need me to come with you?" Mario said.

Miranda stiffened. With all of the commotion, they had not had a chance to talk. Mario had only gotten out of the lab ten minutes before Doug discovered Skye and beat Brock half to death. The intervening time had been consumed with the fallout.

"No, you stay here," Rocco said.

"But I thought you said that the horde messed up the security detail rotation and we're short-handed. I can go with you and not make it worse."

Rocco shook his head. "You've got important work to do. I'll go on my own."

"Alicia is here to keep our experiments on track," Mario added. "And I need a break, anyway."

Even though Miranda wanted to talk to Mario, it wasn't worth

Rocco putting himself in danger. "If you go alone and he manages to escape, do you really want to deal with Doug when he finds out?"

"He really fucked Brock up," Rocco said, approval in his voice. "Never would have thought a skinny guy could do that."

"You are not the first person who has underestimated him," Mario said.

"And it was Skye," Miranda murmured.

Mario and Rocco traded a glance. Mario then studied his fingernails, while Rocco shook his head. They both knew what she meant, but none of them—Miranda included—wanted to be the one who said it.

Rocco sighed. "If you're up for it, Mario, I'd appreciate the help. It would be nice to not leave it so thin on the ground here."

"I'll be here! I know how to shoot a gun and do a watch," Miranda said.

"I know you do, Tucci. I already included you in the headcount, and it's still thin on the ground here." Rocco looked to Mario, grinning, as he pulled Miranda to him. He wrapped his arm around her neck as if he was about to rub his knuckles on her head. "I love this one. When she's old, she'll have Italian Alzheimer's, just like me."

"Which is?" Mario asked.

"When you forget everything but the grudges," Rocco answered.

They all laughed, perhaps more than the joke warranted, but it was nice to get a break in the god-awful tension.

"And," Rocco said. "Skye might want a woman to talk to."

Miranda groaned. "Rocco, you are the most chauvinist gay man I know."

"What can I say? The old school is strong with the Giorginis." He directed his next words to Mario. "I'm guessing we'll head out in thirty minutes or so."

After he had left, Mario asked, "You okay?"

Miranda sighed. She was pregnant, almost two weeks delayed in telling Mario and arranging the abortion, and now he was going to be gone again, perhaps overnight. This was not a conversation she could cram into the half hour before he left for P-Land.

"Yeah. I'm fine. What a fucking day. And who left that door unlocked?"

They left the radio room and walked down the balcony hallway. Voices echoed up from the lobby. At the top of the stairs, Mario stopped.

"Hey, what did you want to talk to me about?"

He looked tired after the long hours in the lab, but his face lit up when he smiled at her. His dark-brown eyes held so much warmth they glowed. She found herself wondering whose eyes this not-to-be baby would have had. His square chin or her pointy one? His dark coloring or her pale Northern Italian redhead? His deep intensity of purpose? Her temper? Not that she would wish her temper on anyone.

I hate this world, she thought, despair threatening to suck her below its murky surface. She hated its stark choices and unrelenting demands. Its hair's breadth margin for error and its raw brutality. She hated it for what it was, but even more for what it prevented. For the dreams it killed.

"You'll be back tomorrow at the latest," she said. "It can keep another day."

"Are you sure?"

As if on cue, Rocco shouted from below. "Yo, James! We're heading out in ten!"

"I'm sure," she said. "Though I have to stop myself from looking around to see who this James guy is. I hear he's quite a dish."

Mario's smile softened, and her heart unexpectedly opened wide to all of the beauty the world still offered, despite all the suffering. A swell of protectiveness for the unwanted creature growing inside her caught her by surprise, and suddenly another twelve hours seemed too soon. She didn't want to tell him, didn't want to make it more real. Didn't want to let this world snatch one more thing away from her, even though she knew in her bones that having an abortion was the right—the only—thing she could do.

Mario's lips found hers, the kiss slow and unhurried, yet one that left her breathless. He pulled her into his arms.

"I love you, Miranda. Please don't run off with James. He's not all that."

The burble of laughter his teasing prompted helped her fend off more tears.

"I'll try and keep my hands off him for now," she said. "But I'm not making any promises."

MIRANDA YAWNED SO WIDE she thought her jaw would dislocate. She checked her watch: half past midnight. Time was she could pull a watch shift until five in the morning no problem. But that time was before her body had been hijacked by a biological process that held her in its thrall like an energy vampire's familiar.

A reflection in the glass of the main door caught her eye. She turned around to see Doug entering the lobby from the hallway below the main staircase. His shoulders drooped, and he limped, favoring his left knee. Even from thirty feet, she could see the split, swollen knuckles of his right hand. The black eye that had been bad a few hours ago was positively spectacular now, running from above his left eyebrow almost to his jaw. When he saw her, he started to offer a wan smile but winced and stopped.

"You literally look like something the cat dragged in," she said when he reached her.

"I feel like it, too."

"How's she doing?"

He sighed, and his face grew pensive. "I don't know... She had a good cry, which seemed to help a bit. Delilah stopped by, which definitely raised her spirits. She's still there, snuggled up with Skye. We both fell asleep, but I woke up 'cause I needed to take a leak. She's so," he stopped, seeming unable to find the right words.

Miranda nodded, unsure of the right thing to say.

"She's so beat up," he said, practically spitting, each word filled with more anger than the last. "The bruises on her neck have gotten so much worse. When I think of what that asshole—"

Eyes flashing, Doug stopped speaking abruptly. He exhaled loudly, relaxed his hands that had balled into fists, and took another deep breath.

"That's why I came out," he continued more evenly. "To get more ibuprofen. I thought there was some in her room, but I couldn't find it. I don't want to wake her up unless I have it to give to her."

Miranda nodded. "How are you?"

The pain that filled Doug's face set the waterworks off. Miranda wiped the tears away quickly. Doug smiled the tiniest bit, despite the pain she could see it caused him, and tousled her short hair.

"Throw in a volcano's worth of anger, and that's exactly how I feel," he said.

Outside, the macaques began to shriek.

"What are they squawking about?" Doug said, cupping his hands on the glass door to see outside.

Miranda nudged Doug out of the way and pulled the door open. She stepped outside, her hand on the hilt of her machete. Doug followed. The volume of the combined troops of macaques grew more agitated.

"Something's got them riled up," she said.

Behind them, the door opened. Miranda turned to see Rich standing in the doorway.

"What's going on?" he asked, yawning as he pulled his jacket on.

"Don't know yet," Miranda said. "Doug and I will check it out."

"Give me a few minutes to get someone else on these doors, and I'll join you," Rich said, heading back inside.

Doug looked at Miranda like he was trying to decide if she had lost her mind and glanced down at her stomach. "Are you sure? With your, you know."

"For Pete's fucking sake, Doug," she said. "If there were zombies coming right at us, you'd never say that. Come on."

"Rich wants us to wait for him."

Miranda ignored him and pulled her machete. After a few feet, Doug fell in step beside her.

"They're louder that way," she said, halfway between the main entrance and the parking lot, uneasiness creeping through her as she pointed to the brig lab, where Jeremiah was held.

They changed direction, Doug flanking the corner of brig lab on the left while Miranda walked farther out on his right. She pulled ahead, now able to get a clear sight line around the building's corner from her slightly better vantage point. In the bright moonlight, nothing looked amiss, except she couldn't see the person on watch.

Who's on the door, she thought, unable to recall the watch schedule.

"It's Miranda and Doug," she called, still not able to see anyone. She doubted he could hear her over the shrieking macaques. It was weird that he had not stepped forward to investigate the racket himself.

She walked faster, closing the distance between herself and Doug, who had also turned the building's corner. The macaques' shrill shrieks echoed off the nearby buildings. Underneath the noise of the monkeys, hers and Doug's deliberate footsteps squelched on the waterlogged ground. Five feet from the door, as he crept along in the shadow of the building cast by the moon, Doug tripped and fell.

"Fuck," Doug said.

Closer now, Miranda could see a body tangled in Doug's feet. He extracted himself and reached for the guard's neck, looking for a pulse. Miranda heard him swear again. Doug straightened, wiping his hand on his shirt.

"It's Axel. His throat's cut."

Adrenaline flooded Miranda's bloodstream—a human adversary

was loose on the Institute grounds. Axel was big and strong and sharp. Or had been, she amended to herself, looking at his body. She held up a hand to indicate that Doug should wait, then swapped her machete for her handgun. Doug did the same. If they were going to knife fight, they might as well be overprepared.

Doug peeked through the inset window in the building's door, then tried the handle. He stepped back into the shadow of the building and crouched beside Axel's body. Miranda heard a soft jangling of keys.

"What are you doing?"

"This door is open, but the other isn't." He stood up, keys in hand. "Wait here, count to thirty. I'll go around to the entrance on the other side. Either I'll click my flashlight, and we'll enter together, or you go in when you hit the count."

"Okay," Miranda said, nodding. "Be careful."

Doug slipped away. Miranda stepped to the door so that she could see through the window and began to count. The main corridor stretched from one end of the building to the other, so seeing Doug's signal would not be a problem. The noise from the macaques faded to the occasional chitter as they settled down again to concern themselves with sleeping. At twenty-six, she saw a pinpoint red flash, three times, at the far end of the building's main corridor. Miranda pulled the door open and stepped inside. She saw the flicker of movement as Doug did the same.

She hugged the wall, her pace quick and steady, stopping only to check the doors along the way. So far all of them had been locked, as they should be.

The lab where Jeremiah's cell had been installed had a door at either end of the long room. The lab was situated mostly on the side of the building by Miranda, so she reached the door she would use to enter the lab before Doug would reach his. Whatever was going on, it had to be Jeremiah. He was the only thing in this building worth killing for.

Between the two doors into the lab the lower half of the wall was solid, the upper windows. Doug's end of the room was dark. A low light was on at this end of the room, which on its face was not cause for alarm. The guard needed a light.

Miranda slowed as she approached the door. Jeremiah's cell was in the section of the lab before this door. She ducked past the door to the edge of the first window, crouching as she turned around to peer inside.

"Goddammit," she whispered.

The door to Jeremiah's darkened cell stood ajar. She could see the silhouette of a woman standing beside the table and chairs used by the guards. The area was half lit since only one of the overhead fluorescent lights was turned on, but not at full brightness. A machete and two guns, a handgun and a rifle, lay on the table.

The woman stepped into the light, holding a coat. Her curly, dark hair was tucked behind her ears.

Courtney.

Then a figure near the open cell straightened up.

Jeremiah.

Even unable to see him clearly where he stood in the gloom, the upright posture, the relaxed authority that radiated from the man still in the shadows... It could not be anyone else. He stepped into the light. The sharp cheekbones in the thin face, the rapacious gleam of his golden eyes.

"Mother*fucker*," Miranda whispered.

Jeremiah took the jacket from Courtney's outstretched hand. He stepped in, stroking her cheek with his other hand. He whispered in her ear, then kissed her. When he broke the kiss, the young woman's face was alight, adoring.

A sudden need to throw up made Miranda's stomach heave. Her flesh began to crawl. Son of a motherfucking asshole, she thought. She stood up, yanked the door open, and raised her gun.

Jeremiah and Courtney jumped.

"Don't even try it, Courtney," Miranda said as Courtney reached for her gun. "I will blow your fucking head off if your hand moves another inch."

Courtney froze. The door at the other end of the room opened. Jeremiah and Courtney both looked to see who had entered. Miranda kept her eyes on Jeremiah and his no doubt masterfully manipulated accomplice.

"Huh," Doug said, walking past the lab tables toward them. He had crossed to the far side of the room to box them in between himself and Miranda. "Step away from her, Jeremiah. Now."

Jeremiah looked at Miranda, a crafty smile playing across his mouth. "Did you truly believe you could thwart the Will of the God All-Father on Earth, Sister Miranda?" he crooned.

"You are not the hypnotic *Jungle Book* snake, and I am not your sister," Miranda growled. "Step away from her right now, or Doug might shoot you. He's had a really shitty day."

Jeremiah's eyes narrowed. "You will not shoot Us. You need Us."

Miranda jumped at the boom from Doug's Glock. A spray of concrete chips exploded from the wall in the cell behind Jeremiah and Courtney.

"We can store your blood properly now, Jeremiah. Move the fuck away from her, into your cell."

Jeremiah backed up. From the corridor, Miranda heard voices. The calvary had arrived.

Miranda glanced quickly at Doug, shocked that he had fired at them, even if his intent had been only to scare. It was the kind of thing she might have done, but not Doug, even if he threatened to.

"Dude, chill the fuck out."

"Was Brock part of this?" Doug asked. "Or just a useful diversion?"

"The God All-Father told me that I would receive a sign, that I would know it when it manifested," Courtney answered.

"Christ," Miranda muttered. Of course. "You silly girl... Jeremiah's big into the hocus pocus part of being a delusional zealot."

Miranda walked over to Courtney. She tucked the handgun on

the table into her coat pocket. She couldn't hold the rifle securely and check for weapons, and she did not trust Doug with it right now. Instead, she shoved the table away a few feet, then relieved the young woman of her handgun, machete, and knife. She frisked Courtney's upper body, then moved to her legs. She had just reached Courtney's knees when the door behind her opened.

And then she was on her ass. Courtney lunged for the rifle, still on the table, knocking Miranda over in the process. She grabbed Courtney's leg with her right hand and yanked. Instead of pulling the young woman down, she got a wobble. Miranda grabbed again with both hands, and Courtney toppled. Pain blossomed across Miranda's face when Courtney's boot kicked back as she fell, connecting with her cheek. Miranda heard Doug shouting for the new arrivals to cover the door, and for someone to get outside and cover the windows.

She had to get Courtney under control so she could help catch Jeremiah. He had darted out of his cell, crouching low behind the lab tables near the windows. Miranda vaulted herself up to lay on top of Courtney. The young woman thrashed below her, screaming.

The room plunged into darkness.

"Keep the doors covered," Doug shouted.

What the fuck, Miranda thought. Had Jeremiah recruited more people than just Courtney?

She got her knee in the center of Courtney's back and cranked an arm back. Courtney screeched in pain.

"Help me All-Father," she cried, shrieking like a banshee.

All around them, the noise seemed to amplify. Miranda dragged Courtney up.

"I've got Courtney," she said.

The lights came back on—all of the lights. Miranda blinked, momentarily blinded.

"Miranda, watch out!"

Jeremiah leaped for her. Under cover of the dark, he had crept over, almost beside her.

Miranda shoved Courtney at him, but he sidestepped. Kept coming.

"Hold your fire," someone shouted.

Jeremiah collided with Miranda, knocking her back. Then her neck was constricted by his arm wrapped around it. People rushed toward them. She stomped on Jeremiah's foot and heard him cry out. When his grip loosened, she twisted to face him. She shoved the heel of her hand, thumb down, against his face. It slipped into his mouth.

"Fuck!" Miranda shrieked.

Jeremiah's teeth chomped into the flesh of her hand. She let go of him and jerked her hand away, stumbling backward. The melee of hand and arms—reaching for her, for Jeremiah—seemed to come from all sides. Courtney rushed into the empty space Miranda's retreat created.

"No! Let him go," Courtney cried, reaching for Jeremiah.

Jeremiah thrashed like a cornered bear. Courtney tried to cradle his face between her hands, but in his frenzy, he did not seem to recognize her. He bit her hand, too. She screamed and was pulled away. Then Doug arrived, his Glock a blur that connected with Jeremiah's head, and the commotion stopped.

The guards dragged Jeremiah into his cell. Rich had arrived from the main building.

"What the hell?" he said, taking in the melee's aftermath. Then he started barking orders.

Miranda held her bleeding hand in the other. "Now he's a freaking cannibal?"

Doug held out a bandana to her. She took it gratefully, wrapping it around her hand.

"I wouldn't be surprised," Doug said. "You okay, Miri?"

Miranda nodded. "I'm fine."

26

"I can't believe the asshole bit me."

The lobby of the main Institute building bustled with activity while Miranda sat, arm outstretched. Alicia had already washed the cuts on the outer edge of her hand twice. Now she swabbed them with iodine. Miranda flinched when the oversized Q-tip touched one of the deeper cuts.

"Sorry," Alicia said. "At least he didn't get your pinky like Courtney and break your finger."

"A broken finger isn't punishment enough for that bitch."

All told, it could have been worse. No one else had been killed. Fucking Jeremiah, she thought. She realized her other hand rested just below her belly button and snatched it away.

Alicia set down the iodine and wound bandages around Miranda's hand.

"Unless River says otherwise, change the bandages twice a day and keep it clean and dry. We'll get you some antibiotics. You'll be good as new in no time."

"Do I need to worry about tetanus or anything like that?"

Alicia shrugged. "I don't think so, but you should ask River. I need to patch up Courtney."

Miranda snorted. *Patch up Courtney, my ass.* She checked her watch—three in the morning. Because of her injury, everyone had insisted she skip the rest of her watch and go to bed. Now that the adrenaline rush had subsided, she was so tired that she had not argued. All she had to do now was stand up. She wasn't sure she had the energy.

"You okay, Miranda?"

Skye sat down in the chair opposite her. A flash of pain flitted across Skye's ethereally beautiful, but now badly battered, face.

"Better than you, I'm afraid. I don't think I've ever seen a black eye that bad."

Skye had looked bad when Miranda last saw her an hour after the attack, but now... Doug had not been exaggerating about how much worse the bruises and swelling had gotten since then.

"You taking pain meds?" she asked.

Skye nodded. "I was out cold until the gunshot woke me."

Miranda thought again about Doug taking a shot at Jeremiah and Courtney to scare them into compliance. He had not meant to hit them. If he had, one of them would be dead.

"That was out of character for Doug," Miranda said. "He's been having a...rage problem. Speak of the devil."

Skye twisted in her seat. Doug trotted down the lobby staircase, looking as falling-flat-on-his-face tired as Miranda felt.

"I thought you were going to bed. Both of you." He stood behind the chair between Miranda and Skye at the square table.

Miranda said, "I'm just trying to summon the energy to stand."

"You can do it, Coppertop. I know you can."

"Where did you put Courtney?" Skye asked. "Where Jeremiah was when you first got here?"

Doug pulled out the chair and sat down. "Yep. She's in the dungeon. Now we just need to figure out how that happened."

Miranda didn't want to talk about how Jere-fucking-miah had

manipulated the stupid young woman and spread his contagion. She gripped the table and dragged herself to her feet. Her body felt like it was made of lead.

"I'm going to bed."

"Me too," Skye said.

Doug's hand slipped under Skye's elbow as she stood. He was not fussing over her, not exactly, but the way he attended to her made it seem like he was.

"I'll walk you back," he said.

"Stay till I fall asleep?" Skye asked.

Doug nodded, and she gave him the tiniest of smiles, the affection of Doug's gaze reflected back to him. There was a lightness between them, a familiarity in the way they stood close to one another, just inside the other's bubble of personal space. But not accidentally on purpose, where they pretended not to notice, like she had seen before. A blind person could see that they were acutely aware of one another, that a longing to touch simmered just below the surface. Even if they weren't ready to act on it yet, whatever was going on between them was out of the box.

"Did you take anything for that, Miri?" Doug asked. "It must hurt like hell."

Miranda looked down at her hand, safely ensconced in strips of clean, white cotton. Alicia had done a good job wrapping the bandages.

"Don't worry about me. I'll live."

"Sleep tight, then," Doug said.

MIRANDA SQUINTED and covered her eyes. The sun was too bright. Blinding. Then it wasn't. She looked up, up, up, until her head could not tip back any more. A perfect circle of blue sky. But she was in the dark, the circle of sky far above her.

She stretched her arms. Her fingers touched cool, wet stone. All around her she heard the sounds of water dripping from the cool rocks, plopping into puddles at her feet. She lifted her face, droplets splashing against it. They felt like kisses, soft and cool.

"I'm at the bottom of a well."

It was dark, except for the circle of sky above. She looked down at her feet. They had plunged into icy water, so cold it hurt. She tried to pull them out, but there was nowhere to put them. She ran her hands along the smooth sides of the well. No cracks nor mortared indentations she could grip. Just dripping stone, smooth and slippy.

"I can't climb this."

The circle of sky was so far away. The freezing water climbed up her shins, but the cool drops on her face still felt lovely.

Miranda!

She turned around, but there was no one with her at the bottom of the well. *Nowhere* for another person to be. Only room enough for she.

To be, for she. She smiled because it rhymed.

Miranda!

She looked up at the circle of blue sky, so perfectly round. The voice came from up there, from the sky. Maybe it's God, she thought. But she knew that it wasn't... God didn't sound like this voice. This familiar voice. But it was nice to think it was, especially now that the frigid water was above her knees.

She would never get out.

She was going to drown.

"Miranda!"

Miranda struggled to open her eyes, but the pain in her head split her skull. Phantom hands touched her shoulders and back, the back of her knees.

"She's coming to! Miri, can you hear me?"

The voice from the circle of blue sky. It wasn't God. She started to sob, swaddled tight in despair. God was supposed to be everywhere, but the voice wasn't God. And the light was so bright she couldn't open her eyes. Her legs almost felt like they weren't there.

An earthquake of pain rumbled through her body.

"Ohhhh," she whimpered, waking up, leaving the well behind in the dreamscape.

"I'm sorry, Miri. Hang on, just hang on."

She knew that voice.

"Doug?" She gasped, knives slicing her throat. "It hurts."

Not just the knives in her throat, but everything. Every part of her. She almost felt like she was flying, moving through the air, but it had a rhythm that pounded with pain. She jerked at the loud bang, then the softer one after. The pounding, flying rhythm sped up, setting her nerves on fire. She forced her eyes open long enough to see Doug's anxious face. Then her eyes slammed shut.

"I know it hurts, Miri," he said. "Stay with me, okay?"

Another voice, far away. "The ice bath—"

Then cold surrounded her, sucked her down.

"DOUG."

Doug jerked awake. Miranda's eyes were open. Relief rushed through him that she was still alive.

"Hey, Coppertop."

She tried to speak, but no words came. She smacked her chapped lips, then tried again.

"Can I have some water?"

Doug picked up the glass on the table beside Miranda's bed. Sweat ran off her body like she was being sprinkled by a hose. It soaked the sheets and mattress, saturating the room with a sour smell.

Doug saw her try to reach for the glass, but the restraint stopped her arm, rattling the tubes of her IV.

"Ow," she whispered.

Doug crouched close, cradling the back of her damp, fiery scalp with his hand, and lifted the glass to her mouth. She took tiny sips, then lay back, looking depleted from the effort. She glanced down at the leather restraints fastened around her wrists.

"That bad, huh?"

Doug couldn't answer. When Miranda wasn't writhing in her bed, mumbling incoherently, she was so still that a few times he thought she had quit breathing. He had laid his hand to her sternum to find its shallow rise and fall continued, but the icy coolness or inferno hot skin leached his relief away.

"He infected me."

Doug shut his eyes, steeling himself, trying to work up his nerve. When he opened them again, he said, "Yeah. He did."

Miranda took a wheezy breath. "How?"

"We don't know. Different strain, or a mutation. You're vaccinated. It shouldn't be possible."

"Would have been nice to know he could do that."

Anger welled up in Doug's chest, pushing up his throat, so bitter it tasted sharp and metallic on his tongue.

"Yeah. That would have been helpful," he said, almost whispering. He hated how defeated he sounded, but for the first time in his life, he could not dredge up a scrap of optimism.

"Mario will be here soon," he continued when she didn't speak.

"Good." A tremor, tiny but insistent, made her body quake. "I'm cold."

Doug reached for the blanket at her feet and tucked it around her. She seemed frail, even though she had only been ill a few hours. Her skin was beginning to look mottled, white and gray, like marble.

"I hurt," she said. "Everything hurts."

She sounded so helpless. Doug felt tears run down his face. He swiped them away before she could see.

"River can't give you anything more or you'll stop breathing."

The spark that usually filled her cornflower-blue eyes was gone. Her gaze looked vacant.

"Don't cry."

"I'm not—" he started to say, but realized he was. "I'm not crying. You're crying."

She laughed, then coughed. It started high and papery, but devolved into a deep, rattling hack.

"Jesus," she said, breathless, when the coughing fit finally subsided. "I'm on my deathbed, and you're teasing me."

Doug clamped his mouth shut tight, but not before a whimper snuck out. His heart contracted, pushing in on itself.

"Don't say that, Miranda. Please don't say that."

She closed her eyes again. "Don't let me turn."

"Miranda," he pleaded, desperate, trying to deny the evidence of his eyes. "Don't give up. You have to fight. We don't know—"

"Promise me. Don't let me turn. And don't let Mario try to do it."

There was iron in her voice, under the rancid-sweet scent of decay. They had promised one another years ago, when they had gained a measure of cavalier swagger that only the young are foolish enough to indulge in. When they had viewed death in the abstract. She opened her eyes and looked at him, some of the vacancy gone from her gaze.

He nodded. Barely. His hair fell into his face, but he didn't push it away like he normally did. His tears fell thick and fast, spattering his shirt.

"Do you love Skye?"

He looked up at her. In just the past minute, the dark smudges under her eyes had become darker, her skin paler. Doug could feel Death circling the bed. It was so like her to press this advantage. She might be gone within the hour, everything that made Miri Miri subsumed by a virus that didn't care how much devastation it wrought, but she was still in there.

"I do. And you have no shame asking me now."

She looked triumphant for a second. "I *knew* it."

He couldn't help himself and smiled. "I thought saying 'I told you so' is bad form."

She coughed again, not as bad as before. The fingers of her hand began to flutter. He took them in his, shocked at their papery dryness.

"Don't waste time like I did."

"Okay," he said. "I won't."

"I'm scared," she said, voice trembling. "Is there really a God waiting for us?"

"Yes, there is," he said, conviction filling his voice. He might be a failure as a priest, but watching Miranda's tenuous hold on life and the pureness of her spirit that shone despite it made his faith stronger than ever. "And He loves you, but it's too soon. Please, Miri, don't give up."

Tears began to slip from the corners of her eyes.

"Is Courtney okay?"

Dread blossomed in Doug's belly. Courtney had turned within an hour of being bitten. It hadn't happened to Miranda yet, but it would. She got sicker and sicker with every passing minute, but he needed her to fight. He would keep his promise, but he wasn't ready to face life without her. Not yet.

"Courtney didn't get sick, Miri. That's how I know you'll be fine."

THE LIGHT WAS SO low that Mario was afraid he'd miss it if Miranda opened her eyes, but she had cried that it stabbed them before when the lights were brighter. Not cried, but whimpered. She'd been too weak to cry.

Wispy breaths rasped in and out of her chest, shallow, scraping. Her skin was cold, and her teeth had chattered almost nonstop until a short time ago. He'd spent six days at her bedside, unable to do anything but watch her get worse. He knew it wouldn't be long now.

And he couldn't believe it.

"Sam?"

Her voice startled him. She asked for her boyfriend when the zombies first appeared. Sam had sacrificed himself to save Miranda.

Mario would do anything, make any bargain, if it let him do what Sam had done. But he couldn't. All he could do was watch her die.

"It's Mario, sweetheart. I'm here."

"Oh," she whispered. "Right. What...happened?"

Her cheek felt like a slab of meat, chilling his hand. Mario tried to bite back the tears as he stroked her hair from her forehead.

"You got sick, Miri." His throat grew tight. He tried to will the tears away. If this was all the time he had left with her, all he wanted her to see, to feel, was how much he loved her. "You got sick after Jeremiah bit you."

"Oh," she whispered, the word drawn out as if she was drunk. "I don't...remember."

She closed her eyes, exhausted from the effort it took to talk.

"You have to fight, Miranda. Do you hear me? *You have to fight.* Fight for me, okay? I love you so much. And I need you. I need you here, with me. You have to fight to stay with me."

"I'm tired," she whimpered.

Anger tangled Mario in its web. He wanted to shake her, to shout at her to try, to fight. To stay alive. He wanted—

Hoarse sobs racked his chest, like an attacker hitting him from behind, where he couldn't see it coming. It couldn't end like this, not now.

"Don't cry," she whispered.

"I love you, Miri, so much," he said, trying and failing to choke the grief back. "Please don't give up. You have to fight."

Her eyes were flitting around the room, as if she could see something he couldn't.

"The baby..."

Grief pierced Mario's heart, flaying him open, while she rambled about a baby that didn't exist.

"There's no baby, honey," he said. "Just you and me."

In the dim room, her eyes looked as gray as her skin. She fought to keep them open but was losing.

"There is."

27

"HEY, BEAUTIFUL," MARIO WHISPERED.

Miranda squinted up at him. She frowned and swallowed, then ran her tongue over her teeth.

"I don't feel beautiful."

Mario laughed out loud. The lightness in his chest made him feel like he was floating. The ache from grinding his teeth had been supplanted by sore muscles because he couldn't stop smiling. And he leaned into that ache as hard as he could, into the kinesthetic promise that Miranda was okay. That she had lived.

"I'm tired," she said.

"You've been on death's door for almost two weeks. You're gonna be tired."

"Two weeks?" She clapped her hand over her mouth. "Get me a toothbrush *right now*."

Unruly tears pricked the corners of Mario's eyes. She wanted a toothbrush. He almost sobbed with relief.

"I'll get right on that."

A few minutes later, her teeth were brushed. She lay back on the pillow, wiped out by the small task. But she was tired because she was alive. He knew he should get River so that she could examine Miranda when she could answer questions, but he didn't want to leave her. He was too afraid that if he did, he would return to a waking nightmare like the last time, when he should have stayed close. When he should have put himself between her and whatever the danger might be, not taken for granted that she would be there when he returned. When she had said that what she needed to talk to him about—that she was pregnant—could wait.

He should have been here.

He sat on the edge of the bed, her hand in his. It was warm again, not the clammy chill that had filled him with dread.

"You scared the shit out of me," he said, throat suddenly tight. Tears filled his eyes and overspilled. He swiped at his face, embarrassed that he could not keep it together. He didn't want to worry her when all of her energy should be spent getting well.

"Hey," she said. She cupped his cheek with her hand. "Don't cry. It's all right."

He looked away, trying to compose himself. From the corner of his eye, Mario saw Doug arrive in the open doorway behind them.

"He's either crying or wearing a shit-eating grin," Doug said. "Get used to it, Miri. You're in love with a two-trick pony."

She laughed, then sucked her breath in with a hiss. Terror crushed Mario in its fist.

"What's wrong?" he said, his chest constricting, stomach collapsing.

"I'll get River," Doug said, his worried voice receding as he dashed out of sight.

"It's okay, I'm okay," she said hurriedly. "Just achy."

Mario reached out to stroke her cheek, so afraid that she would turn out to be a mirage. But touching her, this solid, real, warm Miranda, made the fear leach away. He had never seen her so frail. So helpless. He wasn't sure what to do with this version of her. She looked so fragile. He was afraid he might break her.

"Are you sure?" he asked.

She nodded. The love he saw in her eyes calmed him.

"I'm sure," she said. "And Doug's getting River." She looked down for a second, then raised her eyes to his, looking uncertain. Slowly, she said, "I'm pregnant. Or I was."

Mario blinked, surprised. He had not expected her to bring it up almost as soon as she woke up. But Miranda always jumped in the deep end. He ought to know that by now.

"I know."

Her eyes widened. "How?"

"You said something to me. I thought you were delirious, but when I told Doug, he—"

"He let the cat out of the bag," she said, sounding halfway between annoyed and relieved.

Mario smiled. "You let the cat out of the bag. Doug just picked up the kitten."

She smiled, but her face was pensive. "Am I still, or did this..."

"You are," he said swiftly, wanting to reassure her.

But maybe the fact that she was still pregnant wasn't reassuring. Wasn't what she wanted. Was that a flash of panic in her eyes? He couldn't be sure. It had blinked out too quickly.

They looked at one another.

"Did River say anything?" she asked, her voice trailing.

Mario felt like he was balancing on a tightrope. In high wind. While holding a huge sail. He didn't know what she wanted to do, but based on past conversations, he had a pretty good idea.

"As far as she can tell everything's—" He searched for something neutral. "On track?"

Miranda absorbed the information, such as it was. Her face began to fill with trepidation.

"Do you know what you want to do?" he asked. "You don't have to keep it. You know that, right?"

This was never supposed to happen. Having a child together had never even been on the table. When they knew Miranda would live, he'd finally had the emotional and mental space to think about it.

Once he had gotten over the shock, the ferocity with which he wanted her to continue the pregnancy had astonished him. But Miranda had to want it. It was her decision to make, in the end, no matter how much it might disappoint him.

Her words tumbled out in a flurry. "I want to keep it."

She sounded like she was confessing to a murder, not telling him that she wanted his baby. *His baby.* His and Miri's *baby.* A head rush of relief slammed into Mario's brain. He felt lightheaded, giddy. The world receded behind a haze of light and static, completely apart from the two of them and the tiny tadpole of a baby growing inside her.

She sounded embarrassed when she said, "It makes me the world's biggest hypocrite—"

He kissed her, falling into the cottony softness of her lips against his, the sweet taste of mint, and this wonderful detour that they had not seen coming. When they parted, Mario felt dizzy. He touched his forehead to hers. The tenderness in his heart swelled until it ached.

The dark circles under her eyes could not compete with the way Miranda smiled, glowed, luminesced.

"That's a yes?"

"That's a yes," he said, laughing. "I'd do whatever you want, Miranda, whatever that is. I'm so happy it's this."

If it was possible, and apparently it was, her smile grew even brighter. And then it faded. She pulled away and bit her lip, abruptly apprehensive. Her voice was barely a whisper.

"What about me being sick?"

In the endless hours of helpless waiting, of not knowing if she would live or die, never mind what she wanted to do about a pregnancy neither one of them saw coming, Mario had asked himself the same question. But only once. As she teetered on the edge of life and death, the possibility had been too theoretical to entertain. And when it became clear she would survive, too frightening to think about.

River had said everything was progressing normally despite her illness. All he could think to say was, "We'll figure it out."

"Okay," she said. Relief radiated from her in waves. "Okay. I can do that."

Reassurance was all she had needed. He could give her that. And his love, which was already hers. It hit him again, how fundamentally their lives had changed, and would keep on changing.

He said, incredulous, "We're going to have a baby, Miranda."

"Yeah," she said. "It's pretty fucking weird, isn't it?"

MIRANDA COULD FEEL her eyes drooping, even though she was enjoying her visit with Doug.

"I'm gonna go, Miri. You're falling asleep," he said.

"I'm sorry," she said through a yawn. "Come see me again later, okay?"

Doug smiled and gave Delilah a pat. "Of course, Coppertop. Get better so I can harass you. You almost dying has deprived me of my favorite pastime."

He glanced to the door as he stood. His brow furrowed, concern replacing the indulgent affection he had directed at her.

Miranda followed his line of sight. Skye stood in the doorway. The chalky color of shock, as if she had just seen a ghost, was amplified by the purple and blue bruises on her face and neck. They had finally reached the full bloom of worsening before they would get better.

"What's wrong?" Doug asked.

Miranda's alarm grew as Skye looked from Doug to her, her face a mixture of fear and apprehension.

"I'm sorry, I didn't think," she said haltingly. "I didn't—"

Skye looked desperate, like the world was collapsing around her. She said to Doug, "Can I talk to you later?"

"We can talk now. I was just leaving."

Skye's face showed how much she wanted to take him up on his offer, but she shook her head. "I don't want to interrupt—"

"He really was leaving," Miranda said. She squeezed Doug's hand to get his attention. "Go. I'll see you later."

Doug nodded, giving her a distracted smile, and walked to Skye. Tears shimmered in her eyes by the time Doug reached her. As they stepped into the hallway, he asked, "What is it? What's wrong?"

She couldn't hear Skye's reply, just a low, distressed murmur.

Delilah followed them as far as the door, whimpering. Then she turned back and hopped onto Miranda's bed.

"What has her so shaken up?" Miranda said, rubbing the dog's head while Delilah wormed as close to her as possible.

Miranda watched the retreating forms of her friends through the doorway as they walked down the corridor. Doug put his arm around Skye's shoulders just as they began to hitch. They turned the corner and walked out of sight, leaving Miranda's question unanswered.

WHEN SHE WOKE LATER, the soft March sunshine was gone, replaced by the purples and grays of twilight. The lamp beside her bed was turned low. Doug and Mario huddled near the door. The set of Mario's jaw was tight, and a deep frown pulled the corners of his eyes down. Doug's hunched shoulders, the suppressed anger that radiated off him like heat from a furnace, reminded Miranda of a bomb about to explode.

Whatever was going on, it was not good.

She cleared her throat. "Hey, guys. What's going on?"

They both jumped. When they turned to her, they wore the bland expression of teenagers trying, and failing, to hide that they were stoned off their asses.

"Did we wake you up?" Mario asked, coming to sit on the chair next to her. But not before he and Doug shared a glance that made Miranda uneasy.

"No, you didn't wake me."

Mario's hand felt warm around hers, soft like sunshine.

"I'm going to go check on Skye," Doug said.

"Wait a minute," Miranda said, but he was already out the door. She looked back at Mario. "What the hell is going on?"

Mario sighed. "P-Land got in touch earlier. Brock broke out of their jail. They have no idea where he is."

28

Miranda looked at Mario, puzzled. "Why on earth would I be mad at you?"

"I've been in the lab a little more this week since you're doing so much better, but you've been kind of distracted all day. I don't know." Mario shrugged. "I thought you might be mad at me."

"I don't know where you get these ideas, honey. It's our last night together before I go back to LO. I'm not going to waste it being mad at you."

His whole body loosened in front of her eyes. She hadn't realized how tense he was until he wasn't. He tossed the towel wrapped around his hips over a chair and crawled under the covers. Naked, she was happy to see. She snuggled against him, her head on his shoulder. He smelled clean and faintly of pine.

"You smell good," she said.

She traced her fingers over his chest. After another week in the sick room, she had declared that she was going back to hers and Mario's room. Mario had acquiesced more readily than she had expected. Over the course of the week, however, he had rebuffed her every time she tried to make love, saying she still looked exhausted. She probably had, but she was getting tired of him acting like she was made of glass and would break if he sneezed near her.

"You smell okay," he said. "Not as good as me, but acceptable."

"Do you hear that, Tadpole?" she said, looking down toward her belly. "Do you hear how your father is talking to me?"

He kissed the top of her head. "Tadpole knows I'm teasing."

Miranda sat up, pushing the covers back, and straddled him before he could do something stupid like protest.

"And what do you think you're doing?" he asked, arching an eyebrow.

The T-shirt she had been sleeping in the last few months had grown tight around her swelling breasts. She trailed her hands over them before pulling it over her head, then smiled down at him as she tossed it away. His eyes darkened with desire. She felt him stir below her, already hard, as his hands settled on the small bump of her belly.

"You're beautiful," he whispered. "I don't even have a word for how gorgeous you are."

Her body *was* changing beyond the obvious. Her curves were softening; her breasts were larger and rounder, heavier too.

"Show me."

He sat up, his hands sliding up her body to cup her breasts. They were more sensitive than ever, and a soft moan escaped her lips, her nipples tingling as they hardened under his fingers. His lips found hers, setting the smoldering embers inside her alight.

"Move us to the edge of the bed," she said.

Mario looked at her curiously. "Like I move and you ride on my lap?"

She nodded. He started to scoot them to the edge of the bed, Miranda still straddling him. They moved awkwardly, and Miranda could not suppress the giggles that bubbled up.

"And you're going to laugh at me?" Mario said with a grin.

Miranda kept giggling as she kissed him, even after he bent his knees over the edge of the bed. It was just...funny, moving over the bed together in fits and starts, feeling the anticipation of their hungry bodies bumped off course but growing stronger because of the delay. He was such a good sport about it that it made the giggles worse.

She hooked her feet over the edge of the mattress and kissed him again, a rush of love for him welling up in her chest. She could see how much he wanted her, but it was tempered with a gentleness that made her feel safe and content in a way she never had before. She rose up on her knees before sliding down, gathering him to her.

Mario groaned into her mouth as her body surrounded him. They moved together with a tenderness that felt new, a sweetness that brought tears to her eyes. The gentle swell of her belly brushed against his muscled stomach. She saw his love for her and their baby underneath the haze of lust and desire. He took her hand from his waist, guiding it between them. When she touched herself and her whimpers grew more helplessly urgent, he smiled at her like the Cheshire Cat.

For the first time since her illness, her body felt supple and if not strong, at least not fragile. Mario pulled her deeper into the rising, crackling heat. Waves of pulsing, hot pleasure rippled through Miranda's body from where Mario moved inside her, where she caressed herself with her fingers. She kissed him as she started to come, her shuddering cries lost in the tangle of their tongues and lips. He held her hips in place, his grip growing tighter as he bucked underneath her, coming with a groan.

Mario looked up into her eyes. "I missed you," he said softly.

She pulled him with her to burrow under the covers, drowsy and warm, her arms and legs entwined with his. Mario's head rested on her shoulder. His hand traced lazy circles beneath her belly button that almost tickled.

"I thought I was going to lose you," he said so softly that she almost didn't hear him. "Both of you."

She wriggled down the bed until she faced him. His eyes were dark, finally letting her see the terror that had sucked him into an abyss of despair she had only seen hints of. Mario projected self-assurance. He was so confident, so *competent*, at everything. Maybe because he'd done it for so long it was a habit now, this facade he projected of being strong all the time. But he didn't need to be, not with her.

"I'm still here, sweetheart," she said, taking his hand.

She interlaced his fingers with her own, their joined hands cradling their baby, who had surprised them both with its unexpected presence.

"We're both still here."

———

"TAKE CARE OF YOURSELF," Mario said the next morning. "Make sure you sleep enough, and eat vegetables, and—"

"I'll make sure she does, mom," Skye said as she walked past them.

Despite the shock of learning that Brock was on the loose, Skye seemed to have regained her equilibrium. Miranda smothered a grin. Mario was fussing like a mother hen. It was sweet and endearing and right now, exasperating.

Miranda laid her hand on his cheek and looked into his dark-brown eyes. "I will take very good care of myself and Tadpole. I promise. River is coming back to LO later this afternoon. And I have Liley to look after me."

Mario looked down at Delilah, who hovered nearby. Her tail began to wag, and Miranda saw some of the anxiety in his eyes recede. He smiled, chagrined.

"I worry is all," he said. "Tadpole kicked it into high gear."

"Luckily for Tadpole, he has a kick-ass momma."

"Tucci!" Rocco shouted. "For the love of all that's holy, will you get your ass in gear? I'd like to leave this week."

She kissed Mario, slow and unhurried. Heat began to warm her insides and make her head buzz. Mario broke the kiss first and held her face in both hands.

"I love you," he said. The simple honesty of it shone in his eyes.

"I must be feeling better," she murmured. "Because I really want to jump you again."

Before he could reply, an arm slipped between them, wrapping around Miranda's shoulders to settle over her collarbone.

"I hate to be an asshole, James," Rocco said as he tugged Miranda away, pulling her backward with him. "But we gotta go."

"I'll see you soon," Miranda said, blowing him a kiss. "I love you!"

Mario pretended to catch it and smacked it on his cheek.

"I'd have told you to get a room, but then it would have been another hour," Rocco said. He kept his arm around her shoulders, presumably to keep her from escaping.

"You're not kidding anyone," she said to Rocco. "You love being an asshole."

He laughed. "You two are worse than Doug and Skye."

Miranda stopped and looked up at him. "Did something happen? Have they, you know?"

"Nah," he said, walking to the Jeep again. "But between him holding her hand till she falls asleep every night and the longing looks, the sexual tension is unbearable."

Miranda laughed out loud. Everything he said was true. "You've changed your tune."

Rocco shrugged. "I was worried he was stringing her along for something that wasn't gonna happen, but that guy's still a priest like I'm a ladies' man."

They climbed into the Jeep, Miranda plopping down beside Rich in the back seat. Delilah hopped into the Jeep's front seat, then jumped to the back, squeezing between Miranda and Rich. Rich was rotating back to LO for a week. And he needed it, judging by his red-rimmed eyes and constant yawns. She wished the Jeep had headrests so she could lay her head back and relax, take in the spring sunshine with no effort. Instead, she tipped her face up to the sun and closed her eyes for a moment. Skye and Rocco talked over the noise of the rushing wind for a while, then fell silent. All around them, the already green landscape was dotted with even more light-green springtime shoots and lacy white and pink blossoms.

In approximately four months, she and Mario would have a tiny person who would be completely dependent on them. The thought scared her, but not as much as she had thought it would. They would do what they had to do to protect their child—together. Mario would be ruthless protecting the two of them. Not that she needed protecting, but she did not want to be solely responsible for protecting their child. She had seen the lengths he had gone to in order to protect his family at home. He would do the same with theirs.

A loud pop pulled Miranda from her musings. Delilah yipped as the Jeep listed and skidded across the rough, uneven road.

"Son of a bitch," Rocco said, fighting with the steering wheel as he slowed the Jeep. "Everyone okay?" he asked, looking over his shoulder to check with Miranda and Rich when they stopped.

"Fine," Miranda said.

Skye had already jumped out of the Jeep and stood by the front passenger side tire. "Blow out," she said.

Miranda climbed out to join her. The rupture in the sidewall of the tire that Delilah now sniffed was a foot long.

Rich joined them, jack and lug wrench in his hands.

"If y'all don't mind, ladies," he said, stepping past them. The lilt of his Southern drawl made the request almost courtly.

"I'll help you," Rocco said. He said to Miranda and Skye, "Keep watch?"

Skye said to Miranda, her voice low, "Get the little women out of the way while the men do manly men things."

Miranda snickered but thought she detected a note of relief in Skye's voice that she and Miranda weren't out here on their own. After the news of Brock's escape, Miranda did not blame her.

"They can knock themselves out," Miranda said. "I'd rather watch for zombies any day."

Skye grinned, then winced, putting her hand on her bruised cheek.

"Still smarts?" Miranda asked.

It had been four weeks since Brock had attacked Skye, but many of the bruises were still purplish in spots. The rest were various shades of dark sickly greens and yellows.

Skye nodded. "Much better, though."

Both women fell silent, scanning the area for any movement that might be zombies.

"Gosh darn it," Rich said a minute later. "I think the jack is broken."

"Let me try," Rocco said.

He traded places with Rich, to no effect but with a lot more swearing. Miranda and Skye kept watching, but they moved closer to the Jeep so they could better hear Rocco on the radio with the Institute. They were only about a third of the way to LO, so it was closer.

"Goddammit," Rocco said again a few minutes later. "They'll be here," he said. "But it's gonna be half an hour at least. Something about monkeys... I don't know."

"We heard," Skye answered.

Rocco's brow furrowed. "You two should go to the fallback."

Miranda had heard about the treehouses that LO had built along vehicle and foot routes. She had not seen one, however, since she'd never needed one. Well, except for the day she almost froze to death, but she could not have just sat back and relaxed with Phineas bleeding out.

"It's only going to be half an hour," she said.

"Nah," Rocco said, shaking his head. "They said half an hour at least. They know we're by a fallback, so they know we'll be okay if it takes longer. You two, go. You're still recuperating, Miranda. Rich and I can wait."

"I'll walk y'all over," Rich said.

"We have Delilah to come with—"

"Come on, Miranda," Skye said. "It won't do any harm to have Rich walk us over. Much as I hate to admit it, Rocco's right. He'll bitch and whine the whole time if we don't, and I do not have the patience for that today."

"All right, then," Miranda said.

Letting them change the tire was one thing, but an escort was weird.

They walked down the road a hundred feet to a post with a bright-orange stripe of reflective paint at the top. Delilah disappeared into the tall grass as they left the road and headed for a nearby copse of trees. As they walked under the trees, Miranda saw the treehouse. It was bigger than she had expected, but not huge, and fifteen feet off the ground. She turned back toward the road. Rocco, leaning against the Jeep, waved.

"This isn't even a thousand feet away! You could have just watched us," Miranda said, shooting Rich an incredulous look. "You have rifles, for Pete's sake."

Rich looked sheepish and shrugged. He pushed his sunglasses up on his head.

"Where I come from, a gentleman walks a lady home. If she was still with us, my momma would whip my ass if I didn't, even before all this."

"It's because you're pregnant," Skye said while she pulled on a rope that released a collapsible ladder.

"And because you were doing poorly," Rich added.

"Are you kidding me?" Miranda said, absolutely floored.

"I need to get back," Rich said. "Up you go. Will the dog be okay staying with us?"

"She'll be fine," Miranda said. She climbed the ladder, which Skye pulled up after them. Delilah appeared from the high grass and began to whine.

"It's okay, Liley. Stay with Rich."

Delilah looked up at her, head cocked to the side, then sat down with a harumph.

"I'll leave her, then," Rich said, motioning to the dog. He turned and began walking back to the Jeep.

The treehouse had a roof and shutters that could be closed over the upper half of the walls on all four sides. Cots and camp chairs were folded against one side. Two rectangular metal tool boxes, the kinds that tradesmen used to have in the beds of their trucks, were up against another wall.

"Food and water, radio, sleeping bags," Skye said, when she saw Miranda looking at them. "And some weapons in the other. They're always unlocked."

Skye pulled over two camp chairs and opened them up, then sat and put her feet on the rail of the half-wall at the edge of the treehouse.

"Might as well get comfortable."

Miranda sat in the other chair, resting her hand on her growing belly.

"Are they going to be like this the whole time?"

"Probably," Skye said. "I mean, you know Rocco well enough by now. Pregnant women set his Old School to eleven. I've seen it before. They're all gonna get a little weird."

Miranda tried to absorb this startling information. She had not been surprised when Mario got more protective, but she never thought it would be generalized to include others.

"Are you sure?" she asked, unable to wrap her mind around what Skye was telling her.

Skye laughed. "I don't think Doug will get too weird, but everyone else probably will."

"He better not," Miranda muttered. "I've been sick, but I am a perfectly capable and competent person. I'm not just a vessel because I'm pregnant."

"You know that, and I know that, but things have changed for you, especially where men are concerned. I don't even think they can

help it. I mean, I saw men do it a little bit back in the day, but now."
She shrugged. "It's like their cavemen brains take over and they start
looking for shit to bash with a club."

"It wasn't like this at home." And I never paid attention because I
was never going to do this, Miranda realized. "I am not going to like
this at all."

Skye said, "Doug and I were talking about it the other day. He'll
be *very* disappointed if you do. I think he's looking forward to the
fireworks."

"I'm sure he is," Miranda muttered, but it made her smile, too.
She'd do the same to him if their roles were reversed. A sudden
thought occurred to her. "Has Doug gotten like this with you?
Because of—"

Skye's body language changed without her moving. Tighter, more
constrained. Miranda kicked herself. She had not thought before she
spoke.

"I'm sorry, Skye," she said. "I didn't mean to pry."

Skye pulled her feet down from the rail. "It's okay. I'm just on
edge a little with this whole Brock thing. And you surprised me." She
looked down at her boots. "It's that obvious?"

Miranda stifled a laugh. "I know him really well," she said,
which had the virtue of being true even if just now it was a complete
lie.

Skye smiled, still looking at her boots. She was clearly pleased
and blushing like a beet.

"He's more," her voice trailed off as she searched for the word.
"Around."

She looked up. Miranda thought she would say more about Doug,
but she stood up and said, "They're coming over here."

Miranda looked, too. Sure enough, Rocco and Rich were coming
to the fallback. Skye lowered the ladder.

"What's going on?" Miranda called down.

"It's the monkeys," Rocco said.

Rich reached the top of the ladder and joined them. "A couple of them got inside the building, and they're raising holy heck. They're having a time of it rounding them up."

Rocco appeared, a squirming and unhappy Delilah in one arm. Miranda rushed forward to help with the dog, and Rocco pulled up the ladder.

"I told them to leave it and come get us," he said. "But they're trashing the place, so they have to catch them. Didn't get in the BSL-3 hallway. And they won't get in the lab, of course. They did pull Mario and Alicia out to help."

Skye snickered. "Alicia's laugh and a bunch of macaques running rampant. Oh my God."

"I don't know why y'all are so hard on that poor girl," Rich said.

"I like her just fine, but that laugh." Skye shuddered. "It's brutal."

Miranda looked back at the Jeep. Beyond it, just along the tree line of the ever-expanding forests, a figure stumbled forward.

"We've got company over there," she said, pointing.

"At least we're up here," Rich said. "Doesn't look like too many of them."

How he gauged that Miranda couldn't figure, since the forest area was thick with underbrush, and she couldn't see a thing beyond the tree line. Not that it mattered. It was not a problem yet. Rocco raided the food, which Skye chided him for. Rich settled in for a nap, which looked like an excellent idea to Miranda. She got a sleeping bag, and even a little pillow, out of the supplies box.

Delilah's growls woke her. Miranda could hear the moans but could tell by the volume that there weren't many zombies. They had to be close for Delilah to growl. Miranda sat up, yawning, and pushed her hair out of her eyes. Delilah's nose was glued to the cracks around the trapdoor. Every few seconds, she growled softly. The sun looked high in the sky.

Miranda said, "How long have we been here?"

Skye and Rocco looked up from their card game, where they sat on the floor near the trapdoor.

"Two hours," Skye said.

"Really?" she asked, surprised. "How many monkeys were there?"

"They caught three, four more to go. They think," Rocco said. "Some idiot must have propped the door open to let that many inside."

Rich sat in the chair she had used before, a book on his knee with his finger keeping his place. "Did you rest those eyelids?"

"I did."

Miranda yawned again, then picked up and tossed the small pillow at the empty camp chair, but it sailed right over the rail.

"Goddammit."

Rich grinned at her. "Coulda played for the Yankees."

"I'm from San Francisco, so the Giants," she corrected, looking over the rail to see where the pillow had landed.

Ten zombies milled below. The pillow had landed beyond them but had caught their attention. They stumbled away to investigate. If we're careful about we how we kill them, we can save the pillow, Miranda thought. It wouldn't matter if they walked on it, but zombie goop smell never seemed to completely fade from cloth it soiled.

The first zombie was almost to the pillow when it jerked back and turned away.

"What the hell?" Miranda muttered.

The next zombie staggered closer, then changed course so abruptly it fell over. It stumbled back up to its feet, pretty quickly for a zombie.

I can't be seeing this right, Miranda thought, feeling dizzy.

"Guys," she said. "Come look at this."

Rich leaped to his feet, joined a second later by Rocco and Skye.

"What is it?" Rich asked, his voice tense.

"Watch them and the pillow."

"Watch the pillow?" Rocco said. "From your voice I thought something was wrong."

"Just watch."

A third zombie tottered over. The others had peeled off to follow the zombies that had changed course back to the treehouse.

Just like the first two, this zombie got about two feet from the pillow, then jerked away.

"What is it doing?" Skye said, sounding puzzled.

She wasn't imagining it. Miranda's stomach plunged into her feet.

"I've never seen a zombie do that," Rocco said, sounding both confused and intrigued. "What's on that pillow?"

Through a cottony mouth, Miranda said, "Me."

NINETY MINUTES LATER, Miranda's bra, panties, and both socks —clothing she could manage without and not compromise her outer layers of protection—were on the ground below the treehouse. In every instance, the flutter of fabric had caught the zombies' attention. But when they stumbled over to look for a snack, they never got closer than two feet before jerking away and changing direction. With every new article of clothing, Miranda's dread grew. By the time they tossed her panties, she'd hit full-blown panic.

Miranda sat on the edge of the camp chair, her arms clamped around her middle. She chewed on her lip, wishing one of the waves of nausea roiling her stomach would be enough to make her throw up. She didn't think she would feel better, but it had to be better than this acid burn at the back of her throat that rose and fell but never went anywhere. Delilah lay with her paws and head on Miranda's feet, periodically rising to nudge Miranda's hand until Miranda petted her. When the petting petered out, the tawny pit bull resettled on Miranda's feet.

A vehicular rumble buzzed in the distance—the truck that had radioed ten minutes ago. Skye crouched down in front of Miranda. Her eyes were full of reassurance, but the bruises that surrounded her left eye and colored her jaw and temple undermined it.

"We don't know what this means, Miranda. Don't jump to any conclusions."

Miranda shook her head. Skye's kindness caused the tears that she had managed keep in check so far to rush to the surface. If she repelled bites after being bitten by Jeremiah, what was it doing to the baby?

"You don't know him like I do," she said, her voice barely a whisper. "Nothing good comes from that monster. Not a goddamn thing."

29

RIVER LOOKED SERIOUS BUT NOT ALARMED AS SHE SAT DOWN. Mario wondered if they taught doctors how to do that in medical school... How to Look Like the Shit Has Not Hit the Fan 101. He had been nervous about her leaving earlier. As soon as he saw Miranda, he knew the flat tire had been the least of their worries. He wrapped Miranda's hand inside his own for at least the tenth time since they sat down. She was as outwardly fidgety, anxious, and scared as he felt, but he tried to keep it from showing. Miranda needed him, more than ever. He had to be here for her, reassure her. Which probably wasn't possible, but he still had to try. But he wouldn't be able to if he let how much of a basket case he was on the inside show.

"So," River said. "I can't tell you to not freak out, because you're already doing that. I hate to say this, but on my side, all we can do is wait and see. This is uncharted territory. So far, the pregnancy has been progressing normally. I'll monitor Miranda a lot more closely, obviously. And we will find and fix an ultrasound if it *kills* me. I've already spoken to the commander, and she's made it her top priority."

Miranda sighed. "I knew that was what you were going to say but..."

"Oh, sweetie," Mario said, pulling her close when she started to cry.

It killed him to see her like this. She was still almost too thin from her illness, and she had been so wiped out by the beginning of the pregnancy. The hot, furious anger bubbled up again. He wanted to murder Jeremiah. Wring his fucking neck and watch the light fade from his crazed eyes. And then he wanted to revive him and do it again. With an effort, he tamped the anger down. He would deal with Jeremiah another day. Right now, he had to take care of Miranda and the baby.

"The commander wants to keep this under wraps, and I agree. We have no idea if this repellant effect is permanent or transient, or what causes it, but that's going to be for Mario and Alicia to figure out. I still want you to come back to LO, Miranda," River said. She looked to Mario. "Did you get all the blood draws you need?"

Mario nodded. Alicia had already started to study samples of Jeremiah's saliva and Miranda's blood. Her survival might be the key to being able to replicate the vaccine with this different strain of virus. They still weren't sure how she had been infected in the first place.

We probably need her saliva samples too, he thought, then felt the floor drop out from under him. Would Miranda be an asymptomatic carrier, too? And if she was, had she infected him when they kissed or made love? He shied away from the thought, unable to think about one more thing that might be wrong.

It was personal now. Jeremiah had seen to that.

"If you need more blood, just say so," Miranda said, wiping her face with the hanky Mario had given her.

At her words, his heart broke a little more.

River said, "I don't want to jump the gun, but if the worst should happen, we can terminate the pregnancy safely, even late-term. I had to do it once before, when the fetus died."

A bleak resignation overwhelmed Mario. It had been too good to be true. That Miranda would get pregnant in the first place and want to keep it. That she would survive the illness from the bite. That their little Tadpole would be okay.

"I don't want that," Miranda said, growing more distraught.

"I'm not saying you need to," River said quickly. "Just that it's there. But hopefully this will be the first and last time we talk about it. You're in a different place than you were a few weeks ago, Miranda. I know that."

"I got tired of this world taking everything away from me." She laughed, soft and bitter. "Sure showed me."

"Come on, now," Mario said. "Don't give up yet."

River said, "He's right. Try not to panic *too* much, Miranda. And you too, Mario. This could end up being a big, fat exercise in our imaginations being scarier than anything reality can throw at us."

Mario thanked her, and River hugged them both. They walked to their room, not talking. When they got there, Miranda crumpled on the bed.

"What are we going to do?" she said helplessly.

Mario dropped to his knees in front of her and held her hands in his. She was shaking, he realized. And he couldn't hide it. He couldn't pretend to be stronger than he was, not when it felt like everything was crashing down around him.

"I don't know, sweetheart. But we'll figure it out together," he said, his voice getting tight. Tears pricked the corners of his eyes. "There might not be anything wrong. We might be putting ourselves through this for no reason."

"I know that here," she said, tapping her head, before moving her hand to her heart. "But not here."

"I love you," he said. "Hold on to that."

"I know you do." She sighed. "Lay down with me."

Mario climbed onto the bed and gathered her into the crook of his shoulder. He stroked her hair, which had grown out enough to look shaggy and shapeless.

"I'm going to kill him," Miranda whispered, her voice becoming steely. She looked up at him. A ferocious anger burned in her blue eyes. "Whatever happens, I'm going to kill him."

Mario nodded, then pulled her closer. The rightness of her words wrapped him in a warm embrace.

"We'll do it together."

MARIO LEANED back from the microscope, rubbing his bloodshot eyes. He arched his back from tailbone to neck. Then he looked down at the floor. Every muscle in his neck pulled against the base of his skull and his shoulders. When he rolled his head, his neck crackled.

He checked his watch. It was two thirty in the morning. He had worked for twelve hours straight, just like every other day for the past ten days.

"No wonder I can't see straight," he said, deciding to call it quits.

But today had been a good day—a *great* day. They had confirmed —definitively—that Miranda was *not* an asymptomatic carrier of the ZBZ virus. She could bite people until the cows came home, and she might give them tetanus or any of a number of equally nasty infections, but she could not turn them into zombies.

Half an hour later, because it took that long to store everything properly and get through the decontamination protocols to exit the lab, he collapsed into a chair in the Institute's lobby. He would go to bed in a few minutes. The only people awake at this hour were on watch, at the front and back doors, plus those making rounds inside and outside. He wanted to *be* around people, but not necessarily interact with them, so stopping here for a few minutes worked.

The smell of coffee wafted close. He looked up to see Alicia walking his way, from the hallway below the main staircase where she had set herself up with a room and a study.

"Finally calling it quits?" she said. She carried two mugs. When she reached the table, she set one in front of him. "I don't know how they still manage to find coffee, but I'm glad we have it. Thought I'd bring you some if you were still working. If you didn't want it, I'd drink it myself."

Mario inhaled the nutty, spicy aroma, a little dizzy from the mini head rush it gave him, then took a sip. It felt like liquid gold on his tongue. It was caffeinated, he could tell immediately. But he was so freaking tired he could drink a gallon and still sleep.

"What are you still doing up?"

"Reading, but I'm going to bed soon, too."

Mario took another sip of coffee, then yawned widely.

"What are you reading about?"

"Oh, a lot of things... Just trying to figure out what could break the log jam. Stem—" She stopped abruptly and shrugged. "It's hard to know what will be the thing we need. We'll figure it out eventually."

"Stem cells will definitely help if we're still stuck when the baby arrives," Mario said. "We'll have plenty then."

Everyone who knew tiptoed around the baby, as if mentioning anything about pregnancy or fetal development would upset him. Alicia looked troubled before she schooled her face into a bland expression.

"What?" he said.

"Nothing."

He didn't believe her. He raised his eyebrow. "What is it?"

She scowled, looking reluctant. After a minute of him giving her the stink eye, she said, "Let's talk about it tomorrow."

Alarm scraped at the base of skull. Faint, like it was miles away, but it was there. "What is it? What's wrong?"

"Just something I'm working on. You're too tired right now—over-tired," she said, her voice firm. She tucked a stray curl behind her ear. "You've been up almost twenty-four hours. *Get some rest*. I'll tell you about it in the morning."

The alarm was on the same block now, and it was deafening. "What is it?" he demanded.

She looked at him, plainly trying to make up her mind. Then she sighed. "I did a blood draw every day when Miranda was sick, and I found something."

Mario remembered Alicia doing that. Barely.

"The sicker she got, the more pronounced the anomaly became. I ran every assay I could think of, but I couldn't identify it. Remember the freezers in the lab by the first monkey enclosure? The ones still running because the backup was solar-powered?"

"Yeah," he said softly, bewildered by the pivot she had taken, but knowing in his bones it was bad.

"One had mice and macaque zygotes and embryos at different stages of early gestation. I..." Her voice became reluctant. "Thawed some. And when I exposed them to Miranda's blood—"

Her mouth twisted down. She didn't want to tell him what was next, and Mario suddenly knew that he didn't want to hear it. He felt like he'd been gut punched so hard he'd throw up.

Alicia visibly pulled herself together. "I exposed them, macaque and mouse embryos both. After a few days I could see it in both species, and I had a better idea of what to look for." She took a deep breath. "Because it was pretty clear that we're dealing with a teratogen."

For one beautiful moment, her words didn't compute. Then horror engulfed him. Mario felt light as air, like he might come untethered from his body.

"Tera— what the fuck are you saying, Alicia? You must have contaminated the sample, or—"

She leaned forward and put her hand over his, her eyes full of pity.

"The developing limbs were malformed on every single fetus," she said softly. "Once I knew what to look for—"

"No."

Pictures of babies with stumps of arms and legs filled Mario's brain. Smiling babies in bassinets, still too young to be teased and ridiculed. Little girls with ribbons in their hair whose truncated arms extended past the short, puffy sleeves of their dresses and ended in hands that were babydoll small, or not there at all. Little boys in their Sunday best, Brylcreem in their hair, whose shirt sleeves and pant legs were pinned back because they were not needed. Children whose parents had lived through the Cuban Missile Crisis and Sputnik's launch, who saw a wall divide Berlin and President Kennedy's assassin murdered on live TV. Parents whose children were too young to understand that the drugs given to their mothers for morning sickness had done them this terrible harm.

Children who never needed shoes, who couldn't walk or run. Children who would never survive in the world Mario lived in.

"I want to see the dataset," he said. "We have to run it again."

Gently, Alicia said, "I've already done it twice. I'm not wrong."

"I'm running it again," Mario said through gritted teeth. "You must have made a mistake."

"You've never doubted me before," she said, her face pinched with puzzlement and sympathy.

Anger swept over him, a brush fire fanned into an out-of-control wildfire almost instantaneously. Mario slammed his hands on the table, hard enough to tip over the cups of coffee.

"It's never been my *child* before! I don't need your pity, Alicia. I need you to admit that you're wrong or shut the fuck up."

Alicia flinched away, her eyes wide. Her mouth formed a perfect O of shock.

"I'm so sorry. I know how much you and Miranda want this baby."

Mario felt hot tears run down his face, insatiable grief starting to suck him under until something Alicia had said clicked into place.

"You want the stem cells," he said, his voice rising, the booming accusation echoing off the tiled walls and terrazzo floor. "I've only just found out she's pregnant," he said, shouting now. "And you've already moved on to an abortion and harvesting the stem cells?"

Alicia sat frozen in place, like a rabbit in the path of a wolf. The guy on watch covering the back door had already started walking over but kicked it up to a jog.

The metal back of the chair Mario had been sitting in felt cool against his hands, then sailed across the lobby and crashed off the wall. The table flipped under his fingertips. The impact from another chair jolted up his arms when he slammed it off the side of the staircase.

"No," he shouted with every strike, the jolt of impact traveling up his arms becoming softer as the chair fell apart.

He stood in the atrium, his chest heaving, his heart pounding, adrenaline overloading his system. And grief, burying him beneath it like an avalanche.

One of the watchmen stood between him and Alicia, arms out to the side and behind him. A protective posture, to shield her from harm. Where the hell had he been when Miranda and the baby had needed protection?

"Hey, James," Rich said, his soft drawl almost musical. "I'm not sure what's wrong with y'all over here, but how 'bout you tell me about it?"

Rich held his hands palms up and waist high in front of him. A placating gesture that invited Mario to calm down.

"I have to tell Miranda," he said.

His legs almost gave out, picturing the hope in her eyes snuffed out because of what he had to tell her. Mario searched for Alicia. She stepped out from behind the watchman and crossed to him. Her face was pinched with sympathy as she took his hand in hers.

"I have to tell her," he said again. "How am I supposed to do that?"

"We'll do it again, okay? We'll run the tests again and see. Another week or two won't matter."

A sob welled in Mario's chest. Their tiny, little baby...

"Okay," he said, all the fight draining from his body.

Mario could feel the eyes of every person in the atrium on him. The silence closed in, heavy and suffocating. Rich's posture was still alert, but his eyes reflected that the worst had passed. The storm was over.

"Let's get you into bed, okay?" Alicia said, as if she were talking to a small child. "You're dead on your feet. Get some sleep. We'll look at the data and run a new assay again tomorrow."

"I'm sorry, Alicia," he whispered, ashamed. Alicia was his friend and his colleague. He had focused his fury on the messenger, not the message.

Alicia put her hand on his cheek. "It's okay, James. It'll be okay."

He shook his head, felt tears in his eyes. "No," he said. "No, it won't."

30

MIRANDA HELD DOUG'S HAND TO HER BELLY. TADPOLE KICKED. He looked up at her, smiling.

"You've got a soccer player on your hands, Miri."

She nodded. "I have to count them. He barely kicked all day yesterday. I was getting a little freaked out. But as soon as I went to eat dinner, he started kicking up a storm."

They started down the path through the Big Woods again. Delilah trotted ahead of them, stopping to smell things and peeing to mark the spot. Doug was going to help Skye with her rock-climbing class. Miranda needed to take Delilah on a walk, so she tagged along. If Commander Smith was at the Nature Center, she could thank her for making the ultrasound machine a priority. River had told her this morning that repairs on the one brought back a few days ago were underway. They'd need to wait for Mario in any case. It was too scary to do it without him if—

Friendly Universe, she reminded herself.

Doug said, "It's nice to see you happy, Miri."

"Believe it or not, Skye's book helped."

Doug laughed out loud. "You chose the friendly Universe, huh?"

"Yeah," she said, feeling embarrassed.

Doug shook his head, grinning. "Never thought I'd live to see the day that you, of all people, would read a self-help book, never mind take the advice."

Miranda shrugged. She had worried herself sick about the bite, about how she could still repel zombies and what it might mean for Tadpole. Skye had been downright pushy when she told her to read the book, the kind of self-help crap Miranda hated, but she read it. She would have done anything to distract herself from the never-ending disaster scenarios her brain kept concocting for the two weeks since she had returned to LO. Most of the book was annoying as fuck, except for the part about choosing what kind of Universe you lived in —friendly or unfriendly.

Miranda shrugged. "I thought it was stupid at first, to be honest, but then it hit me that I got to choose. And if I get to choose, I figured fuck it, I'm choosing friendly. If I'm going to have a baby, I want it to live in a friendly Universe even if this particular world has gone to hell." She sighed. "It's totally cheesy and don't you dare tell anyone, but it helped."

"I'm glad," Doug said. "And you are having a baby. It just kicked me."

"Speaking of Skye," she said, a teasing note in her voice. "How's that going? You two are pretty sickening. I threw up in my mouth a little yesterday."

Doug shot her a dirty look before kicking at the dirt path as they walked. "I think it's going okay."

Something about his tone...the uncertainty in it. Miranda's mouth fell open.

"You haven't told her yet."

"Not in so many words," he said, sounding like a kid admitting that he had not done his homework.

"What are you waiting for?"

"I don't want to rush her, since Brock," he said, looking unsure.

"Oh my God," Miranda said as it dawned on her. "You're nervous."

"Of course I'm nervous! It's like I've made just one New Year's resolution: Change Whole Life." Doug sighed. "I'm really out of practice."

Miranda suppressed a grin. This was not the pre-priesthood player she remembered.

They left the Big Woods and entered the Nature Center. Miranda looked around for Delilah, who flashed past her into the lobby. Miranda caught a glimpse of caramel-colored fur as it disappeared into the Community Room where the rock-climbing classes were held. Delilah loved to 'help' with the kids' classes. The kids loved her, petting and wrestling with the pit bull while waiting for their turn to climb, so it worked out.

"Don't get too distracted by those soulful glances and not-really-by-accident touches. Your inattention might kill the wee rock climbers," Miranda said.

Doug flipped her off as he headed for the gym.

"It's like shooting fish in a barrel," she said to herself.

A voice behind her said, "Miranda! I've been looking for you."

She turned to see River coming through the Nature Center's entrance. LO's doctor looked excited.

"The ultrasound is working," River said. "D'you want to see Tadpole?"

Excitement hit Miranda in a rush. She had expected to feel scared about the ultrasound with all the uncertainty from being bitten, but she wasn't.

"Really?" she asked. "Like, now?"

River nodded, grinning.

It took Miranda a second to answer. She had not expected the ultrasound to be ready this week, never mind right now.

"Yeah. Yeah, I do," she said, then her enthusiasm tempered. "But I should wait for Mario. He's coming here later today."

Except she didn't want to wait. She didn't want to wait one more second.

"Of course," River said, nodding.

Miranda took a moment to make sure she wasn't just being impatient. Mario would want to know as much as she did that everything was okay. He wouldn't mind if she didn't wait.

"You know what," she said, making up her mind. "Let's do it."

"Are you sure?"

Miranda nodded, a nervous thrill running through her. "Yeah. I want to know for sure that everything is okay. And I want to see my little guy."

"Okay," River said, smiling broadly. "Let's do it."

FIFTEEN MINUTES LATER, Miranda lay back on the examination table in River's office, a swirl of excitement with just a tiny speck of nervousness filling her. She was going to see Tadpole. Her heart sped up at the idea of seeing the blurry image of her unexpected baby who had changed everything. He had opened her up to possibility again, to the idea that this world could be more than a series of endless losses and disappointments. Being with Mario again had started it. Knowing how rare the second chance they had been given was, and how effortlessly they had come back together, had made the chink in her armor that led to today. But Tadpole was the reason she could believe in a friendly Universe, and believe that this time it would be a happy ending.

River dribbled lubricant onto Miranda's belly and wiped it around. Behind her professional doctor face, Miranda could see excitement in River's dark eyes.

"The definition might not be as clear since we aren't using KY Jelly," River said. "But we'll still see the big stuff."

Miranda nodded, too nervous to speak. The cool metal of the sensor slid over her belly, accompanied by the mechanical *wub wub*

wub of the ultrasound machine. An arc of static-like snow filled the black computer monitor hooked up to the ultrasound.

"There's the head," River said.

Miranda followed the line of River's pointing finger. The rounded white rim of Tadpole's head filled the right side of the screen.

"Oh my God," she said softly, tears filling her eyes. The baby's head moved, its tiny profile coming into view. "Is that his nose and chin?"

"It is," River said. "Head size looks good."

Miranda gasped, tears blurring her vision completely. "Really?"

"Let's see if he's really a he."

Miranda wiped her eyes, which were riveted to the monitor. The slim white bone of the baby's shoulder and upper arm appeared. She could see his bent elbow and started to laugh.

"Huh," River said softly.

River's voice was off. Miranda dragged her eyes from Tadpole to look at River. River's eyes had narrowed, and her lips were pursed.

"What's wrong?" Miranda asked, cold dread falling on her chest.

"Nothing," River assured Miranda, her brow smoothing out. "I'm gonna poke you a little and see if we can get the baby to move for a better view of his arm."

Miranda looked at the monitor again, her brow knitted as she tried to beat back her panic. River pressed on her belly, and the baby stirred, his arm poking out past his torso.

His little forearm almost waved, ending in a tight fist, and Miranda relaxed. River continued to move the sensor, and Tadpole's legs became more defined.

Miranda said, "Are his legs folded back?"

When River didn't answer, Miranda looked at her again. There was no mistaking it this time. River's forehead was creased, her eyes narrowed. She looked unhappy with what the monitor was showing her.

Dread, cold and heavy, filled Miranda's veins.

"What is it? What's wrong?"

"I'm a little concerned about his leg length," River said softly, almost to herself.

Miranda looked back at the monitor, squinting to see it more clearly. Tadpole moved his leg. The bone of his thigh was straight and easy to see, his knee was bent, but his lower leg looked—

"What's wrong with his leg?" Miranda said, panic gripping her chest. She could hardly breathe enough to speak.

River didn't answer. Miranda looked at Tadpole's arm again. It wasn't right, either.

"That's not a fist," she said, her voice, her whole body, trembling. "I thought... River, where's his hand?"

Tadpole moved his head so that his face looked toward the monitor. Miranda could see the darker gray depressions of his eyes, the soft swell of his cheek. Then he kicked. For the first time she could see the motion that accompanied the shove against the inside of her abdomen, but his leg...

Her voice was a whisper, fear sucking the air from her lungs. "Why can't I see his feet?"

She turned to look at River. Finally, the doctor looked at her, and Miranda wished that she hadn't.

"I'm not sure," River said, her voice troubled.

A sharp pain, like a knife driving deep, shoved through Miranda's heart. She wanted to push River's hand away, curl herself around her baby. She looked back at the monitor, at Tadpole's little nose, his perfectly formed head and sturdy, barrel-shaped torso.

"His limbs look..." River said softly as if she was speaking to herself.

Miranda's chest began to hitch, her breaths short and sharp. She could feel the sob building behind her sternum. The black-and-white arc of the ultrasound image still cradled her baby in fuzzy shades of black and white. She couldn't catch her breath. Couldn't stop the lead that filled her own limbs. She realized she was shaking her head, rejecting the evidence of her eyes. Tears ran into her ear canal, cold and itchy.

She had let herself believe and love. Nurtured the small, soft dream of hers and Mario's child and exposed it to her dangerous but still beautiful world. She had chosen the friendly Universe.

It had not returned the favor.

31

"Everything looks great, Miranda. You're healing up nicely."

She knew what River meant, but at the same time, it confused her. Healing up nicely. Was that what people did? How did they do it? How had she? Miranda nodded, even though River couldn't see it. She lay on the exam table, her feet in stirrups. She felt the speculum withdraw from her body, and River told her she could sit up.

A few minutes later, she and Mario sat with River in River's office.

"I'm really glad to hear that," Mario said after hearing that River was pleased with Miranda's recovery. He sounded so relieved, like he had expected to hear she had cancer.

He squeezed Miranda's hand. She gave him a small smile. Not because there was anything to smile about, but because he needed it. She hated seeing him so worried about her, but she couldn't seem to snap out of the fog she had been in after the news had finally sunk in. She rode that fog through the abortion, through being told in sympathetic tones that the fetal deformities had included Tadpole's heart, which was common with teratogen exposure, apparently. Even if

Tadpole's limbs had not been stunted and mangled, he would not have survived. Tadpole had been a he, it turned out, just as she had felt from the very beginning.

She also wanted to hide from Mario. She wanted to strike out and scream and escape his needing. It was sucking her dry, his need. He needed to know she was still the same Miranda. A wounded version, but still that same woman underneath, but she wasn't sure she was. She wasn't sure she could be after being stupid enough to open herself wide for the cosmic sucker punch that the Universe had ordered up. She had never thought of herself as a fool, but this time? Mario needed to be reassured that she was all right, but she wasn't. She couldn't. His need was like a hungry ghost hovering between them, patiently circling for an opportunity to devour her.

"I understand that no teratogens are present in Miranda's blood-work since she got better, just while she was fighting the infection," River said.

Mario nodded. "Yeah, that's right. Alicia took blood samples the whole time. She didn't know it was ter—"

He stopped and took a breath.

"The levels were declining by the tenth day and totally clear by the thirteenth. And nothing in the draw she did two days ago." He looked at Miranda. "Two days ago, right?"

Miranda nodded. She had no idea.

"That's great news," River said. "Really great. It's not a permanent condition then."

Mario sounded tentative when he said, "So if we wanted to try again—"

"We're not trying again," Miranda said, cutting him off.

Silence descended.

"Miranda," River said.

Miranda looked at her. River's almost black eyes were direct—professional—but devoid of sympathy. It was a fucking relief to have someone not look at her like she was an object of pity. Like she was broken.

"I don't know to what degree your tubal ligation has failed. This might have been a fluke, or you might be able to get pregnant again no problem, or something in between. I just don't have the capacity to find out."

Miranda nodded. "Good to know."

"I want to see you again in a week," River said. "We'll talk birth control then. Keep taking good care of her, Mario."

"Of course," he said, squeezing her hand again.

Miranda squeezed Mario's hand back, wondering if he would stop doing it if she did.

"I'M WORRIED ABOUT MIRANDA," Mario said.

Doug took a swig from the dark-brown bottle in his hand before setting it down between them.

"She's taking it hard," Doug said. "I know you are, too."

Mario polished off his cider, the bitter aftertaste lingering on his tongue. He and Doug sat on one of the watch platforms along the palisade around LO. If they had been on watch, they wouldn't be drinking, but they weren't. Rocco had been experimenting with making cider since apples were plentiful, and this batch wasn't half bad.

The platform they sat on had been built too close to the one next to it, so it wasn't used for keeping watch. A rookie mistake from the beginning of the apocalypse, its only consequence being that it gave people a place to hang out, to see LO from a different angle. As far as post-apocalyptic mistakes went, they didn't get much more consequence free.

"I couldn't believe it when she told me she was pregnant. Right in the middle of almost dying. Her timing... Jesus."

Doug laughed as he handed Mario another cider. If anyone was familiar with Miranda's knack for dropping bombshells at the worst possible moment, it was Doug.

"And I *really* couldn't believe it when she said she wanted to keep it. You could have knocked me over with a feather."

Mario knew the figure of speech was trite, but it was true. A puff of wind could have done the job.

"I couldn't believe it, either, and I had a front row seat to all the mixed signals body language," Doug said. "She was always abortion this, abortion that, abort, abort!"

Their laughter pealed down on the passersby walking the path below. Mario remembered how forcefully Miranda had stated her position on the insanity of having children on more than one occasion. When their laughter subsided, he sighed.

"She hasn't cried once, not around me. She won't talk to me. It's like she's totally checked out." Mario shook his head, then took another swig of cider. "I removed every sharp object in the townhouse that I could find."

Doug turned to him, his eyebrows raised. "You think she's that bad?"

"I don't fucking *know*," Mario answered, all of his frustration rushing to the surface. "She won't *talk* to me. She might as well be a sphinx. And I have to go back to work eventually. Soon. She's been tactful, but Alicia needs help. The stem—"

Goddammit, he thought, the word bringing him up short. Tears pricked the corners of his eyes. But he forced himself to keep going. It was the only good thing to come out of this.

"The stem cells have helped. A lot. But I really don't want to leave Miri right now."

"We'll all keep an eye on her," Doug said.

"I don't want to leave because *I* don't want to leave. Not just because she's...whatever the hell she is. I want to be close to her."

Silence settled between them. The soft cacophony of the settlement—voices, dog barks, the soft susurrus of the wind in the trees of the Big Woods—surrounded them, a perfect counterpoint to a soft spring evening.

"I can't even imagine how hard this is for you two," Doug said.

"All of your focus is on Miranda, and I get that, but she's not the only one who lost something."

Mario didn't want to think about how he was, but Doug's question mired him in grief and longing and shame.

"I never thought I'd get another chance," he said softly.

"To be a dad?"

Mario nodded but didn't say more. If he did, he'd probably cry.

"You miss your kids," Doug said.

"Yeah," he whispered, his throat so tight he could barely speak. "I left them. I swore to myself that I wouldn't be like my father, but I did the same thing."

"You didn't abandon them, Mario."

"I did."

"You had to go, Mario. You—"

"No," he said, his voice brooking no argument. "I left them behind." Unbidden, the memory flooded Mario's brain. Anthony in her arms, Michael's hair riffling in the breeze. "What if it's too much for Emily?"

"Hey," Doug said, shaking his shoulder.

Mario looked up. Doug's face was serious.

"She's in a better place than she was, even with how everything went down when we left. When it comes to the kids, she's solid. She always has been."

Mario could hear the desperation in his voice when he said, "Do you really believe that?"

"I do," Doug said. "What Emily did wasn't your fault, Mario. You can't see it because you still think of her as the basket case she was when you met her. There were a lot of ways she could have reacted. She manipulated you—"

"No—" Mario interrupted, but Doug talked over him.

"If she had been serious, she would have gone about it differently, Mario. It would have been so easy to do it right. She wanted you to see, and she wanted you scared, and it worked. We talk, you know, me and Em. She's never come out and said it but... she's my friend, too. Friends can see things spouses can't."

Mario pulled Doug's conviction that Emily would be able to manage close, turning it over in his heart to see if he could hold on, but it felt as slippery as ever. The rest he ignored—Doug didn't know what he was talking about.

"I better get back," Mario said, rousing himself. He didn't want to think about his kids anymore. He had abandoned Michael and Anthony and Maureen, and he hadn't been able to protect Tadpole. The whys and wherefores didn't matter.

Doug said, "Don't be so hard on yourself, Mario, or on Miri. You're both hurting, even if she isn't showing it the same way."

Mario climbed down the ladder, the coordination required to do so making him realize that he'd had more to drink than he thought.

He wanted to go to the townhouse and be with Miranda.

And he didn't.

He felt useless when she shut him out. And it hurt. It hurt that she wouldn't let him be there for her, and that she refused to be there for him. He knew she couldn't help it. He told himself she couldn't. But a selfish part of him wanted her to try.

When he reached the townhouse, he almost left to wander LO for a while. Instead, he opened the door. Miranda sat on the end of the couch, one leg curled under her body, reading a book. Delilah was snuggled beside her.

Miranda looked up. "Someone looks a little toasty."

He held his hand up, his thumb and forefinger almost touching. "Maybe a little."

Miranda arched her eyebrow. "Maybe a little more than a little."

He joined her on the couch, reaching over Delilah to hold her hand. It felt warm in his, the comfort of her touch radiating through him.

"Did you and Doug have fun?"

He nodded, resting his head on the back of the couch. "You know us... It was all sports and titty bars."

He turned his head to look at her. She didn't laugh, but she smiled. She looked almost like herself, except for the tension in her jaw, the stiffness of her posture, the guardedness behind her blue eyes.

"Are you okay?" he asked.

She smiled, a little too brightly. "Yeah, of course."

Wow, he thought. Less than three seconds before she shut him down. He bit the inside of his cheek, using the discomfort to keep focus. He should go to bed. He was more than finger-thumb-maybe-a-little buzzed. Going to bed would be the wisest course of action.

"I'm not," he said. "I'm not okay."

Miranda set down her book. "I know. But... I don't know what you want me to say."

"That's the most you've said to me since the ultrasound. Over a week ago."

She looked down at her knees.

"Talk to me," he said gently.

She shook her head. "I can't."

The generalized dread that followed him like a dark cloud flooded his system. Frustration rushed to the surface, freed by the alcohol.

"What if I need to?" he said, the pain of her shutting him out too sharp, too deep, for him to brush off. For him to be understanding. Between them, Delilah started to whimper.

"We were going to have a baby, Miri. It was never even on the table and suddenly it was. Now it's gone, and you just close in on yourself more every day, fading away. You act like it never even happened."

"I can't *do* anything about what happened," she said. "I don't want to talk about this anymore."

"You never started talking, especially to me."

She didn't look at him. She kept her eyes on her knees like her life depended on it.

"And you have nothing to say," he said, the bitterness sharp in his mouth. "Of course you don't. Of *course* you don't." He sighed. "I need you right now, and you don't seem to give a shit. And you... It's hard to be there for someone who won't let you be."

Delilah's whines grew louder. She looked from Miranda to Mario and back again.

Miranda looked up at him, a glimpse of hurt in her eyes.

"Maybe I don't need you to be here for me," she said, her voice clipped tight. "Did you ever think of that?"

He felt the blow, like a punch to the gut. He knew she didn't mean it. He thought she didn't mean it. Hoped she didn't.

Delilah slunk from the couch and hid behind a chair.

"You should go back to the Institute."

Mario gaped at her, unable to believe what she was saying.

"This hurts, Miranda. And I'm saying it all wrong. I know you're hurting, but you're acting like everything is fine, and it's not."

"You should go back to the Institute," she said again. She looked at him this time. Her eyes were flat, like a shark's. Emotionless. "I know Alicia's been working hard. I don't really need you here, but she probably needs your help."

He stared at her for a moment, surprised to see that she was not clutching his bloody heart in her hands. It felt like she had ripped it from his chest.

"At least she wants my help."

Miranda's eyes widened as emotion rushed back into them— surprise, pain, shock, heartache. His jibe had landed, right on the bull's eye.

"Miri, I'm s—"

"Get out," Miranda said. "Get out and don't come back."

She jumped up, her posture rigid. She ran up the stairs, and Delilah followed, still whimpering.

Shutting him out. Again.

Mario watched her go. Hurt and anger, self-recrimination for saying something so cruel, fury that any of this had happened to them, swirling inside him. He shouldn't have pushed, but he did.

Shouldn't have insisted, but he had. Shouldn't have thought that needing to be comforted mattered to her. That was not something she was willing to do, not a place she was willing to go.

He stood up, debating what to do. Trying to decide if he was enough of a glutton for punishment, enough of an asshole, to try again. He climbed the stairs, stopping outside the bedroom door. Her stifled, hitching breaths as she cried were muffled by the closed door. His hand was on the doorknob when he stopped.

She was crying, but not out here with him. She didn't want him for this. She didn't want him to comfort her, had none to offer him. Which left them...here.

He tried to turn it off, this ache turning his heart inside out. He had seen others compartmentalize their pain, but he had never figured out how to get good at it. He had not protected Miranda, or the baby, or even himself, and everything was falling to pieces around him.

Maybe Rocco has more cider, he thought. Maybe if he got really fucked up, he wouldn't care for a while.

"Like that's possible," he muttered.

But maybe it wouldn't hurt to try.

32

Doug pulled up short at the end of the hallway, his heart pounding, and knocked on the door to Smith's office.

The door cracked open enough for him to see Skye's face before she ushered him in. Mario looked up from where he and Alicia both leaned over Commander Smith's desk. An ecstatic grin stretched across his face from ear to ear. The grin faltered when Mario looked past Doug to the closing door to see that Miranda was not with him. He nodded to Doug, then went back to explaining the papers on the desk.

Rich leaned against one of the overflowing bookcases on the far side of the room. He lifted his chin in greeting, his face bright with excitement. Doug slipped into place between Skye and Rocco. The small office was filled with a palpable fizz of energy.

"Looks like they did it," Rocco said to Doug.

"We're probably a little unpopular with the macaques," Alicia said, laughing.

Everyone winced. It had been a few months now, and Alicia's laugh was still like fingernails on a chalkboard. Judging from everyone else's reactions, it would not get better with time. Alicia was to o excited to notice.

Smith said, "You're both sure about this?"

Both Mario and Alicia nodded their dark heads in unison. "Yeah," Mario said. "In the lab, in mice, and in the macaques, too."

"The macaques being the human testing equivalent?" Smith asked. "And with this final serum, they've all survived?"

Alicia nodded. "Yes. We infected the first monkey with the final serum...fifteen days ago?" she said, looking to Mario for confirmation.

"Yes, that's correct," Mario answered. "Every single one since, and that first one, too, are immune to ZBZ-1 and -2."

"And they're not going to turn down the line?" Smith asked. "You're sure? Because a bunch of zombie monkeys are all we need."

Alicia shot Mario an amused look. Oh God, please don't laugh, Doug thought.

"That's not how it works with the non-human primates, Anna," Alicia said. "If the serum doesn't work, they die. They don't turn like we do."

The straight line of Smith's mouth finally cracked a smile. "So what's next?" she asked.

"A human trial," Mario said. "In the old world, it would be a couple more years before human trials, but..."

Smith nodded. "How many people do you need?"

Mario looked surprised at the question. "One, to start."

"We don't have a lot of people to choose from if we stick to the plan to keep this within the current need-to-know group," Doug said.

"That's still the plan," Smith said. "The last thing we need is this getting out, and then it doesn't work. Will this make whoever gets it ill, like Miranda was?"

Doug saw Mario wince. Any time Miranda came up since Mario had gone back to the Institute ten days ago there was something—a wince, a tightness around his eyes, the corners of his mouth turning down, or a discouraged sigh. Some were more obvious than others.

Everyone had seen this one but Smith, and that was only because she wasn't looking in Mario's direction.

Alicia put her hand on his shoulder before saying, "It shouldn't. Certainly not to that degree. Miranda's immune system was fighting off an active infection from direct exposure to the virus. Vaccines are supposed to trigger the immune response for protection without causing significant disease."

"There have been instances of vaccines causing the disease they were meant to cure," Mario said. "We know what it does in our test subjects to date, and we know what we want it to do, but we won't know for sure until we run the trial. But I think it will work as we expect."

Alicia added, "We can't include Doug and Mario, since they've received the San Jose vaccine. Or Miranda, obviously."

"Okay," Smith said, looking around the room. "Skye, Rocco, let's go through the list of everyone already involved in the project, to make sure we aren't missing anyone, and then we'll ask for volunteers."

"I'll do it," Rich said, the lilt of his southern drawl making the comment sound offhand. "I wouldn't mind going down in history as a lab rat that lived."

"Oh," Smith said, her surprise evident. "I think you should at least talk to Mathilde first. If my husband had agreed to something like this without talking to me first, I'd have killed him."

"You have two kids, Rich," Skye said. "They need you. I'll do it."

Doug felt the room lurch and begin to spin. He turned to Skye. "What?" he said.

Skye glanced at him but didn't answer his question.

Smith asked, "You're sure, Skye?"

Skye nodded. "I've been thinking about it for a while. I'm young and fit. There's no one who depends on me to take care of them, and there's nothing I do that's so specialized that someone else can't do it. Rich has a family; Alicia has skills we can't replace. Most of the people on the project fall into one or both of those categories. And if it works, then Rich can go next if Mathilde will let him." She looked to Rich. "Sound okay to you?"

Rich nodded. Doug felt Rich's eyes on him, then Rich shrugged. I tried, the gesture said.

"Okay," Smith said. "If Skye wants to do it, she'll be the first."

Around the room, conversation buzzed. Mario and Alicia received congratulations and pats on the back. Smith pulled out a bottle of Scotch, and Rocco left to get more glasses.

Doug turned to Skye, horrified. "You can't do this. *Please* don't do this."

She put her hand on his cheek. Her eyes were filled with resolve, and something that looked a lot like love.

"I can. And I am. I've been thinking about this for a while. We can talk, later. Okay? Right now, we need to celebrate Mario and Alicia's work. They deserve it."

She stepped away. Doug stood frozen, his heart pulled out of his chest, his cheek tingling where her hand had touched it. Rocco returned with the glasses.

"Doug, push the door shut," he said.

Doug crossed to the door like an automaton, his body moving but his mind untethered. But instead of pushing the door shut, he left and pulled it closed behind him.

SKYE ENTERED the community room where the rock-climbing wall was located an hour later. Doug's pulse sped up when he saw her. He had been waiting for her, since the only other options were loitering outside her apartment, or the lobby of the Nature Center where everyone would see them. Once he had been able to think straight again, he figured she might check for him here before she left the building.

"Hi," he said, rising to his feet.

"Hi," she said when she reached him.

An awkward silence stretched between them. Doug wasn't used to feeling awkward around Skye. He hated it.

"Thanks for blindsiding me."

"I should have told you," she said. She bit her lip and looked at the floor. When she met his eyes, hers were so blue they almost didn't look real. "I didn't tell you because I knew you wouldn't want me to do it. That you'd fight me on it."

"Because it's *dangerous*," he said, utterly flummoxed. The danger alone should be enough to dissuade her. "Mario's a brilliant scientist. He's probably the smartest person I know, but the first vaccine didn't work right at the start. The first few people turned, Skye! They turned into zombies, and we had to kill them. No one talks about that."

"What you're forgetting is he's done this before and learned from those mistakes. And Alicia is working with him. Mario said she had insights that he had never considered. You were sitting next to me when he said so."

"I don't give a shit if he's working with Einstein. It's too dangerous. You can't do this."

She cocked an eyebrow at him. "You do know Einstein was a physicist?"

Doug's hold on his temper evaporated. "*I'm a fucking physicist!* How can you joke about this?"

Skye took a step back, her eyes wide and lips parted.

He hadn't meant to yell at her, but she thought this was funny? Doug turned on his heel and stalked to the floor-to-ceiling windows that overlooked the back lawn, trying to get his temper under control.

"Crying for fuck's sake," he muttered angrily, dashing the tears in his eyes away.

He wanted to shake some sense into her. Tie her up and throw her in a goddamned closet. Something, *anything*, to get through to her. To protect her from herself.

Skye's reflection appeared in the window over his shoulder. The paleness of her skin and hair made her look like a specter. Like she was already gone. She leaned against his back, arms sliding around his torso. He sunk into the comfort of her body against his and her warm, soft breath that caressed the nape of his neck.

"I'm not trying to hurt you, or scare you, or leave you," she said softly, her voice filled with a tenderness that tore at his heart. "This is something that I need to do. And if you could find a way to be with me on this," she said, her voice becoming tight. "It would really help."

Doug shook his head, and the tears did start to fall, getting stuck in his eyelashes and making the world look sparkly. He took a shaky breath.

"If you felt about me the way I feel about you, you wouldn't do this."

Skye sighed, so long and deep it seemed to come from the center of the Earth.

"That's not fair. You know it's not."

He turned to her and took her face in his hands. He could feel the thin line of the newly healed scar along her jaw, from when Brock had attacked her. From when he might have lost her forever.

Doug searched her eyes. A dark band of blue rimmed the outer edge of her iris, with a gold band inside it. Tiny flecks of gold and amber sparkled from where they nestled in the lighter blues. Her butter-soft skin was warm under his hands, and he realized that he should have told her weeks ago. It was the only thing he could think of that might stop her.

"I—"

The door to the Community Room banged open. Alicia's high voice said, "I've been looking for y— Oh..."

An undercurrent of nervousness accentuated the grating, high-pitched giggle that followed. The giggle that set Doug's every nerve on edge. He wanted to punch Alicia.

Skye turned away from him.

"What's up, Alicia?" she asked.

"Um, I, ah...need to do a blood draw to get a baseline on you. But...I can come back," she squeaked.

Skye looked back at Doug, her smile sad. Then she turned away. "We can do it now."

Her voice sounded calm compared to a moment ago. Doug watched her walk away, dumbfounded. His declaration stuck in his throat like a too-large lump of bread he had swallowed that hurt going down. When Skye reached Alicia, she followed her out the door.

"I HAVE TO SUPPORT HER? *That's* your advice? I thought you were on my side, Miranda."

Doug paced the living room of Miranda's townhouse like a tiger. The pressure continued to build inside his head, making his hammering tension headache worse.

"That's your problem right there," Miranda said. "There are no sides here. It's not Team Doug versus Team Skye."

He stopped pacing and faced her. "Yes, it fucking is!"

Miranda shook her head and pursed her lips. She had the Catholic guilt thing down, because despite the sheer nonsense she spouted at him, he felt guilty for disappointing her. He threw himself down on the couch beside her.

"I need a drink."

"That is the last thing you need," she said.

"I didn't know what else to do to change her mind, so I started to tell her I love her and—"

"You started to tell her you love her?" Miranda said, interrupting him, so incredulous that her mouth hung open. "You were going to tell her you love her to *manipulate* her? Do you know how fucked up that is?"

Miranda's reaction brought him up short. Not because she was right, but because he couldn't believe she would accuse him of doing such a thing.

"No! No! That's not what I was doing at all."

Miranda chuffed, disbelieving. "Then I've got a bridge to sell you, buddy. Yes. It. Was."

He let his head drop back onto the couch cushions and stared at the ceiling.

"There are cobwebs around the light fixture," he said grumpily. "I'm stuck in the middle of a female conspiracy to drive me crazy."

Miranda said, "Hmmm... I see we've moved on to the pity party portion of the afternoon."

He turned his head on the cushion to look at her, then said, "You suck, you know that? You are a sucky best friend."

She got up and walked to the kitchen. He heard her pouring water into a pan, then the click of the stove. He lifted his head.

"You're making tea?" he asked irritably. "Are you seriously making tea?"

"It's what Father Walter does in a crisis. It makes no sense, but it helps."

A few minutes later, she handed him his tea. Black, with honey. It wasn't bad despite being stale. Miranda sat down at the end of the couch sideways and stretched her legs over Doug's lap.

"You have no concept of personal space, Miranda."

"One of my many charms."

He drank his tea, starting to feel the tiniest bit better. He would never admit it, of course. Not even under torture.

"Tell me what to do," he sighed, resigned, finally ready to listen. To quit raging against everything she said to him.

"*Support her.* It's all you can do. You can't fix it, and you can't change it, and you *can't kidnap her.*"

"Is it that obvious?" he said, half laughing.

Miranda smiled. "Yeah, but I understand wanting to snatch her up and take her somewhere safe. Somewhere not here, but you can't. What you *can* do is support her."

"But I'm scared," he said, his throat getting tight, tears in his eyes for what felt like the millionth time.

"Tell her that, too. No matter how much she's set on doing this, she's got to be scared to death. If you *really* love her, support her. Make it easier, not harder. And don't pull away to protect yourself because it won't work."

He almost retorted that she ought to take her own advice, then thought better of it.

"When did you get so smart?"

Miranda smiled again. "It's easy to give advice. I've made every mistake there is. You might as well benefit from it."

"Staying a priest would be so much easier than this," he muttered.

"Braaaaack, brack, brack, brack, brack," Miranda said, imitating a chicken.

He did laugh then. "Fuck," he said softly. "Fuck, fuck, fuck me."

Miranda's voice was teasing. "Only if you play your cards right."

***

BY THE TIME he was halfway to Skye's, Doug had worked himself back into full-blown righteous indignation. Now he wandered in the Big Woods, not paying attention to what path he took. Miranda's advice kept rattling back and forth from one side of his skull to the other, infuriating him.

"She's scared to death... That makes two of us."

What about me being scared to death, he thought. What about what he wanted? How was he supposed to support her when all he wanted to do was tie her up, throw her in a truck, and drive as far away from here as he could? Doug had never thought of himself as a creepy kidnapper kind of guy, never mind a betrayer of every feminist principle he had ever believed in, but he found himself having sympathy for the creepy kidnappers. They must have their reasons, surely.

I'm giving up everything for Skye. I don't even know if she feels the same way about me as I feel about her, and now she's doing this.

Doug stopped in his tracks.

"Oh my God," he said. "I'm sympathizing with kidnapping predators and blaming Skye for my choices, and then acting like she owes me. I did almost tell her I love her to manipulate her... I'm an *asshole.*"

In a few days, Skye would be injected with an experimental vaccine that might kill her. And if she wasn't here, wasn't part of his life...

The next thing Doug knew he was leaning against the rough bark of a tree along the path. Acid burned the back of his throat as his last meal forced its way up through his esophagus. He retched until there was nothing else refusing to stay put in his stomach.

He looked up, finally paying attention to where he was. Otter Pond, Skye's favorite place. A splash from the creek caught his ear. The romp of otters glided through the water, sleek forms glistening as they twisted and dove. The male and female curled around one another, spinning in the gentle current, while their pups splashed one another in a teenaged otter version of Marco Polo.

Doug turned away, running down that path. He had to find Skye, tell her, because he couldn't wait another minute. He checked his watch as he left the Big Woods. Three thirty. It's Wednesday, he realized. She might have decided to still teach her class, which meant she wouldn't be free until four. He'd gone the wrong way, running toward the housing plan, not the Nature Center. He was just about to turn around when he saw a flash of silvery-blond moving in the direction of her apartment.

"I have barf breath."

Doug scoured front yards for a mint plant. He knew there was one nearby. When he found it a few houses away, he stuffed a handful of leaves into his mouth and chewed for a minute, then spat them out. His heart pounded in his chest as he walked to her place. He felt disoriented, like he was in one of those movie scenes where the background moved at a different rate of speed than the people in it. He knocked on the door, feeling like he was going to pass out. He could not remember being this nervous in his entire life.

The door swung open. When she saw him, Skye sighed.

"Can we talk, Skye?" He couldn't believe his voice sounded so steady.

"I don't want to fight with you, Doug," she said, sounding drained.

She looked pale and drawn. And scared. The little anxious line that had only recently begun to take some time off had taken up residence between her eyebrows again. How had he not seen how much she needed him?

"I want to talk *with* you. Not at you."

She shrugged, the gesture noncommittal. "I'm not fighting with you. If you start, I'm kicking you out."

He followed her into the living room, then stopped. He had no idea where to put himself. It must have showed, because Skye tapped the barstool next to her where she sat at the counter between the living room and kitchen.

"I'm not going to bite."

He sat down next to her. This close he could see the softness of her skin, the shine of her silvery-blond hair that hung loose over her shoulders.

"I'm sorry about earlier," he said. "I'm sorry I argued with you and acted like such a jerk. I was scared. I *am* scared."

She nodded, then said, "I understand, I do. It's okay."

He shook his head. "No, it's not."

Doug slid to the edge of the stool, just inches from her now. He pushed her hair back from her face. Ten weeks later, the faintest remnants of sickly yellow bruises were still visible under her eye and along her elegant cheekbone if you knew to look for them.

After the attack, the last thing Doug had wanted to do was rush her. He wouldn't have wanted to rush it anyway. The time just before, when you hoped the other person could tell but you had not worked up the nerve to say it yet, was the part of falling in love that Doug had always found sweetest. He loved Skye and had shown it in every way he could short of telling her, or showing her with his body.

He thought she loved him, but she had not said it, either. There was still the chance he was wrong. Still the chance that he might be projecting his feelings onto her, seeing what he wanted to see. That bit of not knowing combined with not wanting to rush her made him cautious, but so hungry to know. Hungry to know what she felt like, tasted like, to hear the soft noises she would make when they made love. He had let himself sink into the slow, lush dance of lingering touches and too long looks, of longing so deep that it ached, of wanting to know so much and being almost afraid to find out.

Maybe it had taken longer because of Brock. Maybe it would have been like this anyway. Watching her begin to feel comfortable in her own skin again, knowing how comforted she was when he held her hand so she could fall asleep in these weeks since, was the most intimate thing Doug had ever experienced. It was almost as good as those three words and made his hunger to know stronger than the sliver of doubt that he might have misjudged her feelings.

"It's not okay because that's not how you treat someone you love."

Her eyes met his, and he knew that she loved him. He could see it in the kaleidoscope of blue and gold.

"I love you, Skye. And whatever you need to do, I'm with you," he said, his heart breaking open to the bone-crushing fear of losing her, but also to the strength of his love for her.

Her velvety lips brushed his, her mouth sweet like summer berries, and he fell into her headlong. His lips moved to her jaw, down the silky skin of her neck. She pulled his shirt over his head, her hands hot on his chest, her kiss becoming a demand. He gasped when she ran her hands over his stomach, his muscles rippling with want. With need.

They kissed and tripped their way to her bed, stripping each other of clothes so they could touch skin on skin. She sighed deep in her throat, shivered when his lips and tongue explored the swell of her breasts and his hand found the dark heat between her thighs. She was as soft and warm as he had thought she would be, filled with a fiery passion that left him trembling. Just like she was trembling.

And then she broke their kiss and pushed against his shoulders. "You have done this before, right?"

Doug's surprised laughter echoed off the walls. "I'm out of practice," he said, still laughing. "But prepare to be amazed."

It was Skye's turn to laugh before he claimed her mouth again. Everywhere she touched him burst into flames. He sighed when he entered her, whispering her name, the silky embrace of her body beckoning him even closer. Her hooded eyes were soft, shining with love and a happiness he had never seen in them before. Her lips, swollen and pink, the silvery-blond hair that had tumbled across the pillow and tangled in her eyelashes, he wanted all of it. All of her.

"God, I love you," he said softly, losing himself to the rhythm of lust and love lifting them higher, coiling around them, binding them to one another in the oldest, most primal dance there was.

Her hands twisted in his hair. She kept biting her lower lip, radiating heat, whimpering in time to the joining of their bodies. It made him want her even more. Her eyes locked on his, and he saw everything in them...love, desire, amazement. Or maybe the amazement was his, reflected back in her eyes.

He felt the edge rushing toward him, the point of no return suddenly near.

"I can't wait much longer," he said.

Skye nodded, eyes half closed. When she cried out moments later, shuddering beneath him, her nipples hardening against his chest, the connection between them exploded. He let go, falling into the euphoria of their joined bodies that magnified beyond anything Doug had experienced before.

"Holy shit," Skye said afterward, breathless.

Doug rested his damp forehead on her shoulder, catching his breath. He had never felt anything like it, like they had fused together, indelibly, in a flash of heat and light.

"How did I ever think giving this up was a good idea?"

Skye's peal of laughter felt like the softest, coziest blanket settling over them. Doug levered back on his elbows, saw the drowsy contentment that suffused her features, softening her smile, and erasing the little anxious line between her eyebrows. He kissed her eyelids and the tip of her nose. Then he kissed her properly—one that ought to curl her toes—before shifting onto his side and pulling her with him.

They lay facing one another, noses almost touching. An uneven, rakish smile arced to the crinkled corners of her eyes.

"If you get any more endearing, my eyes are going to bleed," he said. Then he grinned like a rogue. "Amazed?"

She laughed again, her eyes sparkling with mischief. "It was a good freshman effort."

Doug's smile faded as he studied her face...the swell of her cheek, the curve of her jaw. She was so beautiful, vital and alive. If his worst fears came true, how would he ever live without her?

"I love you," he said.

Skye's smile had faded, but not the wonder that shone in her eyes.

"I love you," she said. "So much."

He had already seen it in her eyes, in the kaleidoscope of blue and gold, but he hadn't known how he would feel when she said it. That he could love her even more.

"I'm with you, Skye," he whispered. "I'm always on your side, no matter what."

33

"Doug," a voice said, shaking his shoulder gently.

Doug jerked awake, bolting upright. Panic flooded his brain.

"What's wrong?"

"Nothing," Miranda said, crouching beside him where he sat on the floor beside Skye's bed. "Nothing, nothing's changed. I didn't mean to scare you. I just thought you might want to lie on the cot instead of the floor."

His back did ache, and his neck felt like someone had twisted it and driven a spike between the top vertebrae of his spine and skull. He had fallen asleep sitting on the floor next to Skye's bed in the improvised isolation room. Her hand was still in his, hot and damp. Twice her fever had spiked so high that they had to put her in an ice bath, just like they had with Miranda.

She was out again. When she had woken before, she had been delirious, her eyes unfocused before she had lapsed into unconsciousness again. Her face was flushed and sweaty. Her silvery-blond hair stuck to her scalp, its shine gone.

"She wasn't supposed to get this sick."

Miranda ran her hand up and down his back. "She hasn't gotten any worse in the last twenty-four hours, either. She's going to be okay, Doug."

"You don't know that," he said, shaking his head.

He wished he could believe her. He wished Miranda knew for sure, but he couldn't bring himself to indulge in magical thinking to that degree. He *could* extend magical thinking to include prayer to deities and saints that he had no proof were real, but that he believed in all the same. And he had prayed—to God, the Blessed Mother, Jesus, Saints Luke, Jude, Adrian, Sebastian, Rita... He couldn't remember who else. And to every other god and goddess he could think of.

Miranda's eyes were full of sympathy, but also hope. She wasn't putting him on about her belief that Skye would be all right.

"We had five days together."

"During which you were either conspicuously absent, or the pair of you radiated 'Just Fucked' glow so much it was blinding. God's not so cruel to give you that and snatch it away, not you two. Have a little faith."

Exasperated, he said, "Really? You're gonna go there now?"

"Skye's a fighter. And she has you now. She's not going anywhere. I am a thousand percent sure about that."

"I wish I was."

"They haven't tied her down. That's a good sign."

Doug sighed. Miranda was right. She had not gotten that bad—yet.

"Go lay down. The cot's just right there. I'll sit with her and wake you up if anything changes."

"But—"

"It's ten feet away. Go."

Miranda's eyes said, 'Don't make me kick your ass.' He was not going to win this one. Or at least not now, when he was falling-on-his-face exhausted. He climbed to his feet, the muscles of legs and hips tight. He leaned over the cot and kissed Skye's hot forehead. Then he whispered in her ear.

"I'll be just over there. I love you. Keep fighting so I can tell you when you can hear it."

He straightened up. Miranda pulled him tight in an embrace, then pointed him to the cot. He fell asleep almost as soon as his head hit the pillow.

ANOTHER DAY in the chair at Skye's bedside. People kept insisting he eat and drink, and he had to leave to go to the bathroom... It was maddening. Doug sat as still as he could, his eyes closed, trying to meditate. It was the only thing that half worked at getting his anxiety and fear down to just below complete panic.

"Hey."

His eyes snapped open. Skye's eyes were open, too, and looking at him. Her voice had been as soft as a kitten.

"Hey," he said, leaping forward. Her face was no longer flushed. He felt it with the back of his hand. It was cool and dry, as soft as he remembered. Her fever had broken.

"Oh, thank God," he said, tears filling his eyes. He kissed her hand and held it to his face. "You've been so sick. You scared the shit out of me." She smiled tiredly as he leaned in to kiss her. "I love you so much."

"I told you I wasn't going anywhere."

He nodded, never so happy in his life to have been proved wrong.

"I'm just going to call River, okay? I love you, Skye. I love you so much."

Minutes later, Mario stood next to Doug as they watched River examine Skye. Mario's grin stretched from ear to ear.

"This is great, Doug. This is amazing," he said. "I am so happy for you two."

Doug nodded, never taking his eyes from Skye. Word had spread quickly. Alicia joined them right after River arrived. Even her laugh had not been able to penetrate the fog of euphoria and relief swirling around him. Doug glanced at the flash of movement in the corner of his eye. Miranda slipped through the door. She closed in and hugged him, then stepped back, still holding his shoulders.

"I *told* you."

She let go of his shoulder, then leaned against him, her arm around his waist. She ignored Mario. Mario's excitement, which had been so strong Doug could literally feel it sloshing against him, became tempered, replaced by a longing so strong Doug could feel it, too. Something had to be done about these two, but it would have to wait. Right now, the only thing he had time for was Skye.

"You look great," River said, straightening up. "I mean, you're great like someone recovering from a terrible case of the flu and pneumonia," River said, qualifying her earlier statement. "Still a win."

"Can I please get a shower?" Skye said. "I feel gross, and these sheets are disgusting."

"That's because you've been sweating all over them," River said. "We'll change the sheets, but no shower. Maybe the day after tomorrow—*maybe*. You can do a sponge bath." She looked over at Doug and winked. "I'm sure there's someone here who will be very willing to help you."

Everyone laughed or snickered, Doug included. Skye's eyes were already drooping. He could see her fighting to keep them open, like a little kid resisting bedtime. River stepped out the way, and he reclaimed his seat at Skye's bedside. Skye slipped her hand into his.

"Go to sleep, sweetheart," he said. "I'll be here when you wake up."

ALICIA SHRUGGED. "The teratogen effect seems to be transitory. It was there, especially when her fever spiked, but it's gone now," she said, looking from Skye to River. "It's only a risk if a woman is pregnant."

Alicia's looked at Skye again, her face anxious. "You're *positive* you're not pregnant? I know we tested before..."

Doug watched Skye's lips curve into a smile. "I got my period four days ago."

"Oh. Well. That's great," Alicia said, relief filling her voice.

Relief swept through Doug, too.

"You've bounced back much quicker than I expected in just a week," River said. "I still want you to take it easy for another week, but I am very pleased."

"I need another blood draw," Alicia said. "I need to check for the repellant effect."

A few minutes later, Skye's blood had been sucked, and they were left to their own devices. Skye wanted to go outside, so they sat on the stoop outside the main door. The macaques chittered, chasing each other.

"There's Goldie," Doug said, pointing to the blond macaque that had scampered onto the awning above them. Goldie pulled his lips back, baring his teeth. "See, he always smiles at me."

"He's threatening you. You're not supposed to look them in the eye, Doug," Skye said. "You're challenging Goldie's dominance, and you aren't even part of the troop's pecking order."

"Oh," Doug said, looking back to Skye. "That explains a lot, actually."

Skye smiled. "I don't know what I'm going to do with you."

He pulled her closer, going in for a kiss. "Hopefully you will have years to figure it out."

Their lips were just parting when Doug heard footsteps crunching on the falling-apart sidewalk. Miranda and Anna Smith, LO's commander, walked toward them. A guy Doug knew only by sight was still in their vehicle, talking with another of the LO security detail.

"Still kissing all the time, I see," Miranda said, but she grinned at them.

"Yep," said Doug, squeezing Skye to him tighter. "What are you doing here?"

"Alicia wants *another* freaking blood sample," Miranda said. River could have done that, Doug thought. "And they needed a fourth person for the ride. I wasn't doing anything."

"You look good, Skye," Anna said. "I'm glad to see it. I need to check in with Mario and Alicia," she continued. "Figure out how we're going to produce this thing, assuming things go better with the others than they did with you. It would be nice if the vaccine didn't make everyone who receives it deathly ill. And I needed a change of scenery. I don't know if it's springtime or something else, but the uptick in dumbassery lately is driving me crazy."

After they had gone inside, Doug said, "Do you mind if I take some time to talk to Miranda? This thing with her and Mario is ridiculous."

"Of course not," Skye said, starting to stand. Doug leaped to his feet to take her hand. She squinted up at him, shielding her eyes from the sun. "You need to stop."

"Stop what?"

"Hovering. Treating like I'm an invalid. I'm feeling much better. I can stand up on my own."

As if to prove her point, she stood up unassisted.

"Am I really hovering?"

"Just a little," she said, spreading her arms wide. "I understand, and it's very sweet. It really is. Can you please dial it back, just a little bit?"

"Of course," he said, feeling embarrassed. He had never been accused of being a hoverer before. Then a thought occurred to him. "How much better *are* you feeling?"

Skye laughed, a flash of desire darkening her eyes. "I should have known. I think something can be arranged."

Over Skye's shoulder, Doug saw Miranda push open the door to the BSL-3's hallway.

"I've got incoming," he said. He stepped in close and kissed her.

God, she is nice to kiss, he thought. "I'm going to un-hover you back to your room."

"I'll see you later."

The curve of her lips, the promise and desire in her eyes, made Doug want to take her inside and let Miranda figure out her love life on her own.

"You're killing me," he said as the door opened behind her.

"Miranda, hold the door," Skye said, turning away from him.

After Skye was gone, Miranda said, "Why aren't you walking her up to her room?"

"I've been told I'm hovering, so I am un-hovering her ass up the stairs."

"Oh. Well, in that case, well done. You better pay attention because you are hitting so far above your weight it's not funny."

"Believe me, I know."

"You're disgustingly happy. And thank God because the sexual tension was killing us all."

"You're scaring me, Miranda," he said. "I'm not used to almost positive reinforcement from you. Where's Liley?"

"Left her at LO. Gemma, the little girl next door, was playing with her."

Leaving Delilah behind was new. It made Doug uncomfortable, though he couldn't say why. He took her arm and slipped it through his. "Let's take a walk. It's a beautiful day."

She narrowed her eyes at him for a moment, then relented. They started down the path, then cut over in the direction of the pond. It *was* a beautiful day. Puffy, cumulus clouds sailed across deep blue sky. To the east, the snowcapped peak of Mount Hood towered over the landscape.

Doug walked over to a break in the cattails that edged one side of the pond and sat on the carpet of grass and moss. Miranda sat down next to him, her enthusiasm looking tempered.

"So," he said. "You. Mario. What gives?"

She sighed, shooting him a filthy look. "I did not come over here for a lecture."

"And yet you took a walk with me. So spill."

She wore her annoyance like armor, but he could see past it. She would talk, wanted to talk, but needed a nudge. Maybe a hard one.

"Not a lot gives," she said.

"Yeah, I know that part. Why are you doing this?"

She sighed and looked away. "Doing what, exactly?"

"Refusing to talk about losing the baby? Ignoring your partner, who is hurting just as much as you are? Acting like everything's normal while you push him away? I don't think you're trying to be an asshole, Miri, but you are succeeding."

She scowled, then shook her head back and forth, a quarter of an inch at most, while she bit her lip. If the anger Doug saw simmering just below the surface of her skin were a star, it would go supernova any second.

"I'm so angry," she finally whispered. Tears slipped over the edges of her eyes.

When she didn't say anything else, Doug ventured, "You have every right to be."

"No," she said irritably. "I'm angry at *him*. I'm so angry at him, and I don't even know why. And he keeps...pushing. And *wanting*. He wants more than I've got. And I just want to... Mario took everything out of the townhouse," she said, turning to him, her eyes flashing. "Anything sharp, anything at all! I can't even put fucking butter on my bread."

"You have butter?" Doug asked before he could help it. He knew she didn't, but he could almost taste the fatty, creamy goodness on his tongue.

"No, I don't have fucking butter!"

"I'm sorry, Miri... I knew that."

"Christ, you're useless sometimes."

Her anger was directed at him, too, which never happened. And meant she was really hurting.

Doug said, "He's worried about you, that's all."

"Then why doesn't he ask me if I'm going to cut myself instead of doing that?"

Doug tried but couldn't smother the laugh. "Because you won't *talk* to him."

"Don't make this my fault," Miranda snapped.

"I'm not," he said.

They sat in silence for a minute or two. Then Doug said, "*Are you going to cut yourself?*"

"Not at the fucking moment. I don't have the goddamned tools."

Doug mentally sighed, because if she really wanted to, she could find them.

"Are you feeling bad about the abortion?"

"*No,*" she said, her voice a cross of what-the-fuck and don't-be-stupid. "Were we supposed to hope his heart wouldn't be as fucked up as everything else? Pretend his arms and legs wouldn't be like every other thalidomide baby? Teach him to *crawl* away from zombies? There was nothing else to do, unless we wanted to make him suffer before he died."

"Okay, okay," he said, his voice conciliatory. "I'm just making sure, because you wanted the baby."

"Yeah, I did," she said, tears sliding down her face again. She wiped them away and got to her feet. The flash of her eyes was murderous. "I don't want to talk anymore. Don't push."

She marched away, not to the building, but to the parking lot. Doug watched her retreating form. She was angrier than he had ever seen her. With Miranda, that was saying something. And instead of directing it at Jeremiah, who had done this to her, she was dumping it on Mario.

34

MIRANDA SAT IN THE BACK SEAT BETWEEN COMMANDER SMITH and Mario. Smith had not taken the hint, or she just didn't know, because she had insisted that Miranda get into the vehicle ahead of her. Miranda didn't know why Mario was coming along to LO. It had to be something to do with Smith and producing the vaccine. She didn't think he would subject himself to this otherwise.

Now she was stuck between them, wishing she had brought Delilah along. If she had, then she almost certainly would have gotten the front passenger seat to accommodate the dog. But she hadn't, and now she was stuck.

Mario looked out the window, his face in three-quarter profile. He ignored her, mostly. Which was what she wanted. And not what she wanted. The front of this Toyota whatever-it-was mini-SUV had been designed for adults, but the back seat had been designed for kids and car seats. As a consequence, she and Mario touched from hip to shoulder, and knee to hip. There was no getting around it.

Miranda found herself wanting to lean into the warmth of his body, and also wanting to vent an anger toward him that she could not explain. Nothing could mask the feel of his shoulder against her, the rise and fall of his breath. The inch of his wrist below his shirt sleeve, the shape of his hands, almost made her swoon. His snug jeans did nothing to mask the shape of his thighs.

She wanted to push him out of the SUV, be rid of him and the fury he stirred, because she could feel the weight of his legs against her, her thighs wrapped around him, his face above hers. The more she tried to banish the memory, the more detailed it became—his breath hot against her neck, his lips on hers, his voice whispering in her ear all the things he wanted to do to her, and the things he wanted her to do to him. And below the memory this anger, this fury, that percolated just under her skin.

The few times she had chanced a glance, his eyes had been shut, the look on his face that of someone just hanging on. He was doing as she had asked, leaving her alone. It infuriated her. It also made her want to lean into him, melt against him, feel the comfort of his arm around her.

When they got to LO, Mario bolted from the vehicle. She scooted over on the seat to get out, feeling the residual warmth of his body on the upholstery.

Goddammit, she thought. She needed to ask River when her hormones were supposed to level out. When she could expect her body to start feeling like her own again, instead of a vessel overflowing with this anxious, urgent desire and seething anger.

The townhouse was quiet when she returned. Her downstairs neighbor wasn't home. She knew because Delilah would have seen her coming and barked up a storm, her paws on the windowsill as she looked out the window.

Once upstairs and inside, Miranda undid her bra and wriggled out of it without taking off her shirt. It was a little too big now and slid around just enough to be annoying and uncomfortable. She needed to find one of her regular bras that fit her correctly. She closed her eyes and pressed the heel of her hand against her forehead. Thinking about a bra that fit made her think of the house with the lingerie. Images of the night she had surprised Mario with the lingerie leaped unbidden to her mind's eye. The way his lips had curved in an appreciative, hungry smile. The feel of his hard cock in her mouth. His work-roughened hands gliding over her shaved pussy, how he had teased her with his tongue, the tight embrace of her body as he slid into her—

Stop it, just stop it, she hissed at herself. But her body hummed with frustrated desire.

She set the bra on the kitchen counter and gulped down a glass of water. She looked around at the furnishings that had been someone else's, the framed prints on the wall she didn't particularly care for. It had felt like her place, like home for a while, but it didn't anymore. She didn't know why she was so angry with Mario. None of this had been his fault. Of course he needed her. Of course he felt the loss, the grief, of losing the baby. She didn't have a lot to give, that part was true. But she had a little. Instead of trying to share it with him, she guarded it greedily. She would probably feel better if she tried to talk to him, but the anger got in the way every time. It pushed everything else out, blinding her. She had asked herself a thousand times why but never got an answer.

She sat on the upholstered chair by the picture window and tipped her head back. What in the world was she going to do?

WHEN SHE WOKE, the shadows outside her window had lengthened to early evening. The knock. That was what had woken her. She got up, stretching as she walked to door. When she opened it, Mario stood in front of her.

A rush of desire mixed with anger swept through her. She closed her eyes, trying to push them away. Mario looked uncertain. Maybe about being here. Maybe about her.

"Can I come in?"

She took a moment, uncertain herself.

"Sure."

He followed her to the living room but lingered by the junction of the entry hall and main living room. She sat on the couch before realizing this, which made the logistics of talking to him feel awkward. He was both too far away and not far enough.

"I'm sorry about the ride here," he said. "I didn't mean for that... I hope it wasn't too uncomfortable."

She almost said that it was, but he would take it the wrong way. He wouldn't know that she had wanted to sink into him, let him in, but that this anger prevented it.

"I know you didn't plan it any more than I did."

He nodded, a flash of relief in his eyes.

"Doug talked to me," he said.

Of course he did, she thought, annoyed. But she had known that he would, had maybe wanted him to tell Mario. Everything inside her felt so mixed up that she wasn't sure.

Mario looked down at his feet. "I don't know what I've done to make you so angry." He looked over to her, his eyes seeking an answer. "If you, when you figure it out, I hope you'll talk to me. Tell me about it."

"Because I have to be the one to tell you. Because you can't figure things out. Because it's my job to figure out your emotional shit for you."

Mario's eyes widened. "No," he said. "That's not what I meant. You know me better than that."

His response did not give an inch. She could see the flare of temper in his eyes, in the way he took a deep breath before speaking again. "I've said what I wanted to, and I'm just pissing you off, so I'll go."

Miranda was on her feet in an instant. "You're good at that. Leaving."

Mario turned back. "What?"

"You heard me," she said, walking closer. "That's what you do. You drop out and leave, then expect me to take you back."

"You threw me out," he said, looking bewildered. "And if you're talking about before, at home, you know I'm sorry that I ever did any of it."

"I'm not talking about San Jose, but you left me then, too." Only a foot separated them now. The tension in his stance made her fingers itch. "I'm talking about that night. When you left us, and all of this happened."

Mario's lips were slightly parted, breaths coming fast. "I didn't know you were pregnant because you didn't tell me."

"In the five minutes before you took Brock away?"

"I would have stayed, and you know it."

She saw the truth of it in his eyes. Knew the truth before she accused him. But it didn't change that when she had needed him, he had not been there.

"What were you thinking when you went out there? There were other people who could have gone with Doug," Mario said. "Did you even stop to think that maybe it shouldn't be you?"

Icy shock pulled Miranda up short. Doug had questioned her decision to go with him to investigate. She had responded to his concern with annoyance, brushing it aside because it had felt patronizing.

"I didn't know what would happen," Miranda answered, defensiveness filling her voice. "We had no idea what we were dealing with."

"You had no idea what you were dealing with, and you still went to look, because Miranda Tucci's not afraid of anything. She charges in, consequences be damned."

"You'd be dead if I stopped to think about everything the way you do," she countered.

"But it's not me that's dead because you put yourself in harm's way, is it? And it's not you, either. If one of us left the baby behind, it sure as shit wasn't me."

The dagger-sharp pain of his accusation plunged into Miranda's heart. Into the place where she had been foolish enough to nurture the small, soft dream of their child.

"What do you care?" she said angrily, tears springing to her eyes. "You already have three children. You just abandoned ours faster."

Mario recoiled, shock supplanting the anger flashing in his eyes, followed by a fleeting glimpse of anguish. She had landed the blow with just as much skill as he had landed his, weaponizing his heartache because he had trusted her with it.

They stood feet apart, but a wasteland stretched between them. Mario looked at her for another moment, then left without a word.

35

DOUG AND SKYE WERE NOWHERE TO BE FOUND AT THE NATURE Center.

"I can't believe they're late, Delilah. I'm starving," Miranda said.

Delilah's eyes flicked up from where her head rested on her paws and yawped at Miranda, almost disinterested. Miranda reached down and gave Delilah's head a scratch.

"I guess you're not perished with the hunger, little dog, but I am."

Miranda could go to dinner on her own but wanted others around in case she ran into Mario. Doug had mentioned he was back at LO. The less she saw of him, the better.

Miranda checked her watch again. Doug was a punctual person, but Skye took punctuality to a whole new level. It was kind of unnerving, in Miranda's opinion, but she was probably not the best judge. Doug teased her she would be late for her own funeral.

"They're probably fucking in a closet," she muttered.

She wished they would show up because she needed a distraction from the fight with Mario. Two weeks later, it still rattled inside her head on a nonstop loop. She couldn't help the way she felt. Even if the feelings were unfair, they were what they were. But she could help how she acted. Nearly every single thing she had accused him of was unfair or untrue. She'd said the kind of things you can't take back. So had he.

Doug had tried to dissuade her from going with him that night to investigate why the macaques were so noisy, and she blew him off. Where Doug had expressed legitimate if annoying concern, she had seen only a double-standard. She had compared walking into God knows what to an imminent threat, called it even, and done what she always did.

It was too late now. Why the hell was it her job, anyway, to put things back together? The anger always prowling below the surface of her emotional facade broke free, hitting her so hard it felt like it would knock her down. She wanted to strike out at Mario, to hurt him, demand he take the blame. And to shield him from this anger she could not control. To distance herself and protect the man she loved instead of destroying him.

"You okay, Miranda?"

Her head snapped up. Phineas stood in front of her, his hand on her shoulder. She had not even felt it.

"Uh, yeah, yeah, I'm fine," she said, trying to pull herself together. "I, um... You look a lot better."

Phineas' crutches were real ones, manufactured of metal and rubber, not like the pieces of crap she had used at New Jerusalem. The cast from his heel to just past his knee had to weigh a ton.

"What are you doing out?" she asked. "Shouldn't you still be resting?"

"River finally agreed to let me take short walks. For my morale," he said, grinning.

"Through the Big Woods is not short."

"I'm on my way back. Don't rat me out."

"I'm glad you're doing better. You haven't seen Doug and Skye around, have you?"

"They were heading in the direction of the Comm Shack a couple minutes ago."

"Guess I was wrong then," she said softly.

"Wrong about what?"

She laughed a little, almost under her breath. "Oh, I was thinking they might be late meeting me because they were getting it on in a closet."

Phineas' eyebrows shot skyward. "What? But...isn't he a priest?"

"They are a thing," she said, standing. "And he's packing in the priesthood. You really haven't been getting out. Or you're just that young and unobservant."

A rakish grin curved Phineas' jaw. "I haven't been getting out, and I'm not so young that I couldn't handle you, Miranda. I'm still holding out hope."

"Oh, for Pete's sake," she said, laughing.

The kid just did not stop. For a moment she thought how easy it would be. What a relief an uncomplicated, casual fling with Phineas, who was easy on the eyes and probably knew a thing or two, would be. At twenty, his youthful optimism was still intact. There would be no history and no expectations.

She gave herself a mental shake.

"I'll see you when I see you, Phineas."

She crossed the parking lot, feeling unsettled, and took the northerly path that led to the Comm Shack. Delilah raced up the path ahead of her and around a bend, then began to bark. Maybe at Doug and Skye, she thought, hoping to catch up quickly. Instead, she walked the whole way there while Delilah crashed in and out of the brush, barking and chasing squirrels. When Miranda reached the Comm Shack, the door was open. Doug stood in it, leaning against the doorjamb.

He looked over his shoulder and motioned her over. Skye stood just inside the door. She glanced at Miranda, then looked back to Commander Smith. Smith was next to Larry, leaning over the sound defense control board. LO's Comm Shack Operator looked as harried and anxious as when Station Eight had gone off-line. She had seen him in the dining hall this morning, and he had not looked bent out of shape in the least.

Something had happened.

"Station Twelve radioed in twenty minutes ago, said the machines were showing error messages. Then their comms went off-line and I haven't been able to raise them since. None of the other stations can raise them, either. Then Stations Eleven and One did the same thing about eight minutes ago. There's nothing I can see on this end that accounts for it. The system looks like it's operating normally."

Miranda looked at Doug sidelong. His brow was furrowed, and his tongue worried the inside of his cheek.

"So, the stations reported errors but not malfunctions, and now we can't raise them, but things look normal on the board and the system is working. Or, we really do have a problem with two gaps this time," Smith said. "Is there anyone besides Phineas who can go out to see?"

Larry shook his head. "Apart from me, no. Crystal died at Station Eight. Her replacements and Phineas' backups aren't trained up enough for this sort of thing. We could send someone from an adjoining station to meet whoever you send."

"I don't like that idea," Smith said. "Not when we've lost contact with three stations already."

"Then I go," Larry said. "Phineas can hold things down here, no problem. He doesn't need to be mobile for this."

Smith nodded, then looked at her watch. "It'll be dark in an hour, seventy-five minutes at the outside. Goddammit." She took a moment to marshal her thoughts. "Okay, here's what we're going to do. Station Eleven is closest to the Institute, so it's the priority. Doug, I'd like you to go with Rocco and Larry. And you too, Miranda. Get a sit-rep. If you can fix what's wrong, stay there and do it. If you can't or it's not safe, fall back to the Institute."

"I'll go, too, Anna," Skye offered.

Smith shook her head. "No. I need you here. Get patrol group alpha together and brief them. They're tasked with Station One, since it's closest to Portland."

Doug stepped out of the way, and Skye exited the Comm Shack. Larry left ahead of Smith, whom Miranda waited for by the door.

"I just saw Phineas. He said he was heading home," Miranda said. "I'll go get him."

"Thanks, Miranda," Smith said. "But you need to get your kit together and get out of here." She continued, her voice softer. "Are you up for this? I didn't think to ask before."

Miranda appreciated that Commander Smith had thought to ask. Truth was, she was dying to do something that would make her feel normal.

"I'm up for it, Commander. Happy to help."

"Good," Smith said. "We can never have enough people who'll charge in, consequences be damned."

She charges in, consequences be damned.

Unbidden, Mario's accusation echoed inside Miranda's head. She pushed it aside as she caught up with Doug and Skye. Delilah already followed them, as if she knew they were off on another adventure and she was going, too. Charging in was what she had always done, from the moment she decided that she would live when all of this started. The decision to meet danger head-on made her feel in control. It was an illusion, of course, but it was better than feeling helpless.

I can't help what I am, she thought.

And Mario, of all people, should have known that.

SO FAR, the influx of zombies was not too bad. The stench was another story. But any influx meant that at least some of the stations were off-line, and it wasn't showing up on LO's monitoring system. Miranda pulled her bandana over her nose and mouth. The only downside of spring and summer was how much the smell of decay increased in warmer weather. It didn't matter that some of these zombies were almost eleven years old. They still stunk to high heaven.

Rocco turned at a break in the hedge that lined the road. The pickup thumped down a pitted gravel path alongside a tall, thick hedge before creaking to a halt. Delilah swayed gently into Miranda when the truck rocked, then followed her and Doug when they hopped down from the truck's bed. Miranda shrugged into her small pack. She checked to make sure that her gun was loaded, snapping the magazine back into place before holstering it on her hip. Then she checked the other handgun in her thigh holster and made sure the machete on that same hip was secured. She cradled her assault rifle close, like it was precious cargo.

Rocco said, "Station Eleven is about a half mile from here. We go through the fence at the end of this path, then turn right. We'll take a path through the yards of the houses along that street. The Station House has blue siding."

Doug said, "It'll have a fence, right?"

"Yeah, there is that," Rocco said.

Larry looked in the direction of the moans, his face apprehensive.

"Been a while since you've been outside?" Miranda asked him.

Larry shrugged. "I'm fine."

"Stick close to me, if it comes to that," Miranda said.

Larry raised an eyebrow at her. "How's that going to help?"

Miranda remembered that Larry didn't know she could repel zombies. The fact that both she and Skye could was under wraps for the time being. She had meant to reassure him but had not thought it through.

Instead, she said, "I'm a shitkicker extraordinaire. And I have very good luck."

"Okay," Rocco said. "Let's go."

They walked single file, Rocco taking point, Doug bringing up the rear with Larry and then Miranda between them. Delilah mostly stayed beside Miranda but wandered off to sniff or investigate things Miranda could not see. Larry carried himself well. He scanned the area as they walked, carrying his machete lightly in his hand, and didn't startle when a rabbit shot across the path in front of him. They all slipped through the hole in the fence and turned east.

The closer they got to the Station House, the louder the zombies coming from the north became. Miranda found it unsettling both how well LO's sound defenses worked to keep the undead at bay and how quickly zombies arrived whenever there was a chink in the sonic armor.

The shadows lengthened as the sun dropped toward the horizon. Shit, Miranda thought, just a second before Rocco raised his fist to indicate they should halt. Delilah's nose bumped into Miranda's leg at the abrupt halt. Miranda could see the Station House ahead, six doors down, because of the tall chain-link fence that surrounded it. The house was intact, but a fat ribbon of gray smoke rose skyward from it.

"Fire isn't zombies," Larry said. "Who the hell would hit a Station House?"

Rocco turned back to face the rest of them. "I think we should—"

Gunfire erupted around them. Miranda dropped into the high grass. Delilah barked once and darted away. Rocco pulled Larry down, and Miranda lost sight of them.

Behind her, Doug said, "Where the hell are they?"

As abruptly as it had begun, the gunfire stopped. Miranda looked back to Doug. He was on his belly, ten feet behind her.

"The houses?"

Doug snorted, as if that much was obvious. "Can you tell which one?"

The moans and groans of zombies grew louder, excited by the noise of the gunfire. A few sounded closer than Miranda would have liked, but right now, they had more pressing concerns. And I can repel them, she reminded herself. But that only helped the others if they were right next to her. And only if they didn't get shot.

Larry's voice came from a little to the west. "We're okay; how about you two?"

"We're good," Miranda answered, though whatever rock she had dropped down onto was sharp as hell.

She turned her head as Delilah crept close, hunkering down beside her. Relief that her loyal little pit bull was safe hit her in a rush. Delilah whimpered softly as she nudged Miranda's hip with her nose.

"Miri," Doug said. He held a rock in his hand and began twisting his yellow bandana around it. "I'm going to lob this back the way we came. Watch the houses. See if you can see them."

She nodded, but when she started to twist, the pain in her hip flared bright, like the flash from a firecracker.

"Ow!" she hissed.

"What's wrong?" Doug asked.

She reached down to touch her hip where Delilah kept nudging her. Her fingers came away bloody.

"I think I've been shot in the ass."

"What?"

She held Delilah's collar and forced herself onto her knees. A bright flash of pain rushed across her back and down her leg. She didn't bother to try and hold the dog's muzzle shut because any barking would be lost in the gunfire.

"Just throw your rock. I'm ready."

Doug shot her a worried glance. A moment later, he cocked his arm back and threw the rock. Miranda gritted her teeth and poked her head up a little higher. Bright muzzle flashes lit up the upper-story windows of the house two down from the Station House. She had not realized how quickly twilight was descending until she saw the flashes.

"Two houses down from the Station House, toward us," she said, pulling Delilah closer to her.

Rocco said, "I see it. You really hit, Tucci?"

"Unfortunately," she said.

"Okay, here's what we're gonna do," Rocco said. "I'll give you five seconds of cover fire to get to Miranda. Then I'm going to give you a longer one to get behind the houses. The embankment above the stream is at the end of the lots."

"What stream?" Miranda asked. She hadn't seen any streams on the way in.

"I know it," Larry said.

"What about you?" Miranda said.

"You can cover me once you've got cover. Don't worry," Rocco said.

"Rocco!" Miranda said.

"Tucci," Rocco said, his tone indulgent. "I think you're swell, too. Now shut the fuck up."

A second later, a burst of gunfire erupted from Rocco's assault rifle. Doug and Larry appeared beside Miranda from different directions.

"Can you walk?" Larry asked.

"I think so," Miranda answered.

"Get over my shoulder as much as you can," Doug said. "I'll carry you, just till we get there."

Larry pointed behind them, away from the houses. "We're going that way."

When Rocco opened up again, Doug heaved Miranda onto his shoulder. The world jolted and rocked as he ran. Rocco lay down suppressing fire while moving backward in the direction they were headed. When they hit the backyard and veered behind the shelter of the house, Doug unceremoniously dumped Miranda on the ground. She and Larry ran for the embankment, Delilah dashing beside them. Miranda lost sight of Doug as she slid down the embankment to the stream.

A steady volley of gunfire ripped from nearby. Ten seconds later, Delilah barked as two dark forms dove over the lip of the embankment and rolled to the bottom.

Climbing to his feet, Rocco said, "Thanks, Doug. Appreciate it. We'll fall back to the Insti—"

A bright flash filled the sky to the south, accompanied by a deep boom. A bright, flickering light illuminated the sky beyond the tree-tops, followed by a thick column of black smoke.

An explosion.

At LO.

36

"ARE YOU SURE YOU'RE OKAY?" RIVER ASKED.

Mario set down the empty cup of what was passing for coffee these days. The coffee they'd had at the Institute a couple weeks ago had not made its way to LO.

"I'm hanging in there."

The lie tripped off his tongue so easily. He had said it so many times in the two weeks since the fight with Miranda that he almost believed it. He looked out the window of LO's dining hall at the grounds of the Boys' Home. River had arrived at the tail end of the dinner service, and he had waved her over to join him. That had been an hour ago, and he appreciated that she hadn't asked about him and Miranda immediately. The dining hall was almost deserted; just a few people remained, and none of them sat nearby. On the cusp of twilight, the shadows outside the window grew long.

"How's Miranda?"

Mario shrugged. Fuck if he knew. And sometimes, in his lowest moments, fuck if he cared.

"I have no idea," he admitted. "We had an awful fight. I haven't seen her since. She doesn't want to see me, and most of the time, I don't want to see her. I'm not even sure we're still together, to be honest."

He realized the truth of his words as he said them. He truly did not know where things stood or if they would get better. Or if he wanted them to.

You already have three children. You just abandoned ours faster.

Remembering her words felt as painful as when she had said it. She had accused him of thinking that their child hadn't mattered, that one was interchangeable with another.

He had been just as bad. He knew she could be reckless, but it had been cruel to lay responsibility on her for what happened. Maybe he shouldn't have been surprised that she came back with something just as hurtful, but he had no idea how to forgive her for it.

What had happened to Tadpole wasn't her fault, and it wasn't his, but you'd never know it by how they had turned on each other.

River's dark eyes brimmed with sympathy. "You guys really love one another. Anyone can see it. And it's not uncommon in my experience, her pulling away. It's not the case here, it never is, really, but a lot of women feel like their body has let them down. That can really screw with a person's equilibrium."

Mario shook his head. "I don't know how you come back from what we said to each other."

River pushed the braid of her straight, black hair over her shoulder. She opened her mouth but never got farther. A bright white flash and a thunderous boom filled the sky outside, rattling the dining hall windows.

"What the—" Mario said.

The white flash turned into a yellow-orange fireball that billowed above the treetops, lighting up the sky on the far side of the Big Woods. Charcoal-black smoke, visible against the twilit sky only because of the light from the fire, spewed into the sky.

"Is that the Nature Center?" River gasped.

They scrambled to their feet and ran for the exit.

"I need to get my medical bag," River said as she pushed on the exterior dining hall door.

"You have an armory at your place, right?"

River stopped, still holding the door with one hand.

"You think it's an attack?" she said.

"I don't know."

They raced across the Boys' Home grounds and through the sliver of woods separating it from the housing plan. People stood in windows and doorways, on lawns and in the street, everyone asking someone else what was happening. Still others—the kind of people who ran toward danger like he was now—sprinted into the Big Woods. Whether it was the Nature Center or the Woods itself on fire Mario could not tell, but it seemed to be growing.

They burst through the door to River's house.

"In the kitchen," she said, turning into her office. "Straight down the hall. The two cupboards next to the back door!"

Mario walked down the hall as quickly as he could. He didn't dare run since he didn't have a flashlight and the house was filled with shadows.

"There's a lantern on the island counter," River shouted.

Mario found the lantern. It was the kind with a crank, powered by elbow grease. He turned the crank as fast as he could.

There were cupboards on both sides of the back door, but two of them were floor-to-ceiling and vertical, the kind for storing brooms and garbage cans. Mario pulled one open. Rifles lined a stacked rack. He grabbed one, then checked to see if it was loaded, which of course it wasn't. He didn't see any ammo, so he opened the next closet. He scanned the ammo boxes quickly, found the right one, and loaded the rifle. Then he loaded another one for River. As he looked around the room, the lantern died.

"Fucking piece of crap," he muttered, cranking it some more. He started pulling open cupboards, searching for something to carry more ammo in. He found canvas bags in a drawer. He pulled two out and returned to the ammo closet, hastily stuffing the bags. He turned at the sound of footsteps to see River in the shadowy outline of the door to the hall.

"I'm going to the Nature Center, or wherever," she said.

"Here," Mario said, thrusting a rifle into River's arms. "Take this and the ammo."

She only hesitated for a moment, then set down the medical bag in her hand. Mario slipped the rifle's strap over his head and looped the bag of ammo over his shoulder.

"I have a better bag for that," River said.

Mario followed her down the hall. She had left a lighted lantern in her office, and its glow spilled out to illuminate the area by the front door. River bent over a bin and reached inside, then straightened up and handed him a canvas messenger bag. He dumped his ammo into the messenger bag and slipped the strap over his shoulder, taking care that it did not get tangled with the rifle. River went to turn off the lantern. Mario pulled the front door open and hurried outside. As River joined him on the porch, Mario heard a short series of pops.

Gunfire.

"Did you hear that?" River said. "Was that—?"

"Yeah," Mario said, trying to place its location.

Then came another short burst.

"That's coming from the Boys' Home," Mario said.

"I need to see if anyone was hurt in the explosion," River said. "I'll send some people back here. Get more rifles so you're ready for them."

"Okay," Mario said. "Hurry. And be careful."

River nodded and ran down the street toward the Big Woods. Mario watched her for a moment, then looked down the street in the other direction. No lights were on in Miranda's townhouse, and he had not seen her in the street. He had no idea where she was.

Please be safe, Miri.

It was not a thought as much as a silent, undirected prayer. He could already see a group of three people hurrying his way. He ducked back into the house to get more guns.

TWO MINUTES LATER, Mario, joined by Skye and three other people he did not know, were hiding among the strip of trees between the housing plan and the Boys' Home. Mario crouched as low as he could while kneeling with one knee forward. He squinted, wishing he had some night vision goggles. Whoever was behind this might have them, which would leave the five of them hiding in these trees at a terrible disadvantage. The intruders had planned their attack well. There had been a new moon a day ago. The waxing moon's rim of white did almost nothing to illuminate the dark landscape.

A ripple of movement caught his eye. A second later he could make out a figure, mostly because of its bulky outline and the insec-toid-like protrusions sprouting from its head. He had been right about the night vision goggles. The agreed upon course of action before scattering into the trees was simple. Wait until they got close. Kill them all.

Another figure, and then another, emerged from the shadows. Ten seconds later, there were five. The even match was a stroke of luck because once they opened fire, their positions were blown. They had to wait. The intruders might be wearing body armor, and their posture indicated they had semi-automatic weapons at least. They needed them close enough to negate those advantages.

They were fifty feet out. Still crouching low, Mario nestled the elbow of his right arm against his knee, the heft of the rifle cradled in it reassuring. Forty feet. He took deep, measured breaths, because time had slowed down, stretching out like stiff taffy on a cold day. Thirty feet. Behind them—gunfire. Maybe from the Big Woods?

How many of them were there?

Twenty feet. He could hear one of them say something, the soft murmur of a man's voice. Mario raised his torso straight, set the rifle's stock to his shoulder, sighted up, and fired. On both sides of him gunfire rang out into the night. The figure closest to him fell, a quick burst of gunfire flying into the sky. Mario kept firing. He had to make sure the man was *down*.

Mario heard a grunt of pain on his left, one of the people who had come with Skye. He swiveled and saw another intruder pulling himself on the ground. He fired again. The downed figure jerked and shuddered, as if having a fit. There would be no mercy for these people. They had attacked unprovoked, were killing people Mario cared about. A quick death was too good for them.

The rest of the intruders were down and not moving. Mario crashed through the brush to his teammate whose name he didn't even know. He tripped and fell flat on his face. He heard a groan. He had tripped over him! Mario scrambled up.

"How bad are you hit?"

A gurgling groan. Mario flicked on his tiny red flashlight, the kind that didn't mess up your night vision. Gunfire had ripped the guy's throat to shreds. Someone else moved through the brush toward them. Mario checked the man's pupils. They were dilated and fixed. He wasn't breathing.

Mario heard Skye's voice. "Is he okay?"

"He's dead."

"Cindy and Michael have left to sweep the Boys' Home. We need to go."

Blood pounded in Mario's ears as they ran for the Big Woods. His anger burned as bright as the fire still visible on the wood's far side. He hated this shit. People murdered, and no time to even close their goddamned eyes. Just leave the bodies behind because another threat had to be dealt with. These assholes would pay. If it was the last thing he did, they would pay. They ran along the row of houses abutting the strip of woods, then burst into the open of the swampy marsh on either side of the creek. They splashed through the creek and approached the edge of the Big Woods.

"If we go in here, we can catch the Ponderosa Loop. It's the quickest route to the Na—"

Skye's words were cut short by a burst of gunfire in the woods to the immediate northeast. They dropped to the ground. There were small bursts of light from more gunfire, then yet another burst farther away, then another. They had stumbled on a gunfight, with no way to tell which side was which.

"That's where we need to go," Skye said, her frustration palpable. She thought a moment, then said, "We'll follow the creek. We can catch another loop ahead. It's close. And if that doesn't work, we'll go to the next one."

They edged away from the woods into the marsh and took off running to the west. The swampy marshland sucked at Mario's boots. The muck sticking to them weighed his feet down, making the burn of his leg muscles more intense. A few minutes later, Skye slowed, then stopped. She motioned for Mario to follow her as she crept to the tree line. Then they crouched low and waited. And waited. And waited, until Mario wanted to scream. In reality, it was one minute, maybe, but all Mario could think of was where the threat would come from next, who was in danger, and where was Miranda?

Skye said, "Okay, let's go."

Two steps into the woods and he knew why they were not cutting through them. The footing was treacherous. Fallen logs were everywhere. Trees so thick you had to squeeze between them because the other directions offer no better progress. Jaggy bushes, thick with thorns that dug into his flesh. Mario skimmed the ground with his lead foot because taking an actual step in the dark was too dangerous.

They stumbled onto the path.

"Left," Skye said.

They ran side by side. The trail was a shade lighter than the forest around it. At the first convergence with another trail, they turned left. At the next, Skye stopped. Gunfire echoed in the woods.

"If we go right, we'll hit Vine Maple Trail. It goes straight to the Nature Center, but..."

"It goes straight to the Nature Center. I know that path," he said. "How far out of the way does the other one take us?"

"All the way to the north end, by the Comm Shack."

Another explosion caused the ground under them to shake. Mario looked east. More yellow and orange flames leaped to the sky in the vicinity of the Nature Center.

"Fuck it," Mario said. "Let's just go."

When they reached Vine Maple Trail, they turned east. Rounding the last bend, Mario shielded his eyes from the flames engulfing the Nature Center. Bodies lay on the ground. A running gun battle was taking place in the parking lot in front of the burning building. On this side of the burning building, figures darted from one point of cover—a bench, a trash can, a vehicle—to another. Some darted out to drag the wounded to cover. A few wandered, clearly dazed and shell-shocked.

They continued down the path, more cautious than ever. Mario stopped when he heard a grunt ahead, then saw two people farther down the path struggling with one another. One was larger, but the smaller of the two was holding their own. The smaller person turned, her silhouette cast in profile by the raging fire.

"That's Anna," Skye said, taking off.

Anna called out, "It's a zombie!"

They rushed to LO's commander. The zombie had her by the shoulders. Its snapping teeth were held back only by the commander's elbow, which she had managed to wedge against the zombie's cheek. It turned the zombie's face away, but Mario could see that Anna was tiring. The zombie wouldn't.

Skye's arm flashed forward, the arc of her raised knife slicing down for the zombie's neck. Then Anna lost her footing. She fell backward, pulling the zombie with her.

Anna and the zombie thrashed on the ground. Mario grabbed a handful of the zombie's hair, yanking its head back. Skye raised her knife again. But instead of staying intent on the commander, the zombie pushed itself up at Mario. Mario had just enough time to get his arm up to block. He heard the rip of fabric, then felt the sharp bite and sinking tear of teeth.

Skye dove after them, finally able to drive her knife into the vertebrae connecting the base of the zombie's skull with the neck. The zombie collapsed, its teeth releasing Mario's arm.

"Are you bitten?" Skye asked, horror in her voice.

"I've been vaccinated, I'm fine," he said, brushing her concern aside. He felt blood trickling down his arm. The pain from the bite throbbed in time with his heart.

They knelt beside Anna, who had pushed herself to sitting. She held a hand to her side.

"Anna, are you okay?" Skye asked.

The commander looked up at Skye and Mario. She faced the fire at the Nature Center. Anger filled her brown eyes.

"I've been bitten," she said. "But we don't have time for that. We have to repel this attack."

TWO MINUTES LATER, Mario's arm hastily bandaged and Anna's arm draped over his shoulder, they had abandoned a stealthy approach. They stood just inside the edge of the Big Woods. The long, rectangular building across the wide sidewalk from the Nature Center was still intact. They darted behind it at the narrow end. A head popped around the other sheltered corner.

"Skye?"

"River?" Skye said. "The commander's hurt."

"This way," River said, motioning for them to follow her behind the building.

When they rounded the corner, Mario saw a large group of people huddled alongside it.

"Anna, sit down here, and I'll take a look," River said.

Anna shook her head. "No, I've got to organize—"

"Rich is already doing it," River said, pointing to the small group gathered at the other end of the building. "Sit. Now."

Mario recognized Rich's soft drawl as he and Skye drew near.

Rich had driven back to LO with him earlier in the day. Mario was glad he was here.

"Everyone understand?" Rich asked.

"What's the plan, Rich?" he asked.

"James? Glad to see you." He pointed to the parking lot. "Some of them are pinned down in the parking lot. We're circling around to flank them. Once they're dealt with, we'll do the same at the main gate if we need to."

"We just ran into a zombie on the path by the Nature Center," said Skye.

"Yeah, we know there are some inside," Rich said. "I think they brought them."

"We need to capture at least some of the intruders alive," Mario said. "We need to know who these people are."

"We'll give them a chance to surrender, but if they're not interested..."

Mario nodded, not encouraged by Rich's attitude. But he knew what it was like to have your home and the safety of your loved ones threatened.

"Okay," Rich said. "Let's move out."

"Rich, one sec," Skye said. She motioned Rich to her, then pulled him aside. "Anna's been bitten. I thought you should know."

Rich's face went slack with shock for a moment. But when he spoke, his voice was deadly. "Let's get these assholes."

"Don't let your temper get the better of you," Mario said.

"Don't you worry about that," Rich said bitterly. "I could use more people on the other side of the Nature Center. You two up for going around on the Big Woods side so we can catch them in a pincer? I want to know who these people are so we can pay them a visit."

37

LARRY TRIED THE TRUCK AGAIN. THE ENGINE SPUTTERED, sounding like it wanted to start, then gave up the ghost.

"Piece of crap," Rocco muttered under his breath.

Doug looked at Miranda. Delilah was already in the bed of the truck, looking at him anxiously as if to say, 'What are you stupid humans waiting for?' Doug's own anxiety rose with every passing second. The truck would not start, no matter how Rocco tinkered with it. Twilight was rapidly ceding its grip, nightfall almost upon them. Around them, the moans of zombies grew louder.

"We have to get out of here," Doug said.

Over the tops of the row of bushes and trees the pickup was parked behind came another flash of light, followed by a rumble and a crack. They scrambled through the tree line to the comparatively clearer space of the old road. Another fireball billowed into the sky above LO.

"What is going on there?" Larry said.

Doug watched the flames and smoke, his heart contracting. He felt helpless, not knowing what terrible events were unfolding at LO, or if Skye was safe.

"We've gotta go," Miranda said.

"I know, let me think," Rocco said, distress constricting his voice. "There's another vehicle in a stash house, but it's a half a mile north of here."

"That's the wrong direction," Larry said. "That's into where the zombies are coming from."

"Tell me something I don't know, Larry," Rocco snapped. He jumped into the bed of the truck and squinted, looking north. "I don't think we can fall back to the Institute. It takes us away from LO, and if we get cut off, we're screwed." Then he added, more to himself than the others, "And Tucci can't limp along fast enough."

"I can," Miranda said, standing. "Rocco, I'll be fine if I can't keep up. Let's just go."

"How will you be fine?" Larry asked, turning to Miranda.

"Doesn't matter," Miranda said.

Doug said, "The zombies will be inside the perimeter of the next Station House over soon. They're going to cut us off if we wait any longer. It won't get more clear between here and LO than it is right now."

Fifteen minutes later, the smell hit them. Doug gagged as soon as the wind changed direction, blowing from the northeast.

"Jesus, Mary, and Joseph," he said, his eyes beginning to water. The pace they had set was punishing. Doug had worried at first that Miranda and Larry might not be able to keep up, but he needn't have. Imminent death had a way of motivating people.

"We should get up high. See what we're up against," Larry said.

"We won't be able to see anything," Doug panted. It was deep twilight and would soon be dark. "Let's just keep going."

"We need to know what's going on," Rocco said. "The Costco is just ahead."

"A Costco," Doug asked. "Really?"

He had participated in his fair share of end-of-the-world clichés, including raiding two of the three Costcos in San Jose. It had been a great stroke of luck that one of them was technically in Santa Clara, just minutes from SCU's campus. LO must have set this one up as a bolt hole because there was no way it had anything of value left.

A thousand feet later, Rocco and Larry veered off the road. Thanks to the parking lots surrounding the Costco, as soon as they got through the trees lining the road, it was a lot easier to see. The white-and-red canopy of Costco's gas pumps, falling apart and rusted in place, stood sentry over the scrub and small trees that had broken through the weathered asphalt.

Doug put on his headlamp, as did the others. The groans of the zombies were louder nearer to the warehouse. When they reached the Tire Center, Rocco walked to one of the roller doors at a car bay and felt along the wall. A moment later, he came back with a key.

"We should be doing a walk around the building to make sure no one has broken in," Rocco muttered, then opened the door.

"Let Liley in first," Miranda said. "She'll bark if there's anything."

Rocco did, and when there were no barks, they entered. The slightly unpleasant scent of rubber tires, still on the display racks, filled Doug's nose as he pulled and locked the door behind him.

Doug took Miranda's arm, since she was limping pretty badly. "How's your butt?"

"How do you think?"

Delilah walked beside them, panting, two inches of pink tongue hanging out of her mouth. They followed Larry and Rocco on a labyrinthine path that Doug would be hard-pressed to retrace, but then Larry pointed out the arrows in yellow tape on the floor. They reached a set of utilitarian stairs.

Miranda said, "I'm going to wait for you here."

"You sure?" Rocco asked.

"Yeah," she said, leaning against the railing. "I've got Liley. Go."

Doug gave her arm a squeeze. "Be right back."

They left Miranda behind and climbed, their footsteps echoing through the dark warehouse. He heard the clunk as Rocco opened the door to the roof. Doug caught the door's weight from Larry as he walked through. They trotted over the roof, which was in surprisingly good shape. To Doug's right on the south side, he could see LO, only a quarter of a mile away. A huge fire raged on LO's eastern edge—probably the Nature Center. Underneath the noise of the inferno, Doug could hear the call and response of gunfire.

"Jesus," Larry said, sounding stunned.

Doug found the evidence of his eyes hard to believe. It was so different here than San Jose. People got along, worked together. Who would do this?

Doug squinted at the main entrance, a few hundred feet due east of the Nature Center. It was hard to see into LO, since the area was pretty flat, and the Costco was not very high. But enough light from the fire illuminated the main entrance. What he thought he saw hit Doug like a punch to the gut.

"Is the drawbridge down?"

"Holy shit," Larry said.

"Who would do that?" Rocco whispered, sounding like he wanted to murder someone.

Doug tore himself away and ran to the east side of the building's roof. His heart sank. A dark mass of zombies headed this way—thousands of them. The edge of the massive horde was already well inside the perimeter of the Station Houses. It would be safe to assume that some of the horde had gone south. They might already be cut off by zombies on the ground that they couldn't see in the darkness.

"Rocco," he called, running back to them. "There's a huge horde coming. We gotta go."

Larry said, "I don't think we're going to make it."

"I'm going," Doug said.

Rocco turned to Larry. "Stay here. You know where the supply stash is, and there's a radio. In case we don't make it."

Larry's protest was instantaneous. "No!"

Rocco shook his head. "If we're killed, you can at least tell them what happened at the Station House we checked. They'll need to know. Tucci can stay with you."

"She won't," Doug said.

"I'm not either, then," Larry said.

"We need you to get the sound defenses back up, Larry," Rocco said. "You know that stuff better than anyone. Please, stay here."

"I can't do nothing," Larry protested.

"You won't be," Rocco said. "We need you later, alive. But if we don't get the drawbridge up, there won't be anything to save."

WITHIN MINUTES of leaving the Costco, Doug realized it was far worse on the ground than it had seemed from the warehouse's roof. LO was a quarter of a mile south of Costco as the crow flies, but it was a mile to the main entrance on LO's east side. They ran flat-out instead of huddling close to Miranda to be protected by her repellent effect because doing that would be too slow. The drawbridge into LO was down, and they had to get it up. Otherwise the settlement might be overrun. If it got bad enough that they needed Miranda to protect them, they were probably too late to save LO anyway.

Delilah had quit barking at zombies in favor of running. At first Doug had worried about Miranda, but the bullet must have grazed her because she kept up. He could see that it hurt, but stubborn as always, she refused to let it interfere with what she had set out to do. Ahead, Doug saw a field of spring crops trampled under zombies' dragging feet. The discordant symphony of the moans, the reek of rotten bodies, burned itself into Doug's eardrums and sinuses.

He was not getting the familiar thrill underneath the fear when it was life or death like he usually did. But 'people to live for' wasn't as abstract a concept since Skye.

Ahead on the right he saw a gap across the parking lot between the huge office buildings on either end of this stretch of road. If they took it, they could break away from the zombies coming from the east and run along the railroad tracks all the way to the gate.

"Rocco! Miranda!"

"I see it," Rocco said.

Miranda only grunted.

They pivoted toward the gap, Delilah ahead of them, having already identified their escape route on her own. Zombies tripped, limped, and swayed around them. Every zombie within fifty feet changed direction when they saw the trio. Doug darted to the right to avoid a zombie, then sprawled on the ground. He looked up, pebbles and grit ground into the skin of his chin. He had tripped over a zombie, one so old and worn that it seemed to have just collapsed. It writhed but could not lift its arms to grab him. Miranda had turned his direction as he scrambled to his feet, adrenaline pounding through his veins. And then he was down on the ground again, flat on his back, a bolt of pain igniting his arm like a firecracker. Snapping teeth were just inches from his face.

He shoved his elbow under its chin, pushing the snapping teeth away. He writhed, trying to wriggle out from under it, but his right arm would not cooperate with his brain. More zombies were nearby, doggedly making their way to him.

He had to get up. He bent his left leg. Then he pushed, rolling onto his side using his leg and the bent arm underneath the zombie's chin that held its snapping teeth at bay. A thunderclap of agony detonated from his shoulder as soon he moved, becoming excruciating once the weight of his body was on it. Black fuzzed his vision. He was free of the zombie but only for a moment, and up on his knees. But he teetered on the sickly verge of passing out from pain.

He heard a metallic 'shing.' A hand grabbed his right shoulder. He howled at the bolt of pain that traveled down his arm and across his chest.

"It's me," Miranda said. Behind her Rocco hacked off the head of the closest zombie.

Doug couldn't put words together because of the agony ripping through his body from his right shoulder. He gripped Miranda's extended hand with his left hand, pushing up with his feet as she pulled. On his feet once more, Rocco pulled Doug's left arm over his shoulders. Doug stumbled his first few steps when Rocco started running, Miranda on Rocco's other side.

A hand snatched at his right shoulder, then the zombie veered off because of Miranda. The light touch released a fresh wave of pain that rolled down his arm and over his torso. They burst through the tree line at the back of the parking lot. Zombies were here along the railroad tracks, too. Not as many, but the moans were growing louder.

Hungrier.

"Take him," Rocco said, shrugging away from Doug and pulling Doug's good arm over Miranda's shoulder.

"Rocco, stay with us," Miranda cried.

But Rocco had already opened up a lead in front of them. Miranda pulled Doug's arm tighter over her shoulders. She was limping badly. Doug had lost track of Delilah. The chunky gravel crunched underfoot as they ran. The light from Rocco's headlamp jerked against the railroad tracks and trees. Twenty feet. Thirty. Rocco reached the railroad crossing at the road ahead. For a moment, when he turned the corner, Doug could see Rocco's face in the light of the fire burning at LO. Then he turned out of sight.

Doug gritted his teeth. Miranda could repel zombies, and he was close enough to her to be protected, but her ability couldn't raise the drawbridge. They reached the railroad crossing and turned the corner. Ahead, he heard Rocco swearing.

The normally well-camouflaged entrance to LO had been exposed. A large military-style truck was parked nearby. In its bed Doug could see two long benches along the sides. A canvas cover to keep out bad weather was attached to metal supports over the bed. The truck was big enough to transport twenty people and their gear. Whoever had planned this had gone to a lot of trouble.

Doug pelted up the road, Miranda ahead of him. The drawbridge lay ahead. Beyond it, the Nature Center was engulfed in flames. Doug could feel the fire's heat from three hundred feet. Rocco crouched at the corner on the outer side of the zombie trench.

"Son of a bitch," Rocco said. Beside him, Delilah sniffed at the edge of the drawbridge, a deep growl in her throat.

Doug skidded to a halt, gulping lungfuls of air.

"What is it?"

"The cables have been cut."

They pounded over the drawbridge, which started up the moans from the zombies in the trench below. Except for when the sound defenses had failed, Doug had never seen zombies in this part of the outer trench. He looked across the parking lot, bright with the flickering light of the fire. Flashes of gunfire luminesced from the muzzles of guns in different locations, but the people were in silhouette, backlit by the fire. He could not distinguish friend from foe.

Rocco had already disappeared inside the south tower of the main gate. When Doug reached it, he saw bodies on the ground where the drawbridge met the road, people he recognized from LO.

"I'll wait here," Miranda said, breathing heavy and shifting her weight away from her injured hip. "In case anybody comes."

Doug climbed the steep stairs, his useless arm throbbing. He glanced down at his shoulder. Misshapen, and he couldn't move it. Probably dislocated.

"Fuckers!" Rocco said.

Doug reached the covered shelter at the top of the tower.

"What is it?"

Rocco didn't answer. He pounded across the catwalk. Doug looked down at the winch that pulled the cable on this side of the drawbridge. It had been smashed.

"Doug, come here!"

Doug ran across the catwalk to the north tower.

"They didn't bother with this winch," Rocco said. He was already loosening the bolts that attached the winch to the tower. Doug had no idea where he had found a wrench. "I'm going to set this up in the center. We can use it to raise the bridge."

"Will one winch be able to handle all the weight?"

"Yeah. Maybe. We don't have to raise it up the whole way, just a few feet. There are ropes I can throw down. Can you tie them to the bridge?"

Doug shook his head. "I can thread them. Miranda will have to tie them. I think I dislocated my shoulder."

"I'll throw them down. Get them tied. Then lay low, kill whatever you can. And try not to get shot."

38

MARIO AND SKYE CRAWLED ON THE GROUND, JUST INSIDE THE edge of the Big Woods, staying as low as possible. Rivers of sweat ran down Mario's body. His skin hurt from blast furnace temperatures of the burning Nature Center. The bite on his arm itched underneath the improvised bandage that Skye had wrapped around it. Scratches on his hands from the fallen logs, rocks, and jaggy bushes they crawled through stung.

He squinted his eyes against the bright flames. They were just at the start of the Nature Center's back lawn—what was left of it. The floor-to-ceiling glass windows in the community room with the climbing wall had melted. Stalactites of glass hung from the top.

The gun battle still raged. The intruders were pinned down on the south side of the parking lot, between two parked LO trucks and the inferno that the Nature Center had become. The main body of LO fighters were northwest of the intruders on the far side of the parking lot. Mario and Skye were working their way around the edge of the woods to outflank the intruders.

The intruders were stuck, in part because the fire they had started at the Nature Center lit them up from behind like kabuki puppets, casting sharp silhouettes whenever they stepped out from behind the trucks. There was also nothing they could use for cover between their position and the exit to the main gate at the bottom of the kidney-shaped parking lot. If they tried to dash across, they were sitting ducks. They *could* try the Big Woods but as Mario was finding out, unless you were on a path, you had a better chance of breaking your ankle than getting through the treacherous woods. That was why he and Skye were crawling. And there had been at least one zombie in Big Woods. It was safe to assume there were more.

The hot, itchy crawling seemed endless. Finally, Mario could see one of the small utility sheds behind the Nature Center through the trees, about thirty feet from an area with picnic tables. They crawled out to the edge of the forest, fifty feet from the shed. Mario heard voices but could not see anyone. He held his rifle, sweeping back and forth in one direction while Skye took the other.

When they sprinted for the shed, bullets whizzed by them. They both flung themselves to the ground behind the shed.

"Is he behind us in the woods?" Mario hissed.

The muzzle of Skye's rifle flashed, pointed at the closest picnic table. A man fell backward off of it.

"Let's go," she said to Mario, pulling him along.

"Do you see any more?" Mario asked.

Skye shook her head. She had crawled to the other corner of the shed and peeked around the corner.

"I don't see anyone else. I think he was the only one back here."

They waited. Within a minute, the gunfire grew less thick. Then it stopped. Voices began to shout, the message unintelligible.

It was now or never.

They slipped around the corner of the shed and ran across the open spaces around picnic tables and garbage cans, crouching low, to a line of trees that had once offered shade to hikers eating their snacks.

Mario could see them now—three men. They wore dark-green fatigues. At least one of them was badly injured. He lay on the ground beside the closer of the two trucks. Even in the golden reflection of the fire, he looked pasty and gray. They crawled to the last picnic table.

"I don't see that working out," one of the intruders shouted. He was the shorter of the two who were not injured.

"Y'all are surrounded," Rich's voice shouted from across the parking lot. "There's no way you walk away from this. Surrender."

The two men traded words that Mario could not quite catch. The taller, more broadly built man pointed to the man on the ground. His companion shook his head.

The taller man shouted, "Do you have a doctor?"

His companion rounded on him, his back also to Mario and Skye. Skye pointed to herself and left, then to Mario and right. Her lips moved silently: *On one.* Then they burst through the trees.

"Put them down," Skye shouted.

The intruders froze for a moment, then the shorter one started to turn.

Mario said, "Don't do it."

Mario squeezed the trigger when the man did. It could have been his or Skye's bullet, or both, that sent the man to the ground at the feet of his companion.

The other invader froze. Slowly, he raised his hands.

"I surrender," he shouted, his back still to them. He dropped to his knees, keeping his hands in the air. "I surrender."

MIRANDA CAUGHT THE SMOOTH, fat rope and ran to the corner of the drawbridge. Doug did the same, running to the opposite side. Delilah looked toward the road, barking and growling. Miranda could see the shadowy figures of three zombies closing in from the road, with more behind them. She dropped the rope near the massive eyehook protruding from the top of the drawbridge. Then she gripped her machete and walked quickly to intercept the closest zombie. She raised her arm to strike at the scrawny neck of what had once been a teenage boy. As she started the downward arc of her blade, the zombie lurched away from her. Her swing at its neck embedded into the thick bone of its brow. The blade stuck. She held the machete tight and kicked the zombie's stomach. The machete blade didn't budge.

She reached for the knife on her hip as the zombie tried to writhe away from her. The zombie's behavior confused her for a moment—she knew she repelled them, but it still didn't register, especially when she had dealt with them for so long without this advantage. She plunged the knife into the zombie's eye socket, its jellied contents yielding like whipped egg whites. Two more zombies were now just steps away, their hissing moans frenzied. That would change when they reached her, but not if they reached Doug or Rocco.

Delilah pulled on the ankle of the rattier-looking one that was a step behind the first, slowing its progress. Miranda side-kicked the knee out from under J. Crew business casual zombie. She turned to the one Delilah had by the ankle and slammed her knife into its eye, then back to J. Crew. She stomped her boot on its face to keep its head still and plunged the knife into its ear. She stopped at teen zombie on her way back to the drawbridge and tugged free the machete embedded in its brow.

Back at the drawbridge, she dropped to her knees at the eyehook, pulling the rope through the cool steel. More zombies were turning the corner by the truck. She glanced at Doug. He was okay. She tied the rope off as quick as she could using knots Connor had taught her that would not unravel.

A scream pierced the moans and gunfire from the parking lot beyond the trees. She looked up in time to see Doug falling off of the drawbridge. She sprinted over, her heart in her throat.

He had managed to grasp the eyehook protruding from the draw-bridge. His other arm dangled, completely useless. Zombies snatched at his boots, coming up short by inches. Miranda dropped to her knees and grabbed Doug's wrist in both her hands. His eyes, visible in the flickering light of the burning Nature Center, were wide with panic.

"Get Rocco!" he shouted.

She shook her head. He would never be able to hang on that long, not with one arm. Beside her, Delilah leaned over the trench, snarling and snapping at the zombies reaching for Doug.

A yank almost pulled him down. A tall zombie had caught his ankle.

"Motherfucker," Miranda screamed.

She realized she could jump into the trench and ward the zombies away. She shifted her weight to jump in when Delilah left the trench and started to bark. Miranda glanced after the dog. More zombies from the road were closing in. If she jumped into the trench she could save Doug now, but she would not be able to get back out in time to protect him from the approaching zombies, and he couldn't tie off the rope threaded through the drawbridge eyehook.

The imminent feeding frenzy amplified the screeching of the zombies snatching at Doug's feet.

"Tell Skye I love her."

Miranda looked down at him. From the corner of her eye, she saw the slack rope already pulled through the eyehook, piled next to her knees.

She snatched the rope, pulled it through the eyehook, and wrapped the extra length beyond the eyehook around Doug's wrist. Just as she finished a hasty but secure knot, the zombies yanked. Doug's hand slipped off the eyehook with a sickening crack.

Doug's howls of agony filled Miranda's ears, but he didn't fall into the trench. She lay on her stomach, sweat dripping from her nose, and looped the rope under his injured arm. He screamed even more. She ignored him, wrapping it around his torso before tying it off.

Doug looked up. His eyes widened.

Delilah's bark sounded more like a scream.

A house landed on Miranda's back.

That was what it felt like. The stench of a zombie that had to be massive filled her nose as it pinned her beneath it. A fucking dasher, she thought wildly, because she had not seen anything this big. Where the hell had it come from?

The zombie started to writhe like it was trying to get away from her but unlike the tackle, it was not being quick about it.

"Going too fast to stop and now you can't get away," she gasped.

She was pinned, unable to do anything but watch Doug kick frantically at the zombies snatching at his boots. The zombie finally pushed itself up. Miranda sucked in a breath, but it collapsed onto her again, driving the hard-fought breath from her lungs.

It was inert.

Not moving.

Not moving.

And not moving.

Had someone killed it? Where the fuck were they? Did they even know she was suffocating?

She heard gunfire, Delilah's nonstop barking, the moans of zombies trying to make Doug their dinner. As her vision began to swim, Rocco's hands came into view. He heaved on the rope tied around Doug, whose shriek of pain sounded like a troop of agitated macaques. Rocco heaved on the rope again, pulling Doug up so that he was close enough for Rocco to get his hands on him. He dragged Doug over the lip of the trench, and onto the drawbridge. A moment later the weight on her eased enough that Miranda could suck in a breath.

"This fucker weighs a ton, Tucci!"

Miranda squeezed out from under the massive dasher just as the leading edge of zombies from the road arrived. She shook her head, trying to clear the lightheadedness, and hacked at the first upright zombie, even as it shied away.

Rocco shouted, "Is this rope tied off?"

"Yes!"

"Get the winch. I've got him," Rocco said. He slashed through the rope beyond the knot securing the eyehook, then hoisted Doug over his shoulder.

Miranda ran just steps ahead of Rocco to the gate tower. She stumbled up the stairs and found the winch at the center of the catwalk. Frantic, she searched it and found two buttons—one red, one black. She pushed the black one. The scent of machine grease filled her nose, reminding her of carnival rides that smelled the same way. The winch squealed, shuddering against the bolts holding it to the catwalk.

The bridge is too heavy, she thought, but slowly, slowly, the ropes began to wrap around the winch axle.

"Thank God," she cried, almost collapsing with relief.

She peered over the edge of the catwalk. The bridge was rising, slow, like drying mud. Rocco had set Doug down on the ground beneath the catwalk and turned back to cover their retreat in case any zombies managed to stumble onto the drawbridge as it rose. Delilah still barked, hovering near Doug. His wrist trailed a short length of rope and was bent at an unnatural angle. As soon as the drawbridge was high enough that a zombie couldn't accidentally trip over the trench onto it, Miranda hit the red button.

Rocco looked up at her, grinning, then leaned over Doug. The crack of a single gunshot rang out. Rocco jerked and spun away before falling to the ground. In the flickering light from the fire behind them, Miranda saw Rocco's crimson blood bloom beneath him like a poppy.

"Rocco," she cried. "No!"

39

Mario and Skye left securing the captives to others and went to check the drawbridge. A team of people were spreading the word that the invaders had been repelled, and that they should shelter-in-place because there were zombies inside the palisade.

Even though the fire seemed to have reached its apex and was now waning, getting some distance from the Nature Center was a welcome relief. Mario actually felt chilled as they ran across the parking lot.

They reached the road leading to the gate. A scream cut through the noise behind them, raising the hairs on the back of Mario's neck. His chest tightened. He put his arm out to the side to stop Skye, because he knew that voice.

It was Doug.

Doug kept screaming, his cries bloodcurdling. It sounded like someone was breaking his fingers with a hammer.

"That's Doug!" Skye said. She started to bolt, but Mario held her fast.

"Be smart," he said, placing himself in her path and gripping her shoulder tighter. "We can't just charge out there. We don't know who's with him."

"I don't care," she said. But to her credit, she didn't break free of Mario's grip to run. "You take that side," she said, jerking her chin toward the other side of the road. "I'll take this one."

"Don't get ahead of me," Mario said. Doug screamed again. Skye's flinch mirrored his own. "I mean it, Skye. Don't get stupid."

She nodded, her lips pressed in a hard line. Murder filled her eyes. Mario wished he had a tether to tie them together because he didn't trust her to be smart about this. If it was Miranda screaming, he wouldn't trust himself to be.

They crept down the road. It was darker over here, the trees blocking some of the light from the fire behind them. The drawbridge was illuminated inconsistently—brighter in some spots, others deep in shadow. The gate towers cast long shadows, making it hard to see. Doug screamed again, the worst so far. Mario glanced over at Skye. She had gotten ahead of him.

"*Slow down,*" he hissed at her.

She either did not hear him or did not care.

Mario squinted, picking up the pace. There was movement in the darkness, but he couldn't tell what or who it was. The fire behind them flared. Something was different about the drawbridge cables. He saw Doug on the ground, a man bending over him. Doug flinched away from the man, his whimper of pain loud enough that Mario could hear it.

The crack of Skye's rifle felt like a punch to the side of Mario's head. What the fuck was she doing?

Another voice shouted, "Rocco! No!"

It was Miranda.

"Miranda," he shouted, taking off for the gate and drawbridge. "It's Mario and Skye! Don't shoot! Don't shoot!"

They reached Doug and Rocco just as Miranda emerged from the tower stairs.

"Rocco," Miranda said, stumbling to him.

Skye stood over Rocco for a moment, frozen in shock. "I didn't know— I didn't realize it was him!"

She dropped to her knees, covering the gunshot with her hands. Blood welled up between her fingers, slicking her hands as she leaned into Rocco.

Rocco groaned, but it was soft, almost a whisper. Doug crawled over to them. A dog Mario dimly recognized as Delilah whimpered and whined.

"Oh fuck," Skye said, looking up at Mario. "Is he breathing?"

"Yeah," Doug, said, his voice pained and faint.

Mario bolted away, faster than he would have thought possible after everything that had happened today.

"I need River," he shouted, bursting into the parking lot. He kept running, shouting at the top of his lungs.

"I need the doctor! I need River! Rocco's been shot!"

MARIO'S ASS prickled with pins and needles. He had fallen asleep while sitting up against the wall of the Boys' Home dining hall. He climbed to his feet, clumsy because his right foot was asleep, too. Miranda stood between a pushed-out chair and the dining table he had last seen her sitting at, her face pinched with worry. Phineas, the young man with a playful crush on Miranda, stood beside her. Skye and Doug were on their feet next to him. Skye looked as distraught as she had when Mario nodded out.

River approached from the partitioned off end of the dining hall, where a makeshift operating theater had been set up. She lifted the strap of her blood-soaked apron over her head, pulling the scrub cap off with it.

"He's alive."

Mario's whole body felt light, like a helium balloon floating up to the sky. Sighs of relief came from everyone. Skye collapsed into a chair and began to weep, then cry outright, her gasping breaths harsh against Mario's ear.

"The bullet entered between two of his back ribs and lodged against a rib on the front, nicking the edge of his right lung. It didn't hit any other organs. The lung collapsed, but we were able to rein-flate it. Luckily, the front rib didn't shatter and can heal in place. I was able to get the bullet out," she said. She put her hand on Skye's shoulder. "He's strong and stubborn, and it could have been a lot worse. If he does well the next twenty-four hours and doesn't get an infection, he should make a full recovery."

Skye sniffed. "All of our antibiotics are expired."

River crouched down so that she was eye level with Skye.

"Expiration dates don't mean the drugs don't work anymore. They're when the pharmaceutical company could *guarantee* the medicine was still one hundred percent effective. That doesn't mean they don't work. Those jerks probably made the dates earlier than they needed to be so they could make more money. Unless they need to be refrigerated, antibiotics will work up to fifteen years past expira-tion. What we've got is fine, Skye."

"Okay," Skye said, visibly trying to pull herself together.

Doug's attempts to physically comfort her were awkward since one arm was in a sling because of his dislocated shoulder, and the other splinted from his palm past his elbow on account of a broken bone in his forearm. Once River had time to check the splinting done by one of her assistants, it would go into a cast. Mario couldn't remember if it was the ulna or radius that had broken, but the upshot was Doug would be fine. Compared to being eaten by zombies, he had gotten off lightly.

"I'll go tell the commander," Phineas said, hurrying away.

"I should look at that graze, Miranda," River said.

Miranda brushed away River's concern. "It's already been patched up. It's really nothing."

"If it gets red or swollen, come see me right away," River said.

Miranda had received River's concern better than Mario's. When he had asked her earlier if she was okay, she had barely acknowledged him. He had been cutting her a wide berth since. He couldn't handle an argument right now.

"I have other patients. I'll see you all later," River said.

As she walked past him, Mario said, "Well done, Doc."

"Thanks." She paused and smiled tiredly. "The ancestors must be doing their thing today. The attack at the Institute wasn't successful, either."

Mario nodded his agreement. "Thank those ancestors for me."

"Thank them yourself. I'm too busy," she said. Then she wrinkled her nose. "You got that looked at, right?"

Mario looked down at his arm, wrapped in clean bandages.

"Yeah. Zombie bite. Your assistant cleaned it and hooked me up with antibiotics. I'll be fine."

Over River's shoulder, he saw a flash of concern in Miranda's eyes as she walked by. But just for a moment, and it didn't stop her.

River shook her head at him. "I can't wait until everyone can be that blasé about a zombie bite."

"Yeah," Mario said. "Me too."

A FEW MINUTES LATER, Mario was walking down a back hallway of the Boys' Home dining hall with Miranda and Doug. The commander had summoned them to where they were interrogating the healthy prisoner. Smith stood at the far end, talking to Rich. A small knot of people who looked familiar but whom Mario didn't know hovered nearby.

Everything about the situation made Mario uneasy. Rich and Smith looked up at their arrival. LO's commander sweated heavily, her face flushed, with dark circles under her eyes.

"Thanks for coming," she said. At a flick of her head, everyone but Rich moved away. He helped her straighten up, away from the wall. She guarded her side with her hand. "There have been some developments."

She's only got a few hours left, and she's still taking care of business, Mario thought.

When Smith didn't continue, Mario's spidey sense began to tingle. Whatever she had to tell them, it was not good. At all.

Finally, Doug said, "And?"

"They're from San Jose."

There was a moment of stunned silence. Then Doug and Miranda began to talk at once.

"They're from San Jose? How?" Miranda asked.

"How did they even know we're here?" Doug asked, incredulous.

Mario had thought he was tired, but the wave of exhaustion that hit him now felt like a ton of bricks.

"Of course they are," he said. He pinched the bridge of his nose, scrunching his eyes shut. "Of course they're from San Jose. I am so fucking *sick* of this shit."

"As to how," Smith continued, her face filling with...apology? "That's where Brock comes in."

For a beat, no one reacted.

"That mother*fucker*," Doug growled.

Smith took a step back from Doug's murderous expression. She lost her balance for a moment until Rich put his hand under her elbow.

"I should have killed him," Doug snapped. "I should have broken his fucking neck. I should—"

The rage that flared from his friend burned almost as hot against Mario's skin as the Nature Center fire.

Miranda's confused voice said, "But what's the connection? Brock didn't know who we are. How did he— What the fuck is going on?"

Smith said, "After Brock escaped, he managed to reach out to some friends in P-Land. They helped him hole up and got him a short wave radio. Apparently, when Rocco and Mario arrived after Doug rescued Skye, you," she said, inclining her head at Doug. "Called Mario by his real name, not by James. Eventually Brock figured it out."

Mario took a step back, his mind racing. He tried to remember. Sliding to a halt in the door. The broken and out of place furniture. Doug holding Skye, who was half naked and badly beaten, shaking and sobbing uncontrollably. And Brock on the floor behind them, covered in blood, trying to sit up.

Get this piece of shit out of here, Mario, before I change my mind and kill him.

Doug gasped. "Oh my God..." he said, turning to Mario. "Oh my God, I did."

Doug sagged against the wall. Miranda looked over at Mario, seemingly too stunned to be angry with him.

"Brock's a horrible person, but he's never been accused of being stupid. A guy named Mario working on something at the old vaccine institute? It would have been easy to put together after that," Smith said softly.

Mario shook his head and looked at the commander.

"Well, fuck," he said.

"Indeed." She nodded, her voice sympathetic. "You can put together the rest after he got in touch with the people in San Jose. Destroy anything you were working on, kill you all. In return, he would get their vaccine. And Skye."

Doug's face filled with a mixture of anger and disgust. "Jesus," he said.

Mario said bitterly, "They'd promise anything. Life is cheap where we came from."

"We never thought," Miranda said. "It was a risk, of course, but we never meant to bring all this down on you. You have to believe—"

Smith interrupted her. "Of course you didn't. I knew the risks."

Mario looked at Smith through narrowed eyes. There was something else. "What aren't you telling us?"

"He has something else to say," she replied. "But he'll only tell us if you're in the room."

Mario felt everyone's eyes on him.

"Okay," he said, the situation getting more surreal by the minute. "Let's hear it then. I don't see how it can get much worse."

In the room beyond the door, a lithe, muscular man sat in a chair. His blond hair was as dirty as his dark-green fatigues.

Doug laughed, low and bitter. "Christ on a bike," he said. "I'd ask what brings you to this neck of the woods, Victor, but you've made that pretty clear."

The prisoner gave a smug smile. "You're a hard man to track down, Father Doug. The whole group of you, actually."

He looked over the three of them before taking a very obvious moment to check out Miranda. Anger flashed through Mario that this would-be assassin was now taking his time to blatantly assess her figure.

"You know him?" Miranda said.

"Yeah," Doug answered. "Victor's a Navy piece of shit. I've had to deal with him from time to time because of the Missions."

Mario suddenly found it hard to breathe. They had known since Santa Cruz that the Navy was involved, and they had known the Council wouldn't give up easily. But to have it confirmed, right in front of his eyes, made the bottom drop out of his stomach. What had happened at home? What had happened to his family?

When he spoke, Mario was shocked at how even his voice was. "What's your message?"

"This is just a job for me. A contract, you know? Nothing personal. I've got no loyalty to the Council."

Doug muttered, "You've got no loyalty to anything."

Victor shrugged. "Call this a goodwill gesture. Maybe you can keep it in mind going forward."

"Just say it," Mario demanded.

"There was a shake-up on the Council after your little caper." The cadence of the mercenary's speech was deliberate, almost philosophical. "We were supposed to learn what we could and kill all of you. Destroy anything you were working on, the usual stuff."

"You sabotaged the sound defenses to draw us out, and then blew up the Nature Center as a distraction," Smith said bitterly.

"That sound system is really something," Victor said. "I've never seen anything like it."

"Good people died because of you," Rich snapped.

Victor shrugged. "Good people are always dying." He looked at Commander Smith. "We did not count on you, ma'am. If you weren't about to turn, I would love to pick your brain, because you know what you're doing. What branch did you serve in?"

Smith looked at Victor like he was a viper. "Fuck you."

"Air Force is my guess. You have that look," Victor said before returning his attention to Mario. "Our op got the green light from the Council president. This whole thing was his idea."

Mario felt the room jerk forty-five degrees. He almost put his hands out to break a fall he was not taking. Cold sweat slicked his body as his chest tightened.

No, he thought, no, no, no, no, no...

"It's a new guy now," Victor said. "Dominic Santorello."

For a moment, nothing happened. Mario took a deep breath, then another, before a roar of white noise overwhelmed him and snowy television static blinded him. He turned away from Victor, breathing fast, unable to get enough air.

"Get him out of here," Smith said.

Mario heard the door open. Miranda's voice demanded something. The door slammed shut behind him, and hands pulled him down the corridor. A familiar voice buzzed in his ear, talking to someone else, but he didn't understand the words.

He looked up at Doug, uncomprehending. He gulped over and over but couldn't get any air in his lungs. He shook off the man guiding him by the arm. A door with a red 'EXIT' sign stenciled on it opened. Mario walked through it, reeling.

"Sit down," Doug said.

His voice was gentle but brooked no argument. Kind of like how you talked to a dog. Mario looked around, thinking for a moment that Delilah must be with them.

"What?" he gasped, confused.

"Sit."

Doug pointed his splinted arm to a bench against the building. Mario sat down, dazed, not enough air rasping in and out of his chest. He felt sick, light-headed. Someone else showed up and shoved a paper bag in front of him.

"Breathe into the bag," Doug said. "Slowly. You're hyperventilating."

Mario stuck the bag over his nose and mouth like he had seen in countless movies, breathing in and out as he was told.

It's a new guy now, Dominic Santorello.

It's a new guy now, Dominic Santorello.

It's a new guy now, Dominic Santorello.

His head began to clear. He caught his breath and dropped the bag on the ground. The cool night air felt refreshing against his skin.

"It's true. I know it's true."

"Yeah," said Doug. "I think it is."

Mario put his head in his hands. "I actually felt bad, leaving Dom in the shit like that. I knew the rest of the Council would go for him, but there was nothing I could do about it. He would have tried to stop us if he'd known. How the fuck did he end up in charge?"

Doug sat down next to him, his face in shadow. "I don't know what to say, man. I'm so sorry."

"Yeah," Mario said. "Me too."

His own voice sounded far away. *He* felt far away. How in God's name had this happened? He knew his brother was as bad as the rest of the Council, but he was his brother.

But Mario...he's your brother.

His nana's voice ran through his head, her Sicilian accent as strong as the day she stepped off the boat. Dragging out his name and 'brother' as she implored him to do the right thing—again—

when his brother had made a mess that Mario was expected to clean up.

He stood up so fast the head rush made him dizzy. He started walking, not paying attention to the direction he took. He heard Doug speaking to the guy who had walked them out of the building, asking him to follow, in case they had not found every zombie yet.

Zombies, he thought, and laughed. Zombies. Like they were a problem. Like they were even a *concern*.

Mario didn't know exactly when his hysteria-tinged laughter turned to sobs, but it was right around the time he realized that Miranda wouldn't be coming after him and he had to face this alone.

40

THE MEMORIAL SERVICE WAS HELD THREE DAYS LATER ON THE grounds of the Boys' Home. All around her, people wept. Miranda wiped her own eyes and tried to concentrate on what Rich was saying. Except for Tadpole, she hadn't felt this depressed since the third year in a row of Australian wildfires, when the entire continent was ablaze, and she realized it would be lost to climate change within the decade. Then zombies happened, so maybe it scraped through, minus koala bears and kangaroos.

"The last thing that Anna said to me was, 'Memorial services are for the living. I'm an atheist, but if you think it will help then have one.' Anna believed this life was it, and that once she pulled that trigger, there was nothing more."

The sobs of the assembly in the open field on the Boys' Home campus got louder. Doug whispered in Miranda's ear.

"I wish he had let me do this. I may be packing it in, but I know how to do a funeral. This is dreadful."

Rich continued. "I was raised Methodist. I try to be a good person and live my life in a way that people know I'm a Christian without me having to tell them. I know I fail at it, a lot. The last ten years have tried my faith, but my faith is what gets me through. I think Anna was wrong. I believe I'll see her again in Heaven because she was the best example of being a Christian that I can think of. The Gospel of John says, 'Greater love hath no man than this, that a man lay down his life for his friends.'"

Rich stopped speaking. His hand that clutched the paper his eulogy was written on stayed by his side, crumpled in his hand. When he started speaking again, his voice was tight with emotion. He kept wiping tears from his eyes.

"Anna laid down her life for us. She didn't care that she was dying. She didn't care that she wouldn't be here to see how we fared after this...calamity. She served this community to the bitter end. I was getting uncomfortable with how long she insisted on going, to be honest. But she wasn't going to let something as annoying as being bitten by a zombie slow her down."

That one got a few laughs. Doug's shoulders dropped down from his ears a little.

"The best tribute we can make to LO Commander Anna Smith, Full Bird Colonel, United States Air Force, is to continue. Rebuild. And keep LO a place where people help and care about others, whether they've been here from the beginning or have just arrived at our door. Because that's how Anna would want it."

Rich walked over to Mathilde, who stood at the front of the crowd with their children. She wrapped him in an embrace as his shoulders started to hitch. Miranda saw Skye, who had also spoken at the service, pat him on the back. Around her, people hugged one another and began to mill around.

"I need a fucking drink," Miranda said to Doug.

"Tell me about it," Doug muttered. "At least he pulled it out of the bag at the end there."

"See you at my place later?"

Doug nodded. "Yeah. I'll wait for Skye and we'll be over."

DOUG TOWERED OVER HER. He looked thunderstruck.

"You haven't talked to him?"

"I don't even know where he is," Miranda said, defensive. She took a step back and shot Skye a beseeching glance.

"You don't know where he *is*?" Doug's voice became an angry shout. "He was at the service!"

His blue eyes flashed. Miranda had never seen him so outraged.

"It's been *three days,* Miranda. His *brother* put a *hit* on him. I don't care what you said to each other. What the fuck is wrong with you?"

Miranda took a step back, away from Doug.

"Honey," Skye said, her voice placating. She put her hand on his arm, still in a sling. "I can see that you're upset but—"

Doug rounded on her. Miranda could see it was taking everything he had to keep his temper in check.

"Don't get in the middle of this, Skye. You should go."

Skye's eyes were still red-rimmed and puffy from crying at the memorial service. She looked at Doug for a second, then nodded.

"Okay," she said. "I'll see you later."

She stood on tiptoe and kissed Doug on the cheek, then whispered something in his ear that Miranda could not hear. She nodded to Miranda. When she reached the door, she looked down at Delilah, hunkered low and looking anxious. She looped her fingers through Delilah's collar.

"C'mon, Liley," Skye said and tugged the dog out the door with her.

Miranda took the tiny reprieve of Skye's exit to regroup.

"Dominic's always been an asshole," she said when Skye had shut the townhouse door behind her. "I don't know why anyone is surprised by this. I always said he'd sell out his own mother."

Doug took a deep breath, his nostrils flaring. "I don't care what Dominic is or isn't," he said through gritted teeth. "Mario *needs* you. You remember who he is, right? The man you're in love with, who you cried over for five goddamned years. I know things are messed up right now, but why on earth aren't you with him?"

She looked away from Doug because she couldn't come up with a good answer. If the situation was reversed, Mario would be here for her, no matter the horrible things they had said to one another. But every time she thought about holding his hand and drying his tears, offering gentle words of consolation, she choked on the anger and hurt that burned in her belly and leaped into her throat. She couldn't even articulate it, because it was more than just their argument. He must have done *something* for her to be this angry with him. She didn't understand it. She didn't know how, or what, but he had, he must have. And now she was supposed to be there for him?

"Maybe things are different now."

"Is this about the baby?"

Miranda shook her head. "No! It's just..."

"It's just what?"

She glared at him, furious, unable to explain or defend herself. Sorry that she had said it so poorly...whatever the hell it was that she had been trying to say. She wanted Doug to shut up and leave her alone. To quit forcing her to defend what she didn't understand.

Doug lifted his arm that was broken, then stopped. She knew the gesture. He wanted to scrub the back of his head with his hand, but he couldn't. Not in a cast that started above his elbow and ended halfway down his fingers. His other arm was in a sling, so he couldn't use it, either.

"If you don't deal with this, it's going to eat you up inside," Doug said. "It's going to ruin everything good in your life."

"What good?" she demanded, tears springing to her eyes. "What good things are you talking about, exactly? The family surrounding me? They're all dead! The friends I've left behind, who I couldn't even bury because it was too dangerous to stay long enough to do it? Everything this world just snuffs out again and again and again, and it's not even personal, just the way things work now? The man who says he loves me but then leaves me behind? He left us, Doug. He wasn't there—again."

Doug stared at her, openmouthed.

"You actually believe that," he said, sounding stunned. "You know what," he continued, his voice becoming flinty and his eyes and jaw hard. "If he wasn't there for you, Miranda, it's because you wouldn't let him be. You talked to me once. *Once.* And then you froze me out, too. And now you're punishing him for not being able to read your mind?"

Her voice became a growl. "You don't understand."

"*Fuck* understanding you! I'm so fucking sick and tired of having to understand your pain and disappointments, how the world has been so hard on you. Do you honestly think you're the only one?"

For a moment, she couldn't say anything.

"Get out."

Doug laughed. He actually laughed at her. Miranda felt a sob well in her throat.

"Now you're gonna cry?" he said. "Are you gonna take your ball and go home, Miranda? Throw yourself a nice little pity party? Well fucking have at it."

Doug stormed across room. When he reached the door, he lurched to a halt and glared at the door.

"Goddammit," he hissed.

She jumped when he kicked the door. Then he kicked it again. And again. He kept on kicking until she heard a sharp crack. Doug's booted foot had punched through the bottom of the expensive, sturdy door, snapping the bottom third off.

He stood in front of the battered door, seething. He took a few ragged breaths.

"I can't open your goddamn door."

Miranda never thought that Doug would turn on her. Never, and not like this. They'd had their share of disagreements over the years, but he had never directed anger like this at her. Never ridiculed her pain.

She stalked to the door and flung it open. He took a step forward, then turned back to face her.

"I have never been so disappointed in anyone as I am in you right now," he said softly, the anger just under the surface of his voice threatening to explode. "Shame on you, Miranda. Shame on you."

MIRANDA SAT on the bathroom floor, her back against the vanity, a razor pinched tight between her fingers. Her hands rested on her outstretched legs, palms facing one another. Blood trickled down the inside of her bare thighs, puddling on the floor.

This was the best part. Now, just after the very last cut, while they were still raw and new. While they *hurt*. The first few were too overwhelming. It rushed out too fast for her to *feel* the relief. But by the time she switched arms, the deluge began to ease. All the self-recrimination, the knowledge that everything was ruined because she had made that first mistake, because she hadn't stopped to fucking think, began to ebb, and she could focus on the physical sensations. The bite of the razor's corner tip. The slice of the unyielding metal on her flesh. The warmth of the blood welling up and running down her arm. She had done this to herself, to all of them, the voice in her head whispered.

It was her fault.

She pushed it away, quashed the voice through force of will using the calm that the razor had given her. Maybe that was why she was so angry with Mario, because he knew the truth she didn't want to admit. She honestly did not know, but she didn't have the emotional wherewithal to figure it out. She had just enough to claw her way through the day, to hang on by a sliver of her fingernails, to resist resorting to this. Most of the time. She laughed bitterly, then started to weep. This was the only relief she could find, and all it did was confirm how damaged she was.

She had felt better for a while, after she and Mario had reconciled. She had even been happy. She had been kidding herself. It was all still there inside her but tamped down for now. She would be able to breathe again, until she couldn't.

The razor would be waiting.

WHEN SHE HEARD the knock on the door, she knew it was him.

"It's open. Come in."

The door opened. A few seconds later, Mario entered the townhouse. He looked frightened, like a child expecting a monster to gobble him up. When he got close enough for her to get a good look, she was shocked at how terrible he looked. It was as if every bit of spirit that he'd ever had, had been sucked out of him. He looked almost flat, like a piece of paper.

"Can I come in?"

"Yeah," she said, nodding.

She stood before he reached her, pressing one of her arms against her body, leaning into the flare of pain. She needed to hold on to it, pull it close. It couldn't help her otherwise. Mario stopped a few paces away from her.

"I said some really terrible things to you, Miranda. Things that weren't fair. That aren't true. I'm sor—"

She cut him off. "You meant what you said, every word."

Pain flared in Mario's eyes, jagged and raw. He sucked in a breath. "No, I didn't. I was angry and hurt, but I didn't mean it. None of this is—"

"I don't believe you."

She felt the crack, the twisting apart. Maybe if she could still feel it, things might be different—*she* might be different—because it was only getting worse. The razor only helped so much and for so long. But the anger, the bitterness, the desire to strike out at him, magnified with every interaction, with every flicker of his need to connect with her. The angrier she got, the less she could remember what it felt like to love him. She poked at it, like her tongue had once prodded the empty space of a lost tooth.

Every time he tried to connect, her contempt grew. Didn't he have any pride, it whispered. Where was his dignity? His self-respect? To grovel and chase after her... What kind of man did that?

Mario stepped back, the shock on his face filled with surprise, and not. And still, the need to connect with her.

"So that's it? After everything we've been through?"

Maybe if he hadn't said what he said, but he had. And she didn't believe his denials. He had meant it. She didn't see how things could ever be the same again.

Even to herself she sounded detached, like a stranger in someone else's life, when she said, "Yeah. I think it is."

Mario's eyes searched her face, his breath rasping in and out of his slightly open mouth, so quick she could see the rise and fall of his chest.

"Since when do you give up so easily?"

"I don't owe you anything. And I don't love you anymore."

He hadn't expected that. He stepped back, as if he had taken a blow, but then rallied.

"I don't believe you," he said softly.

He turned on his heel, almost reeling like a drunkard but just able to keep it together. Miranda watched him leave, expecting—waiting for—relief that never came.

41

Doug sighed. "I really screwed up."

Skye's eyes were understanding. "You can only do your best, Doug. Most of the time, your worst day is better than a lot of people's best."

Doug rolled his eyes.

"It is," she added. "But other times your best sucks. But it's your best right then, on that day, and you can't do better. You've got to stop beating yourself up."

Doug looked down at his boots, an unhappy scowl distorting his mouth. It was almost too warm where they sat at the bottom of the steps that led up to the observation deck of the old macaque enclosures. The observation decks were too dilapidated to use safely, but the steps were okay. Then he sighed and leaned against her. She slipped her hand into his.

"You're right. I know you're right. You're right about freaking everything." He shot her a sideways grin. "It would be annoying except you're so cute while you're doing it."

Skye laughed. So much of the time he still could not believe any of this had happened. When he thought about the fact that he and Skye were together, that she loved him, it felt like he had hit the lottery.

"It was the wrong way to go about things with Miranda, and I knew it. She'll only dig in. It's been a week, and she still won't talk to me." He stopped, searching for the words. "I just couldn't believe it, and I got so angry. And then she *dumps* him," he continued, incredulous. "Says she doesn't love him anymore, after everything they've been through. If she didn't love him, that would be one thing, but it's obvious she does. I know they had a terrible fight, but..."

He sighed, profoundly discouraged, as if it had been he and Skye and not his friends. "I don't know what is going on with her."

Skye squeezed his hand. "Maybe she'll figure it out and talk to you when she's ready."

"I do think I know what's going on, big picture, just not the heart of it. You know, the part that matters? It's wrapped up with losing the baby, but she won't admit it. It's not getting the abortion. I believe her when she says that's not it. But it's something." A hard edge entered his voice. "It's like she wants to suffer."

"You're still pissed."

Doug looked at her, surprised. "No, I'm not."

"Oh yes, you are," Skye countered. "It's in your voice. You can be angry and concerned about her at the same time."

Bone-deep gratitude enveloped him. He smiled and raised his hand to her cheek. Her skin was soft and warm.

"I don't know what I did to deserve you."

"You just got lucky."

He smiled, then kissed her.

"I don't want to go to a meeting," he said when their lips parted. "I'd rather get you into bed."

"The day is still young," Skye said, a promise in her eyes. She stood up, took his hands, and gave him a pull. "There are lots of nooks and crannies in this building that are not being used."

"You are so full of it," Doug said. "You have a million things to do since you've stepped up to take over for Anna."

"Temporarily," Skye said. "This is just temporary. I do not want the top job at LO."

"Sometimes the job picks you."

She shook her head. "Not this time."

———

"NONE of the last ten people we've vaccinated have gotten sick, apart from slight fevers. That's not unusual." Mario gave a tight facsimile of a smile. "I think we can cautiously say we've got the kinks worked out."

Doug studied the dark smudges under Mario's dull eyes, his pale skin, the exhaustion that accompanied his words. He looked like he had not slept well all week. Which he hadn't, Doug was sure of that. If Doug had not known what was going on, he would think Mario was sick.

He is sick, Doug thought. Heartsick.

Mario should be brimming with excitement delivering this news. Instead, he could not manage the barest enthusiasm. Doug couldn't even bring himself to be more than annoyed with Miranda for robbing Mario of the excitement of this moment. She had looked just as bad this morning, in a zoned-out way.

"That's great news," Skye said, sounding excited. She leaned forward in her chair, her elbows on the table. Her fingers tapped on the tabletop. "What exactly do we need to ramp up production?"

Mario and Alicia ran through equipment requirements for small-scale production, as opposed to the micro-scale in place at the moment. As far as equipment went, there was already enough to scale up quickly. They just needed to get it online and train people to do it. The real challenge were the long lists of organic materials and chemicals. Doug had seen it already, since he and Skye were part of the team that would begin scavenging for those items.

Right now, they had fifteen actual vaccine doses. Mario and Alicia were concentrating their efforts on producing and stockpiling serum now, since it was the key to producing more vaccine. But they were limited in that, too, due to on-hand supplies.

"Still no one else who has developed the repellant effect besides Miranda and me?"

Alicia shook her head in answer to Skye's question, tucking a lock that had come loose from her braided hair behind her ear. "No. At first we thought it might be because of hormonal differences between men and women, but the women we've vaccinated didn't develop it either."

"Any chance it could be a fluke?"

"Anything's possible at this stage," Mario said. "Unlikely, though, since two people have it. It might be the getting so sick that causes it, might be the phase of the moon," he said, sounding discouraged. "We'll figure it out eventually."

"Okay," Skye said. "I'll set up a meeting with the P-Land Council to tell them." She flashed a smile. "I think the next group we vaccinate should be from P-Land, as a show of good faith."

"That's a good idea," Doug said as heads around the table nodded.

"I know I'm beating a dead horse here," Mario said. "But the vaccine must be free and available to everyone. No questions asked. I don't care if they're the scum of the earth or Albert Schweitzer—everyone gets vaccinated."

Skye nodded. "That's always been the agreement. It's what Anna wanted. We'll even vaccinate Brock."

Doug did a double take to make sure Skye was joking.

She wasn't.

"I think we can make an exception there," he said, anger and protectiveness flaring.

A couple people snickered, but not Mario. Doug saw his fierce anger reflected in his friend's eyes.

"Believe me, it's tempting," Skye acknowledged. "But ultimately counterproductive. Rich and I are heading back to LO now. Anyone else coming?"

Rising, Alicia said, "I'll join you."

Skye nodded. "I'll see you all later, then. Leadership calls, though I can't wait until I can ignore it." She paused, then said, "The commander was right when she said it's been an absolute honor to be part of this. She was so proud to be a part of this."

As the meeting broke up, Skye said to Doug. "You coming?"

"No, I'm going to hang out with Mario."

She leaned in and gave him a peck. "See you later then. Love you."

Doug smiled. "Love you, too."

After she left, Mario slumped back against his chair, his head back and his eyes closed.

"How are you doing?"

Mario sighed as he raised his head. He opened his eyes and cast a sidelong glance at Doug.

"Oh...you know," he said. "Getting through. One week down, the rest of my life to go."

"You look like shit."

Mario chuckled, the sound as bitter as medicine. "Thanks a lot."

After a moment, Doug said, "I don't know what to say, man. She's not in her right mind."

"I wasn't exactly a model of good behavior myself. I was a real asshole, and she's not interested in apologies. I wish she'd never gotten pregnant. None of this would have happened." He sounded completely defeated. Looked completely defeated. He turned to Doug, his eyes bleak. "It's really over this time."

"You don't know that," Doug said.

"Yeah," Mario said. "I do."

Doug waited a beat, then said, "I don't care what she says about not loving you anymore, Mario. I know Miranda, and she loves you. If she'll just come clean—"

Mario cut him off. "Just leave it, Doug. Please. I can just about get through the day. I don't have it in me to hope."

"Okay. Sorry," Doug said. They sat in silence for a moment. "Thought about what you want to do next? After everything is up and running?"

Mario nodded. The anger that Doug had seen before, bright and lethal, flashed in Mario's eyes.

"I need to go home and deal with my brother. He tried to kill the woman I love. If she hadn't lost the—"

Mario's voice grew tight. He closed his eyes, blinking away the tears that Doug saw fill them.

"Even if she doesn't...love me, anymore, I can't let that stand. And he might try to hurt Emily and the kids." Mario's voice trembled when he continued. "He may have already."

"Mario," Doug said, absolute confidence in what he said filling his voice, because he really did believe it. "Walter will keep them safe. You know he will. Victor told us the Council hadn't managed to mount a successful attack on SCU. They think everything here went to plan, since that's what Victor told them when he radioed in. Smith promised him the vaccine if he cooperated, and the deal still stands. He's locked up in LO's brig, so it's not like he can change his mind and alert them even if he wanted to. And he won't. He's looking out for number one." Doug sighed. "He's consistent that way. I'll give him that."

"You'll have to pardon me if I don't trust the word of a mercenary. If everything he says is true, it's all the more reason to go home. They'll never see us coming." He shrugged. "Besides, I know my brother. Dominic will try something. And if he fails, he'll try again."

"I don't think that's true," Doug said. He could see Dominic trying to kill Mario, which was horrifying enough, but he could not see him killing his niece and nephews.

"I do," Mario said. "I know my brother better than you do. You, me, my family, Miranda... None of us are safe as long as he's alive."

Doug sat back in his seat, his heart aching for his friend. He didn't know Dominic as well as Mario did. How could he? But killing your own brother? Even if it was to protect the other people you loved, Doug was not sure how a person came back from that.

"We can't do anything for a month or two anyway," Mario said. He sounded as if he was trying to force some liveliness into his voice, which only made his misery more apparent. It made Doug feel even sadder for him.

"Okay," Doug said. "Let me know if you need anything."

Mario nodded. Doug could see that Mario had no idea what he needed.

Doug said, "I'll see if I can rustle up some cider."

Mario's smile was faint, with no enthusiasm to back it up.

"Yeah," he said, then stood. "I should get back to the lab."

"Okay," Doug said. "I'll see you later."

He watched Mario walk out of the room. He had never seen his friend look so defeated, not even after they had put their plan for his 'defection' in motion. He had been distraught at the idea of letting Miranda think he had betrayed her, but this was far worse, by an order of magnitude.

He really thinks this is it, Doug thought with a start.

Doug had just left the meeting room and turned down the hall that led to the lobby when he heard a commotion outside. He picked up the pace.

"Doug! Come help us!"

Miranda's voice? Doug reached the lobby. It *was* Miranda. What was she doing here? She and Phineas half dragged Rich through one of the front doors as several members of security scurried out the other. Rich's left leg dragged, leaving a trail of blood on the terrazzo floor.

"Get him settled," Skye said.

Skye held the door to the BSL-3 hallway for Alicia. Alicia's face was smudged with dirt and her braided hair was coming loose. The two women disappeared into the hallway.

They settled Rich into the nearest chair. He was pale and sweaty and looked rattled. Miranda had already dropped to her knees by his feet. She pressed a cloth against the wound on his lower leg.

"I lost control of the vehicle, and we slid into a ditch," Rich said. He sounded dazed. "I don't even know how it happened."

"I was helping restock the fallbacks today with Phineas." Miranda said. "We were at the one nearest to here and saw them crash."

"Next thing I knew," Rich said, "Miranda and Phineas were pulling me out of the Jeep. The grass was high on the side away from the road. I didn't even see it."

"See what?" Doug asked.

"The zombie," Phineas said. "It didn't have any legs. It bit him."

Doug looked at Rich in horror. "Why weren't you wearing chain mail?" As soon as the words were out of his mouth, Doug kicked himself. Like it mattered now. "Sorry, I just... You aren't slated to be vaccinated until next week."

Rich, who never cursed, smiled weakly. "Isn't that a bitch?"

The doors behind them that led to the BSL-3 hallway banged open. Skye, Mario, and Alicia hurried into the lobby. Mario carried a tray, Skye a first aid kit.

"Miranda! Phineas," Alicia said as she headed for the stairs. "I need help setting up the isolation room."

Miranda and Phineas followed Alicia. Skye removed Rich's boot, retrieved a pair of scissors from the first aid kit, and started cutting away his trouser leg by the bite. Mario set the tray down on the table next to Rich's chair.

"Doug," Mario said, "Roll up his sleeve."

Doug helped Rich out of his jacket and rolled up his sleeve. Rich shivered, even though the lobby was warm.

"We don't know if this will work," Mario said.

"You don't know if what will work?" Doug asked.

"The vaccine."

The contents of the tray—bandages, alcohol, a syringe and needle, and two vials—finally registered. Mario slipped the needle into one of the upturned vials, pulling the liquid serum into the syringe before depressing the plunger again. A jet of tiny bubbles rushed from the needle.

"It's not made for post-bite exposure," Mario said. He looked at Doug, his eyes bleak. "But we have nothing to lose."

42

MIRANDA LEANED AGAINST THE WALL JUST INSIDE THE DOOR OF the isolation room. The dimmed lights matched everyone's mood. Despite being administered a double dose of the vaccine at the start and an additional two doses three and six hours later, Rich continued to go downhill fast. Both Mario and Alicia were pessimistic about the chances that a vaccine not developed for post-bite use would work, but as Mario had said, they had nothing to lose.

Fucking zombies, Miranda thought. Anger flowed through her veins like venom, setting off a cascading reaction of pain that started in her temples. Anger seemed to be the only emotion she felt anymore. Except in the wee hours, when she was so tired she couldn't see straight but still couldn't sleep. That was when the pain would bubble up and try to suck her under. When the tiny voice whispered that all of it was her fault and she was to blame.

She felt like she would die when she couldn't get the voice to shut up, her chest tightening and fear crushing her skull. Someone had brought over two cases of Rocco's cider to celebrate the successful vaccine trials, but it was never touched after Rich was bitten. Last night when the voice started whispering, Miranda drank until she passed out. She had woken up this morning sprawled on the floor, her head pounding, her mouth feeling like something had crawled into it and died.

But the voice was gone.

If she didn't have the wall to lean against, Miranda wasn't sure she would be able to stay upright. Her head felt like it was splitting open. Anything approaching daylight was like an ice pick behind her eyes. The dimmed lights were half the reason she had come to the isolation room. The other was that she liked Rich. He had a steady, calming presence, a soft but sly sense of humor that she enjoyed. He had walked her to the fallback when she was pregnant, *because* she was pregnant. It had been ridiculous and unnecessary and annoying at the time, but she craved the comfort of that unobtrusive care.

And no one talked in here. Not even Mathilde, Rich's wife, who sat in the chair beside his bed, tense and pale. No one tried to engage Miranda here. No questions about why she was being so unfair, so unfeeling, to Mario. No one asked what was up with her and Doug. No one would ask if she had talked to River about trying again for another baby, because apparently Tadpole had been nothing special and could be replaced with another one, like a worn-out pair of boots.

She slid to sitting, her wrists on her knees, her head against the wall. She was surprised that Rich had lasted the night. She didn't think it would be much longer.

MIRANDA CRACKED AN EYE OPEN. Doug leaned over her. She must have fallen asleep.

"Has he turned?"

"No," Doug said, a grin splitting his face. "His fever broke. His vitals have stabilized. He seems to have pulled through."

Her head jerked up straighter.

"Really?"

She scrambled to her feet. The lights were still dimmed, but not as much as before. Mathilde hovered behind Alicia, who was drawing Rich's blood. Tears ran down Mathilde's cheeks that she didn't bother to brush away. Rich was propped up on a pillow. River stood on the other side of his cot, a stethoscope on his chest. A thermometer jutted out from his mouth. He looked coherent and extremely unwell but human, and alive.

Miranda sagged with relief, covering her hand with her mouth. "Wow."

"This is a big deal," Doug said. "It works after the fact. Within the first hour, anyway."

"Mario must be thrilled."

"He is," Doug said, but there was an edge to his voice. An edge that said, like you care.

"How's the shoulder?" she asked, noticing the lack of the sling for his shoulder that had been dislocated.

"Getting there," he said.

They looked at one another. Miranda didn't know what she was supposed to say to him after the argument they'd had.

"I'm going to get some sleep," she said.

She turned and slipped through the door. To her annoyance, Doug followed.

"Miranda," he called after her. "Can we talk for a minute?"

She stopped. She needed this like a hole in her head. She wasn't sure how long she had slept, but her head still pounded. Her mouth felt chalky. She didn't want to deal with Doug and his judgy comments.

She turned to face him. "What about?"

"Home."

Home, not her. She could do that. It might become home, then her, but maybe it was better to get it over with.

"Okay."

Doug poked his head through the door of the closest room, then motioned her inside. Miranda joined him in an old office.

Doug shut the door behind them, then said, "Mario wants to go home soon, while they think their plan has been successful."

Miranda turned the idea over in her mind a moment. "He wants to kill his brother."

Doug's expression became pinched. "He wants to deal with the Council once and for all, just like you and I do."

She let the deflection pass. The Old School was strong in Mario, too. At its core, it meant family. Even if you hated them, they were yours. Mercy was not part of the lexicon when it came to those who threatened your family.

"Dominic's a fuckup, even if he's always landed on his feet, but he went too far this time. If it was just Mario he tried to kill..." Miranda shrugged. "He's not family anymore."

Doug didn't like what she'd said, she could tell by the downward arc of his mouth.

"We'll never get a better tactical advantage since they think we're dead," he said, unwilling to engage more about Mario killing his brother. "It'll only take two weeks to sail to San Jose this time of year."

All the air felt sucked from the room. The pounding behind Miranda's eyes exploded as her heart began to race. Two weeks to get to San Jose. Even if other people came along, the travel party would be small. And contained. Two weeks of Doug's disappointment and frustration. Two weeks with no escape from Mario. She could feel the pull of his pain, his needing, sucking her dry already.

She took a few deep breaths to calm herself. *Two weeks is nothing... Get a grip. You can do anything for two weeks, even travel with Mario.*

Doug continued. "I know Victor said that SCU is okay, but I'll feel a lot better after talking to Walter and seeing for myself."

"Father Walter," Miranda whispered.

Longing to see the old priest welled up with an ache that almost made her gasp. His name rolled over her like a cool breeze. Father Walter would know what to say, would use words that her heart could understand. He could tell her what to do with this anger and pain. He could help her figure this out, and then she might not be so—

"I'm not coming," she heard herself say. "I'm staying here."

Doug's eye went wide. "What?"

"I'm not going home. I'm staying here."

"Miri," Doug said, stunned. "If this is about the other day…"

Miranda shook her head, relief flooding her body at this turn of events that took even her by surprise.

"Is Skye going with you?"

"I think so," Doug said, still looking confused by her answer, but his features softened at the mention of Skye. "She said she was. Says she doesn't want Smith's job."

"I don't blame her."

A long silence stretched between them. Finally, Doug said, "Are you sure you won't come with us?"

"I don't— I can't do it right now."

For the first time in weeks, it wasn't anger that undergirded her words, but she couldn't identify what the feeling was as she studied the floor tiles. She looked back up at Doug. He had become another person she didn't want to be around.

"Someone needs to get the vaccine out to people. I'm good at that sort of thing."

Doug nodded slowly, still frowning. "It'll take a while to get ready. We can't leave everyone here in the lurch with things being so unsettled, so if you change your mind."

She wasn't going to change her mind, but she said, "It's not like you're on a hard deadline. There's time."

Doug blinked, then shook his head. "Says the most impatient woman I know. Miracles never cease."

A tiny smile snuck through before she could school it away. Another uncomfortable silence filled the space between them.

"I'm sorry about the other day, Miri. I—" Doug sighed and shook his head. "I really lost my temper. It was the wrong— I'm sorry."

She could see his apology was sincere. She would be sincere, too. It was only fair.

"You meant what you said, every word. When you said shame on you. When you accused me of abandoning him. When you said fuck understanding me and my," she paused, wanting to get it right so the knife would twist for him like it had for her. "'Pain and disappointments.' You meant every word."

Doug's mouth compressed into a hard line as she spoke. Anger flashed in his eyes.

"I said a lot of things. Poorly. You're not being fair to Mario or yourself, and you're going to regret it."

She met his gaze evenly, clenching her tongue between her teeth so that her temper did not get the better of her. There were so many things she wanted to say, words that would fly as true and sharp as arrows because she knew Doug's soft spots.

"Duly noted. And it's none of your goddamn business."

She turned on her heel so he wouldn't see the tears that sprang to her eyes. Her chest hurt so much it felt like a heart attack. She wanted to lean on someone, *anyone*, but something held her back.

"You're doing a really good job of alienating the people who love you, Miranda."

Doug's words froze her in place. For a split second she almost turned back. Almost let him see that she was afraid to admit what she had done, and that running from it was poisoning her. That it was seeping through her veins and burrowing into her brain and whispering in her ear so insistently that her head felt like an echo chamber of blame and recrimination.

The white-hot misery of what she had lost, and what it had cost, fear of having more scorn heaped upon her, stopped her. Who could she trust if one of the people she had trusted most had used what he knew against her? She wouldn't roll on her back like a dog expecting a belly rub so Doug could kick her again.

She latched onto the anger roiling inside her, as dangerous and devastating as a neutron bomb. She pulled the door open and fled, before she exploded and leveled everything in sight.

"IT'S SUCH a relief to have everything we need from Jeremiah," Alicia said brightly.

Miranda only half listened to Alicia's prattle. Alicia had seen her walking down the BSL-3 hallway with Delilah and cornered her. Miranda had taken this route because she could avoid Mario and Doug, who were in the lobby. She could have kept going, but she liked Alicia, and it felt like she had fewer friends by the minute.

"We've even identified the mutation that causes the repellant effect in people with AB-negative blood," Alicia continued. "That's why Rich repels them, too. But AB-negative is like, less than one percent of the population. That's why it doesn't happen in most people."

"Strange that there are so many of us here."

Alicia's brow furrowed. "It is. The probability of that is, wow. Super low. I don't even want to speculate without doing the math first."

"Yeah, super low."

Alicia crouched and scratched Delilah under her chin. "Who's a good girl? Who's a good girl?"

Alicia laughed when Delilah began to give her kisses. Miranda's nerves jangled at the grating, high-pitched sound. She mumbled a goodbye and turned toward the lobby. Seeing Mario and Doug could not be worse than listening to that laugh.

She walked through the lobby, not acknowledging Mario, Doug, or Skye, even though Skye waved. From the corner of her eye, she saw Delilah detour to Mario, tail wagging furiously. By the time Miranda reached the doors, Delilah had rejoined her.

She pushed the door open and stood on the stoop, tipping her face up to the sun. The macaques chittered, a cry of warning traveling over the grounds. Delilah raced after the nearest one, chasing it up a tree. A moment later, she whimpered while standing on her hind legs with her front paws on the tree trunk, her head cocked to the side as if she was trying to figure out how the monkey had gotten away. Now at a safe distance, the macaque turned back and hurled insults.

God, I love that dog, Miranda thought.

The sunshine warmed her face, its soft caress soothing her frayed nerves. She remembered thinking that Mario's hand on her cheek felt the same way once, like sunshine. She waited to see if the memory stirred anything, but it didn't. A wisp of annoyance, but that wasn't what she had been wondering about.

"Liley, come!"

Miranda turned left, toward the pond. Ahead, she saw Rich and Mathilde. Rich looked gaunt, with hollows under his cheeks. He leaned on his wife's arm, but his color was getting better. They were deep in conversation with one another. Then Mathilde looked forward and smiled at Miranda, raising her hand in greeting. But Rich looked at Mathilde, his face in three-quarter profile. His love for his wife lit his face from inside, so complete and incandescent that Miranda's breath caught in her throat. She remembered Mario looking at her like that, but she couldn't remember how it had felt. She pushed the thought away, frustrated with herself for having it in the first place.

"Hey, guys," she called.

"Hey, yourself," Rich said when they drew near and stopped.

"It's good to see you up and about."

"It's good to *be* up and about."

"Though we are going back so you can rest," Mathilde said, sounding worried. "You are already tired."

"I am," Rich agreed.

"We were very lucky," Mathilde said to Miranda. She shuddered, fear flashing over her face.

"It's all right, ma chere," Rich said softly. His drawl did not accommodate the proper French pronunciation all that much, which somehow made the pet name even sweeter. Mathilde bit her lip and nodded, blinking back tears.

"I hear you're a repeller," Miranda said, trying to lighten the mood.

"I am indeed," Rich said, smiling. "AB-negative. Used to be only the blood bank was interested in me. Who would have thought?"

"I thought it was just because I'm such a bitch," Miranda said.

Mathilde laughed, and Rich joined her, but reluctantly. Miranda suspected it rubbed the wrong way against those Southern manners his mother had instilled in him.

"I'll see you both later," Miranda said. She watched them go, a gentle yearning swelling in her breast. Then she looked down at Delilah. "I need to make a stop before we go to the pond, Liley."

The pit bull looked up at her and groaned.

"Oh, please."

She changed direction and headed for the brig lab. After submitting to a pat down, she entered the lab that housed Jeremiah's cell. Jeremiah sat on the floor, his back against the wall. As usual, he was reading a book. When she got close, she saw it was an old friend.

"Still reading Jack Reacher."

Jeremiah's gold eyes flicked up from his book before he resumed reading.

"Not even a hello?"

He ignored her, but she could wait. Contrary to popular belief, she could be very patient with the right incentive. She sat down at the table and chair. The log book and a pencil were on the desk, to keep track of what they did with the prisoner. When he was fed, when he bathed, when he got outside to stretch his legs, which was never.

That's a Mitsubishi pencil, she thought, noticing its shiny maroon finish. Someone had just sharpened it, the tip pristine. Skye had been right. The Mitsubishi graphite didn't smudge, and it held a point a lot longer, too. She still had the ones that Skye had given her, but she swapped it out with the pencil in her back pocket anyway.

"Your attempts to provoke Us are pointless, Sister Miranda."

She looked up. "It speaks."

"We would speak more if We thought you were ready to hear Our Truth."

"Still obedience and submission?"

His mouth settled into a hard line. It was so easy. Too easy. No sport in it at all.

"You should not mock that which you do not understand."

Her annoyance flared. "You're nothing but a delusional, sleaze-ball rapist. And murderer. And probably more that I haven't witnessed."

She had taken to calling this building the zoo because every time she was at the Institute, she stopped by to poke the bear. And thought about how she would kill him. But some days, like today, it felt so pointless. Killing him wouldn't change anything that mattered. When she thought of him being a wild animal that didn't know any better, that had no say about being caged and deprived of its freedom, she knew these visits were cruel—and not just to Jeremiah. But wild animals weren't sickos, just wild, with different needs and motivations than those of humans.

She could see Father Walter shaking his head, telling her this wasn't good for her mental health. *Like I have good mental health.* Father Walter would say that she should give up this pointless obsession. That it wouldn't make her feel any better. Wouldn't change things.

He would be right of course. He usually was. It didn't stop her getting annoyed at his imaginary side of the conversation. Except that he *was* right, even if he wasn't really here sitting across the table from her. Tormenting Jeremiah had felt so good at first, but the feeling lessened with every visit. More often than not afterward, she thought of Sister John Ignatius, her ancient and soft-spoken sixth grade religion teacher. Sister John Ignatius, who used to say that Jesus was big on forgiveness, so they should be, too. She said forgiveness was more about you than the other person. That it set you free of whatever wrong that person had done you, while wanting revenge kept the violation and harm alive. According to Sister John Ignatius, forgiveness broke that poisonous connection and any power it had over you.

She never met anyone like you, Miranda thought as she studied Jeremiah. But still, she wondered... What was he, really? An insane man, a sick man, who thought he was God's messenger. Who thought he was God's corporeal embodiment, like Jesus had been, but as unlike Jesus as water was to dry, desert earth. What was he but another thing this world had broken? What small, soft dreams had he once held close, only to have them smashed to pieces because some asshole changed a gene in a tomato so a corporation could sell its poison at a better profit margin?

You could forgive him, Sister John Ignatius whispered in her ear.

Miranda looked around the room, just to make sure no one else was there. The idea was startling. She could forgive him for being insane and killing her friends. For killing her child. She could snap in two the power he held over her. The power she let him have, that she handed to him on a silver platter.

The idea made her insides quake. She could choose to forgive him. It would never change how he had wronged her. She would never be able to forget. But she had the power to forgive him instead of hating him, and maybe the crushing pain of what he had done to her would ease just a little bit. She wasn't foolish enough to think it ever would go away. But maybe it wouldn't feel like it did now, like it would kill her. Maybe, if she truly believed that God's grace was undeserved and freely given, even to her, even after all the mistakes and trespasses she had made, as Connor had once assured her it was, maybe she could begin to heal.

She looked down at her scuffed boots, a sudden head rush making her feel light-headed. She could choose to forgive Jeremiah and walk away from this. A lightness began to fill Miranda's chest. She could leave this madman behind her and get on with her life.

"We hear you have recently suffered a loss, Sister Miranda."

Miranda's head whipped up, the lightness in her chest replaced by cement. Adrenaline flooded her body, making it hum.

"What did you say?"

Jeremiah rose to his feet and approached the bars, the Jack Reacher book still in his hand.

"We offer Our condolences. The loss of a child is particularly cruel. It is a loss of possibility. Of what might have been."

She could feel that her face had gone slack with shock. Blood pounded in her ears. Her pulse sped up.

"Who told you that?"

Jeremiah set his free hand on the cell bar. "Your pet name for the child was...Tadpole?"

Freezing, dark fear engulfed her, followed by a rage like she had never felt before. She faced him through the bars, just inches away. She didn't remember walking to his cell.

"Who told you that?"

He smiled at her, sickly sweet, but underneath she saw the venom.

"I am the God All-Father on Earth. There is nothing We do not know about Our Chosen. And you are one of Our Chosen, Sister Miranda. We have foreseen it."

To her right, the lab door opened.

"Miranda, back up," the guard said. "You're not allowed within arm's reach."

Jeremiah's golden eyes held hers like a high-tension wire, mega-joules of electricity sparking between his insane gold and her horrified cornflower blue.

"We never meant your child any harm."

"Shut up," she hissed. "Shut the fuck up!"

She heard the guard say something, but his voice was far away.

"Who told you," she demanded again. Her breath rasped in her chest, fast and shallow. "Who was it?"

"Miranda," the guard said again.

Finally, Jeremiah let the smirk show in his smile.

"You will have Our child one day. We have foreseen that, too." His smirk transformed into a salacious leer. "You *will* submit to Us. You will find fulfillment in Obedience, in pleasing Us. You will serve Our carnal desires and your eagerness to pleasure Us will redeem you."

Miranda recoiled. From his lecherous grin and golden eyes that burned with insanity. From his sick, twisted vision for her. From his hateful words and sneering superiority and his impossible knowledge of her pregnancy and the hopes and dreams she had imbued it with.

Deep in her belly, an eruption of hurt and pain engulfed her, sending its scorching lava coursing through her veins. She reached through the bars, grabbed a handful of his hair, and slammed the side of his head against the unyielding steel.

Jeremiah's triumphant, crazed laughter echoed off the walls. The guard at the door shouted. Miranda could see him coming for her from the corner of her eye, but he moved in slow motion. Jeremiah's mocking mouth contorted with laughter. The force of his head slamming into the bars had cut him, and blood trickled down his face.

She whispered, her lips brushing his ear, "Did you foresee this?"

Surprise, then shock, flashed in his golden eyes as she jammed the sharp pencil into his neck. He started to flail, fingernails scratching her face, panic and fear filling his eyes. She stabbed as many times as she could, like a prisoner with a shiv, before the guard could drag her away. Blood gushed from Jeremiah's neck in pulsing spurts, hot against her hands, spraying her face.

She stabbed until his cries became mangled gurgles, until the pencil snapped. Jeremiah sagged against the bars, shallow breaths still rasping in and out. She let go of his head, and he fell to the floor, bloody foam bubbling on his lips.

Voices and shouts filled the hallway. She looked over at the guard who had cautioned her, blood dripping from her hands. He had backed into the hallway. Miranda laughed when she realized it was the blood. Everyone on-site knew it was contagious.

"You're all so afraid of it," she said, her laughter from the fear on the guard's face sounding unhinged, even to her. "His blood can't hurt me anymore. It's already taken everything."

She felt hands on her shoulders and was steered, unseeing, out of the room, out of the building, into the bright sunshine. Delilah barked, circling Miranda with teeth bared. Fur bristled down the pit bull's back, her pink nose crinkling at the coppery scent of Jeremiah's blood.

Then she was in the parking lot, and Mario stood in front of her, holding her face in his hands. A fierce protectiveness filled his eyes.

"What did he do to you? Did he hurt you? Miranda!"

She pushed Mario away. Why did he still care? Why did he care when she didn't? Then Doug was beside Mario, out of breath, his face flushed and eyes flashing, and Skye just behind him.

The macaques screeched. Their shrill cries echoed off the building, hurting her head. Delilah began to whine while people shouted and ran, amplifying the chaos raging inside her head.

Doug said, "Miranda, what happened?"

She looked at Mario. His dark-brown eyes brimmed with anxiety, glowed with the need to make whatever was wrong right.

"I did what I said I would do."

Mario took a half step back. "Oh, Miri."

Miranda looked to Doug, who watched them, confused.

"I said I would kill him. And I did."

43

"They're leaving soon," Rocco said.

Miranda nodded.

"You're gonna say goodbye, right?"

Miranda rolled her eyes as she looked out the window.

"Yes, dad. I'm going to say goodbye."

Rocco nodded, satisfied, and sat back in his chair. The early morning sunshine poured through the windows of the nearly empty dining hall. Six weeks since the attack on LO, Rocco was still on the mend. That had not changed him being an early breakfast patron. Miranda didn't sleep well lately, so every morning she joined him.

"Because if you weren't going to see them, I was going to tell you that you owe me."

Miranda chuckled. "You are such an asshole."

Rocco smiled. "'Cause you do."

"I know," she said. "And if I didn't, you'd remind me."

Rocco had mitigated the fall-out of murdering Jeremiah and seemed intent on good-naturedly holding it over her head forever. With Skye leaving LO to join Doug and Mario on their journey to San Jose, the consensus at LO was that Rocco was the person who should be in charge, at least until the community decided how to govern itself. While Jeremiah had not had any advocates invested in him personally, Miranda *had* murdered him. Enough people knew about it that there had been dissension about how to respond. One faction figured they had gotten what they needed from Jeremiah and one less psycho in the world could be overlooked. The other faction thought there had to be consequences or LO might end up as lawless as so many other places.

In the end, River pronounced Miranda mentally and emotionally unstable due to recent trauma. Rocco reminded the consequences faction that if he was taking on leadership of LO, then he needed someone he trusted to take over the farming responsibilities. He also pointed out that Miranda had been a friend and an asset to the community since her arrival and made no adverse consequences a condition of taking on Smith's job. Since no one else wanted it, that had been that.

"Is there anything else that I should be planning for the harvest?" Miranda asked, thinking of the list that they had drawn up yesterday.

"Not that I can think of," Rocco said.

"Then I'm gonna jet," she said, standing and picking up her dish. "I know they're leaving early. Don't want to miss them."

Rocco scowled at her. "You could try sounding broken up about it."

"And *you* could try not being an asshole," she said playfully. "See you later."

Miranda left the dining hall, Delilah at her heels. She nodded to a few people, some she knew, others she didn't yet. But she would, eventually, since she was staying.

She followed the path through the narrow strip of trees between the Boys' Home and the housing plan, then took the first path into the Big Woods, the one that went by Otter Pond. Delilah darted ahead, plunging off the path to investigate a scent or chase some poor woodland creature. She never bothered the otters, though. They had not exactly kicked her ass but had instilled in the pit bull a healthy respect for their fierceness. It worked better than Miranda calling her away ever could.

Miranda could smell the scorched scent that lingered in the air before she reached the remains of the Nature Center. The meager salvage and demolition effort was completed. There was nothing to do about the smell but let time pass. In the parking lot, two pickup trucks were at the epicenter of a group of busy people. Both truck beds were loaded with gear and supplies, though one had more open space than the other. For people, Miranda figured.

Doug and Skye stood by the closer pickup. Skye was laughing at Doug. He pulled her close for a kiss, then refused to let go while he tickled her. Her peals of protest rang out.

"Stop it!" she cried, laughing and squirming as she tried to free herself of Doug's hold.

"What's the magic word?" he said.

Miranda approached them, smiling. It was impossible not to. They were too happy.

"I'm going to kill you," Skye squealed.

"That's not it," Doug teased.

He looked up as Miranda drew near. Still smiling, he let go of Skye.

"You better watch your back, buddy," Skye said. "Payback's a bitch."

Doug smirked. "Promises, promises." He turned his attention to Miranda, his eyes flashing with merriment. "Came to see us off, huh?"

"I did," Miranda said.

Skye nudged Doug's shoulder with her own. "I don't know if I'm going to survive two weeks on that yacht with him."

"You'll manage," Miranda said. "There are always pillow fights to pass the time."

"Pillow fights?" Skye said, puzzled.

"I'll tell you later," Doug said.

"I'm sorry you're not coming with us," Skye said. She stepped forward and gave Miranda a hug. "But," she said, letting go, "I'd be lying if I said I'm not glad that you'll be here to help Rocco. He acts like he's back to normal, but he's not. And running the whole show is freaking him out. Not that he'll ever admit it."

Miranda said, "Don't worry about him. I've been dealing with guys like Rocco my whole life. I've got his number."

"I know. I'll see you when I see you. Stay safe, Miranda." Skye turned to Doug and said, "I'll go check on that thing."

"She'll go check on that thing?" Miranda asked when Skye was out of earshot.

Doug grinned. "Subterfuge is not her forte."

After a moment, Miranda said, "So...this is it, I guess."

"It's not too late to change your mind."

"I don't need to change my mind," Miranda answered. "This is better all around, you know that."

The corners of Doug's mouth tugged downward. "I don't. But you think so, so..."

"Be careful, okay?"

Doug nodded. They looked at one another, the pause in their conversation not uncomfortable. She still saw Doug almost every day, but things were different. Doug followed her lead and kept everything light, respected the emotional distance that she had put between them. He didn't like it, but he didn't push. Miranda wasn't sure she liked it, either.

It wasn't that she loved Doug any less. She didn't understand the new terrain of their friendship since their argument. Doug wrapped her in a hug, his tall, lanky frame comfortable and warm. Muscle memory of other hugs of affection and comfort and friendship filled her body.

"I love you, Coppertop," he whispered. "Remember that. We'll figure out the rest."

Miranda nodded against his chest, her throat suddenly tight. Tears prickled the corners of her eyes. Her best friend was leaving.

She might never see him again. She didn't know how to make things right between them, and he didn't seem to know how, either.

"Okay," she said. "I love you, too."

She didn't—couldn't—let go right away. When she finally did, she saw Doug try to wipe his eye without her seeing.

"Tell Father Walter I love him. And I miss him. And Karen, too. Make sure she isn't wearing stupid shoes."

"I will," Doug said with a smile that didn't sit on his lips quite right.

"And don't get dead."

His smile relaxed, becoming genuine. "That's the plan. Don't you, either."

She nodded, gave his hand a final squeeze, and turned away. She knew she was right not to go with them, but she couldn't kid herself that it felt right to stay.

She looked around the parking lot when she reached the edge by the path but didn't see Mario anywhere. She didn't want to see him but knew she should. Everything about them felt like a dream she couldn't remember the details of. That they had been together, loved each other so much, even lost a child, felt like a book she might have read that didn't seem terribly realistic.

Delilah raced over, banging into Miranda's shins before flopping heavily onto Miranda's feet. She looked up at her human, her mouth wide in a goofy pit bull grin.

"You're trying to cripple me, dog," Miranda said.

She reached down and stroked Delilah's silky fur. As she straightened up, she caught sight of Mario on the far side of the parking lot. She had not seen him since the day she killed Jeremiah, when he had held her face in his hands and demanded to know how Jeremiah had hurt her so that he could protect her and make it right.

He looked different, but she couldn't put a finger on the change. His features were as handsome as ever—the dark-brown eyes, the Roman nose, the square chin and full lips, as was the way he moved, so stiffly upright yet as fluid as water. But the tightness around his eyes and in his jaw, the chilly reserve that surrounded him like the cloak of a person who didn't want to be seen, was new, even jarring.

Even at a distance she could feel the longing for something she didn't have to give him rolling off his body like the gravity well of a planet. She had barely let herself feel anything about Mario one way or the other the past few weeks. Now she...didn't. How could she have wanted him so much, and for so long, and now feel nothing?

Mario caught sight of her across the bustling parking lot, his face both lighting and extinguishing at once. His eyes met hers. She searched their brown depths for an ember, a spark. When he spoke, she couldn't hear his voice, but she didn't need to.

I love you.

No flutter of response in her chest, just the echo of a once familiar ache. She held his gaze another moment, the feeling of one epoch ending and another beginning swirling thickly around her.

"Come on, Liley," she said, tearing her eyes from Mario's to look down at the trusty little pit bull. "Let's go."

IF YOU ENJOYED THIS BOOK, please do me a solid and leave a review. Reviews need not be long, the same one can be used in more than one place, and can be left at any retailer where the book is listed (whether you bought it there or not): Amazon, Goodreads and Bookbub are the biggies. Thank you.

DON'T MISS the sneak peek first chapter of Reckoning in an Undead Age at the end of this book!

ABOUT THE AUTHOR

A.M. Geever lives in her hometown of Pittsburgh, Pennsylvania. An avid reader of science fiction and fantasy from an early age, the only job she ever wanted—besides being a writer—was to be a Star Fleet Officer.

When not dreaming of stories of survival in extraordinary circumstances, she spends most of her time with her family and fur babies, and loves to travel to exotic locales.

For more information, check out my website, www.amgeever.com.

ACKNOWLEDGMENTS

No book is written without the community supporting the author. As always, huge and humble thanks, and deepest gratitude, to my family, whose support and love means everything. I cannot think of any positive thing I've done in my life that hasn't been influenced by the love, generosity, and general badassery of each and every one of you.

The Beta Readers

Sarah Lyons Fleming, who is always right about what needs to be cut, what needs to be explored, and what just won't fly.

Terry & Joe Hingston, for your outrageous enthusiasm, and saving me from making an embarrassing Seattle gaffe.

Rhonna Woodie & Roseann Powell, for providing such valuable feedback from gen-yoo-ine fans of the Undead Age universe.

The Editing Team

Arianne "Tex" Thompson, Developmental Editor Extraordinaire. With only a written summary of *Love*, which she had not read, and the outline for *Damage*, Tex fixed the massive problem with the plot that I had not been able to resolve—in ten minutes. *Ten minutes.* This book would have sucked without you, Tex. Thank you!

Kimberly at Kimberly Dawn Editing, who fixed all the crap to make the story shine.

Darcy Prince and Scott Karavlan, nit-picky proofreaders extraordinaire.

There will be typos, I know, despite everyone's diligent efforts (including my own six plus rounds of proofreading), because typos are like fucking cockroaches.

The Creative Geniuses

I cannot say enough about the creative talents of **Doug Dean**, except that he's freaking amazing. I don't know how you raised the bar even higher, but I'm pretty sure it's due (in part) to your willingness to keep looking every time I said, "The hand still isn't right."

The Publicity Team

Many thanks to **Heather Roberts at L. Woods PR** for helping me think about and tackle the big picture of being an author, not just what's right in front of me.

BM, thank you for the advice.

Very Special Thanks

Diana Gordon, Education & Outreach Coordinator for the Oregon National Primate Research Center at Oregon Health & Science University. The last minute tour you were gracious enough to take me on when I was in Portland was not only a fascinating highlight of my research trip, but contributed immensely to the veracity and originality of the story.

Arthur Crivella, for your generous loan of Na-Wak-Wa Lodge, which allowed me to work on the first big re-write without distractions.

Mass Giorgini, for allowing me to use your family name for Rocco. I hope he does it justice.

Last but not least, my **Three Favorite Pieces**. My dad, Eamon, who lifts my heart out of my shoes. My husband, Drew, who still makes me laugh and only occasionally drives me as crazy as I drive him. And my brother, Justin, who continues to inspire me to pursue my artistic dreams by pursuing his own, and whose support and encouragement is off the hook.

— June 6, 2020

SNEAK PEEK: RECKONING IN AN UNDEAD AGE - UNPROOFED & UNEDITED

DOUG FROWNED AS HE STEPPED THROUGH THE DOORWAY INTO the yacht's fore cabin. Mario lay on the berth, limp as a rag doll. He coughed, a deep, wet hack that went on for half a minute, before he spit into the bucket on the floor.

"How are you feeling?"

Mario's fell back against the mattress. He looked spent from the coughing fit. His breath wheezed in and out for a few seconds before he answered.

"Worse."

Doug stepped closer and put the back of his free hand against Mario's forehead. It burned hot against his skin. He held up the mug he carried, a wisp of steam curling from it.

"I've got more pepper-honey tea."

"I'll drink it later."

"No," Doug said. "Now. You have to stay on schedule."

Feebly, Mario pushed to sit up. Doug set the mug down and slipped his hands under Mario's arms to give him a boost.

"How's Tessa?" Mario croaked.

"Pretty much the same."

Tessa actually seemed a little worse than yesterday, even though her cough was not as bad as Mario's, but Doug didn't want him worrying about that. If Doug had not already been concerned, the fact that Mario had just accepted his help to sit up instead of shooing him away would have set alarm bells ringing.

"We're going to find somewhere to put in tonight, find a dry building where we can stop for a few days," Doug said as Mario sipped his tea. "I'll check in on you later."

"Okay," Mario said. "Thank you."

Doug plastered a smile on his face. "Anytime."

He stepped into the parlor, catching sight of the breakfast dishes in the galley's sink that still needed to be washed. He reached the ladder and climbed up into the yacht's cockpit, squinting his eyes despite the overhead canopy that shielded him from the bright sunshine. He twitched his fine, sandy-colored hair out of his eyes.

Everywhere Doug looked, he saw beauty: calm, dark blue ocean, golden sunshine, and a dark, craggy coastline edged with lush, green forest. He zipped up his windbreaker against the chill. The sunshine that seemed to promise warmth might as well be a siren calling sailors toward sharp rocks on which to founder. Oceanside temperatures this far north along the Pacific coast, even in the summer, rarely ventured beyond the seventies. Though less than a mile from the shore, topside temperatures on the yacht hovered another ten degrees cooler due to the ever-present breeze.

Skye looked up at him. "How are they?"

"Worse."

Doug dropped into the seat beside her.

"Watch the helm," Skye said, reaching out to steady the mid-sized, wagon-like wheel that Doug had jostled. "So we shoot for Eureka, and we'll see what we see?"

"Yeah," Doug said, frowning. "Mario didn't protest at all when I helped him sit up to drink his tea. He sounded like he was coughing up a lung, and he would have just gone back to sleep if I hadn't told him he had to drink it right away. Tessa's cough isn't as bad as Mario's, but it's getting there."

Skye took Doug's hand in hers. He looked at her, his breath catching in his throat. Those blue eyes got him every time.

"They'll be okay," she said, giving his hand a squeeze. "We'll hole up somewhere dry and keep them on the antibiotics. They'll be right as rain in a few days."

"If it's bacterial pneumonia, and if the antibiotics we have are the right ones," Doug said, worry creeping into his voice. "Or maybe it's viral, and then we've wasted antibiotics we might need later."

"I know," Skye said. "But we are where we are, with what we've got."

Doug shook his head and scowled. She was right of course, but— But what? She was right. He was already doing all he could, even though it felt inadequate.

"What if he dies?" Doug whispered. "I'll have to tell Miranda, and then she really will... God, I hate this."

"Hey," Skye said softly. When Doug looked at her, she said, "Do you remember Avi Lehr?"

"The rock climber rabbi?" Doug said. "Yeah, of course."

"It will have to be sufficient. He said that all the time."

The corner of Doug's mouth quirked up in a wry smile. Now she was using the Torah to reassure him.

"That's not exactly how it translates, but close enough." The smile faded as quickly as it had appeared. "It's so loud when they cough. Sometimes I think we should just stay on the yacht in case it attracts zombies, but this damp can't be good for them."

"We're talking about sheltering in a city that wasn't even thirty thousand people before, in a part of California that didn't have a lot of people to begin with. There's no way every zombie stuck around." Skye narrowed her eyes. "What's going on? You're usually more optimistic than this."

Doug squeezed her hand, sure that it would sound as stupid out loud as it did in his head.

"He's in the same cabin as Connor, when he..." His voice petered out. "I know it's stupid, but it kind of freaks me out."

Skye grimaced. "That would freak me out, too."

Buoyed by Skye's answer, Doug gave himself a mental shake.

"So," he said, forcing a cheerfulness that he didn't feel into his voice. "Eureka it is. We'll hole up somewhere dry, get some rest, and they'll both be right as rain in no time."

Skye leaned over and kissed him lightly. Her lips were soft and warm.

"That's the spirit," she said. "This is just a quick detour. We'll be back on track in no time."

A FEW HOURS LATER, Tessa said, "We'll be fine. Just go—"

Her attempt at reassurance was interrupted by a coughing fit. When she finally quit hacking, she spit over the rail and added, "Really."

The anxious, vertical line appeared between Skye's eyebrows as she studied Tessa's pale face. Doug felt his lips turn down, a reflection of what Skye's lips were doing, too. Tessa was bundled in sweaters and jackets, a knit cap pulled over her head so low that her eyebrows were hidden. Her cheeks were scarlet, which combined with the many layers of outerwear made her look like a kid coming in from playing in the snow. She shivered, but the chill that caused her to bundle up had nothing to do with the weather.

"If you need us for any reason, send up a flare," Doug said.

"I will," Tessa said. Her pointy chin popped out from under the scarf she wore when she tipped her head toward the dock. "Now go, so I can sit back down. We'll be fine."

Skye turned to Doug. "Ready?"

Doug nodded, then stepped off the yacht onto the dock. He hated being forced to leave two sick people on their own.

"Let's make it as quick as we can," Doug said as they started down the dock. "She ought to be in bed, not sitting topside."

Skye shaded her eyes with her hand as she walked. "At least it looks pretty clear. With any luck, it'll stay that way."

The marina where they had moored, on the south side of Woodly Island near the confluence of the Humbolt and Arcata Bays, looked shabby, years of neglect having taken their toll. Remarkably, several boats along this dock—one a small sailboat, the others cabin cruisers—were still intact, though in need of serious maintenance. But far more had sunk. The tips of masts poked through the water's surface at all angles along the empty slips, the shadowy outlines of the submerged vessels visible only at close range. Another dock, parallel to where they were moored, had twisted along its length before spiraling into the water. Its weathered and rotting support beams at the water's edge were pretty much all that remained.

Their hollow footsteps clunked against the weathered planks, the sound jarring in the silence, but this dock seemed sound enough.

"D'ja think this has been maintained, given that the other has sunk?" Skye asked.

"Maybe. Hard to tell how recently, though. It could be last week or a year ago. Or the other dock suffered damage this one didn't."

They reached the end of the dock. A low building faced them, its fenced, outdoor patio a jumble of knocked over tables and broken umbrellas. A faded sign, Cafe Marina & Woodley's Bar, hung askew from the eave above the patio.

"Must have been nice back in the day," Doug said, picturing a bustling marina in the world before zombies. The tall rigging of pleasure craft would have been silhouetted by the sunsets. Tables of tourists getting pleasantly buzzed on the bar's patio could have enjoyed the view. "Would have been a perfect place to take you on a date."

Skye grinned at him. She re-fastened her hair, tucking the silvery-blond ponytail into her jacket collar.

"Maybe we can have a drink before we go."

A WEEK AND A DAY LATER, Mario and Tessa had improved to the point that Doug figured they could leave in a few days. After a cursory inspection of Woodley Island, he and Skye had decided to venture into Eureka proper. The island had the restaurant/bar, a lighthouse, a National Weather Service station, and not much else. It had meant a mile long trek into the town, longer than Doug would have liked, but they had at least managed to stay along the waterfront. They had a direct line of sight to the yacht and marina from the house they had chosen to shelter in at the end of Eureka's I Street. After scrounging up a row boat they could make the trip across the water to the yacht, moored directly opposite them, in two minutes. Doug didn't think they could have done better location-wise.

He stretched his arms high over his head, groaning a little as he twisted onto his side inside his sleeping bag, and pulled at the zipper. The air in this bedroom of the little beach house was chilly; cool, but not enough to raise goosebumps. He smoothed his hair back as he pulled his long legs out and reached for his boots. Skye's crumpled sleeping bag lay on the floor beside him. Doug had not realized how accustomed he had become to sleeping with Skye beside him until they needed to split the night watches between them. Neither Mario nor Tessa had been in any condition to do anything but rest and, Thank God, get well. Another day, maybe two, and they could get back on the water.

Doug walked down the hallway, glancing through the bathroom's open door as he passed by. Its walls and floor were padded with all the mattresses in the house, as well as several from the house next door. They had muffled the worst of Mario's and Tessa's coughing, even if it had been a little cramped. They had not encountered any zombies so far, but they had not ventured from the house except to retrieve items they needed from the yacht.

He found Skye, Mario, and Tessa sitting at the kitchen table when he entered. The kitchen faced the bay, with lots of windows that gave it a nice view even on a day as overcast as this one appeared to be. Skye's feet were propped on the lone empty chair. Skye looked up from the book she was reading.

"Hey you," she said, smiling.

Mario and Tessa looked up from their game of cards. Both were much improved, and neither had been feverish for several days. Tessa had rebounded from the pneumonia more quickly than Mario had—he was still coughing—but they were both in better shape than when they had arrived here. The delay was annoying, but it had been the right call.

"Good morning, beautiful," Doug said, pecking Skye on the cheek. To Mario and Tessa he added, "How are you two feeling?"

"Good," they said in unison. Then Mario added, "We could leave today, I think."

"Nope," Doug said, shaking his head. He rooted in the small bag of food on the bare kitchen counter, chose an apple, then nudged Skye's feet from the empty chair to sit beside her. "Skye and I are going to see if we can find any meds today. Then we can talk about when to leave." He bit into the apple, breaking its skin with a crisp snap.

"We still have tons of meds. We don't really need more," Tessa said. "We should just get going."

Mario nodded but stayed silent. Doug hadn't missed that Mario had left it to Tessa to argue for their departure the past two days.

"Yeah, we do need more. Nice try," Doug countered cheerfully. He squinted at Skye. "What are you reading?"

She looked up from a fat, faded paperback that had either been well-loved in the days before zombies, or had not fared well in those since.

"*Little House on the Prairie.* It's as good as I remember from when I read it as a kid. And a lot more racist."

"They had different standards for what was considered broad-minded when those were written," Doug said.

Skye snorted, then resumed reading.

"So," he said to Mario and Tessa. "Think you can manage while Skye and I take a look around for a few hours?"

Tessa nodded, while Mario mumbled something that almost sounded like an affirmative. They were all anxious to get underway again, but there was an urgency to Mario's impatience that was different from that of his companions. The pinched expression, the tightness around his eyes and in his jaw, could not be put down to his illness. He rarely mentioned his brother Dominic, who had tried to kill not just Mario, but Miranda and Doug as well. Dominic's plan had succeeded in killing good people at LO. People who had given them the benefit of the doubt when they had no reason to, who had helped them achieve their goal of developing the new vaccine for the zombie virus. People who had become friends after giving them shelter and aid when they had needed it. Mario never mentioned his brother, who had rained down so much destruction on people Mario held dear, including the woman he loved, but Doug caught glimpses of the fury and heartache that his brother had inflicted. Usually when Mario was tired, and especially while he had been so ill. Combined with the rawness of his and Miranda's breakup, Doug found himself worried for his friend, and helpless to ease his suffering.

Doug pushed his worry aside and nudged Skye's foot. She nudged his foot back, a grin tugging at the corner of her mouth, her eyes never leaving the page as she read.

"Leave once I've brushed my teeth?" he said.

"Let me finish this chapter," she said. "I'm just getting to a good part." **find an event to reference.

"IT NEVER STOPS BEING EERIE."

Doug nodded. He knew exactly what Skye meant. Eureka was a ghost town. Lots of human skeletons, falling down buildings, and disintegrating roads relentlessly reabsorbed into the natural world, but so far, no zombies. They had seen foxes, bald eagles, a pack of wolves that had melted back into the trees, and even a fleeting glimpse of a mountain lion. Doug half-expected to cross paths with a Grizzly bear. Before the zombie apocalypse, they had been extinct from California for over a hundred years, their existence acknowledged only by their inclusion on California's State Seal. Doug knew that Grizzlies had reclaimed their place in California, even though they were not the same subspecies native to California. He had never seen one himself. This far north, he reckoned his chances were higher. He hoped that when it happened, it would be at a very far distance.

He said, "Should we keep going or call it quits?"

"I don't know," Skye said, squinting up at the clear sky, then back to him. "We've been gone a good three hours, and we lucked out at the hospital."

"Yeah," Doug said. "That was weird, there being meds after all this time."

"Don't look a gift horse and all that," Skye answered. "We haven't seen a single zombie and none of the animals we've seen have seemed spooked by anything but us. There's no reason to stop."

"Except not pressing our luck."

She smiled at him, the make-his-heart-flutter-in-his-chest smile. "You love pressing your luck."

Doug shrugged, unable to refute it, but also knowing that this truth didn't fit him quite as well as when they had met. He had loved to push the envelope, to balance on the edge of what was prudent and what was foolhardy, even dangerous, for as long as he could remember. He still did. But he didn't enjoy it with the same abandon as before, when it had been just him.

Skye could handle herself. No one survived this long who couldn't. And they were good together beyond the protective walls that sheltered what was left of the human race. Not like he and Miranda, who were almost one organism after the years they had spent partnering on missions and patrols, but that would come in time. He could tell already. They anticipated one another's moves, noticed what the other overlooked, instinctively understood when the risk was worth it and when it wasn't.

But the idea of returning to the world before Skye, to a life that had felt so full until—abruptly—it hadn't, that had become gray and flat until she breathed life into it with her laugh and resilience and the way she moved, tempered the thrill. He didn't know how to tell her this, didn't have the language to parse this feeling of temperance, to distinguish it from hovering or lack of confidence in her capabilities. Maybe one day he would, but not today. Today he had to live with the emotional dissonance and trust in them both. He had to take that leap of faith.

"You know me too well," he said. "Let's give it another hour and head back."

They continued south, continually scanning the wide, flat street, buildings, and parking lots. After a few minutes, Skye stopped in front of what had once been a charming, green cottage turned dentist's office. Now it was now a ruin.

"Maybe we should go back," she said. "It's just going to be more of the same, and you're right. We've already found a lo—"

Doug's mind raced as he tried to identify the threat that had caused her to stop speaking mid-word. His heart jumped into this throat for a moment when he didn't see her before he realized she had crouched down. It looked like she was pretending to tie her bootlace.

"What is it?" he said, keeping his voice low.

Never raising her eyes she said, "Don't look or I think he'll bolt."

"What? Who will bolt?"

"The kid on that balcony."

Doug felt his eyes go wide but stayed still. "Where?"

"The building on the other corner behind you, same side as this one." She pointed to the green cottage, the movement of her arm casual, then looked up at him. "Gray, with blue gutters. Looks like apartments on the second floor."

Irrationally, Doug felt eyes on the back of his neck when the moment before he had not. "What the hell is a kid doing out here?"

Skye shifted onto her other knee and raised her foot that had been tucked behind her. She began to re-tie the shoelace on this boot, too.

"Doesn't look well cared for."

"Feral?"

"Only one way to find out."

Doug held his hand out to her. "Kiss me. We'll hold hands and keep walking so he won't figure out that we've seen him."

Skye took his hand, a grin splitting her face as he helped her up and pulled her to him. He could feel her distraction in the tilt of her head, the angle not quite right since she was trying to peek over his shoulder. When they parted, she kept hold of his hand.

He kept his gaze straight as they continued down the road but held his head a little higher. The building Skye had described was so near that Doug could reach it in seconds. Darkness framed by the jagged edges of dirty, broken plate glass windows lined the building's lower story. Rusting cars were parked, bumpers touching, parallel to the building's edifice to block the ground floor entrances. In the periphery of his vision Doug saw the balcony, which ran the length of the long building. Tucked in the corner at the near end, the top of the boy's head peeked over the handrail, the rest of him hidden behind the solid wall of the balcony. The boy's brown hair looked matted and ratty, his face covered in dirt. Even though he only caught a glimpse, Doug thought the kid looked too thin.

"What about that blue building down there?" Skye said, her voice raised. She pointed to a building farther down the road. "That pharmacy."

"Okay," Doug said.

It really was a pharmacy, one that looked half burned down. Between the pharmacy and the building where the boy was hiding was a large parking lot.

Dropping his voice again, he said to Skye, "The balcony stairs are on the end, by the parking lot between the buildings. Dash over when we reach them?"

"We could," she began. After a moment's pause she continued. "Yeah. If he's following us, he'll see. Might as well make it fast."

As they neared the balcony stairs, a door slammed. They looked at one another for a second, then dashed for the stairs. Skye pulled ahead, both of them knowing by unspoken agreement that a woman might be perceived as less threatening. Doug took the steps three at a time. He turned onto the balcony a few seconds behind Skye, in time to see her tumble through the first door as her shoulder rammed it. By the time he crossed the threshold, a low moan came from the back of the apartment.

So much for no zombies, Doug thought.

Less than a minute later when Skye returned to the main room, wiping her gore-spattered machete on her pants, Doug had finished searching the rest of the small apartment. Doug hadn't examined the balcony before, wanting to be there to back up Skye. He did so as they hurried from the apartment and groaned with frustration; every door was closed. They would have to take them one by one. Even though Skye repelled zombies, it was smarter to stay together.

"We should stay together."

"We don't have time," Skye said, already running to the next apartment. "We spooked him."

Doug entered the third apartment while Skye went into the second. He checked every room as quickly as he could: kitchen, living/dining, two small bedrooms, bathroom, closets, and cupboards, but no boy.

"We're going to lose him," Skye said as they hurried to the next apartments, desperation creeping into her voice.

A muffled whimper stopped Doug in his tracks. Skye whirled around to face him.

"Did you hear that?" she asked, only mouthing the words.

Another whimper, louder, and more distressed than the last. They crept down the balcony. As they reached the second to last apartment, a loud groan was followed by a body slamming against the closed door. Definitely a zombie there. They approached the last door, the zombie in the apartment next door now moaning and snarling as it thrashed and pounded. Underneath the noise made by the zombie, Doug could hear whimpers, now louder and more distressed.

Skye looked over to him, eyes excited. He nodded and she turned the knob.

The door didn't open. From its other side came an anguished cry. "Bunbun!"

Doug kicked the door open. Two voices, one crying, were coming from one of the bedrooms. They raced to the back of the apartment. Doug reached a bedroom door just as two small hands let go of the windowsill.

"Wait!" Skye cried.

At the window they could see that a lower roof extended from the back of the building about eight feet below the window. Two small figures ran across it, the larger of the two pulling the smaller, howling figure along.

"I've got this," Skye said, already halfway out the window. "Go around!"

Before Doug could answer, Skye had disappeared. Racing from the apartment, he sprinted down the balcony. He leaped down the staircase in five soaring strides that left him stumbling on the uneven concrete walk. The tactical soles of his boots found purchase as he sprinted alongside the building's short end. As he skidded around the corner, he heard shouts ahead. A burst of adrenalized energy propelled him forward.

Skye's calming voice competed with high-pitched screams.

"It's okay, it's all right."

Another voice, with a child's high-pitch, shouted, "Let her go!"

Doug saw the boy ahead, down on the ground. He was looking up at Skye, still on the roof. Skye was trying to hold on to a struggling tangle of arms and legs—and lungs. They had to achieve two outcomes at odds with one another as quickly as possible: get the kids to trust them and shut the howler up.

The boy's body tensed, eyes filling with fear, when he finally saw Doug approaching. He backed up a few steps, as if to run, then stopped, unwilling to leave the screaming, squirming child Skye was wrangling on the roof.

"I want Bunbun!" the girl shrieked.

Doug slowed and held his hands out, palms up, about twenty feet from the boy.

"Hey," he said, trying to keep his voice low, but needing to be heard over the other child's shrieks. "It's okay. We won't hurt you."

"Let her go," the boy demanded, fear and fury swirling over his pinched face. "Let her go!"

"Where are your parents?" Doug asked.

At Doug's question, the boy's lower lip began to quiver. So, no parents.

"Let her go," he cried again, but now he sounded on the verge of tears.

Doug looked up to Skye, who seemed to have a secure grip on the now sobbing girl, whose occasional hiccups sounded like *b-b-bunbun*.

"What's Bunbun?" Doug asked the boy.

Tears suddenly filled the boy's eyes. "Violet's rabbit. You were coming and we had to leave him."

"A rabbit?" Doug's brain scrambled to make sense of this development. He was sure that he had finally heard everything the apocalypse could throw at him. "Is Bun Bun back in the room?"

"Mister Bun Bun," the boy said, his voice quivering.

He looked small and frail, and so vulnerable that Doug's heart ached. The boy's chest began to hitch hard as tears trailed down his dirty face. Doug walked closer, waiting for the boy to spook and run. When he was five feet away he dropped down to his knees.

"How about we go get him? Will you let us help you get Mister Bun Bun?"

The boy began to cry in earnest. Doug could see his relief that maybe this adult was someone who could be in charge. Someone who could take responsibility for him and the still distraught girl from his too small shoulders.

He nodded, wiping at his face, smearing the tears and dirt together into a muddy smudge.

"Skye," Doug called, partially turning his head so that his voice would carry, but not wanting to take his eyes off the boy. "We're going to get Mister Bun Bun. Okay?"

"We're going to get Mister Bun Bun?" Skye echoed, clearly bewildered. Immediately, the little girl's crying began to subside. "Okay," she continued, her voice becoming a soothing sing-song. "We're going to get Mister Bun Bun."

Doug returned his full attention to the little boy.

"What's your name?"

The boy looked at him, wary, but the doubt and fear lurking in his eyes was quickly giving way to exhaustion. He looked like a scared kitten, the kind that startled and ran from a leaf being blown on a breeze. Doug would not have been surprised if the kid said his name was Kitty.

"Silas."

Doug smiled and held out his hand. Slowly, Silas extended his own. Doug took hold of his small, grimy fingers.

"It's nice to meet you, Silas. I'm Doug."

Made in the USA
Monee, IL
24 July 2020